T.L. HADDIX

Stormking Road

— A NOVEL —

Streetlight Graphics Publishing
A division of Streetlight Graphics

Stormking Road

Second Print Edition: June 2016
ISBN 13: 978-1-945445-05-7

Visit www.tlhaddix.com for updates, news, bonuses and freebies.
www.facebook.com/tlhaddix

ALSO BY T. L. HADDIX

The Firefly Hollow Series:
Firefly Hollow
Butterfly Lane
Dragonfly Creek
Cattail Ridge
Cricket Cove
Stormking Road
Fern Valley
Snapdragon Way
Stardust Valley
Kathy

The Shadows Collection:
Secrets in the Shadows
Under the Moon's Shadow
Shadows from the Grave
Hidden in the Shadows
In the Heart's Shadow
Deception in the Shadows
Seduction in the Shadows
Redemption in the Shadows

Writing as Mallory Love:
Capturing Colleen (Sunset Motel, Book One)
Seducing Samantha (Sunset Motel, Book Two)

You can connect with T.L. on Facebook and her website:

www.tlhaddix.com
www.facebook.com/tlhaddix

If you'd like to receive email notifications about future releases, please subscribe to T.L.'s newsletter at the address below.

www.tlhaddix.com/newsletter

ACKNOWLEDGEMENTS

Special thanks the following people: Cassie, Kathie (and her dad!), Candace, DeAnn, Anita. Y'all rock.

CAST OF CHARACTERS

Sydney Marie Campbell Gibson - oldest daughter of Emma Campbell and Archer Gibson. First appears in Cattail Ridge.

Sawyer Carson Evans - retired Kentucky State Trooper, age 46. Now owns his own private investigation firm and is up to his eyeballs in paperwork.

Danny Napier - Sydney's best friend, now a preacher.

Neala - Another of Sydney's friends from childhood.

Owen and Sarah Campbell - the folks who started it all. Parents to (in order): John (wife *Zanny*), Emma (husband *Archer*), Ben (wife *Ainsley*), Rachel (divorced, mother of *Easton*), and Amelia (husband *Logan*, brother to *Archer.*)

Owen and Sarah are also grandparents to: Noah, Eli, Molly (*John*), Sydney, Graydon, Carter (*Emma*), Lily (*Ben*), Easton (*Rachel*), three boys and Sadie (*Amelia.*)

Leighton "Lee" Harrison - Rachel's sexy new neighbor and a former co-worker of Sawyer's. Also a state trooper.

Nan Carson - Sawyer's grandmother.

The rest of Sawyer's family - Jordan and Elise (parents), Frank and Matt (brothers), Christie (evil ex-wife.)

NOTE FOR READERS:

Stormking Road takes place twenty years after the last time we got to see the Campbell family, which is in Amelia's book, *Cricket Cove*. A couple of really important things happened to Sydney's parents, Archer and Emma, between that book and this one. If you'd like to catch up with them first and read a short story detailing those important life events, we have included that at the beginning of *Stormking Road*. Happy Reading!

ARCHER'S CAT

CHAPTER ONE

THERE WERE TWO LINES IN the window of the pregnancy test. Two. Not one.

"Oh, God." Emma Campbell Gibson's breath shuddered out of her body. She reached for the hand of her best friend and sister-in-law, Zanny Campbell. "I'm pregnant."

Zanny didn't say anything, simply waited for Emma to get her emotions under control.

It wasn't that Emma being pregnant was a bad thing. But since she'd married Archer Gibson, the love of her life, three years earlier, she'd had two miscarriages. She was afraid now to hope and dream and feel joy.

"Does Archer suspect?" Zanny asked.

"I don't think so," Emma said. "There hasn't been any morning sickness. If I wasn't late... Do you think that's a good sign? It's how things were with Sydney. And I was so sick the other two times."

Sydney was her eight-year-old daughter.

"Maybe. I'll take a positive sign—no pun intended—where I can find one," Zanny said. "What do you want to do?"

That was an interesting question. "Sit here and not move?"

"Okay. I'll have Sam take over your appointments."

They were at the photography studio Emma owned and Zanny ran. They'd come in early so Emma could take the test in privacy. Her assistant, Sam, would be in soon.

Zanny went to open the shop, and Emma did just what she'd said she wanted—she stayed on the couch in the sitting room upstairs and stared into space. After a little while, though, she had to do something. Crossing to the phone, she called her doctor's office and made an appointment, then went downstairs.

"I'm going to go see Dr. Jones," she told Zanny. "They got me right in, considering. Wish me luck?"

Zanny stood and hugged her tight. "Good luck. Want me to go with you?"

"No. I need to do this alone."

Thankfully, she didn't have to wait long at the doctor's office before she was called back. While she got into the gown the nurse had provided her, she thought about the other pregnancies. She and Archer wanted kids so badly, wanted to add to the family they had with Sydney. And since she'd not had a single problem with that pregnancy, there was no reason to expect problems in the future. But twice now she'd made it to eight weeks only to end up losing the baby.

Emma wouldn't say the losses had put a strain on her marriage, exactly, but some of the joy she felt at building a life with the man who was her soul mate was marred. Not a tremendous amount, but enough that the edges of that happiness were burnt. Archer had never once made her feel like he thought she was less than a woman because of the losses, but Emma herself had started to carry a bit of that burden. She'd never confessed that truth to him though she had discussed it with Zanny, who'd suffered her own loss several years earlier.

So this time around when her period was first late, Emma didn't say anything. Archer had to go out of town for one of his rare conferences the same week she was scheduled to start. She didn't tell him she'd missed a period when he returned. Maybe it was duplicitous of her to let him assume she'd had one, but she didn't want to get his hopes up if she was wrong.

When the time came around for her second period and

nothing happened, she knew she had to take a test. She'd put it off so far, thinking that if she didn't know she was pregnant, maybe she wouldn't lose the baby.

Zanny, who was aware of the first missed period, had shaken her head at Emma's recalcitrance. But she'd kept her mouth shut, supporting Emma's decision to wait. That quiet encouragement and love had kept Emma sane the last few weeks.

As she was only a few days late past the second period, she didn't think Archer suspected anything just yet. But she knew time was up—if he didn't suspect now, he would soon. Her breasts were getting tender and fuller, and she'd almost swear she was starting to develop a tiny baby bump. And while she hadn't had any morning sickness in the traditional sense of the word, certain smells were becoming rather off-putting, like that of peanut butter and of tomato soup, of all things.

A soft tap sounded on the door.

"Come in," Emma called.

The nurse poked her head in with a smile, then came inside. "He wants me to get some blood and urine so we can do some labs while he examines you."

"Okay."

By the time her doctor came in several minutes later, Emma was a nervous wreck. "Well?" she asked before he even had a chance to close the door.

He smiled. "Congratulations. You're definitely pregnant. Hop up on the table and we'll see what we see."

Scared to death, she did as instructed. "Are you going to do an ultrasound?"

"That depends. How far along do you think you are? The chart said you'd missed two periods?" He settled in the chair and started the exam.

"Yeah. And I'm not sure how far along. I've been afraid to even consider it, given my history."

"Does Archer know?"

"No. We're doing an ultrasound, right?"

He finished the examination, then moved back and stripped off his gloves. "Are you going to be able to sleep if we don't?"

Emma sat up halfway, propped on her elbows. "You've been my doctor for ten years now. What do you think?"

"I'll get the machine."

Ten minutes later, she was ready to come apart from nerves as he hmmm'd and pursed his lips as he stared at the black and white screen.

"Well?"

He turned it so she could see better and pointed. "Right there's the baby. Everything looks perfectly normal. Heart's beating just fine. Want to see if we can hear it?"

With tears choking her, all Emma could do was nod. He pushed the buttons that turned on the sound, and a minute later, what sounded like a tiny, fast washing machine could be heard.

"Judging from what I'm seeing, you're almost nine weeks along. You've passed the mark," he said quietly. "So stop worrying about that. Is that why you waited to come in?"

She took the tissues the nurse gave her and wiped her face. "Yes. I was afraid to get my hopes up. It's really okay?"

"As far as I can tell," he said, putting the equipment back in its holder. "There's no guarantee, but I'm hopeful. I'll print you out a couple or three of these images. I imagine you'll want to take them home?"

"Please."

Now that the exam was over, she felt like she was going to throw up. As she got dressed and took care of paperwork on her way out of the office, all she could think about was how in the world she was going to tell Archer. She called the office to ask a favor from Zanny.

"Could you get Sydney tonight?" she asked after she'd relayed what the doctor had said.

"Absolutely. I'll pick her up at Mrs. Hendricks' when I get my brood. Want her to spend the night with us?"

"Is that going to be too much trouble?"

Zanny growled. "Emma Jean. I can't even..."

"I had to ask. Thanks, Zan. You're a lifesaver."

"Any idea how you're going to break the news?"

Emma blew out a breath. "None. I've got a little while to figure it out, though. Wish me luck?"

"As much of it as I can send your way, sweetie."

She got home a little past one, having stopped to grab a salad from a drive-thru for lunch. But she was so tired she didn't even want to eat it, so she stuffed it in the fridge and headed up to the bedroom, printouts in hand. Stifling a yawn, she looked at the bed with longing.

"A good, old-fashioned nap sounds like an excellent idea," she muttered. She quickly changed into one of Archer's T-shirts and crawled under the covers with a sigh. "Just a few minutes of rest, and then I'll figure out how to tell him."

Before she could even form another thought, she was sound asleep.

CHAPTER TWO

ARCHER HURT FROM HIS SHOULDERS to his waist. When he walked into the house that evening, all he wanted to do was take a hot shower and relax. The day had been rough, and spending time with his two favorite girls was high on his list of priorities. Even though he'd been married for three years now, he still felt a welcoming rush of love just thinking about home, much less when he walked in the door.

But the house was dark, quiet. Emma's car was in the garage, but if she and Sydney were home, he didn't hear them.

"Em? Syd?" he called, turning on the lights as he went in the kitchen. "Hello?"

Nothing answered him but the welcoming meows of their two cats, Huff and Puff, as they wound around his legs.

"Maybe they went for a walk," he said as he gave them some kibble. He wasn't terribly concerned—they'd been known to get stuck talking to a neighbor here or playing with a friend there—and he decided to head upstairs and get that shower. He'd just reached the door to his and Emma's bedroom when he heard her soft sigh. The rustling of the bedclothes sounded, then a quiet snore.

"Em?"

No response.

Archer frowned and turned on the switch next to the door that controlled the bedside lamps. Sure enough, Emma was curled up in bed, sound asleep.

"She must be sick," he said, inching closer. But when he saw the printouts on the nightstand, his breath caught in his throat. With hands that shook, he picked the top one up.

An ultrasound, dated today. With Emma's name on it.

The shape on the image was fuzzy, a little tiny blob that he wasn't even sure he was supposed to be focusing on. He might not know how to read an ultrasound, but the significance... They were pregnant.

His first instincts were to grab her up in his arms, wake her up and question her, kiss her, love her. But he didn't want to get ahead of himself. He could be reading things wrong. This might not be good news. Besides, he was covered in grease and oil and grime from work, and he'd get her filthy. Some days that had its advantages but not today.

He put the ultrasound back on the nightstand and quietly went to the shower. As soon as he was clean, he'd crawl in bed with her and find out what was going on. He figured Zanny probably had Sydney. Again, he didn't know if that was a good sign or bad. Praying for all that he was worth that it was good, he started scrubbing.

Emma woke up when the bed dipped and strong arms came around her. She smiled as Archer's hand touched her face.

"Wake up, sleeping beauty," he said, his voice low as he kissed her forehead.

"Mmm, no. I like this dream just fine." She snuggled close to him, running her hands over his bare chest. When he jerked and drew in a breath, her eyes flew open.

"Archer?"

"I'm okay."

But he wasn't. There was a large bruise on his chest between his shoulder and his heart. Sitting up so fast she got dizzy, she reached out a hand, stopping just shy of touching him. "What happened?"

"It's nothing. One of the guys at work swung an engine around. I walked into it. It's just sore. I'm fine, Em."

"Did you get checked out? Nothing's broken, is it?"

He moved his arm in an arc, wincing when he stretched it up over his head, but managed a clear range of motion. "I'm fine. I promise. How are you?"

She blinked at him. "Um."

"Something you want to tell me?" he asked patiently. Even so, she could feel the concern coming off of him, as well as the coiled tension.

Emma couldn't find her voice. She bit her lip, staring at him.

Archer sat up, reaching past her to the nightstand. He handed her the printouts. "Maybe this will help," he said, his lips quirking up at the corners.

Trembling all over, she set the pictures aside and wound her arms around him, taking care not to put pressure on the bruise. "I'm afraid if I tell you, it won't be real anymore. And I want it to be real more than just about anything in the world."

He held her close, pressing soft kisses to her hair. "I can wait until you're ready, then. But are you okay?"

She nodded. "I love you, you know that?"

"I do. And I love you back." He kissed her, this time fully on the mouth.

Emma was more than happy to follow him down to the mattress, to help him get her naked, to feel his body pressing against hers as they made love. He knew about the baby without her telling him, and that was sufficient for now. That he understood her fears and didn't press her for more of an explanation only made her love him more.

CHAPTER THREE

THE WORLD BLEW UP THE next morning. As it was Saturday, they'd not set the clock to go off, deciding to sleep in late. Emma hated their alarm clock, had threatened to replace it a thousand times. But she would have preferred its raucous screech to the sound that did wake her—the sound of her husband gasping for air and not being able to find it.

The memory of that morning would be etched on her mind for the rest of her life. Archer's face so pale, his lips blue, his eyes frantic as he tried to breathe but couldn't. The 911 call and miraculously fast response time. Getting dressed in whatever clothes she could find so she wasn't naked when the EMTs got there. The ride in the ambulance to the hospital. The sight of her husband being rushed away from her, and the terror of not knowing whether that was the last time they'd see each other or not.

At some point, someone called her parents. Emma didn't remember telling anyone not to notify them, and she didn't much care how they'd found out. Owen and Sarah were just there. Soon after, other members of her family started trickling in. When Logan, Archer's brother, came in with his wife Emma's sister Amelia, Emma burst into tears.

"What happened?" he ground out as he hugged her. "Em, what happened?"

She shook her head. "I don't know. He couldn't breathe. And they haven't told me anything. I had to sign some papers. He's in surgery."

Sarah had been trying to find out details, and she came back in then with Emma's cousin Michelle, who was a pediatrician. Both their faces were grim.

"It's not good," Michelle said bluntly. "Apparently, when he was shot all those years ago, they missed a bullet fragment. He's got a big bruise on his chest that Emma said came from getting hit at work yesterday. The surgeon thinks that knocked the fragment loose. They've got to get it out. It's lodged between his lung and his heart."

"Wh—what are his chances?" Emma asked faintly, sinking into her chair.

Michelle sighed, taking a seat beside her. She grasped Emma's hands tightly. "The surgeon who's operating has good hands, steady hands. If anyone can get it out, he can."

"That isn't what I asked."

Michelle hesitated. "Not good. Less than thirty percent."

"Oh, God," Logan said. He sat as well, leaning into Amelia, his head in his hands. "That's not enough."

Emma nodded slowly as she took it in. "Where's Sydney?"

John, Zanny's husband, spoke up. "At our house."

"Good."

That was the last thing she said until the surgeon came out three hours later, dark circles under his eyes. His scrubs were soaked with sweat and, Emma saw, there were spatters of blood on the legs. Archer's blood. She steered her mind firmly away from that line of thought.

"He's critical, but he made it through the surgery," the man said. He thanked the nurse who'd followed him as she handed him a cup of coffee. "The next few hours are crucial. He may not survive, and if he does, I don't know if there's going to be any permanent damage. He went into cardiac arrest a couple of times on us. I'm sorry I can't give you any better news."

All around her, the family reacted. Logan was angry, pacing, and cursed under his breath as Amelia tried not to cry. Her parents sagged against each other. John and Ben, her brothers, asked questions about what to expect. Rachel, her other sister, who was seated beside her, put her arm around Emma's shoulders.

"I need some air," Emma said, patting her hand before standing carefully. "And then I want to see him."

"He's being brought to the ICU. You can only stay a few minutes," the doctor said.

"No. I'll stay until he's awake. I know you and your team need to work. I won't get in the way. But I'm not leaving him." She raised her chin and dared him to contradict her.

The surgeon eyed her with a shrewd gaze. "If you do get in the way, that's it. You won't get back in."

"I understand."

She let Rachel and Sarah guide her to the bathroom where she promptly threw up. When she came out of the stall, they watched her with worried eyes.

"Emma—"

"I'm fine, Mom," she said as she splashed her face with cold water. "Will you and Daddy make sure Sydney's okay? She'll be worried."

Sarah's mouth compressed in a thin line, but she nodded. "If you need anything, just say the word."

"Who has all the kids?" Emma asked as they made their way to the ICU waiting room.

"Aunt Gilly, Nonny, and Uncle Eli are at Zanny's, and I'll probably head out soon to help," Rachel said. "Easton's with his dad, but Bear goes on shift in a little while. Do you want me to bring you more clothes? Anything?"

Emma glanced down at herself. "Whatever you think I'll need. Thank you."

The surgeon had left word with the ICU nurses to expect Emma, and they let her and Logan go in.

"You can stay ten minutes, no more," a short, pudgy nurse with a soft voice told Logan. "Mrs. Gibson, Doctor Davies said you'd be staying. If we have to get in there to work, you *will* wait outside the glass. Understand?"

Emma heard the steel in her voice and respected it. "Yes."

When they reached Archer's bay, he was hooked up to

what looked like every piece of equipment in the hospital. Emma staggered against Logan. He caught her easily, but she wondered if she wasn't holding him up as much as he was her.

Archer wasn't a small man at six feet four, not by any stretch of the imagination, but he looked pitiful lying in that hospital bed. It was almost more than Emma could bear.

"I'm okay," she told them after a moment. "I'm okay. How can I help?"

The nurse directed her to a chair on the opposite side of the bed. "Don't touch any of the equipment, and don't try to wake him up. Right now, he needs to stay as quiet as possible."

There was a wide bandage running down the middle of Archer's chest. Realization struck Emma.

"You had to open him up?"

The nurse nodded. "It was the only way to get to his heart."

Logan, on the other side of the bed, laid a hand lightly on his brother's head. "Another scar to add to the collection. Sydney'll love the bandage."

"She will. Can I hold his hand?" Emma asked.

"Of course. And you can talk to him. Just keep your voices low, and like I said, don't try to wake him up. Push that red button on the wall if you need anything."

She left them alone, pulling the curtain part of the way across the glass window in the front of the room.

"I thought we were past this," Logan growled, leaning in toward Archer. "We agreed we wouldn't do this anymore, remember? We're not supposed to disturb you, little brother, so I won't give you too hard of a time right now. But when you get out of here? I'm going to kick your ass for scaring me like this."

She saw the tears on his cheeks and had to look away to keep from screaming.

After he'd gone, Emma carefully wound her hands

around Archer's. That hand was the one spot on his body he didn't seem to have a tube or line or electric feed attached to.

"Don't think you're getting out of parenthood so easily. I made it past the eight-week mark, Archer. This baby is happening. I was so afraid to tell you I thought I was pregnant. You are *not* leaving me to raise your children on my own. I still need you. I'll always need you," she whispered. "So you rest, you heal, you fight this thing. And when you wake up, we'll go on with this happily ever after we've been living. You hear me, you stubborn bastard?"

His fingers tightened around hers. That was all, just a slow movement that could have been a muscle spasm. But she knew better. And that gave her hope.

CHAPTER FOUR

FIVE WEEKS LATER, ARCHER WAS sitting in his recliner, his feet propped up in front of him, trying not to laugh as Emma rattled around in the kitchen, cursing the stove, the recipe, her father, and the universe for not giving her the cooking gene. He'd offered to help her get supper ready, but she'd glared at him with such a ferocious snarl that he'd held his hands up and backed out of the kitchen in self-defense.

Owen, who'd shown up not long after Archer had retreated to the living room, stood with a sigh. "Guess I'd better try to help her."

Archer grinned. "Good luck with that."

A minute later, Emma came stomping out of the kitchen, hands on her hips. "I almost had it," she called back.

Whatever Owen's muffled response was, Archer got the impression from the way Emma's eyes narrowed that he would be better off not asking his father-in-law to repeat it.

"Come here," he said instead, holding his hands out.

With a tiny pout, Emma took his hands. "You did not marry a cook."

He laughed and tugged, not letting up until she eased into his lap. "I didn't, no. But I love you anyhow."

"Yeah?"

"Mm-hmmm," he said, kissing her lightly. "But once I'm allowed back in the kitchen, don't expect to eat spaghetti again until this baby's a year old." Spaghetti was the one dish Emma did well, and they'd had it so much the last few weeks, even eight-year-old Sydney was starting to curl her lip at the dish.

She settled in against him with a sigh as his hand came

to rest on her belly. "We're going to have to tell the family soon."

What with Archer's surgery and recovery, letting everyone know they were expecting had fallen by the wayside. But now that he was almost well again, they were starting to get some funny looks.

"They'll figure it out soon enough. It's getting hard to disguise," he teased.

"Mmm, that it is," Emma said around a yawn as she drifted off. Archer tucked her closer against him, enjoying the feel of her safe and sound in his arms.

When Owen came out of the kitchen a couple of minutes later, wiping his hands on a dishtowel, he smiled. "I saved the chicken. It's in the oven, should be ready in about half an hour. She's wiped out, huh?"

Archer nodded. "I feel guilty about that."

"You shouldn't. Sarah was almost narcoleptic with a couple of her pregnancies. Em doesn't seem overly tired, just pregnantly tired. You may have noticed we've all been pitching in to keep her as rested as possible."

"I had noticed that," Archer said with a happy smile. "Thank you. When did you figure it out?"

"About a week after you had surgery. Sydney told us all that her mommy had a baby in her belly." He sat down on the couch, studying them. "How far along is she?"

"Fourteen weeks or thereabouts. Finally in the safer zone and out of that first trimester, thank God."

Owen's smile grew a bit misty. "Good. When's she going back to work?"

"As soon as I can convince her I'm okay. I should get the all clear from the doctor next week, so hopefully that'll help."

They talked about some of the books they were reading as they waited for Sarah to arrive with Sydney, who'd had her own doctor visit that afternoon. Owen and Sarah stayed for dinner, and after they left, Archer got Sydney upstairs and bathed.

Emma came up soon after. “I locked up downstairs. Once we get her in bed, can we just hold each other? Maybe watch TV in the bedroom?” she asked as she hugged him from behind.

“Sure.”

They’d not been intimate since he had surgery, something else Emma had put the kibosh on despite his doctor’s telling them he was safe to resume those regular activities at last week’s visit. So when Sydney was asleep and they retired to their own room, Archer sat down on the bed and pulled Emma to him, caressing her hips.

“I need you.”

She traced his lips with a finger. “Archer...”

“Em, I’m fine. We can be careful, we can go slow, but I need you.”

“I’m afraid.”

“I know. I’m asking you to do this for me.” He slid his hands under her top and eased it over her head, then undid her bra. She’d already had to go up a size, and he cupped the tender flesh gently. “I promise you’ll enjoy it,” he cajoled.

A reluctant smile spread across her face even as she arched into his touch. “What if I hurt you?”

“I’m already hurting.”

She scowled, not amused, and he sighed. Sliding his hands to her hips, he drew her so that she was in his lap, her knees on either side of his hips.

“You didn’t hurt me before. Making love is not what put me in the hospital.”

Emma tugged his shirt off, then placed her hands carefully on his chest on either side of the new scar. “If we do this and you have any chest pain, any pressure, you tell me right away. We’ll stop. Promise?”

“I promise.”

She stared at him for another minute, then shook her

head. "I've missed you like this," she confessed as they kissed.

There were no more words as they touched one another, the heat building to a flashpoint that made going slow impossible. When Emma settled over him, warm and welcoming, Archer buried his face in her throat. Their movements were fast and frantic after that, need driving them each to a stunning climax. It came too soon and not fast enough, and Archer could hardly wait to do it again.

The second time they made love, the pace was slow, unhurried, and just as intense. "I don't think I'll be able to get enough of you until we're ninety and living in a home somewhere. Not even if we do this every single day," he whispered once they'd come down. "And I have my doubts that I'll be satiated even then. You're addictive."

Emma wrapped her arms and legs around him and held on tightly. "So are you. I love you."

Though he would have been more than happy to go for round three, she wasn't willing to risk it. So he pulled her into his arms instead, more than content to hold her close as they drifted off to sleep.

CHAPTER FIVE

THE PURRING WOKE HER. "HUFF, Puff, ask Archer to feed you," Emma said as warm cat breath lifted her hair off her face. She buried her head deeper into the pillow. "After last night, I think he's more than able to open a can of cat food."

A hoarse *rawr* answered her as the purring faded, and the bed shook hard. Harder than it normally would have with Archer or the cats getting up. Opening her eyes, Emma glanced at the bedroom door. It was closed. The room was bathed in morning sunlight, even though the clock only said seven.

A second *rawr* sounded, this one closer, as the purring resumed. A very solid head butted her behind, and a large tawny paw came across her hip, resting there. A paw that was as big as her own hand, bigger even.

With a shocked gasp, Emma rolled over and sat up, coming face to face with a beautiful mountain lion who was gazing at her with something akin to impatience.

"What...?"

The cat yawned, showing off impressive teeth, then licked its paw. Satisfied she was awake, he rolled over and into the floor. From the twitching of his tail, she wondered absently if he'd intended to fall off the bed or not.

"Logan, this isn't funny." She clutched the sheet to her, grateful beyond words she'd had to put her nightgown back on last night after she and Archer had finished making love. "What the hell are you doing here?" she demanded in a whisper. "It's not even eight o'clock in the morning! Where's Archer? I'll skin you two alive for this."

Letting out what sounded suspiciously like a sigh, the

cat padded to the door and scratched at it, not using his claws. He looked back over his shoulder at her as if asking her to let him out.

Emma scrambled off the bed. "Does Amelia know about this?" She let him out, then closed the door behind him, hanging her head. "Shape-shifters. God bless 'em, I'm going to strangle those men."

Archer didn't know quite what to do. He'd never expected Emma not to realize it was him. He knew she didn't typically come fully awake until she'd had a cup of coffee, but for her not to know what was going on... Maybe it was pregnancy brain, he thought as he twitched his tail, annoyed and frustrated at not being understood.

Thanks to his enhanced hearing, he knew she was in their bathroom. With an aggravated huff, he crossed the hall to Sydney's bedroom door, which was slightly ajar. Emma might not recognize him, but he was betting their daughter would. She rolled around and played with Logan every time she was around him after he shifted.

More than a decade earlier, Archer's first wife had decided widowhood was cheaper than divorce. She'd pumped two bullets into his chest, not counting on him surviving. But he had, for the most part. The part of him that could shift into a mountain lion? That had died on the table.

Or so he'd thought.

Sydney, who could sense certain elements about some people, had said ever since she was five that his cat was asleep. His brother Logan's cat, on the other hand, was not. The family had long taken that to mean Archer's cat was dead.

When he'd awakened a short time earlier, his entire body tingling from head to toe, Archer had thought he was dying. He'd gotten to his feet, then fallen to his knees, somehow without disturbing Emma. He was terrified he'd not be able to wake her in time to say good-bye. But then he'd shifted. The change into the cat had happened so fast, he hadn't realized what was going on until it was done. Even then, he wondered if he'd died or was dreaming. He'd gone through some strange things while he was unconscious in the hospital, after all.

But after a couple of minutes, he figured he wasn't dead. He wasn't in a weird coma or something. He had, somehow, someway, gotten his cat back. And he desperately needed to run.

Easing Sydney's door open, he crossed to the bed. One of her little feet was sticking out from under the covers, and he butted his head against it, purring loudly as he rubbed.

"Uncle Logan?" she said, coming awake almost instantly. She rubbed the heels of her hands against her eyes, then reached for her glasses. Archer rolled onto his back, then got up on his feet and stood there, watching her patiently. He saw the moment when she put it together.

"Daddy?" she whispered, her eyes huge.

He nudged her bed again with his head.

She was off the bed in a flash, her arms thrown around his neck as she squealed with excitement.

"Mommy! Mommy, Daddy's a cat! Daddy's a cat!" Sydney ran across the hall to their bedroom, opening the door without knocking to dash inside. "Mommy!"

Archer followed.

Emma was coming out of the bathroom, dressed, toothbrush in hand, frowning. "What did you say?"

"He's a cat, he's a cat, he's a cat!" Sydney grabbed her hand and danced in place for a second, then dashed back to where Archer stood and hugged him. "Look!"

Emma's face paled. "He can't be."

Archer let out a rumbling, growling purr and did his best to nod.

"Oh, my God." She leaned against the doorjamb. "Oh, my God."

"Can we take him to the farm? Please?" Sydney begged. "And let Grandma and Grandpa see him?"

As that was exactly what he wanted to happen, Archer prayed Emma would agree. He chattered and paced, not taking his eyes off her.

"You need to run?" Emma asked faintly.

This time, the roar he let out was louder than he'd intended, and she jumped.

"Okay. Okay. I'll call Daddy and then we'll go. Sydney, grab your robe. Get dressed. Shoes. You'll need shoes. *I* need shoes," she said as she went to the closet. "Shit, the phone."

She was panicking, the last thing Archer had wanted. Desperate to calm her down, he went to where she stood and raised up on his back legs. Pinning her to the door, he licked her neck and face, trying to tickle her and make her laugh.

It worked.

"Stop it!" she said, dodging his tongue even as she giggled. He'd never heard her giggle before, and he chuffed at the sound, amused. He let his head rest on her shoulder for a moment, then got down. She was laughing now, still shaking but no longer completely freaked out as she grabbed the phone off the nightstand and dialed.

"Daddy? I'm bringing you a cat."

Archer went back in the closet while she got her shoes on and tugged on a pair of his jeans. He pulled so hard the hanger broke, pieces of plastic flying everywhere.

Emma got the message. "You'll need clothes. Okay. Stop that and move before you tear something down." She hastily pulled an outfit together, including shoes when he nudged them, and they were out the door.

"Sydney, we're going to cover him up so that no one else sees him," she said as they piled in her SUV. She grabbed a blanket from the back and tossed it over him as he settled in the backseat next to Sydney. "Thank God I parked in the garage yesterday."

Archer was concerned that she'd wreck, but before she backed out of the garage, she drew in several breaths. He peeked out from under the blanket and was relieved to see that she'd calmed considerably. "Okay, I have this. Let's go."

He couldn't tell how fast she was driving, but she handled the vehicle well enough. *That's my girl*, he thought. It seemed to take forever to reach the farm, but they finally did.

As soon as she opened the door and uncovered him, he was out. Owen and Sarah were standing on the porch, their mouths open with shock. A quick glance around showed him he was in the clear. Letting out a loud roar, he ran like hadn't been able to in years.

CHAPTER SIX

OWEN AND SARAH HURRIED DOWN the steps, meeting Sydney and Emma halfway to the car.

"What in the world? When you said you were bringing us a cat, I thought you meant one like Huff or Puff. Was that Logan?" Owen asked.

Emma shook her head, laughing. "It was Archer." And she promptly burst into tears.

Half an hour later, she was sitting on the porch steps, alternating between laughter and tears. Owen had his arm around her, laughing as much as she was. Sarah'd taken Sydney in for some breakfast.

"I can't believe it," she said, her voice hoarse. "I thought he was Logan when I woke up and he was in the bedroom, and that they were playing some kind of trick on me. I was ready to skin them both."

"I imagine so."

They watched as Archer trotted around the side of the barn across the meadow, then turned ninety degrees to dash as hard as he could toward the spot the family often set up for picnics at.

"He's *playing*." She sniffed back her tears. "Oh, Daddy. How is it possible for your heart to break from being so happy?"

"It just is. Happened to me every time one of you kids was born. Every time we have a new grandchild to love on," he said, sending her a sidelong glance.

Emma smiled. "Yeah, about that."

He kissed her temple. "Congratulations, sweetheart. I couldn't be happier for you."

She sighed happily and watched Archer roll down a grassy slope. "I wish I'd brought a camera."

"Your mom might have one inside somewhere."

An hour later, Archer was having some bacon and eggs when Logan and Amelia arrived. He'd been running nonstop, and he'd needed to refuel. But when he saw his brother's truck, he stiffened, every muscle in his body going on alert. Before Logan could even get the driver's door open, Archer was beside him.

Emma's tears, which had calmed down, started again. Sarah just patted her shoulder and handed her a box of tissues.

Logan had been devastated when he'd learned about Archer losing the cat. It had taken him a long time to get over that loss. Now, he got out of the truck and sank to his knees, laughing as Archer nudged him and head-butted him.

"How much do you want to bet me they run together?" Owen said as they headed to the truck to help Amelia with the kids.

"Oh, I'd put money on it," Sarah said.

Logan looked up as they approached, the biggest grin Emma had ever seen on his face, not counting when his and Amelia's two sons had been born. Tears were coursing down his cheeks. Unashamed, he wiped at them with his hands.

"Can you believe it?"

Archer took advantage of his position to knock him over, then settled across him and licked the top of Logan's head. He let out a self-satisfied purr as he glanced at Emma and chuffed.

She snickered, wiping away her own tears. "No, I can't. I thought the two of you were playing some kind of trick on me this morning. Oh, Logan."

He stood and hugged her, then went to the barn to change clothes and shift so he and Archer could run together. As the rest of the family sat on the porch, Amelia—who was also a shifter—shook her head.

"If he hadn't gone through what he did a few weeks back, he probably never would have been able to do this. All this time..."

"It's hard to think about him losing the cat, especially now," Emma confessed. "He'd accepted it. I never saw real regret in his eyes when you all would shift. But now, I wonder."

Owen patted her hand. "I think he'd made his peace with it. He's happy, no doubt in my mind about that, and he has been since you two got married. But sometimes you don't know how much you miss something until you get it back after you think you've lost it and you've accepted that loss."

When they'd finally run enough, the brothers shifted and got dressed, then made their way up to the farmhouse. Logan was still smiling, even though he was rubbing his hip. Archer was as relaxed as Emma had seen him... well, since ever.

"How do you feel?" she asked.

He kissed her hard. "Human again, if that makes sense. And starving to death."

They all laughed, and Sarah waved a hand toward the door. "Sandwich fixings are laid out in the kitchen, boys. Help yourselves."

That night when they were home, once again wrapped around each other in bed after making love, Emma propped herself on an elbow and studied him.

"What?"

She shook her head and traced his scar, which had healed quite a bit more since the previous night, one of the benefits of being a shifter. "Just thinking. Feeling beyond grateful for everything we have."

"It's a lot," he said, touching her face. "I was scared to death this morning. I didn't know what was happening at first. I kept thinking 'I can't go out this way. I can't do this to

Emma, to Sydney.' And then I shifted, and if a cat can cry, I did. Did you see Logan's face, Em?"

"Oh, yes. Daddy said this morning that you'd made your peace with losing the cat, but I don't think Logan ever did. You gave him a part of his heart back today."

He pulled her down and kissed her forehead, then tucked her under his chin. "I love you. Thanks for calling him."

"You are very welcome. And I love you, too. I'm so glad you fought for us, did I ever tell you that? That you never gave up on Sydney and me? On our family?"

Archer rolled them so that she was on her back, then gently placed his hand over her belly. "You tell me every day."

The look they shared was more intimate than words, deeper than a touch.

Emma smiled and ran a hand through his hair. "My very own big cat."

"Forever and ever," he whispered as he lowered his head. "Amen."

CHAPTER ONE

HOME. FUNNY HOW THE WORD could mean different things to so many people.

To Sydney Marie Campbell Gibson, home was the two-story adobe house in Hazard, Kentucky, that she'd grown up in. The sound of her parents' voices echoing quietly up the stairs at night after she and her brothers were tucked safely in bed. Ink stains on her grandfather's fingers from where he'd been writing and illustrating the books he authored. The smell of her grandmother's apple spice cake that embraced a person when they walked into the farmhouse in which Owen and Sarah Campbell had raised their family.

Today, Sydney was coming home. But for the first time in her life she wasn't going to that adobe house or to her grandparents' farm. Today, she was bypassing town, driving to the new house her parents had built on a private, out-of-the-way piece of land not far from where her grandparents lived.

Emma and Archer Gibson had been planning their dream house for close to ten years now. Archer had bought the land the year before he'd married Emma when Sydney was five. They would have built the house sooner but the everyday craziness of raising three kids, working, of Emma running her photography studio, and simply having a life had interfered. Now that Sydney's brothers, Graydon and

Carter, were teenagers, Emma had seized the opportunity. And the land that had sat empty for the twenty-some years Archer had owned it had become the site of the family's new home.

Sydney hadn't seen the house in the flesh, so to speak, only in pictures. As far as that went, she hadn't been back to Hazard and Perry County for over two years now. She wasn't ready before. Now, at twenty-six, she was.

As excited as she was for her parents, she was a bit apprehensive. Feeling so full of trepidation was ridiculous, but there was a part of her that worried everything would have changed, that she'd not have a real home to return to now. That home wouldn't be *home* anymore.

And Sydney desperately needed to be able to come home.

So much had happened to the family in the last decade or so. The loss of her great-grandmother, Eliza, and of Owen's uncle, Eli. A bitter feud that had erupted between her cousins, Noah and Eli. Her aunt Zanny's bout with breast cancer. Sydney's own divorce. She needed to come home now, to try to figure out where her place was in the world. To try to reach for happiness and permanence, whatever that ended up meaning.

Finding the house was easy. She'd been to the property countless times over the years as she grew up, either to go hiking or to have a picnic or just to have a place to go and think. But when she saw the stone and glass structure that rose up from the side of the hill, looking as natural in the landscape as though it had sprouted there from a seed, she had to stop the car for a few moments to take it all in. To admire the beauty and peacefulness of the setting. Flowers bloomed along both sides of the wide gravel driveway, cheery red, yellow, orange, and white emissaries whose heads bobbed in the early June breeze. It was a warm welcome, and letting out a deep sigh, she continued up the drive.

Wanting to surprise everyone, she hadn't called to let them know she was coming. So it was with some relief that she saw her father's truck, the bed loaded down with mulch, parked in front of the three-car garage. Pulling in beside the truck, she took a sip of water from the bottle tucked into the car's console, then got out and made her way to the wide covered porch.

Archer Gibson pulled the door open before she could ring the bell. The stunned pleasure on his face assured her that her arrival was not an unwelcome surprise.

"Oh, my God! Sydney? What are you doing here? Why didn't you tell us you were coming? How long are you staying?" Archer's laugh was soggy as he wrapped her in a bear hug and lifted her off her feet, twirling her around.

Laughing, crying, Sydney hugged him back just as tightly. He was still as solid as a rock, though his hair was shot through with gray and laugh lines fanned out from the corners of his eyes. Sydney knew a lot of those gray hairs had come from her antics as a teen. He'd earned every one of them, something for which she still felt regret.

"I'm home. I wanted to surprise you all. And I'll stay as long as you want me to."

Archer sat her on her feet, grinning down at her happily. "Well, then, you'll be here until you're old and gray. Your mom is going to be so happy. I can't believe you're here!"

"Where is she?" she asked as he led her inside. "And the boys?"

"Emma's shooting a wedding, and your brothers are out riding around in Graydon's car. I'm piddling around here on my own today. Have you eaten? When did you leave Georgia?"

"A couple of days ago. I took the scenic route, came up through Tennessee. And no, I've not eaten. I'm starving."

Archer winked at her. "We can remedy that. What sounds good?"

"Honestly? Mom's spaghetti."

They both laughed. Emma was a very talented, very competent woman in nearly every area of her life. Cooking, however, was not one of those areas. There were only a few dishes she could make with consistent results. Spaghetti was one.

"I think we can probably arrange that for dinner tonight. She'll be so happy to see you," he said. "I can't believe you're here."

Sydney slipped her arm around his waist and leaned against him. "I can't, either. I've missed you all so much. So show me this place. It's gorgeous, Daddy."

"We're pretty happy with it."

She looked around the wide foyer that opened onto the great room, trying to take it all in. While the house itself was new, many of the contents were familiar, and she felt the last of her nerves settle down.

Archer gave her the tour, stopping in the door of a bedroom upstairs that held very familiar furnishings. "This is your room. It's probably not what you'd put together now that you're an adult, but we wanted you to have a place to come to."

Tears pricked her eyes and she had to sniff them back. She couldn't speak, just hugged him again.

He kissed the top of her head. "Let's get some grub and we can catch up on things."

She followed him downstairs to the state-of-the-art kitchen, whistling when they walked into the airy, clean space. "You know, I'd figured I would find my own place once I got here but now, after seeing this house... I'm not too old to move back in, am I?"

Archer laughed. "You'll never be too old to move back in. So how are Kathy and Charles? I imagine they didn't want to see you leave."

Sydney smiled ruefully. "No, they didn't. And honestly, I hated to leave them. But Charles's nephew and niece and their spouses and kids are there, and they'll be okay. He's settling into retirement finally, and for once, he's leaning on

Kathy. The hip replacement took a lot out of him. I think it's actually made her stronger, having him need her."

"I can see how that would."

Kathy was Sydney's great-aunt, her grandmother Sarah's older sister. She'd been in a fragile emotional state for decades thanks to a horrific and tragic event more than fifty years ago that had cost Kathy the man she loved and her children. She'd moved to Georgia to escape the memories, where she'd eventually remarried. Her second husband, Charles, was an attorney in the Savannah area. Sydney had worked as his assistant for the past three years.

"So what are you planning to do now? Live a life of leisure? Eat bonbons and hire cabana boys to fan you all day?" Archer asked.

Sydney rolled her eyes even as she smiled. "Daddy, you're outrageous. I don't know what I'm going to do. Something I can stay busy at, that's for sure. I don't need the money, and I'm not sure what jobs I'm qualified for around here. Something like what I did for Charles, maybe."

After coming back to Kentucky for a few months to lick her wounds after her divorce nearly four years earlier, she'd fled to Savannah. Though her degree was in history, Charles had hired her. She'd always been close to Charles and Kathy, and he'd offered her a job at the law firm he was partners in when he saw that she needed to do something to stay busy. Since he was nearing retirement by the time Sydney was hired on, the work hadn't been terribly intense, but it had succeeded in keeping her mind off the tatters of her personal life.

"I might know something," Archer told her now. "Let me see what I can come up with."

"Ooh, what kind of something?" she asked as they sat down at the table in the kitchen's breakfast nook.

"Remember Sawyer? He needs a receptionist. Secretary. Assistant. Hell, whatever you want to call it. He needs someone to take care of the office for him."

Sydney's heart stuttered at the name. Sawyer Evans. Tall, dark, too handsome for words, broody. Totally out of reach and quite naturally, therefore, the man she'd had a crush on for what felt like most of her life.

"I'm hardly liable to forget Sawyer, seeing as how he arrested me when I was a teenager. But don't the state police have people to do that kind of work?"

"He's retired. Been out of uniform for about a year now. He set up his own firm, private investigations and the like. His office is only a few doors down from your mom's shop. You should swing by there next week. He's had a couple of people in there, but they haven't worked out. You might just fit."

"Um, sure. I bet we'd fit well," she told him, her voice full of laughter. "But Sawyer isn't old enough to retire. What is he, forty?"

Archer snorted. "More like forty-six or seven, I think. He's about six years younger than me. He was with the state police over twenty years, kiddo. Time's marching on. We're getting old."

"No, you're not."

The concept was impossible for Sydney to grasp. A fluttering disturbance went through her belly at the thought.

"Oh, we're definitely feeling our age some these days. Sawyer had to have major knee reconstruction last year, which is what spurred his retirement."

She shook her head. "I can't imagine him not being active."

She thought about the last time she'd seen him, when she was nineteen and foolish and head-over-heels in love with him. He'd been so virile and masculine then, thinking of him withering away into retirement caused her breath to hitch painfully in her chest. Thankfully, she was able to cover the hitch with a sip of cola.

"I didn't say he wasn't still active. If anything he's more active now than he was," Archer said. "He's not riding a desk all day, and he's able to get out and about. The knee surgery was due to injury, not to his being old and decrepit. We're not ready for the grave yet, thank God."

Sydney lightly punched him on the shoulder. "Good. I'd hate to have to go pick out a nursing home."

"Watch it, missy, or you'll be grounded before you even bring your bags in. I still can't believe you're really here." He ran a hand over her dark hair, his smile soft as he looked her over. "You look so much like your mom, personality and all. Just a smaller version and with glasses."

"Gee, thanks, Daddy. I'm going to tell Mom you said that."

Archer stuck his tongue out at her, causing her to laugh. "You know what I mean. When you were a tiny little thing, I figured you'd eventually hit a growth spurt and be her double. But you never did. You're her mini-me."

Sydney shook her head, chuckling. "I'm five-four, not what I'd call 'mini,' thank you very much." But she smiled at him, pleased with the comparison. Emma Gibson was a very beautiful woman, and Sydney could only hope she was half as pretty and smart and funny as her mother.

As they finished eating and cleaned up from the meal, they caught up on the goings-on of the rest of the family. As Emma had four siblings, it took a while. By the time they were done and heading back out to the front of the house, it was nearly one o'clock.

"So what time is Mom going to be home, do you think?" Sydney asked as they stood side by side on the front porch, looking out across the clearing that made up the yard.

"She was hoping to be back around three or four."

"Hmmm... I wonder what Grandma and Grandpa are doing."

Archer put his arm around her shoulder and squeezed. "Why don't you go see?"

She looked at the truck full of mulch. "Seems to me you could use a pair of hands to help you spread that."

He shrugged. "I have it. If I'd needed help, I could have commandeered your brothers."

"Why didn't you? A little hard work would do those two lazy sots wonders," she told him with a wink.

Archer grinned. "Oh, they'll work plenty this summer, believe me. But school just ended last week, and we figured they could use a little free time to have fun before the drudgery begins. Go see Owen and Sarah. You'll make their day."

"They might not be home."

"I'll bet they are."

She tilted her head to the side, pushing her glasses up on her nose as she studied him. "You're trying awfully hard to get rid of me for someone who was so excited when I showed up. What are you up to?"

Archer kissed her temple. "Not a thing. I don't want you to feel obligated to stay here and help me when I know you're itching to get to the farm."

"Daddy, what am I going to do with you? Stubborn man, you could have been a Campbell." With an exasperated sigh, she started down the steps toward the driveway. "Help me carry my bags in? Tomorrow will be plenty soon enough to go to the farm. You all *do* still do Sunday dinner, right?" she drawled.

"Yes, Miss Impertinence," he shot back with a grin. "And Logan, Amelia, and their brood are planning to be there, too. So you'll get to see them in addition to everyone else. Only Ben, Ainsley, and Lily won't be there."

"Good. I'll bet Amelia's kids are nearly grown."

Archer nodded. "Colin is. And the rest are getting that way, yes. It's been six months since you've seen everyone, and you won't believe how much they've changed."

She'd come in to Lexington, where Ben and Ainsley and their daughter lived, for Christmas. The visit had been wonderful but brief. "I'm looking forward to getting to spend some quality time with everyone. Short visits here and there just don't cut it, you know?"

"Yeah, I do."

As much as he'd tried to get her to go to her grandparents' house, Sydney could tell Archer was pleased that she'd chosen to stay with him as they worked on the mulch. He wasn't her biological father, even though he'd been in her life since the day she was born and had formally adopted her when she was five. He was the only father she'd ever known, the only man she'd ever *wanted* as her father despite the rough patch they'd hit when she was a teenager. And even though she was one hundred percent a daddy's girl, going out of her way to never let him think she wasn't, she knew he still had insecurities from time to time.

So, yes, she was itching to get to the farm, but she didn't mind spending the rest of the day with her father in the least. There'd be time for everything else later.

CHAPTER TWO

THE WATER SLUICING OVER HIS back and shoulders was warm, invigorating, and just what he needed the morning after the disastrous Saturday night before. Sawyer Carson Evans swam hard and fast against the current provided by the swim spa, working out most of the frustration that had kept him tossing and turning through the night. When he finally let his feet touch bottom, he was out of breath, but he felt worlds better than he had when he'd gotten in the pool.

He was still surprised to feel the longer hair that met his hands when he ran them over his scalp. For more than twenty years, he'd worn his hair in an extremely close-cropped style common among law enforcement officers. After his retirement, he'd let it grow out. He'd gotten quite a bit of teasing about the new look, but he liked it. To his mind, the growth signified something new, a different path than the one he'd been on. That old path hadn't been a bad one, but it was in the past. And Sawyer wasn't the kind of man who dwelled on the past. At least not the distant past.

Last night, however, was still fresh enough in his mind that it rode his back like an annoying monkey. He'd had a date that had sounded promising on paper, a blind date set up by a friend. But almost as soon as the evening had begun, Sawyer had known it wouldn't turn out the way he'd hoped.

Oh, the woman had been nice enough, attractive, intelligent. But she'd been overeager, so much so that her attitude had ridden roughshod over her charms, leaving him cold. Five years younger than him and fresh off her second marriage, she'd made Sawyer feel like nothing more than a piece of meat served up on a platter. If he'd wanted to spend the night with her, he could have. No doubt about it. But he hadn't wanted to.

The days of him having sex for the sake of having sex were gone. While he wasn't really after a permanent relationship, he wanted more than just a slaking of lust with the woman of the week or month, as the case might be. At forty-six, he was looking for more from his bed partners than a good time.

Sure, a nice romp between the sheets would've been nice. It had been a long, dry spell, over a year if he was being honest. But even with that being said, he couldn't bring himself to bed the merry divorcée. He wasn't willing to offer himself up as a sacrificial lamb to someone who was looking to take out her anger at her ex-husband or worse, snag a third husband. And more than anything in the world, that's the vibe Sawyer had gotten from her.

He got out of the pool and grabbed his towel, blotting away the majority of the wetness so he wouldn't track it inside. He'd hit the shower, then grab a light breakfast while he looked over his paperwork as he waited for lunchtime to arrive.

Thinking about lunch brought a small smile to his face as he turned on the shower and waited for the water to heat up. He'd be spending the afternoon with Owen and Sarah Campbell and their large, extended family. Family that, after twenty years, they insisted he was part of. From what Sarah's e-mail invitation had said, most of that family was going to be there. John and Zanny and two of their three kids, Emma and Archer and their sons, Rachel and her son, Amelia and Logan and their four kids... And who knew what other assorted cousins and nieces and nephews might show up. It would be a noisy madhouse, one Sawyer hadn't visited in a while.

He'd first interacted with the family twenty years earlier when he was put in charge of an investigation Amelia was involved in. Out of self-defense she'd shot and killed the abusive husband of a friend, a man who'd been stalking her for months. Once she was cleared of any wrongdoing, the family had added Sawyer to the fold. He'd just moved to the area from out of state, was recently divorced, and had basically wanted to be left the hell alone. But one of his co-workers, Burke Lockhart, was engaged to Sarah's niece, Michelle. Sarah had put pressure on Burke, who'd in turn put pressure on Sawyer. Michelle's brother Rick, a county sheriff's deputy, had happily jumped on the bandwagon.

Against his better judgment, he'd found himself spending holidays with the family, in addition to the occasional Sunday dinner. He had an open invitation, though Sarah had learned early on not to press him too hard, so when she did explicitly invite him, he only turned her down if he had a prior obligation. When this invitation had come earlier in the week, he'd been happy to accept.

The connection to the family had grown stronger when Rachel, Sarah and Owen's second daughter, had married another colleague, Ken Boyd. Though the marriage hadn't lasted, Sawyer's connection to the family had endured. He and Rachel had developed a very solid friendship, and he thought of her almost as the sister he'd never had. Even so, he still didn't quite consider himself an insider, as he'd especially tried to keep his emotional distance from the kids as they were growing up. But he was closer to the Campbells and all their kin than he was to just about anyone on the planet, save his grandmother. They'd become his surrogate family of sorts, and Sawyer valued their friendship.

With a reluctant groan, he shut the water off and got out of the shower to dry off. Though he was looking forward to dinner, he'd really prefer to skip the tasks he had to do before the time came for him to leave for the Campbell farm.

When he'd started his own business as a private investigator, one of the things he'd been looking forward to most was a reduction in the amount of paperwork he had to do on a weekly basis. For most cops, paperwork was the bane of their existence, and Sawyer was no exception.

Owning a business—particularly a business that relied on meticulous record keeping, he was learning—was about as far from paperwork-free as one could get. If he'd had any idea how much of it he'd have to plow through on a weekly basis, he might have moved to Florida with his grandmother and taken up fishing.

"You've got to find someone, Evans. Surely to God there's somebody out there who's willing to work for a pittance and get you lined out."

He wasn't making a fortune doing private investigations, but he was doing okay. And he hadn't really gotten into the business for the money. He'd done it so he'd have something to do in order to stay sane. That said, his budget didn't allow for paying someone an exorbitant salary to do his busywork. He'd had two assistants already, one who'd lasted four months and one who'd only lasted three weeks. *That* experience had been so ugly he'd decided to forego hiring anyone else for the job. But the workload, nearly eighty hours a week, was starting to wear thin. He was retired, for crying out loud. He was supposed to be able to take some time off and do the things he wanted to do.

"I'll place an ad tomorrow, see what comes of it. Who knows? Maybe the perfect person will fall into my lap. Stranger things have happened. Right?"

And right after he placed that ad, he'd head over to the animal shelter. He was starting to talk to himself more and more these days, and while a cat or dog wouldn't warm his bed at night the same way a woman would, they'd at least be a companion to talk to so that he didn't feel quite ready for the looney bin.

When he got to the farm, most of the family was already there, a good-sized crowd of Campbells and Campbell relatives already milling around under the picnic shelter Owen had built a few years back.

"We've grown so much now that it just makes sense. After all, we have the land," Owen had said when his son John teased him about it.

The farmhouse was situated on top of a mountain in the middle of hundreds of acres of land that Owen and Sarah owned. It was private, secluded, and peaceful, and access was invitation only. Though no one had ever told him exactly why Owen was so determined to have such a large safe cushion for his family around his home, Sawyer had his suspicions. In any event, as many family gatherings as they held, building a structure that was big enough for everyone to fit in was a logical step.

Rachel was coming out the front door of the farmhouse, plates in hand, and Sawyer changed course to intercept her. "Hold up, Teach."

She laughed up at him and accepted his one-armed hug. "Where've you been, stranger? And what did you bring?"

He held the large bowl of fruit salad down so she could see through the clear plastic. "The usual. Where's the kid?"

"Easton is at the beach with his father, enjoying an early summer vacation," she told him as they walked toward the shelter. "How've you been? You haven't come around much lately. I was starting to think we'd offended you."

Sawyer laughed. "No, I've just been busy. Very, very busy."

A woman's laughter rang out across the meadow, carried

by the wind, and the cheerful sound caught his attention. Looking around, he saw a dark-haired, attractive young woman who was playfully flirting with Rachel's nephew Noah as they came toward the shelter from the opposite direction. "Who's that? Don't tell me Noah finally got a girlfriend. At least the kid has good taste. She's gorgeous."

Rachel's laughter sputtered out. "What are you talking about. You don't mean Sydney?"

Sawyer stopped dead in his tracks, his jaw dropping even as his cheeks flushed. "That's *Sydney*? Little punk-rocker in-your-face rebellious *Sydney*?"

From the cheeky grin Rachel was wearing, he knew he'd stepped in it big time. They were close enough friends that she knew Sawyer didn't make casual observations about women.

"Yes, that Sydney. I can't believe she's changed *that* much since you've seen her. How long has it been?"

He shrugged. "Five, six years?" More like seven, if he wanted to be accurate. Almost seven years to the day.

"Hmmm. She has changed, I guess. She went and grew up on us. She looks so much like Emma that it's scary."

"Says the woman who's practically a doppelgänger for her own mother. You all have strong genes."

Rachel's smile was pleased. "That we do."

In the ensuing chaos that surrounded the family as they got ready to sit down to eat, Sawyer didn't have a chance to say hello to Sydney. To be honest, he didn't go out of his way to greet her, either. He wanted a few minutes for his brain to accept what his eyes had seen.

The last time he'd seen her, she'd been nineteen and in trouble for something that she hadn't done. As the LEO who'd pulled her over, Sawyer had been drawn into the scheme she and her friend had cooked up to hide the truth about what had happened. He'd been coerced into helping her, not unwillingly. He'd made her a promise then that he'd kept for years now, a promise freely given. But that wasn't all.

The last time he'd seen her, she'd kissed him.

It had mortified them both.

Given how viscerally he'd reacted to the sight of her now, that innocent kiss from seven years ago felt different. The context had changed. And he had to admit to himself, even as he carried on conversations with the people around him, that if this Sydney kissed him? He might have had an entirely different reaction than the one he'd had back then.

CHAPTER THREE

SHE'D SEEN SAWYER COME ACROSS the yard with Rachel. He'd been hard to miss, especially since she'd been looking for him. As soon as her grandmother had mentioned he'd be attending, Sydney had gone on alert.

As covertly as she could, she examined him. There was no limp, no obvious sign that he'd had knee surgery. Clad in jeans and a polo shirt, he was as handsome and masculine as ever. His hair was different—longer, softer, though still incredibly short compared to non-law-enforcement types. Though there was gray at the temples, it in no way took away from his attractiveness. If anything it added to it, God help her. And if his flat stomach and wide shoulders were an indication, her father was right—the man was more active now than he'd been while he was wearing a badge.

The noise of the crowd around her was almost overwhelming, and once lunch was mostly finished, with only a few people lingering over their food, Sydney got up. "I need to stretch my legs," she told her grandfather, kissing him on the cheek. "I think I'll head into the house for a few minutes."

Owen winked up at her. "Need a break?"

"Something like that."

He patted her hand. "We'll be here when you come back."

Grabbing some empty bowls, she hurried inside, sighing with relief as the noisy chatter from outside faded with the closing of the storm door. In the kitchen, she set the dishes down and closed her eyes, leaning against the counter as she took in the quiet.

Though she'd grown up in the middle of the loud, boisterous family, she'd been away now for long enough that it felt a little foreign.

Once she was settled, she glanced around. There were several empty dishes on the counter that she could get a start on washing, and starting the hot water in the sink, she lined them up in preparation. She'd just dipped her hands in the water when a man spoke from behind her, causing her to jump.

"Steal any cars lately?"

Even though she'd been half expecting someone to sneak up behind her, she hadn't been expecting Sawyer. And she hadn't heard him come in, the dratted man. He'd truly startled her. She closed her eyes against the shiver of awareness that went through her, even as she laughingly answered, her wet hand going to her face.

"Not lately, no. Sorry to disappoint. Damn, Sawyer, you need to wear a bell or something. You scared me half to death!"

A wide, ever-so-slightly off-center grin met her when she turned around. "Sorry." He reached out and wiped the soapy bubbles off her forehead, blowing them off his hand and back to the sink before folding his arms across his chest and leaning his hips against the edge of the counter. "When did you get in?"

"Yesterday." Sydney grabbed a nearby dish towel and wiped her hands, holding on to the fabric to keep her hands from reaching out to him. To put a little distance between them, she casually moved into the corner opposite where he stood. It was only a couple of feet, but every little bit helped. "I hear you exchanged the badge for a trench coat. Congratulations."

"Thanks. It's been an interesting road."

Silence descended between them, and a warm flush spread across Sydney's cheeks as he studied her.

"What?"

He shook his head. "I'm just trying to reconcile the two Sydneys. You went and grew up on us."

She laughed softly. "That does happen, you know." Knowing that if she didn't do something she'd embarrass herself, she moved back to the sink and started washing the first dish.

"Seen Danny yet? I'm surprised he isn't here today, what with you being back in town."

Danny was her best friend, her partner in crime. They'd been attached at the hip since sixth grade when she'd saved him from a bully.

"He doesn't know I'm back yet. I sneaked into town, wanted to surprise everyone. I'm planning to stop by his office tomorrow. Why? You aren't afraid the crime rate will skyrocket now that I'm back in town, are you? You might have to bring that uniform out of storage."

Sawyer chuckled, the sound going through her to tickle places best left alone, at least as far as she knew he was concerned. "Nah, I'm not worried. The two of you never were hardened criminals."

Sydney snorted. "Tell his mother that. She thinks I'm the devil incarnate."

He leaned closer and lowered his voice as though imparting a secret. "Miriam thinks every female who crosses Danny's path is the devil incarnate, determined to lead him down the path of self-destruction. Don't take it personally."

"Seriously? She would have arranged for me to disappear if she could have when we were kids. Heck, probably more recently than that if she could have figured out how to do it. She hates my guts. Always has." Sydney cast him a look over her shoulder, daring him to argue. From the way he hid his smile behind his hand, she figured he agreed with her assessment.

"He was in the office Thursday. He's turned out pretty well, you know."

She paused in rinsing the bowl she held as a familiar pang of relief winged its way through her chest. "I do know. And I know you're part of why he did. So what did he come in for, if I may be so nosy as to ask?" She set the bowl in the dish drainer and turned toward him.

"He has a couple of kids who need some guidance this summer. I was getting him some contact information for the guys who've taken that over."

"You didn't keep a hand in it?" She knew, both from experience and from what Danny had told her over the years, that Sawyer had quietly helped a handful of troubled kids stay on the straight and narrow, stepping in as a role model when they didn't have anyone to turn to. "I figured you would."

"You know about that?"

She let a tiny smile out. "Of course."

He gave a shrug, clearly uncomfortable. "I'm on the sidelines. I can do more from there now than anything. So who told you?"

"I have my sources. I also hear that you need an assistant to help with that new business of yours." She couldn't believe the words had come out of her mouth, and as soon as she said them, she wanted to call them back. As that wasn't an option, she kept her mouth shut.

Sawyer was eyeing her with consternation. "You're as bad about knowing stuff as Amelia is," he said, referring to her aunt, Emma's youngest sister, who seemed to have a finger on the pulse of everything that happened in the family. "Yeah, I do need someone. I just can't find anyone I can trust to run the place. Why?"

It was Sydney's turn to shrug. "I might know someone."

"Who?"

She propped one hand on her hip, pushing her glasses up with the other. "Duh. Me."

When Sawyer blinked at her, speechless, she threw her hands in the air. "Surely it isn't that odd a notion."

His lips twitched. "Channeling Owen, are you?"

She had to fight to tamp down her own smile. "Hush. I'm serious. I need a job, you need help. I have experience."

"Yeah, stealing cars and taking them across state lines, getting caught with a concealed deadly weapon without a permit..." His voice trailed off when she crossed her arms over her chest and narrowed her eyes, though his mouth moved into a wide grin. "It's a hectic job, doesn't pay much, and it can get hairy from time to time."

The first thought that went through her mind was of the television detectives she'd seen on shows in reruns on late-night cable. She shook her head. "So you're telling me you go around breaking people's knees and camping out in your car while they have liaisons in seedy motel rooms, huh?"

He scowled. "Not hardly. I don't handle divorce cases, and I only break knees when it's absolutely necessary. I just don't think you'd be a good fit, that's all."

Sydney blew out a breath to hide how much the words hurt. "Why not? Because of my criminal past?"

Sawyer cocked an eyebrow. "No, because you're more suited to...to an art gallery or something. Not a half-retired PI's office."

She couldn't help but laugh. "Oh, dear God. Sawyer, you're a snob. How would you know what I'm suited to? You haven't seen me since I was a kid."

The look he sent her told her he hadn't forgotten their last encounter any more than she had. Just the idea almost made her run out the door. But Sydney was made of stern stuff, sterner than she had been at nineteen, and she'd be damned if she'd run again.

"Tell you what, I'll swing by one day next week after I've had a chance to catch up with everyone and find a place to live, and we'll talk. You can show me how 'hairy' this job of yours is. I'll even bring a few razors, just in case."

He opened his mouth to protest, but before he could, Amelia came in. Rachel was close behind her, and the opportunity was lost. Sydney smiled at him with satisfaction, knowing he was stuck. She was glad as her heart was pounding. She'd only barely managed to stop short of throwing herself at his feet and begging for the job. If there was a surefire way not to get it, that would be it.

As her aunts joined the conversation, Sawyer excused himself. Sydney turned back to the sink and the dishes, sighing with relief. She didn't see the look Amelia sent Rachel, or the speculative gazes they studied her with as the three of them talked about books they'd read recently. If she had, she really might have made a run for it.

"What do you think that was about?" Rachel asked Amelia as soon as they were alone. It was late in the day, almost early evening, and she'd been itching to get her baby sister by herself so she could ask Amelia whether she'd imagined the heat in the kitchen between Sawyer and Sydney or not. "Did you see how they were looking at each other?"

"When the other one wasn't looking? Yeah, I saw it. And I felt it," Amelia said, rubbing her hands over her arms. A natural Cupid, she could pick up on a couple's attraction to and suitability for one another in ways most people could not. "They just about sparked me out of the kitchen. Damn!"

"Sawyer and Sydney? Really?" Rachel was stunned.

"Really. It's been a while since I've been around a couple that hummed like that. Probably since Archer and Emma. What should we do?"

"I don't know. Should we do anything? He's a good man."

Amelia frowned. "I know he's a good man. I also know he's determined to remain unmarried the rest of his life and why."

Rachel blew out a breath. The warm breeze blowing across the meadow lifted her long hair, whipping it gently around her face. They'd walked out to the barn for privacy.

"I'd like to see Sydney happy," Rachel hedged. "And Sawyer, for that matter. He really is a good man, a kind man. Too kind to spend the rest of his life alone."

"She's young enough to be his daughter. What? It had to be said," Amelia protested when Rachel shot her a dirty look. "And no, I don't think it matters in the least. Not to me, it doesn't. It *will* matter to him. And I don't even want to think about how it will matter to Archer if it comes to that."

"Yeah, that could get... interesting. They really sparked?"

Amelia nodded. "And hummed."

"Good or bad?"

Her baby sister's smile was soft. "They have a very nice resonance. That aspect of things reminds me of Mom and Daddy." She sighed. "I think we have to keep our mouths shut and our eyes open. He's a good man. And she deserves a good man."

"He is and she does," Rachel agreed. "But he's got pretty deep scars, too. Shoot, we've known him for twenty years, and I've been what I'd consider close friends with him nearly that long. There's still a lot about the man I don't know. I have my doubts that he could let her in even if he wanted to."

Amelia linked their arms. "I guess we'll have to wait and see, then. But I'm not planning to say anything to Em or Archer. No use starting trouble if there's not any to start. And that could put a stop to things before they get off the ground."

Rachel laughed. "This is true. So we'll watch and wait and keep our fingers crossed. Sound like a plan?"

"Yes, ma'am, it does."

CHAPTER FOUR

SYDNEY PULLED HER CAR INTO the parking lot of the picturesque church a little after ten the next morning. For a couple of minutes, she sat there looking at the building and its surroundings. It wasn't the largest church in Perry County, but anyone with eyes in their head could see it was well loved. The building itself was in good repair, with tidy black shutters against the white clapboard siding and a cheerful bed of petunias and marigolds around the perimeter of the building.

A few times in her youth, she had attended the church with Danny and his family. While it hadn't been neglected by any means back then, the small touches of hominess, like the baskets of ferns and discreet little statues of woodland creatures peeking out from behind the greenery that flanked the wide front steps, made it clear that whoever was in charge of the congregation now wanted to make it feel welcoming. Sydney had a good idea who was behind that change.

She detoured past the front door, instead going to the small building that sat beside the church, separated from the main church by a covered concrete pad. The door was open to let in the June breeze, and she stopped in the doorway, pecking softly on the doorframe.

"Can I help... oh, my God." The tall blond-haired man

seated behind the desk laughed incredulously, coming to his feet without taking his eyes off her. "I'll be hanged."

Sydney's smile was as wide as Danny's as she met him midway across the room for a tight hug. "I was in the neighborhood, thought I'd stop by and see what kind of trouble you're up to this morning."

"Just the usual quarterbacking of yesterday's sermon." He squeezed her extra tight, then pulled back to look at her, shaking his head. "In the neighborhood. I'll be hanged."

"I've missed you." Her eyes searched his face, taking in the changes. He'd gained a little weight, but it looked good on him. Danny had always been a little gaunt, the stereotypical ninety-eight-pound weakling, even after he'd hit a growth spurt as a teenager. The wheat-blond hair and hazel eyes were the same, though. "It's so good to see you, Dan."

He cupped her face in his hands, examining her just as thoroughly. "Are you in trouble or are you just in for a visit?" He asked the question with a wink.

"I'm home. Out of a job, no roof over my head..."

Danny settled down on the edge of his desk, a mock frown crossing his face. "Are you pregnant?"

Sydney smacked his shoulder lightly, then took the spot beside him. "Not unless it was an immaculate conception. Speaking of religious occurrences and the like... The church is beautiful. You've done an amazing job from what little I've seen. I'm proud of you."

"Thank you. It's been a lot of hard work but oh, so worth it."

Danny had been appointed pastor of the small congregation close to two years earlier, after having served as associate pastor for a couple of years before that.

"Do you have time to show me around?" she asked.

"I'll not only show you around, but I'll buy you lunch if you're interested."

Sydney grinned at him, feeling ridiculously happy to see him again. "Lead the way."

After he'd shown her the church, they drove the short distance to town to a popular diner. Once they were seated, he leveled a look on her. "So are you in trouble? Or did you just decide it was time to come home? And why in the world didn't you tell me you were coming? Don't think I'm not happy to see you, because I'm thrilled. But I'm wondering whether I should be concerned, as well."

"I'm not in trouble. You know Uncle Charles was retiring, and I was contemplating traveling. I just decided to travel here. I packed up my things, put them in storage, and when I got in the car to figure out where to go... something said 'home.' It was that simple. I didn't say anything because I wanted to surprise you."

"You really are planning to stay?" he asked as the waitress brought them their drinks.

"I am. Someone has to be around here to keep you in line," she said as she wadded up the paper from her straw and tossed it at him. "I may even have a job lined up already. I just have to convince Sawyer to give it to me."

Danny nearly choked on his soft drink. "Sawyer? Sawyer Evans?"

Sydney scowled at him. "Why is that so surprising?"

The waitress returned with their salads then, saving Danny from having to answer immediately. Sydney gave him a minute after she left to answer, and when he didn't, she asked again. "Is it so incredible, the idea that I might end up working for him?"

Danny paused, cracker in hand, clearly trying to figure out how to answer. "Not incredible, no. Just... knowing your history with the man, it's a little unexpected. That's all."

"Damn. You don't think I should do it, then."

"I didn't say that," he protested. "God knows Sawyer needs someone to help him out. I'm just not sure you two would be a good fit, that's all."

"He said you'd been in to see him last week." When Danny quirked an eyebrow, she shrugged. "He was at the farm yesterday for dinner. We spoke briefly. And as to us fitting, he's not convinced, either. Said I'd be better suited to working in an art gallery or some such."

Danny grinned across the table at her. "I can see that. Until you had to open your mouth and sell something."

Sydney grunted as she chomped on a cherry tomato, enjoying the blast of flavor that hit her mouth as it exploded. "Amen to that, Pastor. A salesman I'm not. I don't have the patience to schmooze people. Either buy it or don't."

There was something very comforting about being able to spend time with someone who knew your flaws and yet didn't judge you for them. Danny was that person for Sydney. He always had been. As far as that went, she played the same role for him. They didn't have secrets from one another, and if Danny hadn't been gay, they probably would have ended up married.

"You ever think that we could have had a couple of kids by now?" she asked softly.

His smile was quick and just a bit sad. "I do think about that. Usually during christenings or Mother's lectures. We'd have made some cute kids, wouldn't we?"

"Hellions. They'd be hellions and you know it. And I love you dearly, but I don't think I could handle your mother on a regular, marriage-induced basis."

"I can barely handle my mother on a regular basis. I'd never subject someone else to her." He winked, letting her know he was joking, though Sydney also knew there was some measure of truth to the words. "I'm still on the fence as to whether or not to come out."

Sydney studied him. "What does your church mentor say?"

The decision to stay in the closet was one he'd battled for years now, at first because he wasn't strong enough emotionally to face his family's reaction, and then because he simply didn't want the bother of dealing with his mother's histrionics.

"He says I should come clean, at least to the family. As long as I stay in, I'm not being honest with them. He's right. I just have to muster up the courage to do it. Mother still isn't sold a hundred percent on my vow of celibacy. I just worry that if I come out, she'll try to institute an exorcism."

Sydney reached across the table, clasping his hand with hers. "You know I'll be here for you whatever you decide."

Truthfully, knowing he was close to a decision was one of the reasons Sydney had wanted to come home. She was too aware that things could go very badly for him with the family and if they did, she wanted to be close by so he would have a support system if he needed it.

"I do know that. And I love you for it."

Sydney winked at him, even as she misted up. "Back at you."

"Now, let's get back to that subject you seem to want to avoid. Are you seriously going to try to work for Sawyer?"

She sighed and sat back. "That depends on him. The job sounds interesting enough. I could probably do most of it in my sleep, and it would be familiar. Daddy said he needed an assistant. It's investigations. I'm guessing there's probably a lot of interaction with law enforcement and colorful characters."

"Sydney, this is me you're talking to. It isn't the job that interests you."

She wet her lips and looked out the window at the traffic passing by on the road beyond the diner's parking lot. "It doesn't sound boring," she hedged.

"But the boss man's the real draw," Danny finished in a low voice. "I don't want to see you get hurt."

She wanted to argue with him. She couldn't. "Maybe if I spend time with him in an office setting, I'll get over this ridiculous crush. Maybe he burps and farts and smells like onions and liver on closer acquaintance. Besides, I don't know if I'll be able to convince him to give me the job no matter how badly he needs someone in there."

Danny gave a quick shrug. "He really does need help. I don't know. Like I said, I just hate to see you get hurt."

"I've got some visiting to do today, tomorrow. I'll probably go in Wednesday or thereabouts and see what he says. As much as I'm jumping in with both feet, my eyes closed, I don't think he'll give me the job. The sad thing is, I *am* qualified for it. And I really might like it. I guess we'll have to wait and see."

"Well, however things turn out, I'm here for you," Danny told her quietly. He smiled across the table at her. "It's good to have you back."

Sydney tipped her head to the side and smiled back at him. "It's good to be back."

CHAPTER FIVE

HE KNEW SHE'D SHOW UP. Oh, he'd hoped she'd not but in his heart, Sawyer knew Sydney'd been serious about the job. When she walked in the door ten minutes after he opened the office Thursday morning, he cursed under his breath. Looking fresh, young, and too pretty for his peace of mind, she greeted him with a sunny smile and a bag of pastries.

"I'm not above bribes," she said as he took the bag. "Are you terribly busy?"

Sawyer huffed out a breath even as he opened the bag and sniffed. "No. Let's get this over with."

"Gee, Sawyer, you'll give me a complex. You sound like me when I have to go to the dentist. Surely I'm not that daunting." She followed him from the reception area into his office, taking in every nook and cranny of the place as she sat down in the guest chair. When he sat and pulled a bear claw from the bag, she handed him one of the paper plates she carried, along with a napkin.

Sawyer raised an eyebrow. "What makes you think you'd be able to do this job?"

"Well, now, since I'm not entirely clear on what the job is, I'm not sure I *can* do it. Why don't we start there? Tell me what you need."

The phone rang, and after glancing at caller ID, he ignored it.

“I need someone who can answer phones, greet clients, be discreet, handle transcribing reports, do a craptastic load of paperwork and payroll, make me coffee, keep the office clean, and generally run things while I’m not here. The pay’s lousy, the hours are long, and there’s little chance of promotion.”

Sydney nodded. “I can do that. I don’t need the money, so the lousy pay isn’t a problem.” When he snorted, she shrugged. “Sorry, but it’s true. When you walk in after a family member’s funeral and find your husband banging the maid on the dining room table, you get a bit of bargaining power in the divorce. Especially considering that your father-in-law and his business partner are with you when you catch dear hubby *in flagrante delicto*.”

Sawyer’s eyebrows clashed together in a mighty scowl. “Son of a bitch. I’m sorry.”

She waved the apology away. “It was a blessing in disguise, but thanks. Regardless, it left me in a very comfortable position financially. Plus, I’ve not spent the last three years idle. I worked as Uncle Charles’s personal assistant at the law firm in Savannah where he was a senior partner. I helped him close his end of the business out during the past year, and I’m familiar with how an office works. I also realize how important discretion is in this kind of business.”

She paused, giving him a chance to offer a rebuttal. For the life of him, Sawyer was having a hard time coming up with one. The phone rang again, the same caller as before, and as before he ignored it.

“I’d need you at least forty hours a week for a while.”

“I’m used to working sixty to eighty. Forty will feel like a vacation.”

He narrowed his eyes as he sat back, wiping his hands on a napkin as he studied her. “Why do you want this job?”

Sydney pushed her glasses up, her gaze dropping to his desk. “You need help. From what I’ve heard, you’ve had trouble finding it. And it sounds interesting. I need something to do, and I might just enjoy this. At the very least, I can help you out of a pinch."

There was more, Sawyer knew. He just didn't know what that something else was. He didn't want to hire her, but the hell of it was, she did sound perfect for the job.

"You'd have to pass a background check."

"Hmmm. That might be a problem. Except you already know every criminal thing I've ever done," she countered, though her cheeks were flushed. "I've walked the path of the good girl since I was nineteen. I've not had so much as a speeding ticket."

"Where are you going to be staying? With your folks?"

To his surprise, her mouth tightened. "That's still up in the air. They haven't done anything with the old house, and if we can get past Mom and Daddy's stubbornness, I'll probably move in there."

It was entirely nosy of him, but Sawyer's curiosity was aroused. "Why are they being stubborn?"

"My parents are genetically programmed to be stubborn, you know that."

"Runs in the family."

She laughed softly, but the question made her uncomfortable, no doubt. She was clearly reluctant to answer, which made him even more determined to know what was going on. When he just stared at her, waiting, she finally gave in with a sigh.

"You know Archer isn't my biological father, right?"

Sawyer nodded.

"When Mom came home from Georgia all those years ago, when she was pregnant with me, she bought that house with money my biological father had given her to take care of me with. So she and Daddy are trying to say that the house is mine to begin with. I'm arguing that it's their house, they're the ones who've maintained it all these years, and they should either rent it or sell it to me. Not give it to me outright like they're trying to do." She frowned. "Why are you smiling?"

He shook his head. "That's just a very adult thing of you to do. I'm imagining the 'discussion' you all've been having, that's all."

Sydney growled. "It's hard to tell who's winning. At this point, we're at an impasse. If they keep insisting on giving me the house, I may end up renting an apartment somewhere just to prove a point. Whose point I'd be proving, though, I don't know." She crossed her eyes and stuck her tongue out, then gave another soft laugh.

This time, Sawyer laughed with her. "You all will figure it out. What if you get bored and decide you hate the job, leave me high and dry here all by myself?"

The change of subject didn't throw her, but the question did make her angry. If he wasn't mistaken, it also disappointed her. "I'm not a quitter. If I make a commitment, I honor it. And if I did get bored, I'd at least give you notice. Can it be worse than the situation you're in now?" She gestured around the office.

As though to validate her words, the phone rang again. Sydney raised an eyebrow and waited expectantly for him to either answer it or ignore it.

Shaking his head, cursing under his breath again, Sawyer stood and went to a nearby filing cabinet. "Fill this out," he said, handing her an application. "Front and back. Assuming you pass the background check, when do you want to start?"

"I'll pass the background check," she told him confidently. "And I can start whenever you want me to."

The phone rang again. This time it wasn't a call he could ignore, and he answered. "Evans Investigations."

Sydney smiled and stood, going into the reception

area. Sawyer kept an eye on her as she sat at the desk out there and filled out the application, his attention mostly on the phone call. He made some notes pertinent to the conversation after he hung up, his mind racing as he asked himself what the hell he was doing.

He knew she'd pass the background check. Her qualifications were ideal. She'd definitely brighten the place up. And he couldn't ignore the fact that the pay didn't matter. But damn it, he'd really been hoping he would be able to say no.

He'd had disturbing dreams about Sydney ever since Sunday, dreams that had him seriously contemplating calling the divorcée for a second date. Given the difference in their ages, Sawyer was horrified. He blamed the dreams on the fact that it had been so long since he'd had sex. And he told himself that he hadn't spent that much time around Sydney when she was a child, only a handful of encounters here and there. It wasn't like he'd watched her grow up. Knowing that didn't make it better, though.

When he saw her sign the application, he stood and went into the front room. She handed him the paper, and as he glanced at it, he saw that she'd filled it out fully, her handwriting neat and not the frilly girlish scrawl he'd been expecting. He had a feeling there was a lot about Sydney that would turn out to be not what he'd expected.

"Give me your driver's license and social security card," he said gruffly. "I'll make a copy of those. If you can come back after lunch, I'll have the background check done. We can go from there."

"I'll be here. What time exactly?" she asked as he made the copies.

"Let's say one." Handing her the IDs, he nodded. "See you in a bit."

She smiled up at him. "I can hardly wait."

After she'd gone, he crossed to the desk and picked up the pen she'd used, watching out the window as she exited the stairs and headed down the sidewalk in the direction of her mother's photography studio. "You're a pathetic, dirty old man, Evans," he growled. "And you're an idiot."

He'd had to fight not to draw in a deep breath as she stood beside him while he made copies of the IDs. Her perfume was subtle, not light and floral as he'd imagined, but darker, more seductive. Hiring Sydney was definitely not a good idea, he thought for the hundredth time since she'd walked in the office, but he'd be damned if he could come up with a good reason not to. Maybe he'd be able to figure something out by the time she returned.

CHAPTER SIX

IT TOOK EVERY BIT OF willpower Sydney had as she walked downstairs to the street not to break into skips and giggles. She had to remind herself that she was a twenty-six-year-old divorced woman who'd just applied for a position with a man who didn't particularly want her working for him, not a nineteen-year-old kid getting a summer dream job with the hottie who'd caught her eye.

She'd gotten the job! Thankfully, she was far enough down the street now that she was around an ever-so-slight bend, and when the giddy laugh escaped her, she didn't try to hold it back.

She practically skipped past the bakery where she'd gotten the pastries and opened the door of the photography studio Emma Gibson had set up all those years ago when she'd come home pregnant with Sydney.

Her Aunt Zanny greeted her with an expectant smile. "Well?"

Sydney's excited squeal served as an answer as she danced in place.

Zanny clapped her hands, laughing at the antics. "Congratulations! I'm so happy that you're happy! And that Sawyer will have you helping him. The poor man's been run ragged. When do you start?"

Sydney pirouetted across the room to land not lightly on

the sofa. "If I have my way? Today. If he has his way? Never. But I think I won this round."

"So you got it?" Emma asked as she came in from the back room. "You'll really be working just a few doors down from us?"

"Yep. Think you can stand having me that close, Mama?"

Emma walked over and placed a smacking kiss on her forehead. "I'll manage. I knew the man would have the good sense to hire you. Now, we just need to get that housing situation straightened out. Zanny, maybe you can talk some sense into her."

Zanny, who'd been her mother's best friend since she and Emma were seven, pursed her lips. "She has plenty sense. And she has a point. Charge her a pittance for rent, make her pay utilities, and call it done. Save the money in a special account and buy her something huge for her birthday next year." Zanny winked at Sydney, and Sydney winked back.

"It's her house!" Emma protested.

"It's not *just* her house. It's your house, too. You're both right about this, and you're both wrong. Compromise."

Emma flopped down beside Sydney. "Fine. Two hundred a month. You're in charge of everything else the house needs. And what do you want for your birthday?"

Sydney laughed. "I don't care. I don't need anything. Give the money to the animal shelter or something. Deal?" She held her hand out, biting her lip as Emma contemplated the offer. When her mother groaned and gave in, sealing the deal with a handshake, Sydney smiled.

"So when do you start your job?" Emma asked.

"We'll see. Maybe today if I can twist his arm. He didn't want to give it to me. I could read that as plainly as I can read the newspaper. He really must be as desperate as everyone says." That hurt a bit, she wasn't going to lie. But in the end, she'd gotten the job, and that was what she was holding on to.

"The first girl he had was pretty good, really," Zanny said. "But it was a lot of work and she had a small child. The second girl? You know those old TV shows where the secretary sits there chewing gum, talking on the phone, filing her nails?"

Sydney was astonished. "Surely not?"

"Yep. Two-hour lunches, coming in late, the whole nine yards. It was a disaster. She confused a couple of his clients with one another, from my understanding, in a way that nearly caused a fistfight right in the office."

Eyes wide, Sydney looked at her mother.

Emma nodded. "I don't think I've ever seen anyone run that fast in three-inch heels as she went by to her car. We heard him roar at her from in here. Literally. Not that I blame the man."

"That was when he vowed never again. But then he had to start keeping up with all the paperwork, and he's been reconsidering that vow," Zanny said.

"It sounds like the two of you see quite a bit of him." Sydney looked from her mother to Zanny.

"We do," her aunt confirmed. "He'll stop in on slow days for coffee or a pastry or the like, just to have someone to talk to more than anything I think. As solitary as he is, he's not used to being completely alone with only clients to interact with."

Emma snorted. "If Myrtle from downstairs has her way, he'd interact with her."

"That's true." Zanny shook her head as she sipped her coffee. "Even if she is old enough to be his mother."

"She's not *that* old," Emma protested. "Only about ten years older than him. She's just been rode hard."

"Still, she's not who I'd pair him with. She's... a bit of a corncob. Sawyer needs a sleek fox."

"Who's Myrtle?" Sydney asked, tamping down on her jealousy.

"She owns the beauty salon on the first floor of Sawyer's

building. She moved in a couple of years back after the place she'd had for decades burned down." Emma stood as the phone rang. "That's my cue. Can you stick around for lunch?"

"I might head over to the library first, then come back. I'm supposed to be at Sawyer's at one."

"You might see Noah and Daddy there," Emma said. "Daddy wanted to do some genealogy, and Noah usually drives him these days."

"How come?" Sydney asked, concerned. Although both her grandparents had seemed to be the picture of health yesterday, they were eighty-one and seventy-five respectively, and Sydney knew they wouldn't always be as sprightly as they were now.

"I think Owen just likes spending the time with Noah," Zanny answered. "They're two of a kind, and he knows Noah tends to stay in more than he should. If he's not working, he's home. And Owen tries to get him out and about. I think he's looking for a woman for Noah, between us and the fencepost."

"Awww... that's so sweet! Grandpa's matchmaking? Does Noah realize that's what Grandpa's doing?"

Sydney knew Zanny worried about Noah. He was her oldest son, and he had abilities that were uncommon even in the Campbell family. He could see, hear, and talk to the dead, and had been able to since he was small. Those abilities had weighed heavily on Noah, who craved solitude as a result.

Emma's snort was amused. "No. Noah's your typical male in that regard. For the record, I hope it works. I hope Daddy does find him someone. I know he worries that Noah's too much like he was before he met Mom."

Zanny nodded. "There's a reason Sarah likes to call Noah her 'little Owen' and it isn't because he looks just like his grandfather at that age. Maybe now that you're home, you can help Owen find him someone."

"Whew. I don't know. If you all haven't had any luck, I probably won't. But I can try. Maybe Danny can help."

After giving them both excited hugs, she left and headed for the new library. Once there, she looked around for her grandfather and cousin but didn't see them. She did find a few books she'd been trying to find the time to read, though, and she snatched them up. It wasn't until she got to the checkout desk that she realized she didn't have a valid library card.

"Would you like to apply for one?" the girl behind the counter asked her. "I just need two forms of ID and proof of a current address."

"Yeah, I don't have that yet, not the Kentucky license or address, I mean. I only got back in Kentucky this weekend. Um, my grandmother is Sarah Campbell. She used to be the director here. Well, at the old library, not *here* here. If I call her, she can verify my information. Will that work?"

The girl bit her lip. "I don't know. I'll have to ask. I remember Mrs. Campbell from when I was a little girl, and she and Mr. Campbell are in here pretty often still with that yummy guy. I guess he's your cousin?"

"Mm-hmmm. He's single, too," Sydney said, all too happy to throw Noah under the bus if that's what it took to get her library card. After all, he and his brother Eli were as close to her as brothers, and what else was a little sister to do? "I could get you his phone number."

The girl glanced over her shoulder, then back at Sydney. "You'll be staying here in Kentucky?" she asked, her voice low.

Sydney nodded. "I just haven't had a chance to get moved in yet."

"But you know the address?"

"Yes."

The girl blew out a breath, going to the end of the counter to pick up a form and set of cards. She brought it back to

Sydney. "Fill it out with the Kentucky address, then. We'll let it slide by this time, given who you are."

Once she was done, Sydney handed the form back. The girl slid a sticky note across the counter.

"Um, the phone number?"

Sydney laid her book bag down and pulled her phone out, thumbing through her contacts to find Noah's number. "He does custom woodworking—cabinets, staircases, the like. This is his business number. If you have anything around the house that needs done, you might set up an appointment with him, have him come out and do an estimate or something. It would give you a chance to talk to him."

The girl pushed a strand of hair back behind her ear. "I'm in an apartment over Mom's garage, but she's been talking about redoing her kitchen. That'd be perfect. Thank you so much," she said with a shy smile as Sydney handed the number over. "We're really not allowed to use the patrons records here to access their numbers for anything personal, and I never can seem to catch the call when he has a hold in."

"No problem. Good luck. And thanks for the card."

"It was a fair trade. See ya around."

As she went to her car, Sydney thought about what Noah would say if she knew he'd just been set up. The girl seemed sweet enough. And she was honest enough not to abuse the library's policy, so that was a point in her favor. That said, Sydney didn't have much hope that Noah would return the girl's interest. He was a bit of a recluse who simply preferred to be left alone. He'd moved into Rachel's old house nearly ten years ago when he'd come home after spending a few years in Europe, and aside from short trips here and there for weddings and funerals, that's where he stayed.

Since she had the keys to the old house, she decided to swing by there before heading back to Sawyer's. Her parents had left some of the furniture in the house, and if she was going to be moving in, it made sense to make a list of what she needed beforehand.

Even though the house was vacant, it didn't have that neglected air some houses got when they were empty. The grass was cut, the flowers were blooming, and the windows still wore curtains. That said, it felt lonely. It was a bit stuffy inside, but that would clear out with open windows and air-conditioning. They'd left the couch and tables in the living room, she saw, as well as the dining room table and chairs.

"There were a lot of good years in this house," she said, stopping in the kitchen door and remembered watching her parents cook dinner, helping as she got older, chasing her brothers around the open archways that led from room to room, playing with Noah and Eli and their sister Molly when they'd come over... As nice as her parents' new house was, Sydney was glad they'd held on to this one. She wasn't ready to let it go just yet.

A glance at her watch told her she'd better hit the road. She had about twenty minutes before she had to meet Sawyer, but she didn't want to risk getting stuck in traffic. Even though it only took about ten minutes to drive from one side of Hazard to the other, she'd rather be safe than sorry.

Sydney was nervous. There was no hiding it. She hadn't even been able to think about food, even though she was getting a little hungry. It wasn't simply that she'd be working with Sawyer in fairly close quarters but that she didn't want to let him down. She didn't want to disappoint him. She wanted to show him she was competent, professional, and yes, she wanted to make herself invaluable to him.

Before her marriage, she would have entertained the idea of making the man's head spin so much with her overwhelmingly terrific skills that he'd fall to his knees in gratitude and head over heels in love with her.

Now? She knew better than to even entertain that idea.

Just thinking about the goal her younger self would have set made her cringe with embarrassment.

"After that stunt you pulled when you were nineteen, it's a miracle he let you in the door, Sydney Marie, much less agreed to hire you."

But he had let her in the door, and Sydney was going to do her best not to make him regret it. It had taken a while and some tough knocks that she'd wondered if she'd survive, but she'd finally grown up. Now all she had to do was prove it.

CHAPTER SEVEN

MUCH AS SHE'D HOPED, SYDNEY convinced Sawyer to let her start that very afternoon. It wasn't hard—all she had to do was walk in the door to find him faced with a ringing phone, a tearful client, and a screaming baby.

"I'm sorry, Sawyer," the woman was saying, her voice raised over the baby's cries. "He's tired, and he's teething. I'll have to come back another day to talk."

From the frustration and concern on Sawyer's face, Sydney guessed that whatever they had planned to talk about, it didn't need to wait until another day. Fond of the notion that if a person acts like they know what they're doing people would believe they do, she jumped in with both feet.

"Hi. I'm Sydney, Sawyer's assistant. Why don't you let me hold him and try to calm him down?" she asked, tossing her purse on the desk and extending her hands out to the baby. She was as surprised as anyone when he only hesitated a moment, then lunged for her.

"O...okay," the mother stammered. She handed Sydney the large diaper bag she carried. "His teething ring is in there. I can dig it out."

The baby had calmed down some, still crying but not as loudly as before. Sydney didn't want to disturb that growing peace. "I'll find it. You two go on in and talk."

"Thanks, Sydney. Mina, come with me. He's in good

hands and we'll only be a room away." Sawyer shot her a grateful look over the woman's shoulder as he ushered her into his office.

"He doesn't need to know that I know next to nothing about babies, now does he?" Sydney asked the little boy in a soft voice as she settled him in closer against her. "No, he doesn't. As long as we can figure this out, we're good."

She continued to speak in a low, soft voice as she eased around the desk to sit. Once the baby was situated on her lap, sniffling wetly but calm, she pulled the bag across the desk.

"Let's see what we have in here, shall we, big guy?" The bag was tattered here and there, and Sydney could see that it had been mended carefully more than once. The contents were neatly arranged, and finding the teething ring didn't take long. As soon as she pulled it out, the baby reached for it, grabbing it and taking it from her with surprising strength.

"Wow, Popeye. What have they been feeding you, huh? You've got muskles."

The baby leaned against her, drool dripping down his chin as he gnawed on the hard plastic ring. His eyes drooped closed as he started drifting off, and Sydney took advantage of his quietness to clean his face with a wipe.

"There you go," she whispered, placing a soft kiss on his head. "All better now."

Nearly twenty minutes had passed before the door to Sawyer's office opened and he emerged with the baby's mother. She was still pale but appeared to have calmed down. When she saw the baby asleep in Sydney's arms, she smiled tensely.

"I'm so sorry he was a bother. And thank you so much for taking him."

"He was a sweetheart," Sydney assured her as she handed him over. "What's his name?"

"Carter."

Sydney chuckled. “My baby brother’s named Carter. It’s a good name.”

This time the woman’s answering smile was more natural. “Thanks. He’s named after my grandfather.”

“Mina, I’ll be in touch as soon as I know something,” Sawyer told her. “Try not to worry too much. We’ll figure this out.”

She nodded, and something very much like resolve flashed in her eyes. “I know that. It just gets overwhelming from time to time. Thank you both.”

Once the door closed behind her, Sydney sagged back in her chair. “Wow. That was terrifying.”

Sawyer’s eyebrows quirked up. “How so?”

“I’ve not held a baby in years. Probably since Aunt Pip’s kids were that size. We got lucky that he liked me. She seemed nice. What’s her story?”

His mouth tightened. “Her father just remarried, and Mina thinks the woman he married is trying to kill him. At the very least, she’s determined to gaslight him and Mina. She lives at home with her dad and stepmother—Mina’s a single mother, works a lot of hours. She can’t afford childcare and she’s terrified of leaving the baby with the woman.”

“Good Lord. The poor thing.” Sydney was horrified. “And she can’t go to the police? Not that you’re not kind of law enforcement, I mean…”

Sawyer leaned against the desk beside her chair and picked up the small glass paperweight from the corner of the blotter, turning it over and over in his hands. “There’s nothing the cops can do. She did go to them, and they told her she needed to see a shrink. She knew me from a couple of years back when she got into trouble and still had my card. Dug it up and called me. I kept the same cell phone number when I retired just for that reason.”

“So people you’d helped in the past would still have that lifeline?” she asked softly.

The question made him uncomfortable, she could tell,

but he answered. "Yeah. Though I wouldn't call it a lifeline necessarily."

"Mm. Of course not. What kind of trouble did she get into?"

"Running with the wrong crowd, mixed up with the boy's father. She's a good kid, just got put on the wrong path."

Sydney's smile was a little sad. "I know the type. So how can I help?"

He blew out a breath. "Start by answering the phone. For right now, take a message with every call unless it's Nan Carson. I'll always take her calls, especially if they're urgent, no matter what."

"Girlfriend?" she teased lightly even as her heart sank.

"Grandmother. And I'll bring you the mail, have you sort through that. I've been putting it off. If you can find something else that needs doing, have at it. Just don't start organizing records or redoing my filing cabinets or anything like that. I'll show you that system when I have time." He headed into his office, coming back out a minute later with a small box from the post office that was chock-full of mail. "Here you go."

Sydney knew her eyes were huge. "Holy hell, Sawyer. How long's it been since you went through the mail?"

He had the grace to look embarrassed. "A couple of weeks? I glanced at it, got the important things out."

She shook her head. "Mom and Zanny were right. You do need help." She made a shooing motion with her hands. "Let me at it. You take care of Mina."

"Are you sure you want to do this? Work for me, I mean?" he asked, concern clear on his face.

"It sounds interesting. Like I said, I'm somewhat familiar with the industry as I worked in a law firm for the last three years. I think it might be a good fit. Where are the message pads?"

He didn't look convinced, but since frustration was practically rolling off the man in waves, Sydney figured he knew she was his best bet. "There should be some in the drawers of the desk. If not, grab some paper from the printer and use that. Holler if you need me."

She saluted him with a cheeky grin. "Will do, Boss."

Once he'd gone into his office, leaving the door open halfway, she started looking through the desk. She found everything she'd need to get started easily enough, and once she had the desk lined out, she blew out a long breath.

"Showtime, girly girl. Let's rock and roll."

As she answered the phone and sorted the mail, she was surprised to find that her nervousness at the idea of working for Sawyer had largely faded. The routine felt familiar, like coming home, and she realized then how much she'd missed her job with Charles, even though it had only ended a few weeks ago.

One of the lessons her marriage had taught her was that feeling needed, feeling necessary, was vital to her mental wellbeing. Looking around the room at the somewhat disorganized office, she knew she could make a difference in Sawyer's business life. While that might not be the position her girlish self had dreamed about having years ago, it was certainly one that her adult self could appreciate.

CHAPTER EIGHT

SAWYER WAS LATE. AS SYDNEY stood in the doorway of her mother's photography studio Monday morning, staring at the street, she tapped her foot impatiently, trying to mask her concern. "Where is he?"

Emma's laugh sounded from behind her. "Honey, he's only ten minutes late. He'll be here."

"I expected better of the man," Sydney responded dryly. "As by the book as he is, I really expected better. Think he's okay?"

"He probably got caught up in something. Did you try his phone again?"

"Yep. No answer. Straight to voice mail."

"That's a little odd," Zanny put in. "If he isn't here soon, we may have to send out a search party."

When Sydney shot her an irritated look over her shoulder, Zanny grinned.

"Who would we call? Wait, there he is!" Sydney couldn't pretend she wasn't relieved to see his black truck coming down the street. "He'd better have a good excuse. Else I'll never let him live this down." She grabbed the small box of personal belongings she'd brought from home, shaking her head the whole time.

"Have fun, sweetie," Emma told her.

"You two do the same." She opened the door and stepped

onto the sidewalk as Sawyer came past. "Hey, you. Where've you been? The boss will dock your pay, you know."

He grimaced. "I slept late, got called in to look at something for a former colleague, and completely forgot about you. I'm sorry. I need to get you a key and the security code," he said as he took the box from her, tucking it under his arm as they headed up the stairs.

She gasped, holding her hand over her chest. "You forgot me? Oh, I'm heartbroken. Do you know that I had to hide out at Mom's? I was slinking on the steps, and the scary lady with Texas hair was heading out to defend her territory."

"Texas hair—you mean Myrtle?"

"Yep."

His lips quivered, but he managed to get control of the laugh before it escaped. "That's scarily accurate. You work here now, you know. You have as much right to be here as she does."

"Yeah, but *she* doesn't know that yet. And from what Mom and Zanny said, she thinks you're her personal property. Did you see the nails that go with the hair? Nearsighted or not, I'm rather fond of my eyes. Getting in a cat fight over my boss on Monday morning is the last thing on my agenda. Why didn't you answer your phone?"

"I'm not Myrtle's personal property," he responded with a deep scowl. "What in the hell did your mother tell you that makes you say that? And I didn't answer because the phone is dead. DOA. As soon as I get you settled in and check a couple of things, I have to head out and get a new one."

Sydney lifted her eyebrows and sighed. "*You* might not think you're hers, but Myrtle apparently has other ideas. She'll be up here quizzing me by the end of the week, wait and see."

"I've only ever been polite to her. She'd better not be up here," he grumbled as he put the box down on her desk. "I swear if I'd known about Myrtle, I'd have rented office space somewhere else."

"Poor Sawyer." She laughed outright when he huffed out an exasperated breath.

A short while after that, he was ready to leave again, promising to return as soon as possible. "You think you have things in hand here by yourself?"

"Sure. If I have any questions, I'll figure it out or bluff my way through it. Not my first rodeo, and you won't be gone all day, right?"

"Right."

She worked on getting his files back into shape while he was gone as he'd familiarized her with the system during a lull on Friday. By the time he got back, she had a good start on things. This time, he was the one carrying the bribe.

"Peace offering, apology, whatever you want to call it. Fresh strawberry cupcake," he said as he handed her the small pastry box from the bakery next door to the photography studio. "Your mom said you liked them."

More pleased than she knew was healthy, Sydney smiled up at him widely as she accepted the package. "I love them! I found some great bakeries on the East Coast that made some pretty damned good desserts, but none that made strawberry cupcakes that came close to these. Thank you."

"You're welcome. And here's this," he said, giving her a key. "I'll get the code for you before you leave today. I really am sorry I wasn't here on time this morning."

She waved the apology away. "It's not a big deal. The cupcake more than makes up for your tardiness. It's hard to stay angry when you're confronted with buttercream."

He smiled. "I'll have to remember that for future reference."

"Are you planning on upsetting me frequently, then?" she teased.

"Me? I'd never do such a thing. I'm easy to get along with," he said with a grin. "Just ask anyone."

"That's a likely story. Get out of here, Boss. I have work to do. I put your messages on your desk."

After a quick salute, he headed into his office. Sydney made sure the door was closed fully before she opened the box containing the cupcake. As much as she'd joked about the confection's superiority, eating one of the bakery's cupcakes really was an experience. She took a moment to admire it visually before she lifted it out of the box and took a big bite out of the side. When the sweet saltiness of the buttercream hit her tongue, her eyes drifted closed.

"Oh, that's good."

A click sounded, and her gaze flew to Sawyer's office door. She was horribly embarrassed at being caught enjoying the cupcake so much. To her relief, the door was still closed. Regardless, she carefully placed the rest of the treat back in the box. She didn't want to chance Sawyer catching her for real.

"I'll take care of you later," she whispered as she closed the lid. "And I might stop by and get a dozen of your friends to take home with me tonight. Strawberry cupcakes for dinner sounds like a plan I can really get behind." She might have to run twenty miles to work the calories off, but it would be worth it.

Inside his office, Sawyer leaned against the door, exhaling as quietly as he could. He'd intended to sneak and open the door, to tease Sydney about eating the cupcake. But the look of pure ecstasy on her face as she took that first bite had taken his breath. The moment had turned into something hot, erotic, and his reaction had been nearly instantaneous. How he'd managed to close the door without making a sound, he'd never know. But as he stood there, his mind reeling and his nerves humming, he called himself ten kinds of fool.

"She's young enough to be your daughter. You've known her since she was a child," he muttered under his breath as he paced to his desk. "You really, really need to get laid, Evans."

As much as he'd grown out of the days when he'd indulged in casual sex, he might have to make a couple of phone calls, see if he could arrange a date. Otherwise, he'd soon be howl-at-the-moon crazy with lust, and all because he had the misfortune to be attracted to his assistant.

CHAPTER NINE

LATE MONDAY AFTERNOON, SYDNEY ASKED him a question that shoved all thoughts of how delicious she might be covered in buttercream out of his head.

"Have you filed your quarterly taxes yet?"

Sawyer was ashamed to admit all he could do at first was blink at her. "Quarterly taxes? I don't file quarterly. I file annually."

It was Sydney's turn to be dumbstruck. "But you're a small business. You have to file quarterly or you pay a penalty. How are you structured?"

He told her. "But my accountant said filing quarterly was optional. Same with payroll taxes, though I suppose now that you're on board, I'll have to start that up again."

If looks could maim, he'd be short an arm or leg. "They told you *what*? Sawyer, if you're set up to file payroll taxes, you can't just quit. You can probably get away without filing quarterly in a pinch, but payroll's a different story. Please tell me that isn't what you've done."

He shifted his feet. "Um..."

Sydney whimpered, her head falling into her hand. "Oh, my God. Who's your accountant?"

"Tracy Ward. She's been doing my taxes for about ten years now."

Her eyes narrowed. "Tracy Ward. Why does that name sound familiar?" She pursed her lips and stared at him. "I know that name. I'm going to call Uncle John. You'd better cross your fingers and your toes, buddy. I'm afraid you might have a real mess on your hands."

He folded his arms over his chest. "You really think that's necessary?"

"Yes." But before she could pick up her cell phone, her face went blank. "Wait a minute. Oh, my God. Tracy Ward." Eyes huge, she stared at Sawyer for a moment, then grabbed her phone.

"What's wrong?" he asked, stepping closer to the desk.

Sydney held a hand up, shushing him. "Mom? I have a question for you. Is Zanny around? No? Good. Remember that woman John worked with that kissed him? What was her name? Was it Tracy Ward?"

She listened to Emma's response, nodding grimly. "I thought so. She's Sawyer's accountant, and she's a fricking lunatic. I've got to call John and see if he can help get him straightened out."

Sawyer didn't like the sound of what he was hearing, not for an instant. "Now wait just a second," he protested as Sydney ended the call with Emma. "You don't know that I'm in a mess."

"One of my duties with Charles was helping him get his paperwork lined out for taxes. I worked for him for three years. How long have you been self-employed?"

He stared at her, tapping the fingers of his right hand on his left arm. "Thirteen months."

"Exactly." She thumbed through her contacts.

"So let me get this straight. John used to work with Tracy?"

Sydney nodded slowly. "And the woman set it up so that Zanny walked in on them kissing. Not that John was interested in her in the least, you understand. Your accountant took advantage of the situation. He and Zanny were going through a rough patch at the time, and it almost caused a divorce. They were separated for a few months. It was right before I was born. I've heard Mom and Zanny talk about the woman, and that's how I knew the name."

He sighed, rubbing a hand over his face, then pulled a chair up to sit in front of her desk. "Call him, then. If you think you should, call him."

She did. An hour later, John was in the conference room, papers spread out around him as he went over Sawyer's tax returns. If the look on his face was any indication, he wasn't pleased with what he was seeing.

"I can't believe this. Sawyer, I'm sorry. This is... This is going to take some unraveling to fix. Damn."

"How bad is it?" Sawyer asked from across the table.

John grimaced. "It's not 'hire a tax attorney' bad, but it's a tangled ball of yarn. We can fix it. I'm just... I can't believe she'd do this. For all her faults, she's a good CPA. It's almost like she's deliberately set you up to get in trouble. But that wouldn't make any sense."

Sawyer had the sinking feeling it did make sense. "Um, yeah. It would."

When Sydney and John both looked at him expectantly, he felt his face heat up. He really didn't want to have to explain to them that he'd rejected the woman's advances several times, and while she'd finally accepted his refusals, it had strained their professional relationship.

"Well?" Sydney asked. "Are you going to tell us?"

"I wouldn't go out with her," he finally admitted.

John whistled. "Damn."

"Yeah," Sawyer agreed. "I hate to ask you to get involved with this. I know you stay pretty busy with your regular job. Can you refer me to someone?"

"Don't be ridiculous. I'll be happy to help. You know I've cut back to part time now so Zanny and I can take time off and do some things. Besides, I used to work with Tracy. I feel kind of like I owe you the help if we're being honest. She caused a situation a long time ago that I never felt like

I made proper restitution for. This might be a good way to balance out the karma."

Sawyer exchanged a look with Sydney. There was no reason for him to mention that Sydney had told him about the kiss. "If you're sure, then I'd really appreciate the help. What do we do?"

"First, we sit down and go through your taxes every year she's worked on them. And it wouldn't hurt to pray or cross your fingers or whatever you feel comfortable doing."

A glance at his watch told him it was nearly five o'clock. "Okay. I have the business records here. My personal records are at home. When do you want to start?"

"If you want to get started tonight, we can. If you trust me with your files, I can take them home and review them," John offered. "Or I can make some schedule adjustments and come back tomorrow. That might be better. Bring in everything you have, personal and professional, and we'll see what we see."

Grimly, Sawyer nodded and stood. "I'll have it here first thing."

John looked over his shoulder to the reception area, where Sydney was taking a phone call, then turned back to eye Sawyer hesitantly. "If you don't mind my being nosy, when did you turn her down?"

"Right about the time I was setting up the business. I'd probably had the doors open a month? Maybe two?"

"That fits with what I'm seeing," John said, "so we may have gotten lucky if you'll forgive a bad pun. All the paperwork from where the company was set up looks fine. It's just the tax reports after that which are messed up."

Sawyer rubbed the back of his neck, his cheeks hot. "I feel like an idiot. You'd think I'd have had the sense to know that I couldn't just stop filing payroll taxes."

John shook his head as he stacked papers. "Not necessarily. You're plenty smart. But smart has nothing to do with this. You had a professional whose opinion you trusted to advise you on what to do. There's no reason for you to think anything would have been amiss with what she said. Like I told you earlier, she's a good CPA. She's just a really nasty piece of work personally."

"I appreciate the sentiment. Doesn't make me feel like less of an idiot, though."

John smiled. "Sawyer, you're about as far from an idiot as anyone I've ever met."

Sawyer chuckled ruefully. "Thanks. You know, I had serious reservations about hiring Sydney. But I'm very glad now that I did. I probably shouldn't tell you that."

"Eh, I understand what you mean. The last time you had any interaction with her, she was a somewhat wild teenager who had a penchant for finding trouble whether she wanted it or not."

"She was," Sawyer agreed, keeping his voice low so that it didn't carry to the other room. "And now she's so competent it's scary. Do you know, as soon as I explained my filing system to her Friday, she had it in hand? The other women who worked for me, at least the one who was familiar with office management? It took her a week."

John's smile was a little bit wicked as he asked, "What about the other one?"

In response, Sawyer simply lifted his hand and raised his middle finger.

John laughed. "That's what I heard. In all seriousness, Sydney's had a rough way to go the last few years. She's kind of forged in fire, thanks to her piece of shit ex-husband. And she really enjoyed her job with Charles, took a lot of pleasure out of helping the clients who came in. Archer was pretty sharp to put you two together. I think once you get past the idea of her being that troubled kid, you'll be trying to figure out how you made it this long without her."

Sawyer agreed. "I think I already am."

CHAPTER TEN

When Sydney came back from lunch Thursday, John was leaving, having dropped off Sawyer's taxes.

"Hey, Uncle John. Did you get him straightened out?" she asked as he gave her a hug.

"I did. And now I'm going to head next door and grab my girl. We have a date."

"Try to stay out of trouble," Sydney told him with a smile as he left.

"I make no promises," he called over his shoulder, his grin wicked.

"He's a good guy," Sawyer said. He sat on the edge of her desk as she put her purse in one of the drawers. "He's going to handle my taxes from here on out. I hated to ask him to do it, but he wouldn't take no for an answer."

"He enjoys it. He has a gift for seeing patterns, doesn't see numbers the way the rest of us do. And if he didn't want to take you on as a client, he wouldn't have offered."

"I know."

Sydney came around and perched on the edge beside him. "It's good to see him and Zanny taking some time for themselves. After her breast cancer diagnosis and everything that's happened between Noah and Eli, it would have been too easy for them to lose sight of each other. Instead, it's made them stronger than ever."

Sawyer nodded. "So things aren't any better between Noah and Eli? I thought they'd patched things up a bit after Eli's wife was killed."

She shrugged, thinking about everything the family had been through in the last few years. Noah and Eli had fallen out when they were teenagers, still in high school. As soon as he'd graduated, Noah had gone to Europe, where he'd stayed for several years. It wasn't until Zanny was diagnosed with breast cancer, when Sydney was sixteen, that he'd come home for good. Eli had just graduated from high school, married his long-time girlfriend, and had enlisted in the Army, his absence being the only reason Noah had been able to manage moving back to Kentucky.

"They called something of a truce when Zanny was sick, but the animosity didn't start to fade until after Erica died. And it's been better since then, but it's still tense whenever they're in the same room, which isn't often. I know that's really weighed heavily on John and Zanny. With that feud, the cancer, and getting Molly through her teenage years, they've had a lot of stress. Even though Molly was nothing approaching a troubled child," she said with a soft smile. "Unlike some people I could mention."

"You were okay. Trust me, the things you did? You could have been a lot worse. A lot worse."

"I do know that, but I was bad enough. For heaven's sake, I stole Daddy's car and took it to Virginia when I was fifteen. Fifteen, Sawyer. Do you know what could have happened?"

He laughed and she nudged him with her shoulder.

"I do know. You had enough sense to take Danny with you, though. And like I said, in the grand scheme of things, what you did wasn't that bad. You turned out okay."

Sydney grinned. "Most days. I still get a wild hair every now and then."

When the phone rang, she reached behind her and answered it. "Evans Investigations."

"Yeah, I'm Bret Varney with McElty and Jones of Charleston. I'd like to speak with whomever's in charge."

"That would be the owner, Sawyer Evans. If you'll hold one moment, I'll put you through."

She pursed her lips as she pushed the hold button. "Sounds impressive. McElty and Jones, Charleston?" she asked Sawyer.

He shook his head and stood. "No idea. I'll take it in the office."

With a groan, Sydney headed for the restroom. She started a pot of coffee on her way back to the reception area, all too aware now of Sawyer's addiction to the stuff, and settled in to check e-mail.

A few minutes later, Sawyer came out, a pensive look on his face as he stared down at her.

"What's wrong?"

"I don't know," he said slowly. "Do you know anyone from Charleston, South Carolina, who would be looking into you?"

Sydney raised a hand to her throat. "Into me? What are you talking about?"

"Varney's a PI. His client's based in Charleston, and they're looking for a thorough dossier on one Sydney Gibson Tate. He knew you were back in Hazard, and he was looking for someone local to do the legwork."

Her hand clenched involuntarily, and she cursed under her breath when Sawyer's eyes dropped to follow the movement. She forced herself to relax.

"I don't use that name anymore. I legally took Gibson back. But to answer your question, no. I don't know who would be interested in investigating me."

Sawyer lifted a pen out of the cup on the desk, twirling it end over end as he studied her. "Is there anything you're not telling me, Sydney?" he asked softly.

"No! Honest to God, I-I don't know... Adam and his family would know to call Mom and Daddy. Shoot, they could call me—my cell phone number's the same. I can't think of anyone who would have any reason to hire a PI to find out about me."

"What about your biological father?"

She sat back in her chair, her gaze falling to the blotter calendar on the desk. "He died about eighteen months ago. And you were there the one and only time I ever met the man. Do *you* think he'd have any interest in finding me?" She chanced looking up at Sawyer, hating the sympathy she saw in his face. "What did you tell him?"

"That I'd ask around and call him back. He didn't want to let go of too many details, such as what his client's name is, until and unless I agree to take the case."

"If you don't do it, someone else will."

He dropped the pen back in the cup and paced to the window beside the door. "I know. How do you want me to handle it?"

Sydney didn't have a clue how to answer. She told him as much. "What do you advise?"

"I'm not providing a perfect stranger with a detailed file on your life, Sydney. That's out of the question. But at the same time, like you said—if I don't do something, he'll just hire someone else."

"How'd he find you?"

"Called the sheriff's department, asked for recommendations for local investigators. I think our best bet is to call him back, let me lay the cards on the table. Tell him I know you, who you are to me, and ask bluntly why he's looking at you. But I'm going to look into his agency first, see who we're dealing with."

"I can call someone at Uncle Charles's firm, talk to them. Charleston isn't that far from Savannah, and the legal community is fairly closely connected down there. I have a couple of people in mind who can probably tell us what we need to know."

"Make the call."

As she picked up the phone to dial, she let out a quiet sigh. Knowing someone was trying to get detailed information about her life was eerie, scary. It could be perfectly benign and harmless, but then again, it might not be.

"Thanks for backing me up on this," she told Sawyer as she waited for the call to be answered.

He shook his head. "Call it even for the tax advice."

"I don't know if that's even or not," she said, serious.

"Sure it is."

When the man she'd been hoping to reach answered, she swallowed back her nerves and explained the situation. "I figured calling you might be the smartest move, Lenny. Have you ever heard of them? I'll put you on speaker so my boss can hear," she said as she hit the button.

"McElty and Jones? Sure. They're not that big, but their client list reads like a who's who. If you don't have an annual income or assets totaling at least ten million, they don't even answer your calls."

Sawyer whistled. "No kidding?"

"Nope, not even a little," Lenny answered. "So whoever's looking at Syd, they've got resources and influence. You didn't break some playboy's heart did you, kid?"

She laughed, amused even through her tension. "You know better than that. Do you have any connections at the firm, Len?"

"No, but I know someone who does. Want me to give 'em a shout?"

"I hate to ask you to do that," she hedged.

"Sydney, don't make me drive up to Kentucky and put you over my knee. I'll see what I can find out. What's the best number to reach you at?"

She gave him the office number and her cell phone. "I appreciate this, Len. Seriously."

"Enough to come home and work for me? I probably shouldn't ask you that in front of your boss," he said with a laugh.

Sydney smiled and winked across the desk at Sawyer, who was scowling. "You know Kentucky's home for me. But if I ever do decide to head south again, you'll be the first person I call. Give Dora a hug for me?"

"Always. Talk to you soon, kid. I'll light a fire under my contact. We need to know who's looking for you."

The buzz of the disconnected call filled the room. Sydney lifted the receiver and let it fall back into the cradle, then sank back with a groan. "Knowing Lenny, he'll drive up there if he can't get answers. He's persistent."

"Who's Dora?"

"His wife. They're two of the sweetest people you'll ever meet. She's a lawyer with the firm, and he's the investigator. They have a daughter my age who lives in California, and when I started working with Uncle Charles, they kind of adopted me. Holy crap, Sawyer. Ten million minimum? I don't like this. I left that world behind when I got divorced. I don't want any part of it now."

His right eyebrow shot up. "I knew your husband's family was wealthy. I didn't know they were that wealthy."

Sydney sent him a sardonic grimace. "Oh, they were up there. If I'd known Adam was from that kind of money, I'd never have started dating him. Not that there aren't nice people in that income bracket, but a lot of the kids in my generation are entitled assholes even without all that privilege. Of course, I could just have a biased point of view, all things considered."

"Can't imagine why," Sawyer teased gently.

There was speculation in his gaze, and Sydney could tell he wanted to ask her something. "What is it you aren't saying?" she asked as she stood.

"I'm trying to think of a nice way to put it," he said.

She grabbed a couple of folders off her desk and crossed to the cabinets to file them. "Then ask in a not-so-nice way. I'm a big girl, fairly hard to offend most days."

"I'm just thinking about what you were like when you left here."

Despite her best efforts, her back stiffened a bit, even though she wasn't upset at the observation. "And you're wondering how in the world someone like me fit in with a family like that?"

He had the grace to look ashamed when she glanced at him over her shoulder.

"Kind of."

Sydney snorted. "It was a square peg, round hole kind of situation for a while. And I'm embarrassed to admit that I wanted to fit in with them so much that I turned into something of a sheep, at least the first couple of years. I had school, and that's where I was myself. When I went home, I conformed to Adam's expectations." She closed the drawer and leaned against the cabinet. "His parents are good people. They really are. Kind people, even if they're a bit standoffish. They remind me a lot of Ainsley, Uncle Ben's wife. You know?"

Sawyer nodded. "Reserved but warm."

She smiled. "That's Ainsley. And that's Ray and Helen. I don't think they expected my... courtship, I guess you could say, with Adam to last beyond a few weeks. They certainly didn't expect us to get married after six months of dating. Helen confessed that to me after the marriage fell apart. It wasn't that they didn't like me or approve of me. They just knew their son. If I could have kept them in the divorce, I would have."

"They sound nice."

"They are. She still calls me occasionally just to chat. In any event, she and Ray did what they could to make social situations easier for me. And it wasn't like Mom and Daddy raised a heathen. A hellion, yes."

"No arguments here."

She smacked him gently with the stack of mail from the top of the filing cabinet. "Hush."

"Don't forget who's the boss here, young lady."

"Mm-hmmm."

Sawyer crossed his ankle over his knee as she sat back down. "So you don't miss it?"

"Being part of that world? No."

"Being married."

The question stunned her, coming from Sawyer, especially considering the seriousness with which he asked.

"Um, I guess... yeah. I do miss some aspects of marriage. Not enough to risk it again, at least not at this point in time. Do you miss it?" she countered softly.

"Some aspects."

They exchanged a long look. After a minute, Sydney laughed sadly. "I never expected to be a member of this club, you know. The 'divorced' club. I was stupid with youth and love, and that's a dangerous combination. I expected it to last forever, and in hindsight, now that I'm out from under Adam's spell, I know there's no way in hell it could have lasted. The miracle was that it lasted as long as it did. How in the world did we get on this subject?" she asked, tucking a strand of hair behind her ear.

"My fault," Sawyer said as he stood. "And now that I've thoroughly depressed us both, I guess we'd better get back to work. How long do you think it'll be before Lenny calls you back?"

"Probably late today or sometime tomorrow, depending on how easily he can get up with his contact. He won't dawdle. When are you supposed to call Varney back?"

"Tomorrow. I'll be in here if you need me."

"Thanks, Sawyer. I mean that," she told him as he went into the office.

He shrugged. "It's the least I can do."

"Still, I appreciate it. Whatever *it* turns out to be."

Desperate to have something else to focus on, she turned back to her computer and pulled up the e-mail program. Maybe there'd be something in there that would distract her. Otherwise, she might just get in her car and drive to Charleston to ask Bret Varney herself what the hell was going on.

CHAPTER ELEVEN

THEY FOUND OUT THE NEXT morning what was going on, though not via the phone call Sydney had been expecting. Or rather, not through a phone call from Lenny. Instead, the news came from Emma, who called just after ten a.m.

"Hey, Mom. What's up?" Sydney asked.

"Are you terribly busy? Could you come down here?" Emma's voice was strained, tense. Right away, Sydney knew something wasn't right.

"What's wrong?" She stood as Sawyer stepped into the reception area. When he held his hands up questioningly, she shrugged.

"I just need you to come over here."

"On my way." Disconnecting, she shoved the phone into her pocket. "Something's wrong. She needs me down at the shop."

"Want me to tag along?" he asked.

"Please?"

He didn't say a word, just followed her down the stairs. In less than a minute, they were walking in the door at Emma's studio. Emma was standing in front of Zanny's unoccupied desk, staring quietly at two clean-cut young men who were seated on the couch across the reception area.

"Mom? Are you okay?"

Emma smiled tensely and held her arm out. "I am. I didn't mean to worry you. Hey, Sawyer."

"Hey."

But Sydney could see she wasn't okay. Her mouth was pinched, and she looked like she'd break if someone touched her. And she was staring at the two men as though they were a threat to everything she held dear. Sydney hugged her tightly from the side.

"Who are you?" Sydney asked the men. They'd gotten to their feet when she and Sawyer had come in, and upon further inspection, she was startled to see they were twins. Identical twins, unless she missed her guess, the only difference between the two being their haircuts and the fact that one of them wore glasses. She started to get a sinking sensation in the pit of her stomach.

"We, um, we're... I'm Grant," the one without glasses said.

"And I'm Cade," his brother answered, staring at Sydney with an intensity that unnerved her. "We're sorry to cause such a disturbance, ma'am," he said to Emma. "Truly."

"We are," Grant reiterated. "She looks just like you, Mrs. Gibson. Wow. She's so pretty." Cade elbowed him, causing Grant to scowl. "What? She is."

"You sound like you expected her to be a hag or something," Cade said.

Grant pulled his gaze off Sydney long enough to make a face at his brother. "You know better. I knew she wouldn't be a hag, not that it would matter if you were," he quickly reassured Sydney. "But it's a relief to know that we won't have to pay someone to date her."

"Excuse me?" Sydney asked, incredulous. "What the hell are you talking about? Who are you?"

Emma let out a long, shuddering breath. "You don't recognize them, do you? Though I guess there's no reason you should. Sydney, they're your brothers."

Stunned beyond words, all she could do was stare

at her mother. That sick feeling in her stomach rose up, threatening to choke her. Before she could come up with anything, the door opened and Archer came in, anger and fear on his face. He went straight for Sydney and Emma, moving so that he was between them and the men.

"What do you want?" he demanded.

"Daddy..." Sydney edged around him to stare at Grant and Cade, who were looking very uncertain. Though they weren't small men, Archer was six feet four and heavily muscled, an imposing figure even when he wasn't upset. And right now, "upset" didn't begin to cover the tension coming off his body.

"We just wanted to meet her, sir," Grant said. "That's all."

When she tried to step forward, Archer shot her a displeased look. Trying to reassure him, she slid her arm around his and clasped his hand. But she didn't back down.

"Are you the ones who're looking into my background?" she asked. "The investigator from Charleston?"

"What?" Emma asked. "What investigator?"

The twins exchanged a silent look, and Sydney had the eerie sensation they'd held an entire conversation with that glance. She'd always heard about "twin speak" but she'd never seen it before.

"That's probably our mom. She worries," Cade said with an embarrassed shrug. "We're..."

"...all the family she has," Grant finished. "She knew we were thinking about contacting you, and she'd want to be sure you weren't dangerous or something." His cheeks flushed.

"Yeah, she's not much of a threat, she's so tiny," Cade said. "I don't think Mom has anything to worry about."

Grant rolled his eyes. "I don't think Mom was afraid she'd beat us up, Cade. I think she was more concerned about..."

"...other things. Yeah, I know. Mom tends to think we're naive or something," Cade said. "Sorry."

Sydney couldn't help it. She laughed. They were so cute, so funny, finishing each others sentences. And she'd never responded well to certain kinds of stress, laughing when other people were dead serious.

"They're like puppies," she said, smiling at them. "Polite, somewhat clumsy puppies."

Grant clearly didn't like the comparison. Judging by the way he stood, the close-cropped haircut, he was either military or law enforcement. But Cade took her words in stride and grinned back at her.

Archer didn't seem any more pleased than Grant. "That still doesn't answer my question satisfactorily. Why are you here now?"

Cade answered. "We've always been curious, ever since we learned about Sydney. We were upstairs the night you showed up," he told her. "Did you really drive all the way from Kentucky when you were just fifteen? And you stole a car and everything?"

"Anyhow," Grant said before she could respond, "we saw you stand up to Dad. And then after you left and things calmed down, Mom explained who you were. Who you all were," he said, his gaze dancing to Emma and Archer. "We..."

"...didn't have the best relationship with our father," Cade said quietly. "He wasn't the nicest guy in the world, as you might have gathered. You really, really hit the jackpot by not having him raise you."

Archer's hand flexed involuntarily, and Sydney squeezed it even tighter. She knew he'd often worried over the years that she was missing out on something by not having known her biological father. Hopefully, if the twins were telling the truth, some of that fear would be allayed.

"So after that, any time things got rough, we kind of had this thing we'd ask ourselves. Mom even picked up on it, and she started playing along with us when we were teenagers," Cade finished.

"'What would Sydney do?'" Grant told them. "Any time

we had something to get through, that's what we'd ask. 'What would Sydney do?' And it helped to imagine how you might handle things, even if we didn't have the courage to implement what we came up with."

Cade chuckled. "We came up with some pretty crazy things."

Grant nodded. "I guess that sounds pathetic now, but we kinda looked up to you. Like you were a superhero or something. And so when Dad died, we started thinking maybe we should try to meet you. It wasn't possible before. That's all."

Even Archer wasn't immune to the story. He sighed roughly, and Sydney could feel his muscles relaxing. "Does your mother know you're here?"

Grant cleared his throat. "Not so much, sir. She knows we're traveling but..."

"...We didn't want to worry her. If we got here and Sydney wasn't what we were expecting, there was no need for her to know about it. Right?" Cade asked his brother.

"Right."

Sawyer pushed away from the wall beside the door. "Looks like you folks have things under control. I'm going to head back. Sydney, if you need to take today off, feel free."

"Thank you. I probably will."

"Thanks, Sawyer," Emma put in. "Sorry to disturb you."

"Don't mention it. Call if you need me."

"Is he your boss?" Grant asked as Sawyer left.

"He is."

"LEO?" he persisted.

She tilted her head, confused. "LEO? Oh! Law enforcement officer. Yes, he's retired from the state police. Why?"

"Grant's getting ready to start his senior year, pre-law, and then he's heading to the FBI academy," Cade said. He pushed his glasses up. "I'm just a bookworm."

"An archivist is not just a bookworm," Grant argued.

"He does that, sells himself short like it's something to be ashamed of."

Cade nudged him again in the ribs, this time a little firmer. "Shut up."

Archer shook his head. "Puppies. Yeah. So do you boys have a place to stay? How long *are* you planning to stay, exactly?"

"Daddy!" Sydney chided at the same time as Emma's "Archer!"

"It's a legitimate question," he told Emma, then sent Sydney a scolding look. "Well?"

"We figured we'd get a hotel," Cade said. "And we can't stay long. He has to get back home to his girlfriend," he teased Grant.

"She's getting ready to go overseas for an internship," Grant said through his teeth. "She's leaving next weekend and I want to spend some time with her before she goes. That's all."

"He's going to ask her to marry him," Cade whispered, his eyes sparkling. "That's why he's so nervous."

"Very much more of this and they'll be rolling around on the floor," Emma laughed. "Boys, we have room. You can stay with us."

A hopeful look crossed their faces as they exchanged another silent message. "We really don't want to impose," Grant hedged.

"I'd rather have you close at hand," Archer grumbled. "That way I can head off any trouble before it starts."

Cade nodded. "Then if you're sure, we'd really appreciate the hospitality. We're curious about you all, too. You made quite an impression."

"Well, it wasn't one of my finest moments," Archer protested. "I never should have hit him the way I did. I especially wouldn't have done it if I'd known the two of you were watching."

Grant shook his head in protest. "No. You don't realize what that meant for us. We never saw anyone stand up to Dad like that, before or since. I guess it showed us he was just human, that he wasn't some god or something."

"That's when we stopped being so afraid of him," Cade said quietly. "We never had the courage to stand up to him while he was alive. But knowing that someone else could, well..."

"...it made things bearable. So thank you."

Sydney's heart broke. She didn't know them well enough to accurately judge whether or not they were telling the truth. But if they were, she didn't know if she could stand it.

"I need to go get my purse from the office," she said. "Do you want to go get lunch or coffee or something? Mom, Daddy?"

Archer ran a hand over her head. "Sure. Boys?"

"Sounds good. But could we see where you work?" Grant asked.

Sydney laughed. "Sure. I just started last week, but come on. I'll give you the nickel tour."

Emma named a local chain restaurant. "Is that okay?"

Cade nodded. "That's fine. We'll meet you there?"

"Of course. Sydney, you drive separately," Archer told her. He scowled at the twins. "I'm willing to let you into my home, probably, but until I know you two a little better, I'm not letting you in the car alone with my daughter. Understand?"

"Yes, sir," they chorused.

"See you at the restaurant," she said, giving Archer a quick, tight hug. "Love you both."

Archer pulled her back to him for a longer hug. "Be careful, sweetheart."

Sydney knew he was scared, and she swallowed back tears. “I will. See you soon.”

As she led her brothers down the street, telling them about her job, she sent a heartfelt thanks heavenward that she’d been raised by Archer Gibson and not her biological father. Even though Emma hadn’t had it easy, being a single mother for the first five years of Sydney’s life, she’d be the first to admit Archer had been worth the wait. Not for the first time, Sydney thought about how differently things could have been, and she thanked God they’d turned out the way they had.

CHAPTER TWELVE

As curious as Sawyer was to see how Sydney was faring with her brothers, he didn't particularly want to go to the Campbell farm Sunday for dinner. Not because he didn't enjoy spending time with the family, but because of the reason for the gathering—his birthday. He wouldn't be forty-seven until Tuesday, but that small technicality didn't matter to Sarah.

"You know I hate drawing attention to myself," he told her when he arrived.

"I do know that, sweetie, but sometimes you need attention," she said, kissing his cheek. "Happy early birthday. I hope it's a good one."

"Thank you."

"So how's your new assistant working out?"

Sawyer laughed. "So far, so good. She's already saved me a ton of trouble and heartache. I think it's going to be like John said. Pretty soon I won't know what I ever did without her. Speaking of Sydney, have you heard from her?"

"She brought the boys up here yesterday to meet us," Sarah said, tucking her arm through his as they walked to the picnic area. "That's something Emma never anticipated happening, her brothers showing up. Or the fact that they really seem to be good, nice boys. Full of mischief, from what I saw, but good. They fell far from the tree, thank God."

"So they're getting along?"

"Like gangbusters. I think Emma and Archer's boys are a little jealous—after all, they're used to being her only brothers. But all in all, the meeting has gone well. I hope they stay in touch after they go home. Time will tell. In any event, let's have a birthday party."

Sawyer groaned when he saw the modified trooper's hat in Amelia's hands. "Not the hat. Really? Aren't you too old for that nonsense now?"

Instead of being insulted, Amelia grinned broadly as she came over to him. "Not even close, buddy. Come on, lean down here."

"Give in gracefully now," her husband, Logan, advised. "You know she'll win this argument."

He did. "I have to give my annual protest. This is ridiculous."

The hat, which she'd made for him several years ago, was a family tradition with the Campbells. It represented aspects, little and big, from Sawyer's life. There was a badge, a gun, and a pair of handcuffs, as well as a detective's notebook and now a private investigator's license. All the items were in miniature, and they were arranged around the brim of the hat along with a fishing pole, tackle box, hammer, and saw.

Once it was on his head, Sawyer straightened to cheers and whistles from around the table. He touched the brim in a salute, shaking his head with chagrined amusement.

"There's the birthday boy," Sydney teased from behind him. "Are you ready for your spanking?"

The hot flush that rushed into his cheeks didn't surprise him, nor did the thoughts that crossed his mind which caused the flush. At least he was getting more used to this whole idea of Sydney the temptress, he thought as he turned to face her.

"I'm not volunteering to hold him down," Logan said. "Archer?"

"Nope. Not even on a bet. Happy birthday."

"Thanks. What'd you get me?" Sawyer asked.

"Sydney wasn't enough?" Archer responded, pretending outrage.

"Daddy! Seriously, these guys are trying to marry me off," she said, pointing at the twins, "you're giving me to Sawyer. What am I, chattel?" Rolling her eyes, Sydney flounced away, throwing a laugh over her shoulder after she'd passed Sawyer.

"Archer, I don't know whether to thank you or not," Sawyer joked. "Half the time I don't know who's the boss, me or her."

"I know who it is!" Sydney called.

"That's what I was afraid of."

Archer just grinned at him and slapped his shoulder. "Happy birthday again."

By the time they'd gotten around to the cake, Sawyer had endured more good-natured teasing than any man should have to, and he'd laughed more than he had in at least a year. At least since his last birthday at the farm.

Sydney, who was sitting beside him, leaned in during a lull. "Having fun?"

"It's okay, I guess." He winked at her. "How about you? Doing okay?"

"It's been interesting. And yes, I guess for the most part I'm okay."

"Sarah said the boys seem nice."

Sydney ducked her head. "They do. I think they've even almost won Daddy over."

"High praise," Sawyer said, completely serious. "I'm glad."

"So am I. Although I'm not sure about Uncle John... You should have seen the way Cade's jaw dropped when he met Molly. And when he found out she's in school to be a nurse?" She waved a hand in front of her face, her eyes alight with laughter. "You could just see the thoughts running through his mind. He even asked her if she had to wear a white uniform. Poor kid, he didn't know whether to howl like a wolf or tuck his tail between his legs when he turned around and saw John standing there."

Sawyer laughed out loud. "Oh, I'd have given good money to see that."

Sydney scooped up a bite of cake and ice cream. "I feel so old around them. Cade, Grant, Molly, Graydon, and Carter? It's like they speak a language I don't know. I'm only five years older than them, but good Lord, it feels like fifty. And poor Noah... he *really* didn't know what to think. It was a madhouse last night up here. He came in, stayed about five minutes, and left."

"Danny seems to be fitting in pretty well with them," Sawyer said. He nodded at the group, who was standing next to the table that was loaded with food.

"Yep. He speaks their language. He speaks just about every age group's language."

There was a good amount of wistfulness in her tone, and Sawyer figured as soon as her brothers left, Sydney would be feeling some fallout from the surprise of their arrival. He wanted to volunteer to be the shoulder he thought she'd need, but some remaining sense of self-preservation stopped him. Besides, she had Danny. Regardless of the fact that the other man was gay, there was a bond between him and Sydney that Sawyer hadn't seen too often, not even between couples who were romantically involved. As much as he was tempted to step in and comfort her, the plain truth was that she didn't need him.

When they'd had the conversation the other day about marriage, it had surprised him as much as it had Sydney that he'd confessed to missing some aspects of being married. It surprised him, and it disturbed him. Most of the time, he was good at pretending he wasn't lonely. He'd learned through the years how to cope with the long nights, the solitude. And it wasn't like he didn't have friends, good friends, close friends, to whom he could turn when he needed someone. But the intimacy of marriage, of having someone to talk to and bounce things off of, someone who would help carry the burden of life in the simplest ways, that was something he'd never been able to replace.

When his wife had divorced him when he was twenty-four after finding out he was sterile with no chance for ever having children of his own no matter what kind of medical intervention was involved, she'd ripped part of his soul out. He'd gone to a very dark place emotionally for a couple of years after that. When he'd finally emerged, he'd locked a big part of himself away. And he'd never unpacked that part, not even to this day.

So as much as he was tempted by Sydney, he knew that even in the best-case scenario, all they could ever have would be a fling. He'd been hurt too badly, burned with scars that went too deep, to ever try building a permanent relationship with someone else. That reluctance was part of who he was now, as much as his brown eyes and dark hair. And as he felt the soft press of her along his side, listened to her sweet voice as she teased Noah, who'd come over to their table to sit, he let himself experience a moment of sharp regret for what might have been.

CHAPTER THIRTEEN

THE DREAM DIDN'T COME AS any surprise to Sydney. In fact, she'd been expecting it from the first moment she'd realized who the twins were. She was just grateful it waited until Sunday night, when she was back in her own bed at the house in Hazard, to raise its ugly head.

It was nearly always the same, step by step, and after having had it off and on for so many years now, she'd think she'd be used to it. But it still had the power to disturb her, to turn her upside down emotionally.

"I suppose that's because it's mostly a memory of things that really happened," she told the quiet backyard that was drenched in shadows and starlight. It was close to three in the morning, and the neighborhood was quiet, most of the residents sound asleep. She took another sip of the whiskey she'd poured before coming outside, shuddering as the alcohol burned its way down to her stomach.

In the dream, she was fifteen again, full of anger and hormones, raging at the injustice of the world around her. She'd been testing her boundaries, smarting off to and talking back to her parents, and the tensions had escalated between them to the breaking point. That point had come when she'd missed her curfew by thirty minutes.

School hadn't been out very long for summer break, and Sydney was tasked with watching her brothers during the day. Normally they would have stayed with Owen and

Sarah, but Sarah had just undergone elbow surgery and wasn't quite up to having two active young boys under her care. Sydney didn't want to watch her brothers. Instead, she wanted to hang out with her friends and have fun, and her resentment at being tied down had combined with the typical angst of being a teenager.

That night, Sydney had escaped the house as soon as her mother had gotten home, heading straight to Danny's and their friend, Neala's. And they'd just been playing video games, but the time had gotten away from them. She wasn't about to tell her parents that.

When she walked in the door, everything had boiled over.

"Young lady, where in the hell have you been?" Archer demanded to know as she came in. "In case you hadn't noticed, it's ten thirty. You're late." She knew now he had been more frightened than angry at her missing curfew, but back then, only his anger had come through.

Sydney snubbed up, defiant and scared to death at the same time. "Out. And now I'm not."

He stopped her at the front door, standing in the hall at the foot of the stairs, hands clenched at his sides. Emma stood beside him, worry etched on her face as much as disappointment was.

"You missed curfew, Syd. You know the rules. You're grounded," Emma said. "One week."

"No. You can't ground me. I'm fifteen!"

"Young lady, watch your tone," Archer warned.

Sydney lashed out at him. "You're not my father! You're just some guy my mother married so she could have a real family. You don't get to tell me what to do. Fuck you!"

As soon as the words left her mouth, she wanted to call them back. The hallway filled with silence, so quiet that she thought it had to be what being dead sounded like. A look crossed Archer's face that Sydney hoped to God she never had to see again, pure heartbreak and pain, and then it was gone. In its place was a stony cold mask whose distance was almost worse than the hurt.

The left side of her face exploded in heat and pain, leaving her gasping. Sydney hadn't even realized Emma had moved until she slapped her and had her pinned up against the door, her toes dangling two inches off the floor.

"How *dare* you say that to him?" Emma hissed, even as her lip trembled, tears threatening to fall. "How *dare* you say he isn't your father? Answer me, Sydney! Answer me!"

Archer pulled her back, his jaw set. "Stop. Both of you, just stop. Maybe I'm not your father," he told Sydney, "but by God, I am the head of this household and you'll damned well do what I say as long as you live here. Go to your room. Now."

He didn't raise his voice, but he was as angry as Sydney had ever seen him. Scurrying around him, she ran up the stairs, slamming her door behind her. She made sure she locked it before she flew across the room to her bed, where she collapsed, sobbing into her pillow.

"What have I done?" she whispered, over and over again as the ramifications of her words sank in. She didn't mean it. She'd *never* have hurt Archer like that intentionally, not in a million years. But Neala had been talking for weeks about how they should look up Sydney's real father, and she'd been raging about all the mean things her new stepfather was doing. He wouldn't let her wear the clothes she wanted to wear, date the boys she wanted to date, and her resentment at being confined had transferred itself to Sydney.

In the dream, time jumped ahead. Instead of the week passing slowly, painfully, instead of the quiet in the house being deafening, especially between Sydney and Archer, the week had simply vanished. She and Danny were on their way to Virginia in Archer's classic car, an electric-blue Camaro that had been his father's, determined to meet the man who was her biological father. The road twisted and turned and curved in the dream, unlike the clear interstate that had unfolded in reality. In the dream, with each curve and hill and obstacle she had to go around, Sydney's anxiety grew.

Sometimes she got lucky, and she woke up before they reached her father's house. Sometimes she managed to avoid reliving the ugliness that had unfolded once she and Danny had arrived. Tonight she hadn't been so lucky.

No, tonight she got to relive the scene in all its hideous glory. Pulling up in front of the mansion, knocking on the door. Coming face to face with the sniveling, sneering man who had looked at her like she was less than the dirt on the bottom of his shoe.

"I thought she'd gotten rid of you. God knows I tried to," he hissed. "Little white-trash slut, just like your mother. You're probably not even mine, though I paid through the teeth to make her go away."

Danny was tugging on her arm, frantically trying to get Sydney to turn around and just go, but she was frozen in place. She couldn't look away from the man standing in front of her in dress pants and a half-unbuttoned white shirt. He was handsome, but the pure meanness and evil radiating off of him terrified her.

"What, are you retarded or something?" Ted Hughes had yelled. "I don't want you. I never wanted you. Your mother was just a dumb bitch I screwed to pass the time. She wasn't the first, wasn't the last. I barely remember her face or name."

"What in God's name is going on here, Ted?" a pretty, shocked-faced woman asked, hurrying down the stairs. "Why are you yelling at these kids?"

"Because they're worthless trash," he sneered at Sydney. "I should have kicked your mother harder when I had a chance to get rid of you."

A blur of motion passed by Sydney and Danny, tackling Ted and taking him to the floor. Archer. The woman screamed as the men slid across the slick marble tile of the foyer, pure chaos erupting. Emma was there, pulling Sydney and Danny away from the fight as Sawyer and the Hughes' butler worked to separate the two men. Given that Archer's hands were clamped around Ted's throat, the task wasn't easy.

"Archer, let him go," Sawyer said, his voice calm even as he forced his way between them. "He's not worth it. Let him go."

"I'll kill him for what he said about them," Archer growled.

"And then where will that leave us?" Emma cried. "Let him go. They're safe, Archer. Please, let him go."

With a mighty growl, Archer shoved Ted as hard as he could, nearly pushing him into a marble statue.

"Leave now or I'll call the police," Ted's wife, Julianne, had warned as she hurried to her husband. "Just go and get out of here, leave us alone."

Sometimes in the dream, they left. Sometimes, Archer killed Ted and ended up going to prison for the rest of his life. And sometimes, he turned to Sydney and Emma with hatred in his eyes.

"I never should have gotten involved with you people. You can have them," he'd say before walking away. Those were the worst endings to the dream by far, and that was what Sydney had tonight.

In real life, they hadn't wasted any time leaving the house. As soon as they were outside, Sydney was running to Archer, sobbing. "Daddy! I'm so sorry. I'm so sorry."

"Hush, baby. I'm here. I'm here, Sydney. It's okay." He picked her up in his arms, lifting her off the ground completely as he held her close. She'd been nearly hysterical by that point, and Sawyer, who'd come along in case law enforcement had been needed to intervene, had to drive the Camaro while Emma drove her SUV, Sydney in the backseat with Archer, to a nearby motel.

It had taken weeks for things to return to anything approaching normal within the family. Sydney had been grounded for months, and Danny's mother had flat refused to let him have anything to do with her outside school. And even though Sydney and Archer had worked hard on rebuilding their relationship, she always felt like she'd broken off a part of his heart that night, a part that she'd never be able to replace.

The guilt over that hurt had driven her to walk the line, and aside from a few small things, she'd not gotten into trouble again until she was nineteen. She hadn't wanted to give him any reason in the world to question her, to doubt her love and affection. And she hadn't wanted to ever disappoint him again.

With the whiskey gone, some of the tension was leaving her system. Fatigue was starting to set in, and with a tired sigh, she headed back inside.

"I doubt sleep will come, but I have to try," she said into the quiet emptiness of the bedroom. As much as she was happy not to still be married to a lying, womanizing cheat, the need and longing to have someone she could crawl into bed with just so she could be held on nights like this was almost overwhelming.

"Maybe I'll get a cat or something," she said around a yawn. "Or several cats."

As she dozed off, the notion of what it might be like to have Sawyer to lean on through the night drifted through her mind. It would never happen, she knew, but of all the solid, dependable men in the world, if anyone could make a girl feel like things were going to be okay, he'd be the man to do it.

CHAPTER FOURTEEN

"Do you think she's okay?" Archer asked Emma. It was early Monday morning, not quite six, and they'd just hit snooze on the alarm clock.

Emma snuggled back into his warmth, loving the way he pulled her into him even tighter. "I think so. This hasn't been an easy weekend for her, for any of us, but I think it's turned out really well, all things considered. I mean, it could have gone in a completely different direction. You know?"

"Mm. I do." He buried his face in her neck with a sigh. "Do you think she's curious about him still?"

"About Ted? No. I don't think she's been curious about him for several years now. I *do* believe she's worried to death that you still feel like you're second best or just a substitute. She never has forgiven herself for what she said that night."

Archer raised up on his elbow. "But I've told her a hundred times I understood. That I forgave her almost as soon as it happened."

Emma turned over, resting her hands on his chest. "She hurt you that night. You know how she is—she can't stand to see people in pain. It's part of her abilities. She's a born nurturer. So the pain she inflicted on you, it came back to her. And she'll never forget that."

He traced her eyebrow, then let his hand rest alongside her face. "You still think she's a healer, don't you?"

"I do. Unintentional, unknowing. She can't control it,

but if she wants someone to be better strongly enough, something happens. I just hope she never figures it out."

From the time Sydney was little, she'd had the ability to touch some people and tell things about their health. She'd known Zanny was pregnant with Molly, known Ainsley was pregnant with Lily, and had known Archer and Logan were cats inside. She'd also known Archer's cat had gone to sleep, while Logan's hadn't, a revelation that had come during a wedding planning session at Owen and Sarah's when she was just five years old.

"I can still see the look on her face when she felt that Zanny was sick," Emma said softly. "I think it was the first time she realized the people around her could get sick, and that they could possibly die."

Archer kissed her forehead. "I know. She was terrified."

When she was sixteen, Sydney had hugged Zanny after she and John had returned home from a month-long vacation. As soon as she'd touched Zanny, Sydney had stiffened. She'd pulled back, staring at her aunt with befuddled fear.

"I need to do something," she said. "I need to touch you."

Zanny, puzzled, had laughed. "Okay. Go ahead."

Sydney put her hand flat over Zanny's chest on the right side on the curve of her breast. As Emma watched, every bit of color faded from Sydney's cheeks.

"You need to go to the doctor as soon as you can. Something's here... something's wrong," Sydney whispered. "Promise me you'll go."

The three of them had been alone in the studio, thankfully. Sydney's words had shaken them all.

Zanny, to her credit, never hesitated.

"Okay. I'll call right now." She'd crossed to her desk, made the call, and gotten an appointment for the next day. A week later, the breast cancer diagnosis was made.

"There's no other way to explain it, you know," Emma told Archer now. "When they did those initial scans, that tumor had metastasized to her lung. We never told the kids. But Sydney wouldn't let go of her that weekend after she'd had the scan. She stuck to her side like glue. When Zanny had the second scan, the mets were gone. Then there's Ainsley and her inability to have kids. Sydney spent a lot of time around her right before she got pregnant. And Mom's doctor still doesn't know what to think about the fact that her hip, which needed replacement three years ago, is in better shape now than it was when she was sixty."

In a family whose abilities included shape-shifting, extreme pattern recognition, and botanical enhancement, Sydney was still a bit unusual. Her paranormal skills, as well as Noah's ability to communicate with the dead, stood out. Noah's skills came through Zanny's mother. Owen, who was the family expert on such things, theorized Sydney's gift came from a recessive gene.

"Does it make me an awful mother to say that I'm glad Graydon and Carter are just cats?" she asked Archer.

He smiled. "No. That has its own burdens, but they're minor compared to what Sydney and Noah have to deal with. Do you think she's happy?"

"I think she's working on it. And I think the job has helped a lot. Archer... Sawyer looks at her."

"I hope he does. Otherwise he might run into her or something," he joked. Emma goosed him, and he jumped. "What? He might. He's almost as tall as I am. He could hurt her."

"I mean he *looks* at her. Like she's a woman."

That got his attention. He sat up and turned the lamp on beside the bed. "No. He wouldn't. Would he?" He frowned.

Emma sat up, placing a kiss on his bare shoulder. "I think... I don't know. Maybe all it is, is looking. But she looks back."

Archer stared at her for a long minute. "I should go have lunch with her today. Just to make sure she's okay." When she laughed, he scowled. "What?"

"I love you. Do you know that? Overprotective daddy."

His lips twitched, even though he tried to maintain a stern face. "She's my baby girl. And he's old enough to know better."

"He's a good man, and you know it. Besides, you're the one who 'gave' her to him. You said as much yesterday."

When she went to get out of bed, he caught her and pulled her back, rolling on top of her. "I didn't mean he could have her like that!"

Emma laughed softly as she ran her hands down his sides, enjoying the weight of him. "No, but that might be what ends up happening. She could do worse."

"I guess so. But he's not a long-term commitment guy. He makes Logan before Amelia look like a homemaker."

"I know that. However, our daughter is a grown woman. And she's as aware of Sawyer's commitment issues as we are. I'd like to see her have fun, even if it means she has a fling with him and that's all it is."

"I really don't want to talk about this," he muttered, letting his head fall to her shoulder. "I realize she's an adult but there are some things I'd prefer to leave in that gray area of the unknown."

"Then we won't talk about it. I love you, husband."

When Emma bit down lightly on his shoulder, he sucked in a breath and raised his head.

"Yeah?"

"Oh, yeah. Maybe you'd better hit the snooze button again," she told him as her hands became bolder in their explorations. "Your luscious body has distracted me, and I think you're going to have to do something about it before we get ready for work."

The smile that she loved so much spread across his face, slightly wicked, completely endearing. "My pleasure."

CHAPTER FIFTEEN

THEY'D NOT BEEN OPEN LONG Tuesday morning when Sydney heard footsteps on the stairs outside. A few seconds later, the door opened, admitting an older gentleman. Dressed in a snazzy sports jacket, dress shirt, and dress slacks, he wore a plaid golf cap and carried a cane. He looked to be around the same age as Owen, maybe a little younger. When he saw Sydney, he removed the hat, nodding a greeting.

"Hi. Can I help you?" she asked.

"I hope so, young lady," he replied, lifting his chin to study her through his glasses. "Are you Sydney?"

"I am."

"Hmmm. You're awfully young."

She smiled. "Time will take care of that if I'm lucky."

He gave a bark of laughter, acknowledging Sawyer with another nod when he came to the door of the office. "Depends on your perspective, I suppose. I ran into a man at the library, said he was your grandfather. Said you might could help me out."

Sydney gestured to the chair in front of her desk. "I'll do my best. What sort of help do you need?"

"My name's Leslie Grainger. My wife, Zelda, is from here originally. Grew up over on Big Creek. She grew up hearing how her great-great-grandfather was in the Revolution, and she wanted to trace that lineage, join the DAR," he said, referring to the Daughters of the American Revolution. "And I'm trying to achieve that goal for her. I need someone to do the genealogical research. I'm a retired pharmacist, and I don't have the patience to sit down and learn about computers. So I drove down here from Lexington to see if I could find someone who could do it." He punctuated his sentence with a thump of the cane. "Ran into your grandfather, and he sent me to you."

"Um, well... Sawyer?" She knew they handled insurance fraud investigation, background searches, and other personal information-gathering tasks, but Sawyer had never said anything about genealogy.

"We don't really offer genealogy services, sir," he told the man with some regret. "I'm assuming your wife isn't able to do the work?"

A stillness came over Mr. Grainger very briefly. "No. She's in an assisted care facility. Alzheimer's. She only was ever able to complete the basic information needed before she... couldn't do anymore."

Sydney swallowed hard against the lump that rose into her throat. Her great-grandmother, Eliza, had developed stroke-related dementia during the last few years of her life. The disease was insidious, evil, and Sydney couldn't think of a crueler fate for the patient or their loved ones.

"I'm sorry, Mr. Grainger. What sort of research exactly are you needing?" she asked, ignoring Sawyer's raised eyebrow.

"She was only able to trace her lines back three or four generations, depending on which side we're talking about," he said. He handed Sydney a folder. "That's all I have right there."

"So they weren't able to help you at the library?" Sawyer asked. "I thought they had a list of people who offered this sort of thing."

"Well, I didn't get that far, you see. I ran into Owen Campbell and we got to chatting before I could talk to the girl at the desk. He said that for what I'm after, his granddaughter might be my best bet. But it doesn't sound like that's the case."

Sydney looked at Sawyer. "I know you're booked up solid, but I could do this. I tagged along after Grandpa enough growing up when he was doing genealogy, and I do have a history degree."

He rested an arm on top of one of the filing cabinets. "How long would something like this take? I wouldn't even begin to know how to bill for the services."

She glanced back through the file, biting her lip. "As long as I can do most of the research locally... probably no more than fifteen or twenty hours. I might have to go over to Virginia, though, for some of it. That's where some of these names appear to come from if this information is correct, but luckily, the places I'd need to go to access the records are only an hour or so from here. And the DAR has pretty strict regulations on what they'll accept for proof of lineage, so I would have to find the actual court records, deeds, probated wills, that sort of thing."

"If it makes any difference, money is no object," Mr. Grainger put in.

"It isn't about the money so much," Sawyer said. "It's more about whether or not we can adequately meet your needs."

"How about this," Sydney suggested. "Let me do some digging, see what I can find out. Are you planning to be in Hazard long, Mr. Grainger?"

He waggled his hand. "I'd thought to head home this afternoon sometime. Even though I'm not from here, I have a couple of friends we've made over the years I'd like to stop in and see."

"Then why don't you let me make a copy of this," she said, holding the file up, "and I'll do some rudimentary research. I can do that from here. I can get a better idea of how easy or difficult this project would be, as well as an estimate of how much it would cost. You can come back this afternoon on your way out of town, and we'll see if we can come to an agreement."

"I have no problem with that. Do you, sir?" he asked Sawyer.

Sawyer studied her closely for a moment. "Okay. But no promises."

"I appreciate your honesty," Mr. Grainger said as he stood with a grunt. "You could easily have taken me for a ride. You still might, for all I know. But I don't think so." He held his hand out, and Sawyer shook with him. "You can keep those papers, young lady. That's a copy of what I have at home."

"Okay. Thank you. About what time do you think you'll be back by?"

He glanced at his watch. "Oh, I'd say around three. Is that all right?"

She nodded. "That's plenty of time for me to do what I need to."

"Then I'll see you two then. Good day." He donned his cap, tipping the brim, and left. Sawyer followed him to the door, watching as he went down the steps.

"Thanks for letting me do this," she told him. She could tell he wasn't thrilled with the turn of events.

"I want to go over what you find before he comes back."

"Sure. I should be able to get a report pulled together in about three hours, maybe less. I'd like to call Grandpa first, see what he thinks. He *is* something of an expert in genealogy in this area."

"He is. And that's the only reason I'm letting you do this," Sawyer told her. "I know you have backup if you get into trouble. See what Owen says, and we'll go from there."

"You don't think I can do this on my own?" she asked, trying to mask her hurt.

"I didn't say that. You've proven ten times over how competent you are at running this place, and I don't see that your doing genealogy research would be much different. But what little I do know about the field, the research can be tricky. It's a whole 'nother world. And if Evans Investigations' name is going to be on this project, it has to be done well and done quickly. That's nothing personal against you."

That made her feel better, went a long way toward smoothing her hackles. "I'll do my best not to let you down."

Sawyer smiled. "Sydney, if there's one thing I'm sure of, it's that you'll do a damned fine job at this. *If* you can find the resources you need. Let me know if you need anything."

"Yes, sir." She gave him a sharp salute as he went back into his office. The first place she'd need to start was with the expert. Grabbing her cell phone, she called Owen while she started working her way through the e-mails that had come into the general mailbox overnight.

"I've been expecting your call," he said in lieu of a greeting. "How's my girl this morning?"

"Excited. How are you?"

"I'm enjoying watching Noah try to avoid going on a date. I'm not sure he's going to be successful, thankfully. Did you talk to Mr. Grainger?"

Sydney laughed. "I did. And I have a ton of questions—we're going to try to help him, but before we do, I need to pick your brain."

"Ask away, my dear, though the pickings might be slim."

"I know better, Grandpa. So who's Noah possibly going on a date with?"

Owen cleared his throat. "The young lady at the front desk here at the library. Apparently, someone gave her his business number and he gave her mother a quote for a new kitchen last week."

A satisfied grin spread across her face. "I wonder who in the world would do such a thing."

"I'm sure you don't know a thing about it."

"Nope. I'm completely innocent," she told him with a laugh. "So about these questions I have."

"Why don't I head over to Sawyer's office and answer them?" he proposed. "I've wanted to see where the boy works now for a while."

"That would be wonderful, but what about Noah?"

Owen sighed. "I think I'm going to have to rescue him. He's looking awfully vexed, and if I don't step in, he's liable to do or say something unwise. We'll see you in a bit."

A deep peal of laughter rang out as she imagined how harassed Noah must be feeling, and the sound drew Sawyer's attention. He stopped in the reception area on his way back from the coffee pot.

"What's funny?"

"Noah," she told him, snickering. "Grandpa's trying to play matchmaker and it isn't going so well."

Sawyer's smile was slow, wickedly amused, and made her stomach turn somersaults. "Who's the girl?"

"A really sweet young woman at the library. I *may* have given her his phone number the other day. Apparently, she followed through and called him, set up an appointment for her mother to get a kitchen estimate."

He shook his head as she laughed. "Better watch it. You might find yourself on Owen's Cupid list."

That sobered her up. "Oh, no. Forget it. That's not happening."

It was Sawyer's turn to chuckle. "Don't bet on that."

"You hush, or else I'll tell Grandpa to find *you* someone," she warned, shaking her finger at him. "As a matter of fact, I'm surprised he hasn't tried to do that before now."

"What makes you think he hasn't?" With a wink, he went back into his office.

Sydney stared after him, her mouth hanging open. "You booger!"

His response was a low laugh that affected her much the way the smile had. The stinker knew her well enough by now to know that curiosity over who Owen had set him up with and how it had turned out would eat her alive.

"I'll pay you back for that. You'd better watch it," she called.

"Good luck with that."

As she went over the genealogy file so she knew what to ask Owen, she realized she was excited about the project for the project's sake, not just so she could prove herself to Sawyer. While she'd enjoyed the work she'd done for Charles, none of that had been anything she'd taken lead on. She'd had a lot of responsibility in her duties as his assistant, yes, but the nuts and bolts of the work had been his. This one would be all on her, and she was more than ready for the challenge.

CHAPTER SIXTEEN

WATCHING SYDNEY INTERACT WITH OWEN in a more professional setting gave Sawyer some surprising insights into what made her tick. He knew of Owen's passion for history, a passion Rachel shared to the point that she'd made a career out of teaching the subject. Many times over the years, Sawyer had been present for discussions where she and Owen had debated this settlement theory or that historical finding, and the depth of their knowledge on the subjects they discussed had amazed him. For some reason, he'd never expected Sydney to share that love of history. Clearly, though, she did.

"So that's where I think I need to start," she said as she finished going over the job with Owen. "What do you think?"

"I think that sounds like a solid plan. I know a lot of work has been done on at least a couple of these families," he said, tapping the file. "I can tell you what books to look at in the library. If he's just after one or two lines to tie into DAR, you should be able to follow those two easily enough. If he wants a full genealogical profile, that might be a bit harder. Not impossible but harder. Just keep in mind that not every branch of every tree leads to information. You'll have some dead branches that the information simply doesn't exist on anymore."

Sawyer heard regret in the man's voice. "Why would they be dead branches?"

"A lot of reasons. The families might not have been record keepers or they might have been isolationists—in which case the traditional routes of research such as census records and birth records won't exist—or the records might have been lost over the years. Back in the day, burning down courthouses to make a mark during wartime was a common practice. Shoot, the courthouse here in Perry County has been burned three or four times since the county was founded in 1821."

Sawyer was astonished. "Seriously? Three or four times?"

"Yes, not counting expansions. We're on the fifth or sixth version now. Thankfully, this last round was just a renovation, but it's not been that long ago that feuding families went in to get rid of land transfer records by whatever measures it took."

"Even knowing what kind of people I interacted with as a state trooper, that still surprises me," Sawyer confessed. "I guess there weren't any duplicates of the records that burned, either."

"Not often, no. The 1890 census is a great example of records that were lost," Sydney said. "Also due to a massive fire, this time in the National Archives in 1921. They're still finding bits and pieces of it here and there, thanks to the government's typical bureaucratic inefficiency, but most of it's gone as far as we know. And that's vital information we'll never get back."

Owen nodded. "A lot can happen in twenty years—marriages, divorces, relocations, births, deaths. They do the census every ten years, and so losing that decade's censuses... it's a painful blow to historians. If you need access to the online databases, come up to the house and use my subscription," he told Sydney. "There's an amazing amount of information to be had right there, and we'll feed you."

Sawyer raised his coffee mug. "Can't beat that offer."

"You should come, too," Owen said. "I know this isn't

your particular field of inquiry, but it might behoove you to see how the process unfolds."

"I don't want to bother you and Sarah," Sawyer hedged.

Owen's look scolded him as effectively as though he'd spoken. "I won't tell Sarah you said that. I'd hate to see her blister your ears. Will an evening work better for you two?"

Sydney shrugged. "I'm free whenever. The only thing I have planned is dinner with Danny Friday evening. You?"

"Tonight or tomorrow would work," Sawyer said, giving in. "I'll be happy to bring food, though."

"Me, too. Or I can come up and help Grandma cook," Sydney said.

"You can cook?" He hadn't meant to ask that, but the words slipped out before he could stop them. Sawyer knew, as did anyone who was close to the Campbells, that Emma wasn't a great cook.

Sydney scowled at him. "Why wouldn't I be able to cook?"

"Um, because you're Emma's daughter?" he answered tentatively.

Owen laughed. "You've stepped in it now."

Sydney straightened, shooting Sawyer a dirty look. "I may be Emma's daughter, but I'm also Archer Gibson's. And I'm Sarah Campbell's granddaughter. 'You can cook?'" she mimicked. "Oh, it's on now, buddy. It's on."

Sawyer struggled not to laugh at her outrage, and seeing Owen's clear amusement didn't help. "I stand corrected. I'm sorry for doubting your culinary skills."

"Mm-hmmm. You just go right on and try to make nice. Won't do a bit of good. That horse is already out of the barn," she said as she straightened the file. "Grandpa, I'll call Grandma and coordinate with her about the food. Is this evening, six o'clock okay? I get off at four thirty and I'll need a little bit of time to get to the farm and get cooking."

Owen grinned at her proudly. "I look forward to it." He stood. "I'd better meet up with Noah. He's a bit miffed at me right this moment. Something to do with interfering in his personal life. The things these kids come up with. Like I'd try to find him a girlfriend. He has me confused with someone else."

"Uh-huh. Sure he does," Sydney said, coming to her feet. "If it's okay with Sawyer, I'll walk over to the bakery with you. My breakfast bar's wearing off. Do you want anything?"

"Surprise me," Sawyer told her. The mischievous look that flitted across her face made him wish he'd chosen better words, but they were out.

Judging by Owen's expression, he was enjoying watching Sawyer dig himself a deeper hole. His words confirmed it.

"The two of you should take this act on the road. You could charge admission."

"I don't know what you're talking about," Sawyer said, somewhat desperately.

Owen squeezed his shoulder. "Sure you don't. See you this evening."

The office was quiet after they left. Sawyer took the opportunity to close his eyes for a moment, to sit back in his chair with a groan and ask himself again what he'd gotten into. Hiring Sydney had not been a mistake. He didn't believe that now. But his quiet, regimented life was being turned upside down bit by bit, and it was unsettling. He wasn't sure where the pieces would land when they came back down. All he could do was hold on for the ride and hope they settled into something resembling normal.

CHAPTER SEVENTEEN

BY THE TIME DINNER WAS over, Sawyer was so stuffed he didn't know if he could push his chair away from the table. From the smug, knowing smirk on her face, Sydney was very aware of his predicament.

"Gee, Sawyer, you act like you've never had a home-cooked meal or something," she said as she stood to clear the dishes.

Forcing himself to his feet, he scowled across the table at her. "Okay, smarty pants. You can cook. I was wrong, I was judging you, and I'm sorry."

She shot him a coquettish glance over her shoulder, then snubbed her nose in the air. "Hmmph." Her dark hair, pulled back into a ponytail, swung with the movement.

Sawyer gave a put-upon sigh. "She'll never let me live that down," he told Sarah and Owen as he gathered up empty dishes.

"Probably not. And what do you think you're doing? You came here to do genealogy, not dishes," Sarah said, trying to shoo him away from the dining room.

"You are not waiting on me." He ignored her efforts and followed Sydney into the kitchen. "I'm perfectly capable of helping with the cleanup."

"Good luck with that," Sydney said, taking the plates from his hands. "You're a guest. You'd have to come to more family dinners than you attend now to qualify for dishwasher duty."

As Sydney went back for a second load, Sarah came in, the plate with the leftover biscuits in hand. "Would you like me to wrap these up for you to take home?"

He barely managed to hold back a whimper. "Yes, please. Unless you and Owen want them."

The biscuits had been amazing, as had the rest of the meal—crisply fried potatoes and onions, soup beans, homemade apple butter, sautéed mustard greens, and fresh tomatoes and cucumbers from Sarah's garden.

She smiled as she bagged the food. "I have a direct line to the chef. I can get a dozen of these anytime I want them."

"I wonder if that line would work for me," he said in a low voice.

Sarah winked at him. "Can't hurt to try. I hear she can be bribed with cupcakes."

"I heard that," Sydney said, coming back with more dishes. "I can hardly wait to grow a garden next year so I can have fresh veggies right outside the back door. I've missed the planting season now for the most part, though I can still do some greens later this summer when it cools down."

"You know we have more than enough growing here," Owen said. He brought the rest of the dishes in and set them on the counter. "Noah always plants enough to feed an army. He's got some of Ben's talent with plants, I think."

"I know, and I fully intend to raid his bounty as soon as I can," Sydney said. "But I'd like to be able to step out the back door and get some fresh lettuce or a tomato. I won't always have time to run up here and get a quick snack."

"Do you garden, Sawyer?" Sarah asked as she gently moved Sydney away from the sink, taking the dishes from her.

"No. I've never had the time or the inclination to do it, to be honest."

"I thought you might be an avid gardener, what with you being vegetarian," Sydney said. "Don't you like to get your hands dirty?"

He had to bite his tongue to keep from responding with a comeback that would likely get him slapped. "I have no problem getting my hands dirty, thank you very much. We never had a garden growing up, and I figure I can keep the local farmer's markets going, get what I need there. That's a fair trade."

"You kids go on in the living room. Owen has you set up in there," Sarah said. "I'll finish up here and be with you in a minute."

Seeing that she wouldn't take no for an answer, Sawyer gave in gracefully and followed Owen and Sydney to the living room.

"So where did you grow up that you didn't have a garden?" Sydney asked.

"In a trailer park in a little town near Pittsburgh."

"Pennsylvania?"

He laughed. "That's the one."

She settled in on the couch and organized a clipboard with paper, a couple of pens, and the Grainger file on the table beside her. "How'd you end up in Hazard?"

"You're Miss Detective tonight."

"Familial trait. You may have noticed we're all insatiably curious." She pushed her glasses up and tucked her bangs away from her face. "So? How'd you get here?"

Deciding to torment her a little, Sawyer settled in beside her, leaving a few inches between them. "In a car. Well, a truck if you want to get technical."

She grabbed a throw pillow from behind her, smacking Sawyer with it before putting it in her lap. "Smart ass. You know that isn't what I meant."

Owen chuckled from across the room. He adjusted his own glasses as he turned the TV on, then handed Sydney the remote. "Tickets, I'm telling you. I'll get the keyboard."

Sawyer shrugged, enjoying her aggravation. "I was a trooper up there, and I was ready for a change. A friend of mine knew the commander at the post here, and I put in an application. I got the job, and I moved. End of story."

He could tell she knew there was more to the story than that, but he wasn't willing to give up any of the details. His time in Pennsylvania wasn't, for the most part, filled with pleasant memories and he didn't like visiting them.

"Here we go," Owen said, coming back in with a wireless keyboard and mouse. "We don't watch much television these days, and I've started using this one as a computer monitor. Sydney, you know how to drive from here?"

"I do. Thank you." With her legs crossed under the pillow, she positioned the keyboard and maneuvered the mouse to open the browser. "Here we go."

All Sawyer could do over the next two hours was sit back and watch as she deftly sent queries out and gathered information. A large part of what he did now, as well as what he'd done with the state police, was to track down information from various sources. But he'd never realized how similar genealogical research was to investigating. And to have so much of the data in one place, organized in collections that were easily accessible?

"Amazing," he said. "I wish the databases I use every day were as user-friendly as this one." He'd asked so many questions and learned so much this evening he felt like he'd been in school.

Owen nodded. "It's worlds different now than it was just a few years ago. There's still a need, especially for the kinds of records she'll be looking for, to do some physical legwork. But so much is available now that was closed off to the public... I can't overstate how thrilling it is to have all that information at your fingertips."

"Speaking of fingertips," Sydney said, groaning as she straightened and flexed her hands. She'd been hunched over the keyboard, searching and make notes and searching again, for most of the time they'd been in the living room. "Why did you let me sit here this long?"

"Sweetie, I recognized that on-the-hunt look on your face," Sarah told her with a smile. "I knew better than to interrupt you. What do you think?" She held up a crooked pink and white square of knitted yarn.

Sydney did a double take. "Um. What is that supposed to be?"

Sarah huffed out a breath. "It's a baby blanket." She lowered it to her lap and frowned. "I didn't think it was *that* bad."

"It's not," Sydney hurried to assure her. "It's just..."

But Sarah was waving a hand. "No, don't try to spare my feelings. I know it's hideous. But I found this sweet, soft yarn, and I had to get it. Now if I can just get one of you grandkids to produce me some babies, we'll be set." She sent Sydney a pointed look that clearly asked "what are you waiting for?"

Sydney had taken a sip of tea, and Sawyer thought she was going to choke to death as she sputtered and coughed.

"What? No. Oh, no. Don't you even look at me. Noah's the oldest. He's the one who's neglecting his duty as a grandson." She set the drink aside and shook her head, her hand going to her chest.

"That boy's so danged ornery, he might stay single for the rest of his life out of pure stubbornness," Owen grumbled. "I think we're going to have to resort to having them adopt us some babies, Sarah."

She sighed. "Well, I don't much care how we get babies. We just need some. It's been almost twelve years since we had a baby in the family. Sawyer, any chance you'll be getting married soon?"

"Uh... that's not on my radar, n-no," he stammered. He narrowed his eyes at Sydney, who was snickering at his discomfort. In retaliation, he reached out and tugged on the end of her ponytail.

That was a mistake. Her hair was softer than he could believe, silky and seductive. Everything in him shifted, his fingers itching to take it out of its ponytail holder and comb through the luscious, dark-chocolate strands. It took every bit of control he had to move his fingers away to a safe spot on the back of the couch.

"Well, I think we've gotten a really good start here tonight," Sydney said, oblivious, as she turned her attention away from him. "I appreciate the help and the time, you two. I should be able to take this and run with it tomorrow."

Owen spread his hands. "Glad to help and you know it. Mr. Grainger seemed like a nice enough guy, and I figured he might have better luck with you than with the people the library recommends. Don't get me wrong—they're good people. But he needed a professional, not a hobbyist."

"I'm not anything approaching a professional genealogist," Sydney protested as she set the keyboard on the coffee table in front of her and stood. "But I think we can definitely provide him with a professional result."

"Absolutely we can," Sawyer agreed. "As a matter of fact, if this goes well and if you don't get overwhelmed, it might be a service we can add. I don't know how much call for it there is, but at least we'll have it if someone else comes along."

He stood, as well, realizing as he looked down on her just how petite she was. She usually wore heels in the office, and seeing her without shoes on now was a bit of a jolt. Her forehead barely came up to his chin.

"Well, before you go, I was hoping I could ask a favor," Owen said. He grimaced a bit as he got out of his chair. "They delivered a package here this afternoon that actually belongs to Noah. Given how peeved he is with me at the moment, I don't particularly want to face him. Could you walk it down to him, Sydney?"

"Sure. I'll be glad to."

Sarah led Sawyer into the kitchen, where she got the

biscuits and a small jar of apple butter while Sydney was getting her shoes on. "I hope she takes a flashlight. It's not fully dark yet, but there could be snakes or elk or anything."

"I can walk down with her. It's not that far."

"Would you? Oh, Sawyer, that would be so nice of you. I know she's perfectly capable of making it down there and back by herself, but ever since Owen and I were dating and I almost stepped on a snake, I've been horrified by the creatures."

"I'll be glad to provide an escort."

Sarah smiled up at him, pleased. "Do you have a flashlight in your truck? I can get you one if you don't."

"You really think I'd not have a flashlight? You know me better than that," he teased.

She reached up and pinched his cheek gently. "Yes, I do."

They met up with Owen and Sydney on the porch. "I'll walk down with you," Sawyer told her, taking the package from her. "I could use the exercise after that meal. I'll just drop this food off at the truck first."

He was a little surprised Owen hadn't delivered the package himself, but maybe Noah *was* that upset. And remembering the older man's grimace as he got up, Sawyer wondered if maybe age wasn't catching up to Owen a bit. He was, after all, eighty-one. Even if he was slowing down, he was still the most active octogenarian Sawyer had ever seen. Regardless of the reasoning, Sawyer was glad to help out. He didn't particularly like the idea of Sydney walking the half mile down the ridge to Noah's by herself in the near dark any more than Sarah did.

Sarah waited until they'd disappeared behind the barn

before turning to Owen with a narrowed gaze. "The grimace was a nice touch."

He grinned, unabashed. "I figured it couldn't hurt. But what was with the baby blanket? You hate knitting."

She walked over to him and slipped her arms around his waist, gratified to feel him return the embrace. "Was it too much?"

"Eh, maybe a little. Probably not, though. How'd you get him to go with her?"

"Oh, I just mentioned how I've loathed snakes ever since you and I were dating and I almost stepped on one. And I worry so about my grandbaby being out there in the dark by herself."

Owen kissed her soundly. "Think they'll figure it out?"

"I doubt it. They'll be so busy being thankful that we're not focusing our matchmaking on them with other people that they'll never realize what we've done. Do you really think they're attracted to each other?"

"You saw the way they interacted. What do you think?"

She rested her head on his shoulder. "I think they're circling each other and the potential is there. What they end up doing with that potential, I don't know."

"Amelia was watching them like a hawk this weekend. I asked her why and she brushed me off," he said, taking her hand. They moved to the porch swing and sat down. He put his arm around her shoulders, covering her hand with his as he spread her fingers out on his knee. "But I've not known that little Cupid for her whole life and not learned how to read her. They set something off with her. That's what initially made me start looking at them."

"It would be nice to add him to the family," Sarah admitted.

"Yes, it would. He's a good man. A bit stubborn, but God knows he'd need to be to deal with Sydney."

Sarah laughed and placed a kiss on the hand that rested

on her shoulder. "That's the truth. We should go in, just in case. I'd hate to embarrass them."

"Go in? I suppose I could go to bed early tonight," he said, his voice dropping as he feathered a kiss over her temple.

"I wasn't necessarily thinking about bed, but now that you've mentioned it, that does sound nice." Sarah closed her eyes briefly, thanking God for the man beside her. Even after more than fifty years of marriage, he was still her world just as she was his, emotionally and physically.

"We've had a good run, you know that?" he said as they went inside.

"I do. And it isn't over yet. I'm not ready to finish our book, not by a long shot."

Owen kissed her again. "Neither am I."

CHAPTER EIGHTEEN

SYDNEY DIDN'T KNOW IF SAWYER was aware of what her grandparents were up to or not, but she wasn't about to point it out to him. She knew good and well that nothing would come of their walk, but that didn't mean she couldn't enjoy the man's company while she had it.

The evening was gorgeous, warm without being hot, not a cloud in the falling-twilight sky. She slowed to a stop as they came around the far side of the barn, taking in the magical sight unfolding across the rolling land on top of the mountain.

"Look at that," she said, her voice hushed with something approaching reverence.

Sawyer whistled low, turning around in a circle to take it all in.

Hundreds, if not thousands, of lightning bugs danced and sparkled in the trees and floated above the wildflowers that covered the pasture. Sydney knew the science behind the show, but right that moment, the science didn't matter. A night bird called from somewhere in the distance, its cry haunting and soulful.

"I never get tired of watching this," she confessed. "This is one of the things I missed the most, not counting family, when I was away. I don't know how I lived anywhere else, seeing this now."

Instead of teasing her for being softhearted, Sawyer

surprised her by agreeing. "My place is like this in the evenings and in the mornings. Different creatures, obviously, depending on the time of day, but it's peaceful, it's quiet, and it's kind of a sanctuary. Of course, I don't have anything approaching the scale Owen and Sarah have here. But it's home."

Sydney crossed her arms over her chest, feeling vulnerable as they started walking again. The path to Noah's house was more than wide enough for them to walk side by side, but thanks to the canopy of trees on either side, it felt intimate. "How long have you lived there? Since you came to Hazard?"

"No. I bought the place about ten years back. Helping me rehab it was one of Noah's first jobs when he came home." He glanced at her. "How are things with you and Archer?"

The question was unexpected. "They're fine. Why?"

"I just wondered, that's all. I know you worry about him with regards to your biological family."

Sydney shrugged. "I kept a close eye on him while Cade and Grant were here. He seemed okay with the idea of us meeting. And he told me yesterday that he liked them, hoped they came back. That he was glad we'd connected." She let out a long sigh. "It's hard to explain. I don't wish I'd known Ted or that I'd grown up with him instead of with Daddy. But there's some curiosity that's been there. I kept tabs on him and his family via the Internet, or at least I did until a couple of years ago. That's one of the reasons I was so surprised to see the boys—they don't look anything like their pictures. They've grown up."

Sawyer's quick flash of a smile was visible in the growing dark. "They look a bit like you. I always thought you were Emma's double, but there's something of the boys there, too."

"I know. And that makes me sad. Not because I don't want to look like them but because I don't want Daddy to... I don't know how to explain it. I'm probably being ridiculous."

"No. I understand what you mean. I don't know my own parents all that well. Nan raised me for the most part. And I always felt guilty when I did spend time with Mom and Dad because I thought it meant I was taking something away from her."

Sydney stopped walking. Tipping her head to the side, she studied him. "I had no idea. And yes, that's exactly how I feel—like I'm stealing from Daddy if I think about them."

"You know Archer doesn't believe that any more than Nan does," Sawyer said quietly.

She scuffed the toe of her shoe on the ground. "I hope he doesn't. But that fear's always there. So how come she raised you and not your parents?"

He didn't answer immediately, just shifted the package from one hand to the other. "My mom was just sixteen when she had me. Just barely sixteen—she got pregnant when she was fifteen. Dad was a few years older. He supported me, but he didn't have much to do with me, and they didn't get married until Mom was twenty-one. And when they did get married, at first Nan kept me to give them a little time to adjust to being together. You know how it is—no matter how well you think you know someone, the game changes when you get married."

"Right."

"Well, by the time the first year came and went, she was pregnant with my first brother. And then my second brother came along after that, and before anyone realized it, time passed."

Sydney was horrified. "Time passed? You were their child, Sawyer. You don't just forget a child like it's a...a purse or something you stopped using."

He shifted, uncomfortable. "It wasn't like I never saw them. We visited. I had sleepovers. And they didn't live that far away, only about twenty miles or so."

She wasn't buying it. He was too defensive, too stoic about the whole ordeal. "Bull. I don't think I like your parents very much. Nan? She's adorable and feisty and we'd get on like gangbusters. But your parents? Oh, no. You just don't do that to a child."

To her surprise, he laughed. "What are you going to do, drive up to Pittsburgh and punish them?"

"Don't give me any ideas," she said. "They left you with Nan, all by yourself? I can't get my head around that."

"It wasn't like they abandoned me. Dad supported me until I was eighteen. You don't have to defend me, you know. I survived just fine."

She had to pinch her lips together to keep from protesting. Finally, she shook her head. "At least you had Nan."

"Yes. Sarah reminds me a lot of her, if that makes you feel any better."

It did. A child could do a lot worse to be raised by someone like her grandmother. "Let's get this package to Noah before we get eaten by some woodland creature," she said, changing the subject and resuming the walk. "Have you ever been down here?"

"To his house and workshop? No."

"You're in for a treat, then."

When they reached the clearing that surrounded the small house, there was just enough light left in the day for Sawyer to look around. As she watched, wonder dawned on his face.

"Oh, my God. This is unreal."

"It's pretty impressive," she said with a smile.

Noah had filled the acre or so of cleared land with a cottage garden, with gravel paths leading to various beds of flowers and plants. Along the paths and around the perimeter of the garden, he'd placed intricately carved animals and fairy-tale creatures, the carvings so lifelike Sydney often had to take a second look to make sure they weren't real even though she'd seen them before.

"This is unbelievable," Sawyer said. "How is it that he doesn't have tourists stopping by to see this?"

"You know it's set back off the road a good way, and even if they did get lost and find their way here, there's a big, tall fence along the front of the property. Plus he has that gate down at the foot of the driveway. You may have noticed my family guards its privacy quite rigorously."

His look was hard to interpret. "It hadn't escaped me. And I know why Noah is so reclusive."

"You do?" Sydney was skeptical.

"Yes, I do. He worked on my house, remember, and that wasn't a short project. The place was falling down. I worked alongside him quite often. I know about Moira and what he can do."

"He told you?" she asked in a hushed voice.

Sawyer gave a half shrug. "He didn't have much choice. I kept finding him talking to himself, or so I thought. I was starting to worry. He had to explain who he was really talking to."

"Oh."

The idea was staggering. As far as Sydney knew, Noah had never told anyone outside immediate family about his abilities. The threat of the secret being exposed was what had led to his rift with Eli.

"I just... he doesn't trust people. Even if you did catch him talking to Moira, for him to admit that... And you don't seem freaked out."

He spread his hands. "I've seen a lot over the years I couldn't explain. I was shocked at first, and no, I didn't believe him immediately. He had to prove it. But it kind of made sense once he told me and the shock had worn off. I don't envy him."

"I don't, either. I think it's a big part of why he's still single, if you want the truth." She wanted to ask him if he knew any other of her family's secrets, but she didn't quite know how to approach the subject. Besides, they'd reached Noah's door, and she could see him coming through the house to greet them.

"What are you two doing here?" he asked, stepping outside.

"Playing mailman." Sawyer handed the package over. "This got mis-delivered."

Noah smiled. "Sweet. New router bits! Come on in." He held the screen door open.

"No fiddle tonight?" Sydney asked.

"You just missed it."

"Hmm. Maybe next time." Sydney led the way inside, stopping by the tall counter that divided the hall from the kitchen. A large calico cat was perched atop a barstool, waving her plume of a tail slowly as she raised and lowered her front feet in a soft rhythm.

"Hi, Fig, how are you?" Sydney gave her a finger to sniff, then accommodated her by scratching the side of her face. "Are you keeping Noah in line?"

The cat gave a happy purr in response, then reached out her front paws to grab Noah as he went by. He set the package on the counter and picked her up, holding her like a baby.

"That's a big cat," Sawyer said as he watched them interact. "What in the world do you feed her?"

"The good stuff. And she *is* big, twenty pounds plus all this fur. She's got some Maine coon in her family somewhere. Don't you?" he asked.

Fig nudged his chin, and Sawyer laughed. "Where's the name come from?"

"What, Fig?" Noah asked. "She has an orange patch that looks just like a fig on her side."

"You need a cat," Sydney said. When Sawyer looked at her with a frown, she held her hands up. "You do. Out there in that house all by yourself."

"They are good company. I know someone who has some kittens, if you're interested. They're about three months old, so they're not as dependent as the little ones." Noah let the cat down on the back of the couch. "Do you two want something to drink?"

"No, thanks. I'm still stuffed from dinner," Sawyer said. "And I have biscuits in the truck for breakfast tomorrow. Someone made them to prove she could cook. Is there anything you can't do?" he asked Sydney.

"She sucks at math, and she can't drive a stick to save her life. You made biscuits and you didn't bring me any?" Noah glared at her. "I see how it is."

Sydney narrowed her eyes. "Excuse me? Where's my marinara, cuz? Seems like I remember you saying something about six quarts. And I can't sew or knit or anything like that," she told Sawyer. "Speaking of knitting, Grandma's making baby blankets."

Noah growled as he opened a cabinet. "They're driving me nuts. Can't you get them off my back? And I know who gave the chick at the library my number, by the way. Karma, Sydney. Karma."

"Her mother needed a new kitchen," Sydney protested. "What was I supposed to do? Send her to a box store? I thought you might appreciate the referral."

"Sure you did." He crossed to them, handing Sawyer two jars. "Here's some marinara and some pesto. A gift."

"You brat! That's cruel, Noah. He makes the best marinara you've ever eaten in your life," she told Sawyer, eyeing the jars with longing.

"Comes from living in Italy for so long. I told you, marinara for biscuits. Two dozen, please." Her cousin watched her, an arch look on his face as he waited for her to cave.

She blew out an exasperated breath. "I haven't had time to make them. I'll try to do it this weekend, okay?"

Sawyer was grinning at their back and forth. "I'm so glad I never had a little sister."

"They can be more trouble than they're worth," Noah conceded. "I have two if you count this one."

"I'm not your sister."

"Close enough." He stuck his tongue out at her and Sydney made a face back at him, causing them all to laugh.

"We should probably go, get out of your hair," she said.

"Just a second." He went back to the cabinet and got another jar of sauce down, this time giving it to her. "Call it a bonus."

Sydney held it to her, grinning with pleasure. "I know what I'm having tomorrow for dinner! Thank you!"

"Yeah, well, you know the price if you want more."

As she and Sawyer walked back to her grandparents' house, an easy silence fell between them. With crickets chirping, frogs calling, and lightning bugs still flashing, the night bore a distinctly romantic feel.

As much as she tried to convince herself otherwise, she couldn't. Walking beside Sawyer in the dark felt too right. He was solid, giving off a strong presence both mentally and physically even through his quietness. She knew women who'd be afraid of him because of that, because of his height, but Sydney was used to tall men. Instead of being nervous, he made her feel safe, protected. Not that she thought she had anything to be afraid of up here on top of the mountain, but still. Her heart ached at the notion of how differently the night might end if he were attracted to her.

The lights were off in the farmhouse when they reached their vehicles.

"Do you think they're okay?" he asked her. "It's barely nine o'clock. I thought they were night owls."

Sydney's face heated, and she was grateful for the dark that hid her blush. "Um, I think they're fine. They probably just turned in early." There was no way in the world she was going to tell him they'd probably gone to bed but not for the purpose of sleeping. But Sawyer being the smart man he was, he picked up on her embarrassment.

"Oh. Oh, I see. Okay. That's... encouraging, I suppose."

"Sawyer!"

"What?" he said, laughing. "It is."

"You're incorrigible."

"Look who's talking."

Sydney shook her head as she put the marinara in her car, tucking it safely into the mesh pouch behind the driver's seat. "Thanks for letting me do this project. I'm eager to see what I can do with it."

He came to the window when she slid behind the wheel. "I'm happy to help Mr. Grainger. It's a noble mission he's on. Just so you know, my main concern wasn't the money."

Very briefly, Sydney laid her hand on his where it rested on the door. "I know. I never thought that. Still, I appreciate the opportunity." Her hand tingled where their skin had touched, and once it was back inside the vehicle and out of his sight, she curled her fingers around her palm. "I'd better go. You, too. I'll see you in the morning."

"Drive safely." He stepped back and dug his keys from his pocket. "The biscuits were really, really good, by the way. In case I didn't mention that."

Pleased, she smiled. "I got that impression. Wait until you see what I can do with yeast bread."

The man actually swallowed at the words. "Cinnamon rolls?" he said hopefully.

"Maybe. Goodnight, Sawyer."

She started her vehicle and got her seatbelt on as he got in his truck. Once he had his engine going, she backed out, then headed down the driveway.

"You're going to get your heart broken like it's never been broken before, Sydney Marie," she said in the quiet cab, classical music from the local NPR station playing in the background. "And you've practically begged for it to happen. Stupid girl."

Instead of Sawyer being less attractive or her girlish crush fading upon closer interaction with the man, she was more drawn to him now than she had ever been in the past. The difference now was that she had a good idea of exactly what she was missing by not being romantically involved with him, whereas before, when she was nineteen, all she'd had to go on was what she'd read in books and seen in movies.

She didn't know what in the world she was going to do with that knowledge, other than slowly go nuts lusting after her boss. There was no way Sawyer would ever see her as anything more than an impertinent, competent assistant or that troubled teenager she'd once been, she knew that. And if she didn't figure out how to stop wanting more from him, she was in big trouble.

CHAPTER NINETEEN

SAWYER'S MOOD WAS FOUL THE next morning though he tried to hide it from Sydney. Even though he knew he was being ridiculous, he partly blamed her for the lousy night he'd had and the subsequent mood. After all, dreams of her had kept him tossing and turning most of the night.

His mood wasn't enhanced when one of the young Lotharios from the state police post came in at eleven and started flirting with her. The only thing that kept him from losing his temper entirely was the fact that Sydney didn't seem to be receptive to the man's overtures in the least.

Still, he couldn't resist a jab. "I didn't realize you were divorced, Zander. I'm so sorry."

The other man's face flushed. "I'm not."

"Huh. Well, this is awkward, then. I thought you were trying to pick up my assistant. My mistake." Sawyer stared at him, daring the burly state trooper to say a word to the contrary.

Leighton "Lee" Harrison, the senior trooper who'd come in with Zander and the one who'd requested the meeting, rubbed a hand across his face to hide his smile. "Why don't we go over these files?" he suggested, his tone conciliatory.

"Sure thing. Come on into the conference room." Sawyer glanced back at Sydney as the other men went through the door. She was shaking her head, her own cheeks pink, and she wouldn't look at him.

Shit. He hadn't meant to embarrass her, too. There was nothing he could do about it at the moment, however, so he went on into the meeting.

An hour later, they'd finished going over the case Lee was working on. Since Sawyer had worked with the people involved several times in the past, Lee had wanted his opinion.

"Thanks for letting me bounce this off of you," Lee said, gathering up the papers he'd brought. "This helps."

"If you'll excuse me, I need to make a few calls. I'll be in the car." Zander stood without a word to Sawyer and left, barely acknowledging Sydney as he passed her desk.

"You know he'll hold a grudge over what you did out there," Lee told him quietly. "He thinks because he lives in Breathitt County he can do whatever he wants up here. And he's been called on it a few times now but not so publicly."

"He's young, he's stupid with self-importance, and he'll be on his third marriage within ten years." Sawyer didn't bother tempering his words. "He thinks with his dick, and if he's not careful, that's going to get him or whoever he's working with killed."

"I'll talk to him. He's a good cop when he's not trying to pick women up."

"Just watch your back. I probably shouldn't have said what I did, but he caught me on a bad day."

"Yeah. I'm sure that's what it was."

Sawyer knew Lee didn't believe that was all to the story any more than he believed in the tooth fairy. And damned if he could come up with a reasonable excuse.

"How's the new house?" he asked, standing, trying to change the subject.

Lee grinned, his blue eyes sparkling. "It's great. And my neighbor across the street is even greater. I think I'm in love. She comes out on the porch wearing these little shorts and does her paperwork. Wears glasses. Nothing sexier than a bookworm with mile-long legs."

Sawyer laughed, even as his mind drifted to his own glasses-wearing assistant. "You've only been moved in what, a week? Two? You aren't wasting any time."

"Doesn't take long to spot someone like her. I've not really introduced myself yet, but I will soon."

For all his friendly and outgoing personality, Sawyer knew Lee wasn't really a ladies' man. He had an active social life, but he didn't use his badge and uniform to rack up notches on his bedpost like some LEOs did.

"You never did tell me where you live now," Sawyer said.

"Tennant Avenue over in Airport Gardens. You should stop by sometime, check the place out."

They'd walked into the reception area, and Sydney overheard the tail end of the conversation. "That's where Rachel lives. Did you buy that house next to the brick wall?"

"That's it," Lee said. "Who's Rachel?"

Sawyer grinned, then laughed out loud. "Sydney's aunt, and your sexy neighbor who comes out onto the porch to do her paperwork, unless I miss my guess."

Sydney's mouth dropped open, then curved into a wide smile. "Oh, boy."

Lee was shaking his head, his jaw set as he fought down embarrassed amusement. "That's great. Any chance this conversation won't get back to her? Is she single? And I'm Lee Harrison, by the way." He held his hand out for Sydney to shake.

"Nice to meet you, and I won't say a word. I can't speak to Sawyer's intentions, though. He and Aunt Rachel have been friends for decades now. And yes, she's single, but her ex-husband was a state trooper, so you won't even get in the door," Sydney told him. "Sorry."

"She has a thing against cops?"

"Only against dating them," Sawyer explained. "Like Sydney said, she's been one of my best friends for twenty years now. The Campbells that I spend holidays with?

That's her family. Sydney's mom is her sister, Emma, who owns the photography studio two doors down."

"Oh, okay. So you're kin to Burke Lockhart and Rick Browning, I guess," Lee said to Sydney.

"I am. And Aunt Rachel's son, Easton? He's in school now going for a degree in criminology. As soon as he's old enough, he's planning to become a trooper."

Lee blinked at her. "Her son? Um, what'd she do? Have him when she was twelve or something?"

Sydney snorted. "Rachel's going to love you for that."

"She's my age, Lee." Sawyer didn't bother hiding his amusement at the other man's discomfort. "How old did you think she was?"

He shrugged. "I dunno. Around my age, I guess. Mid thirties, maybe. Wow."

"At least you don't have to worry about dating her now," Sydney said.

"Why? Because she's older than me? That doesn't matter. Age is just a number." He made the declaration so nonchalantly, Sawyer knew then he was seriously interested in Rachel, and it wasn't just a case of his having the hots for his neighbor.

"Rachel's fun. We go out a couple of times a month usually, just as friends," he said to turn the knife a little and give Lee a push. "If she ever does decide to date again, whoever she picks would be a lucky guy."

"Well, good luck if you go after her because you'll need it." Sydney got her purse out of the desk and stood. "I'm going to head to lunch, Boss. See you in an hour. Nice meeting you," she told Lee with a brief smile, then left.

"Why do I get the feeling she's offended?" Lee asked as they listened to her footsteps fade.

"I don't know. Maybe she's jealous you're interested in Rachel?"

Lee stared at him, an unholy gleam of amusement lighting his eyes. "Yeah. I'm sure that's it. She's jealous. Of *me* and her aunt. Yep."

Sawyer crossed his arms over his chest and scowled fiercely. "Spit it out."

"Nothing to spit out. You just about take Zander's head off for being his normal, 'charming' self, even though she wasn't the least bit interested in what he was offering. You can't stop looking at her when you think she isn't watching you—which she does, by the way. She puffs up and leaves when you sing the praises of her 'sexy' aunt. No, nothing to spit out that I can think of."

"I'm old enough to be her father," Sawyer told him quietly. He decided to open up a bit. Keeping the growing attraction he felt for Sydney to himself was driving him nuts, and aside from Rachel, Lee was his best friend. "I've known her since she was little. I can't just have an affair with her and then have the two of us go our separate ways."

"So what about having more than an affair?" Lee asked, serious. "I know you think you can't take that chance, but maybe she doesn't want kids. Some people don't. I don't."

"Sydney does."

Lee watched him closely for a moment, then sighed. "Too damned bad there's no way to get kids other than to create them yourself. You'd think they'd come up with something, I don't know, where you could borrow other people's kids or um... what's it called?" He pretended to think, tapping his fingers against his temple, then snapped them. "Adopt. Yeah, adoption. Too bad that's only something you can do with dogs and cats."

"Smart ass."

"Chicken shit."

Sawyer flipped him off. "I'm too old to adopt."

"Well, then, you're too old to have kids the normal way, too. Better get you a cane, an adult diaper, and a room in a nursing home." Lee was relentless, even though his tone wasn't harsh. "Big former state trooper, too scared to take a chance at being happy. I've never seen you so torn up over a woman before. And I'll bet a month's paychecks she's as torn up over you. Just think about it, okay? Try to take your emotions out of it. Ask her out for dinner or something."

"Hadn't you better go check on Zander? He's liable to leave you or find a heap of trouble on his own."

Lee took the hint and moved toward the door. "Call me if you want to talk. Any tips on Rachel?"

"Let me know when you plan to introduce yourself so I can bring popcorn and watch?" Sawyer teased. He shrugged. "Seriously, though, I think Sydney's right. You've got an uphill battle. That said, she could use a good guy in her life and I know you are one. Good luck."

"Thanks."

Sawyer didn't go back to his office for a while after Lee had gone. Instead, he sat down behind Sydney's desk, looking at the pictures and geegaws she'd arranged on its surface. It wasn't cluttered or overstated, but it very clearly reflected her personality.

Lee was right. If he didn't do something soon, the tension was going to build to the point that the wrong thing would slip out at the wrong time, and Sydney could get hurt.

About halfway through the walk back up to their vehicles last night, he'd realized just how expertly Owen and Sarah had played him. He tried to convince himself he was imagining it, but no. They'd set him up to take a romantic stroll with their granddaughter, he was sure of it. But what he couldn't figure out was why. Surely they knew any sort of relationship between him and Sydney wouldn't be appropriate.

He groaned and rubbed his eyes. Like Lee had said, he'd not been this torn up over a woman in... well, probably in twenty years. And he didn't like the sensation, not one bit.

"I'll let it ride for now," he muttered. "Hell if I know what else to do. Maybe the situation will rectify itself."

But he didn't believe that any more than he believed his feelings for Sydney would disappear overnight. No, he was in trouble. He just hoped he could find his way out of this mess before someone got hurt.

CHAPTER TWENTY

Sydney hadn't known what to expect Wednesday morning, but it wasn't what she got. Sawyer was late getting in, and when he did arrive, he was standoffish. She was on the verge of asking him if she'd done something wrong when the two state troopers arrived for their eleven o'clock meeting. The shorter one, Lee, seemed nice enough, but his burly companion, Zander, turned her stomach. He'd taken one look at her when they'd come in and instantly assumed she'd be an easy target.

When Sawyer had called him on the flirting, Sydney had wanted to cheer. And when he left after their meeting without stopping to try to pick her up again, she almost got out of her chair and danced.

Discovering that the charming, black-haired Lee was her aunt's new neighbor had thrilled her. He seemed to be a bit quirky, even for someone in law enforcement, and he took the news of Rachel's age in stride. But hearing Sawyer sing Rachel's praises had been unpleasant to say the least.

The unhappy realization that she was jealous of her aunt was something Sydney had to deal with as she ate lunch, or rather as she picked at her food. Danny had been trying to set her up with a friend, someone he'd met through work, and so far, she'd refused. But she was getting pathetic as it pertained to Sawyer, and the last thing she wanted was to turn into a moping, lovesick caricature.

"I'll call him tonight," she promised herself as she threw away the remnants of her meal. "Get it over with. Or maybe I'll just wait until dinner Friday." She really didn't want to have to put herself through the ordeal of joining the dating pool again.

When she went back to work after lunch, Sawyer was leaving. "I'll be out for the rest of the day," he said. "I'll have my phone on, so call if you need anything."

"Okay." As much as she hated to admit it, she was glad he was gone. She wasn't in any mood to deal with Sawyer, his attitude, or his admiration of Rachel anymore this afternoon.

Thursday morning was a little better. He seemed less touchy, even unbending enough to joke around with her. But when he stepped out for lunch, trouble stepped into the office in the form of Myrtle Grimes.

"So you're Sawyer's new girl," she rasped in a voice that sounded like she'd smoked two packs of cigarettes a day since she was born. "And lawd, if you don't look just like your mama. I'm Myrtle from downstairs."

"I'm Sydney. How do you do?"

Myrtle laughed. "So polite and professional. You're nothing like his usual type, that's for sure."

Sydney tried to take the reality of the woman in. Big bleached blond and red hair, bigger boobs that were outlined in a skin-tight shirt that said "Real Boobs Rock," and jeans that Sydney feared might literally split if the woman bent over. She'd clearly had work done on her face, and there was an edginess about her that made Sydney wonder if she was here for reconnaissance or to issue a warning.

"You're never going to catch his attention if you keep wearing clothes like that." She gestured to the red silk wrap-style blouse and grey skirt Sydney wore. "Most girls your age dress like little tramps. You've gone the other way, dressing like a damned nun. Sawyer prefers women who aren't afraid to show off their assets."

"Excuse me?" Sydney doubted her hearing even as she knew she hadn't misunderstood.

Myrtle didn't wait for an invitation, just sat down in front of Sydney's desk. She picked up one of the pictures beside the computer monitor and looked at it. "Brothers?"

Sydney stood and reached across, snapping the frame from her hands. "Yes. Is there something I can help you with?"

Myrtle raised a perfectly sketched-on brow. "No need to get snippy. Guess you've not done him yet, not with that attitude. That isn't a surprise, I reckon, given how you dress. Bet you're locked up like Fort Knox."

"I *beg* your pardon?" The fuse to her temper was lit, icy hot. "If you've not come up here to conduct business, I have work to do. Thanks for stopping by."

The woman didn't budge, just pulled a cigarette out of her cleavage—her *cleavage*!—and held it without lighting it while she gave Sydney a once-over.

"Are you a lesbian dyke or something?"

"That does it. You need to leave," Sydney ground out. "I don't know who the *hell* you think you are, but my life is none of your business."

"Hoo, boy, that hit a nerve." Myrtle leaned to the side and pulled a lighter from her pocket. "Got anything I can use as an ashtray?"

Sydney picked up the thirty-two ounce fast food soft-drink cup she'd picked up on the way in that morning. She'd refilled it with ice water an hour ago. Taking the lid off, she held the cup back.

"So help me if you light that thing, you're going to swim back downstairs," she gritted out between her clenched teeth. "Now *git*."

"What the hell is going on here?" Sawyer stepped inside. "Sydney?"

She'd been so intent on Myrtle she hadn't heard him come up the steps. She put the lid back on the drink with a growl. “My dressing habits, sexual preference, and life in general are *none* of her business. She doesn’t seem to understand the concept of polite behavior. I’m more than happy to teach her a lesson or two if she persists.”

“Honey, this girl needs to ride a pole or three and chill the hell out,” Myrtle told him, finally getting to her feet. She stopped beside Sawyer to trail a hand over his arm. “Surely you can find one of your old buddies that would be willing to break her in. I can’t imagine how unpleasant it has to be for you, up here having to work with her every day.”

“Leave now. Don’t come back,” Sawyer said. His eyes were cold, his face like stone as he glared at Myrtle. “And leave Sydney alone. You understand me?”

Myrtle looked from him to Sydney, then shrugged. “Whatever floats your boat. You know where to find me when you get tired of poking the dried-up prude over there.”

There was dead silence in the office for a couple of seconds, and then Sydney let out an outraged screech. Sawyer had to stop her from going after Myrtle, who’d taken one look at her furious face and hauled ass down the steps.

“Easy, now. Let it go. She’s not worth it.”

Sydney’s face felt so hot she thought she could fry an egg on it, and she was perilously close to tears as she struggled a little against his arms. “Nasty shitheaded bleached-blond bitch. You should have let me take her.”

His lips twitched. “You know I couldn’t do that. Sydney, I had no idea she would… I’m sorry.”

Swallowing hard, praying she wouldn’t embarrass herself further, she backed up. “No. Not your fault. But I am going to go now, get some fresh air.” She went to the desk and grabbed her phone and her purse.

“Okay.”

Sawyer didn’t try to stop her again, but she could feel the weight of his gaze as she left. Walking fast, she headed to her car, to the privacy it would afford her. Once there, she tried to figure out where to go. She had an hour, and the way she was feeling, it might take that long to calm down.

"I can't believe I lost my temper like that. I guess I might as well go home." But she didn't want to be cooped up. She needed to move. Making a decision, she pulled out. She'd go to the local park and walk or simply sit and watch the river go by.

Nearly forty minutes later, she'd finally started to calm down when her phone rang. Looking at the display, she groaned. Helen. Normally Sydney didn't mind talking to her former mother-in-law, but today wasn't one of those days. Deciding to put the conversation off, she sent the call to voice mail. She took a few more minutes to get a good grasp on her temper and her ego, and then she headed back to work.

Sawyer kept a solicitous eye on her the rest of the day, going out of his way not to cause ripples. By the time four thirty rolled around, she was more than ready to go home.

"I'm not glass, you know. And I appreciate your being careful with me, but I'm a big girl, Sawyer. My ego got dented, that's all," she told him before she left. "Still, thank you for not asking me to talk about it. And for backing me up. I'm sorry for the drama."

He sat back in his chair, steepling his hands together. "You don't have a thing to apologize for. I'm stunned she came up here and acted like that. I'm sorry—if there was any way I could go back and erase that little episode, I would."

"It's over, it's done, and there's nothing to do now but move on. I'll see you tomorrow."

She changed into a soft tank top and pajama bottoms when she got home, then headed for the kitchen. Thanks to skipping lunch, she was starving. In a few minutes, she'd heated up the leftover marinara and made some fresh pasta to put it on. With a couple of slices of garlic toast and a tall, frosty beer, she was set.

Once she'd eaten, she went to the screened-in back

porch and stretched out on the swing. Comfortable, she returned Helen's call.

"Hey, you. I'm sorry I missed you earlier. Are you busy?"

"Not at all. How are you? Liking the new job?" As warm as her tone was, Helen's voice was strained.

"It's fun most days. Today? Not so much. Is everything okay?"

There was a pause, then Helen expelled a tight breath. "I have some news. I'm afraid it might upset you, but I thought you had the right to know. Adam's getting married."

"Oh. Well, that's... I can't say it's entirely unexpected. I figured he would someday."

"Sydney... There's no easy way to say this. She's pregnant."

All the breath in her body vanished, the punch was so unexpected. For what felt like forever, she couldn't seem to get her lungs to work. When she finally did, she gasped.

"She's what?"

"I'm so sorry, honey. I debated on whether to tell you or not, but I know you still have friends up here. I didn't want you to hear about it from someone else."

Sydney hated her reaction, hated the pain and betrayal she felt. "But he had a vasectomy. She can't be pregnant. Who is she?"

"A co-worker. And they've been seeing each other for a while now. He had a reversal."

"I see."

She couldn't say anything else. She literally couldn't form the words, not even in her mind. All she could do was hurt.

"Anyhow, like I said, I thought you had the right to know. And I know there are people out there who might try to use the information to hurt you. I'm sorry, Sydney."

Taking in a deep breath, Sydney forced herself to pull it together long enough to finish the conversation. "I know.

And I appreciate you telling me, I really do. I should probably go."

"Will you call me sometime? Once you've had time to... once you've had time?" Helen asked.

"I will. Bye for now."

Sydney ended the call, tossing the phone down onto the swing by her hip. She wrapped her arms tightly around her body, cold anger freezing her from the inside out.

When she'd married Adam, she'd been barely twenty years old. They'd met the fall after her disastrous kiss with Sawyer, and Adam had swept her off her feet. Married that following spring, they'd only ever talked about children in the most general terms. She had school to finish, and he was establishing himself at his father's company.

After she graduated, though, she'd started thinking about kids. She'd known she hadn't wanted to work but instead was ready to start their family. At first, Adam had put her off.

"I'm too busy right now for kids. Don't you want it to just be us for a few years first?"

"We've had three years of just us. I want babies, Adam," she'd said. "I want a little boy who looks like his daddy."

She'd not told him that to placate his ego. She'd genuinely wanted that child. Looking back, she knew that part of her desire for children stemmed from not wanting to see the holes that existed in her marriage. But at that time, all she knew was that she wanted to be pregnant more than anything in the world.

After her admission, Adam had been more open to the idea, but he'd still put her off. "Give me a year to get used to the idea. Twelve months."

Sydney'd caved. And eleven months later, she'd walked in on him boning the maid.

"Don't get me pregnant," the woman had gasped. "Pull out."

"I got snipped years ago," he'd said. "I can come inside you all day, sugar."

Sydney hadn't had any idea. None. He'd had the surgery before they even met. He'd never intended to have children, not ever. So in addition to having her heart ripped out by his infidelity, she had to deal with the betrayal stemming from his deception. That, more than anything, had been the hardest part to deal with. That she'd trusted him with her heart and had chosen poorly.

After she caught him, after she'd fled their townhouse, he'd given her a few days to "cool down" before he'd come after her. Sydney had holed up in a hotel, too ashamed to go home, too torn apart to know what else to do. When he'd found her, the truth about their marriage had come out.

"I never wanted to have kids with you or anyone else. I just wanted to have fun. You caught me at a weak moment and I proposed. I wish to God I hadn't. By the time the wedding was planned, I was ready to back out. But if I had, my mother would have killed me. So I went through with it."

"So all these years when you've told me you loved me? The nights we've spent together in bed, making love? The life we've built together? All that was a lie?"

He wouldn't meet her eyes. "I care for you, Syd. But I don't love you. I want a divorce."

"I've already filed," she had the satisfaction of telling him. "How many other women have there been, just out of curiosity?"

"I don't know. Ten? Twelve?"

She'd tried to kill him when he made that confession. She'd literally picked up a vase from the table beside her and gone after him. He'd barely made it out of the hotel room without serious injury. She'd called Emma, who'd immediately flown out. Together, they'd retrieved Sydney's belongings and prepared to move her back to Kentucky while Adam's parents pushed his attorney for a large, hasty settlement. They'd been as angry as Emma on Sydney's behalf, especially his father, who'd had the misfortune to be present when she'd discovered Adam's infidelity.

Two days later, she'd gone in to see her gynecologist. As devastated as she was, Sydney wasn't stupid. If Adam hadn't used a condom with the maid, chances were excellent he hadn't used any with his other affairs. Sure enough, he'd given Sydney gonorrhea. She knew she should be thankful that was all he'd given her. But the humiliation was almost more than she could bear.

She didn't remember much about the next few weeks, not the move back to Kentucky, not the treatment for the STD, not the final paperwork for the divorce. She'd stayed locked away with her parents and at the farm with her grandparents for close to six months.

When she finally started coming out of her stupor, she'd lost a lot of faith in the world around her. She didn't look at love and marriage the same way she had before. Her perspective was so skewed and negative, it started to affect her relationships with her family and friends. The job in Savannah had come open, and desperately needing a new start, Sydney had jumped at the chance to start over.

It had taken her two good years before she was able to look at the people around her and see them as they really were. Not the rose-colored glasses view she'd had before, not the scarred and jaded vision, either. But real people with human fallacies and flaws who loved each other and were determined, no matter what the obstacles, to stick together no matter what life threw at them.

The lessons Adam had taught her went deep. Even though she was able to finally stop thinking of love as a four-letter and dirty word, she was a long way away from being able to trust anyone enough to date them seriously or let them near her body, much less her heart. It didn't matter how lonely she got, she couldn't trust another man not to hurt her the way Adam had.

That was one of the reasons she'd come home. She knew

she wanted a family someday, and she figured her best bet at finding someone to have that with would be to come back home, to be someplace where the people around her were looking out for her. To be in a place where anyone she dated would come under close scrutiny, and she wouldn't have to rely solely on her own judgment, which she no longer trusted.

Learning that Adam was getting married again truly didn't surprise her, and aside from a little ping of hurt, it didn't bother her. She didn't want him back, hadn't loved him for a long time now.

But knowing he'd found someone he loved enough to have a child with? That turned her inside out. She was hard pressed to explain even to herself why that was the case. It wasn't like she was pining away from unrequited love for the man. If she had the opportunity right this moment to snap her fingers and become pregnant with his child, she'd pass.

"I guess it's because he's moving on, building what I wanted, and I'm still alone," she whispered. "It isn't fair that he should be rewarded with something he didn't even want."

She'd learned a long time ago that life wasn't fair, that bad things happened to good people just as much as good things happened to bad. There wasn't always balance in the world. Knowing that didn't make the news easier to take, though. Not by a long shot.

CHAPTER TWENTY-ONE

SOMETHING WAS WRONG WITH SYDNEY. Sawyer knew that as much as he knew his own name. He knew yesterday's debacle with Myrtle had thrown her for a loop, but he felt like it was more than that. She was sad in a way he'd not seen before.

"Are you sure you're okay?" he asked her for the third time. It was close to two o'clock, and she'd been quiet all day.

"I'm fine. You can stop asking me."

He rested his hands on her desk, leaning in a bit. "I don't believe you. But I'll back off. If you need to talk, I'm here."

"I won't need to talk, but I appreciate the offer. I think I have most of the work done for Mr. Grainger that I can accomplish from here. Do you want to go over that? I'll probably need to head to Virginia one day next week."

Sawyer let her change the subject, but his concern wasn't diminished. He mentioned it to Rachel that evening at dinner.

"She wouldn't tell me what was wrong." He glared down at his menu as though if he stared at it long and hard enough, it would tell him what was going on. "Has she said anything to you?"

"No. Could it just be that she's had a long week?"

"I don't think so. Myrtle upset her, but she was okay

after she came back from lunch. I don't know what's going on, but mark my words—something is."

The restaurant was noisy, busy, and they'd had to take a table near the back of the place. When he glanced up toward the front door, he was surprised to see Sydney come in. The hostess led her to the bar, where she took a seat and ordered a drink. She had her back to him, and from the way she kept glancing at the door, he figured she was waiting on someone. He remembered then that she'd mentioned dinner with Danny earlier in the week.

"Who are you looking at?" Rachel turned in her seat to see. "Oh. Speak of the devil."

"She's supposed to be meeting Danny. I didn't know they'd be here, though."

"He'll get to the bottom of what's bothering her, then. I always thought it was a shame those two didn't get together."

Sawyer's brows snapped together in a scowl. "I'd hate to wish his mother on Sydney."

Rachel's smile was tinged with amusement. "There is that. But if he wasn't gay, they'd have already had a couple of kids."

"Well, he *is* gay. Why don't they have more vegetarian options here? This is the healthiest place in town and everything is still deep fried and smothered in gravy," he grumbled, hating the thought of Sydney with the other man. When Rachel laughed, he shot her an irritated glare. "What?"

"Sydney's not the only one in a mood, I see. Maybe she's just playing off you."

He didn't bother to answer that. The waitress came to take their order, and after she'd gone, he kept stealing glances at Sydney. A good-looking man who appeared to be about her age took the barstool next to her, his eyes roaming a bit too freely for Sawyer's comfort over her exposed arms and neck.

"What was she thinking, wearing that dress? If Danny

doesn't get here soon, she's going to have to fend that guy off." The dress was purple and green, a swirly pattern whose top was held up by tiny straps that tied on top of her shoulders. It wasn't skintight, but it wasn't a tarp, either, and Sydney was entirely too attractive in the garment.

Rachel twisted again to get a look at her niece. "There's nothing wrong with that dress. It's perfectly decent. And even if it *were* more revealing, she shouldn't have to fend off some letch who can't mind his manners because she wore it."

"I didn't mean it that way and you know it," Sawyer said, flustered.

"Mmm. Okay."

"I ran into your new neighbor the other day." He hoped that by talking about Lee, he could get his mind of Sydney. "Have you met him yet?"

"The state trooper who bought the house across the street? He introduced himself. Why?"

"Lee's a good guy. He's not one of the hotshots."

Rachel leaned back as their salads were delivered. "Do you think he'd be a good connection for Easton to make?"

"Probably. He's a solid investigator, knows his job well and enjoys it. He mostly deals with marijuana growers and some of the less routine things, isn't out on patrol as much these days. You should get to know him." He tried to keep his voice casual, but he didn't think he succeeded.

"Just to be friendly and all, right?" she asked. "You're not trying to play matchmaker, are you?"

"You know me better than that. What the hell is he doing?"

The guy next to Sydney was making his move, and unless Sawyer was mistaken, he was ignoring her very clear "hands off" signs.

Rachel picked up her tea. "You might need to go over there."

He was already out of his seat. “She can come sit with us until Danny gets here. She’ll be safer.”

He would have been appalled to see the knowing grin on Rachel’s face as he walked away or to read the text she sent to Amelia telling her they’d been right about him and Sydney. And he would have been stunned to know that instead of disapproving, she was planning to do whatever she could to encourage what appeared to be a budding romance between the two of them.

None of that even occurred to him, though. All he could think about was getting Sydney safely away from the creep who needed a lesson in personal space.

CHAPTER TWENTY-TWO

SYDNEY WAS ON THE VERGE of saying something pointed and vulgar in an extremely loud voice to the jerk beside her. A suggestion of what he could do with his revolting pick-up lines would be where she started. And if that didn't back him down, she wasn't above using a knee to the groin.

"Just because I'm wearing a dress doesn't mean I'm on the prowl, you dipshit," she growled into her drink.

"What's that, sweetheart?"

"I am *not* your *sweetheart*," she hissed.

"Sydney, hey." Sawyer stepped between her and the jerk just in time to keep her from going completely nuclear. "Is there a problem?"

The man looked from her to Sawyer, then shifted away. "Nope. She's all yours."

For the third time in as many days, Sawyer had come to her "rescue." Knowing he meant well was the only thing that kept her from lashing out at him.

"What are you doing here?" she asked.

"Rachel and I are having dinner. Grab your drink and join us. You waiting on Danny?"

"Yes. He shouldn't be long. I hate to bother you two."

She was dismayed. Dinner, with Rachel, her sexy aunt. And now she was going to be the third wheel who got to sit by and watch them make goo-goo eyes at each other. Could the week get any worse?

"Don't be ridiculous. It's just Rachel. It isn't like we're on a date. And even if we were..."

Sydney wanted to refuse, but the jerk was still sitting there, and he was listening to every word. She picked up her drink and followed Sawyer to the back of the restaurant.

Rachel smiled at her, concerned. "Hey, kiddo. What's shaking?"

"Not much. Trying to stay sane. You?"

"That sounds about right."

Rachel was sitting on the end of her booth, her purse taking up the spot beside her. Instead of sharing that bench like she'd expected, Sydney had to slide in beside Sawyer. She tried to ignore his proximity.

"You're meeting Danny?" Rachel asked.

"That was the plan, but he has an emergency with one of his parishioners. He wasn't sure he was going to make it the last time he texted me." When the server came over to take her order, Sydney grimaced. "I don't know if I should go ahead and order or not."

"Sure you should. Danny'd hardly expect you to starve yourself," Rachel teased gently.

"I guess not. I'll have the grilled chicken house salad with vinaigrette, and another mojito, please," she told the girl.

"How was the marinara?" Sawyer asked.

She grinned. "Oh, it was okay. Have you tried yours?"

He nodded. "What sorts of bribes does Noah take? If he ever decides to close up the wood shop, he could bottle that stuff and sell it."

Rachel laughed. "Oh, *that* marinara. It's pretty danged good. Shoot, he'd make a ton of money just keeping the family stocked."

Right after the server brought her salad, Sydney's phone rang. "It's Danny. Hey, are you on your way?"

"No. Syd, I'm so sorry. This lady's husband just went back for surgery, and they aren't sure he's going to make it. I can't leave her."

She closed her eyes, sending a quick prayer up for the family even as she cursed her own luck. "Oh, the poor thing. I understand completely. You stay there and do what you need to. I'm fine—I met up with Rachel and Sawyer here at the restaurant. We'll catch up later. Call if you need me?"

"I will. Are you sure you're okay?"

She forced herself to smile, knowing he'd hear it in her voice. "I'm fine. I'll say a prayer for her, and for you. Call me."

"Everything all right?" Rachel asked as Sydney slid her phone back in her purse.

"He's at the hospital with the lady. Her husband's in surgery, and it doesn't sound good. So I guess I'm flying solo tonight." She really didn't resent Danny having to stand her up. But God, she'd needed to talk to him.

"What all did you have planned?" Sawyer's arm rubbed against hers as he shifted in his seat.

"Just dinner and talking. We've not had a chance to spend any time together much since I got home, and I was looking forward to catching up. That's all."

Rachel's concern was clear on her face. "Are you okay, honey?"

Sydney nodded. "Mm-hmmm. Have you made a decision about work yet?"

Her aunt regarded her with skepticism, but she answered. "I'm taking the sabbatical. Right now's the best time, what with Easton being in school and not living at home. I'm excited to get started."

For the first time in over twenty years, Rachel wouldn't be teaching classes at the local community college. The opportunity had come up for her to take a few semesters off while she worked on a non-fiction book for a local historian, and she'd decided to take the chance to go for her Ph.D.

"I'm glad you're doing it. You should have some fun now and then," Sydney told her. When she ordered a third mojito, Rachel's concern morphed into a frown. Hoping to stave off any further questions about her wellbeing, Sydney held up her empty glass. "I'm not driving. I caught a ride up here with Mom and Daddy, and I'll call a cab for the trip home."

"A cab? No. One of us can take you home," Sawyer said.

"It'll have to be you," Rachel told him. "I have an... appointment after we finish dinner."

Sydney narrowed her eyes. "An appointment."

"Yes." That was all. The stubborn look on her face dared Sydney to question her further.

Once they'd finished their meal, they declined the server's offer of dessert. Feeling pleasantly buzzed, Sydney slid out of the booth.

"I can still call a cab," she said as they walked to the front of the restaurant.

"Or you could just go back in, pick up the jerk from the bar, and let him take you home," Rachel said. "Good lord, girl, you are stubborn."

"I came by my obstinance honestly, you know. I get it from you and Mom. And I don't want to be a bother."

"Then stop acting like you're putting me out." Sawyer unlocked the truck and held the door open for her.

Between the effects of the alcohol and the lousy week, Sydney was just about out of steam. Deciding her best option was to shut the hell up and do as she was told, she got in the truck.

"See you Sunday, Syd," Rachel told her with a wave. "Sawyer, thanks for dinner."

"I'm sorry I interrupted your meal," Sydney told him once he was behind the wheel. "Even if it wasn't a date."

He chastised her with a look. "I'm just happy we were there. That guy looked like he was getting aggressive."

She let her head fall back on the headrest. "There's a

good chance that if you hadn't stepped in, I would have ended up assaulting him. It's been that bad of a week."

"You ready to tell me what's wrong?"

The evening was as gorgeous as the other night had been, even though there were some clouds in the sky, and Sydney almost felt insulted by the beauty. It should have been pouring rain to match her mood.

"My ex is getting married to his pregnant girlfriend," she confessed in a low voice. "This is the same ex who had a vasectomy before we were married because he didn't want kids."

Sawyer cursed long and low, questioning everything from Adam's parentage to the size of his testicles. "I'm sorry, Sydney. When did you find out?"

"Helen called me yesterday. She didn't want me to hear it from someone else."

He pulled his truck in her driveway and turned the engine off. One of the joys of living in a small town was being so close to everything, but one of the drawbacks was that it made going for long, contemplative drives a bit difficult. Now that she'd admitted what the problem was, the thought of going in her house for the night so she could stare at four walls held less than no appeal.

"I thought you wanted kids," he said.

She laughed, even though she felt like crying. "I did. I do. Do you know when I found out he'd had the surgery?" She turned her head to look at him.

"When?"

"When I walked in the door after Eli's wife's funeral, my father-in-law and his business partner in tow, and heard Adam tell our maid that it was okay if he came inside her because he'd gotten snipped."

Sawyer winced, but he didn't look away. "Are you kidding me? God, Sydney. How is it that you didn't castrate the bastard on the spot?"

"I was so stunned and so hurt, it was everything I could

do to get out of there after he saw us. I wasn't expecting it, not at all. It turns out she wasn't the first woman he'd cheated on me with. She was far from the first, truth be told. And he brought his cooties home with him. Do you have any idea how humiliating it was to have to go to the doctor and get tested for STDs? And then to find out that I had gonorrhea? He gives me the clap and tears my life apart, and he's the one who gets to have kids now? I can't believe I just told you that." She cringed, hiding her face. "Oh, my God. I'm so sorry."

Sawyer was utterly silent across the cab for so long that she had to force herself to face him. When she did, he held his hand out, palm facing upward.

"My wife divorced me after a year of testing to determine why we couldn't have kids. Turns out it was me. I have the rarest form of male sterility. There's absolutely no chance whatsoever that I'll ever be able to have children. That was a deal breaker for her. Didn't matter that we'd been together since high school, that we'd gotten married as soon as we'd graduated. A year after we got divorced, she was giving birth with her second husband. It isn't quite what you went through, but I think it's close enough that I can say I adequately understand where you're coming from. And I'm sorry."

Sydney tentatively laid her hand over his, letting their fingers curl together. Before she knew it, she was crying. Sawyer used their connection to pull her to him, and she felt his arms come around her as she grieved. She wasn't sobbing, but for several minutes, every time she tried to stop, a new wave of tears would hit.

She couldn't even enjoy being tucked into Sawyer's side or the feel of his hand rubbing up and down her arm, she was so miserable.

The tears finally slowed to a stop, and with a hiccupping sigh, Sydney apologized. "I know this is way more than you signed up for."

Sawyer handed her a bundle of tissues. “Would you please stop saying your sorry? I’m glad I can help.”

“It’s a good thing your windows are tinted.” Reluctantly, she sat up, sliding back to her own seat.

“That could have lead to some interesting questions from the neighbors,” he agreed. “Feel better?”

“I do. Thank you.”

“Thank me with some coffee,” he suggested. “I don’t want to leave you by yourself until I’m sure you’re okay.”

“You don’t have to do that.” As much as she loved the idea of him spending some more time with her, she couldn’t help but think she was putting him out.

“Maybe I don’t want to spend the evening alone,” he surprised her by saying. He picked at the wrap on the steering wheel, playing with a loose end of leather string. “So if you don’t mind the company, I don’t mind staying. Unless you have something else to do, I mean.”

She gave a soft laugh. “In that case, how does cappuccino sound? And I might be able to scrounge up a brownie or two to go with it.”

He sent her a winsome smile. “Sounds great.”

It wasn’t a date, even if she felt a bit like it was, she kept reminding herself as she led him inside. “I’ve still got some furniture I want to get for the house. It’s probably changed a bit since the last time you saw it.”

“Actually, I’ve never been here. I’ve seen the new house, but that’s it.”

“Mom and Daddy never invited you?” she asked, shocked.

“Sure, but it just never worked out that I visited. Most of the get-togethers I’ve gone to were at the farm.”

“You don’t want to risk being added to the kitchen duty list. I know what it is.”

He shrugged, spreading his hands. “Maybe.”

“Well, I’ll give you the tour, then. You might have to return the favor someday. I may show up on your doorstep one weekend.”

"The door's open."

She grinned at him over her shoulder. "Yeah, you say that because you know I don't know exactly where you live. Out off Highway Eighty somewhere, that's all I know."

"Stormking Road," he said "I'm the last house on the road, a quarter mile past the gate that has the No Trespassing signs up."

"How much land do you have?" she asked as she showed him the dining room.

"About a hundred acres."

Sydney's eyebrows lifted. "A hundred acres? Wow. I had no idea you had that much."

"I got really lucky, got a good deal on it. And getting it in shape has been a good project. It's kept me busy for ten years now."

"I'll definitely have to come check it out. Now I'm curious."

"Like I said, door's open."

As she got the coffee and sweets ready, she asked him about the property. He had the same peaceful air talking about the spread that her grandfather did when he spoke about his place.

"It's your sanctuary, isn't it?" she asked. She settled in on one end of the couch, pulling a blanket over her bare legs. When his lips twitched with amusement, she made a face at him. "Don't you start. It's a habit—shorts and a tank top in the summer, cover up with a blanket. Or in this case, a sleeveless dress. Regardless, it's one of my quirks."

"I didn't say a word," he responded. "And yeah, I guess it is a sanctuary. I've got a small pond and a dock with a nice tree hanging over it, and I've used that spot more than once in the last decade to go and get some mental clarity. In the line of work I was in, I had to have something."

"I'm glad you had it. You know how Grandpa and Noah feel about the farm. Ainsley feels the same way about her place in Lexington. Shoot, after the divorce, I hid out at the farm. I can't imagine what it would be like not to have had someplace like that to go."

He took a sip of his coffee. "It helps."

"Are you glad you retired?" she asked softly. "Or do you miss it?"

"I don't miss most of the job. Some of it, yes. But most of it? No. People have always been... well, people. There've always been bad seeds to interact with, evil to contend with. That sounds dramatic, but I mean it in a very matter-of-fact way. Evil exists in this world. Ask anyone in law enforcement. But the last few years, things have deteriorated. I'd gotten to where I didn't enjoy it very much, to be honest. So I'm glad to be out."

"What about the badge bunnies? Do you miss them?"

He sat forward, setting his mug on the coffee table as he shot her an amused grin. "Sydney, you're something else. Badge bunnies."

She worked her foot out from under the blanket to nudge him on the hip. "Don't even try to tell me you didn't get chased by badge bunnies. I know better."

He laughed, his cheeks turning a bit red. "Persistent much?"

"Evasive much?" she came back with, putting her own mug on the table. She came to her knees and edged closer to him before sitting back down. This time, she poked him in the ribs with a finger. "Now I'm convinced there's a story there. Give it up."

Sawyer captured her hand, watching her with a sidelong look. He kept her hand in his, tangling their fingers together even as she tugged against him. As he answered, he traced the tips of her fingers.

"I tried to ignore the badge bunnies as much as I could, especially after I got a little older. Maybe not so much when I was young. I don't do relationships, you know that, but I also wasn't much interested in women who were only after me because of the badge and uniform."

"Is that no-relationship rule because of the infertility?" she asked quietly. "Or because you still love her?"

He spread his hand out, palm up, hers on top of his as though comparing their sizes. "At first it was both. I did meet someone a few years after the divorce, but it didn't work out. She had a couple of kids from a previous marriage, and we got pretty close. Her ex didn't like that, and he started causing trouble between me and the kids. We decided to go our separate ways. It wasn't fair to put the kids in that position."

Sydney wondered just how seriously he'd been interested in the woman. "That was her loss, you know."

"Ah, I don't know. I kind of look at it as a lucky escape on my part. I found out how things were going to be before I was in too deep. If we'd ended up married or something, it would have been a disaster. He did the same thing to the guy she ended up with after me. They got divorced because of it."

"You've never tried again?"

He shook his head. "No. It was safer not to."

Taking a chance, Sydney reached out and touched his shoulder with her free hand. She let it rest there for a moment, then trailed it down his arm to rest on the bend of his elbow. "You never considered adoption or fostering as an answer to the question of children? Or did you only want kids if you were their genetic father?"

He turned to stare at her, his expression solemn and contemplative. "The few times it came up, the woman in question wasn't interested. In the case of my ex, it was out of the question. She had this fear of not having a perfectly healthy, happy child, and she saw adopted kids as damaged goods. And the other woman... she didn't really want any more kids. Said something to the effect of not taking on another child of her own, much less someone else's problem."

Sydney was appalled. "Sawyer, that's awful. Oh, my God. You did get lucky getting them out of your life. Damaged goods? Are you kidding me?" As much as the sentiment was revolting, it was also hurtful. "Thank God not everyone feels that way."

"More do than don't," he said. "To answer your question, I don't. But it wasn't just me in the relationship."

She squeezed his arm, then stood to pace, needing to move. Arms crossed under her breasts, she muttered curses. "Why didn't you just adopt or foster on your own?"

He sat back, crossing his ankle over his knee. "High-risk job, single parent? There's not an agency out there that would let me sign up for that. And now... I'm not a spring chicken."

She rolled her eyes. "Please. You're like Grandpa—you'll still be running around doing whatever you want even when you're in your eighties. And you've got more years than I've been alive to go before you get to that mark."

Sawyer laughed. "Thanks for the vote of confidence. If you knew how much getting out of bed hurts some days, you might reconsider that."

"Bull. Not that don't you hurt, I don't mean that. But I don't see age slowing you down much."

"I've gotten used to being on my own. It'd be hard enough to add a woman to the mix, much less a kid or two or three."

"I guess I understand that. I know there are a lot of people out there who are perfectly content living solitary lives. I just don't think you're one of them." She raised her chin, daring him to contradict her.

Sawyer stood and came to stand in front of her, not stopping until less than two feet separated them. "You have *got* to be one of the most stubborn women I've ever met in my life."

"I'm perfectly meek and pliable," she quipped back. "You're just projecting your own flaws onto me." She tempered her words with a wink.

"Impertinent imp."

She couldn't hold her laughter back. "Guilty as charged."

The evening had grown dark, and the only lamp on was the one behind the sofa. The room wasn't completely shadowed, but the atmosphere was decidedly intimate. As they stood there watching each other, tension built. The ringing of Sydney's cell phone broke the spell, and she sucked in a breath as she moved to answer it.

"Molly, hey."

"Are you busy? I'm here by myself and I'm going nuts. Mom and Dad are out on date night, all my friends are working, and I need something to do. Do you mind if I swing by?"

Sydney wanted to scream that yes, she was busy. She was on the verge of jumping Sawyer's bones and taking him to the floor. But she couldn't. Some tiny sense of self-preservation reared its head.

"No, that's fine. You can head on over."

"Great! I'll be down in a few minutes."

She ended the call, staring down at the phone for a few seconds before turning to face Sawyer. "That was Molly. She's home alone and needs a friend. I'm sorry."

He shook his head. "It's fine. I need to go, anyhow."

Regret warred with disappointment. "I figured as much."

She walked him to the door, wanting to grab him and tug him back with every step. "Thank you for looking out for me, for the shoulder, the... the friendship," she said softly as she rested her hand on the doorknob. "I'm glad you were there tonight."

"So am I. And if you need me, I'm just a phone call away. Even if it's the middle of the night."

Sydney tilted her head and met his eyes. "That works both ways, lawman. Now that I know how to find you, just call. I'll bring brownies and coffee and we'll solve the world's problems."

When he lifted his hand to cup her face, his thumb brushing across the fullness of her bottom lip, Sydney lost the ability to breathe. The sound of a car pulling up outside stopped him from doing anything else, however, and he took a step back.

"See you Monday."

She could have wept with frustration, but she managed to hold it back. She swung the door open, instead, as Molly was coming up the walk. "Unless I show up on your doorstep with goodies."

The heated look Sawyer gave her made her toes curl. He tapped the tip of her nose with a finger. "Impertinent. Hey, Molly."

"Hey, Sawyer. What are you doing here?"

"He gave me a ride home," Sydney answered. "Goodnight."

"Ladies."

They watched him walk to his truck, Sydney holding on to the door for support. After he left, she sighed.

"He's so hot," Molly said as she came inside. "Please tell me I didn't interrupt the two of you."

"You didn't interrupt anything that didn't need to be interrupted," Sydney assured her. "So what kind of trouble are we going to get into?"

"Mani/pedi? And gossip?"

"Sounds good to me. Let me get into some jammies first. You want to spend the night?"

"I was hoping you'd ask," she said as she held up an overnight bag. Molly grinned, looking more like the wholesome redheaded urchin who was John and Zanny's miracle baby than the femme fatale nursing student who'd captured Sydney's brother's interest.

While she changed clothes, Sydney bit her lip, imagining she could taste Sawyer's touch. She loved Molly like a sister, and she knew the timing of her call had been fortuitous, but *damn*, she wondered what might have happened if that phone hadn't rung.

CHAPTER TWENTY-THREE

SAWYER TRIED VALIANTLY TO FORGET his Friday night with Sydney. By the time the Fourth of July rolled around a week later, he'd convinced himself he'd done it. At least half the time, anyhow.

Once again, an invitation to join the Campbells had been issued. And this time instead of trying to figure out an excuse as to why not to join them, he accepted without hesitation. He didn't examine why. He knew he wouldn't like the answer to his query.

When everyone sat down shortly after five o'clock to eat dinner, Sydney lobbed the first salvo in a teasing game. "So are you looking forward to your conference? He has to go Knoxville next weekend for an investigators' convention," she told everyone around them.

"That sounds like fun," Danny said. He saluted Sawyer with his lemonade.

"It's okay. And it's in Gatlinburg, not Knoxville."

"That does sound fun," Rachel chimed in. "All that shopping. Em, we should tag along."

"Oh, no," Sydney told them, her grin full of mischief. "Sawyer has plans. He's already gotten calls from three ladies confirming his arrival. Charlene, Monique, and Laurie. And that nice state trooper, Lee? The one who lives across the street from Aunt Rachel? He's going, too."

Sawyer glowered at her across the picnic table as everyone laughed.

Noah whistled. “Make sure you take some ties to hang on the doorknob,” he joked.

“That is not funny,” Sawyer said, half serious. “And Lee isn’t going. The conference starts Friday, so we’d have to leave Thursday afternoon. He’s scheduled for court both days.”

“Uh-oh,” Rachel teased. “Three to one? Forget the ties, better take your vitamins.” When Sawyer narrowed his eyes at her, she held her hands up. “What?”

“Vitamins, hell. Take a video camera,” Easton said.

“Easton Michael!” Rachel smacked him on the head, causing most everyone at the table to laugh.

“What? Geez, Mom, I’m joking!”

“You’d better be.”

Sawyer blew out a slow breath. “You’re going with me,” he told Sydney, the words slipping out before he had a chance to consider their implications. “No way I’m going down there on my own with those three calling. Nope. I was going to throw Lee to the wolves. You’ll have to take his place.”

That caused more laughter, but not from Sydney, who was staring at him, incredulous.

“What? I can’t go with you. I’m not a PI or a cop.”

“I’ll get you in. You might enjoy it. And yes, you are too going.” He forked up some of Sarah’s excellent potato salad with a triumphant grin. “Job requirement. If you don’t go…” He left it at that. He’d never fire her for not going, but she didn’t need to know that. Not right this moment.

“Now, wait just a minute, buddy—” she started.

Archer interrupted her. “You should go, Syd, have fun. It’d be educational.”

Beside Sawyer, Rachel almost choked on her drink.

Easton had to slap her on the back. “You okay?”

“Mm-hmmm. Just swallowed wrong.”

Sawyer turned his attention back to Sydney. “You can

keep 'em off my back. Lee made the reservations for us, and he got a suite. You'll have your own room, but you'll be right there where I can use you as an excuse."

She rolled her eyes. "Are you kidding me? You can't say 'no' to these women on your own?"

He shrugged. "You never know what might happen. They could take advantage of me. No, the only answer is that you have to be there to protect me."

Her jaw dropped, and she was clearly struggling for something to say. "Take Rachel," she finally got out.

"I would love to go," Rachel said. "But I'm tied up. Isn't Charlene the one who was so pushy last year?"

"She is. Very nice woman, extremely competent detective with a small town in Alabama. But she drinks, and when she drinks, she gets grabby. If I hadn't been on crutches, who knows what would have happened?"

The hell of it was, he wasn't joking about that. He'd been appalled at the woman's lack of ability to take no for an answer. Lee had been with him for that trip, and he'd stepped in, calling the woman's partner in to manage her and stop the harassment.

"I know men can be assaulted," Sydney said, "so please don't think I'm downplaying the seriousness of the potential situation. But you can't really want me along as a chaperone. Can you?"

"I can protect myself, but I think it'd be beneficial for the job, yes. I wish I'd thought of it sooner." He stubbornly stuck to that explanation, flat refusing to admit even to himself there might be another reason he wanted her along.

"You should do it, Syd. Free vacation," Danny told her. "You know you love the Smokies. How long does the conference last?"

"Until Saturday night. We'd have a lot of the day on Sunday that we could explore since it's only four hours from here," Sawyer said.

Sydney pushed her glasses up with a sigh. "Fine. But if

I don't have fun or I come back with scars, I'm holding you accountable. Are these women anything like Myrtle?"

Sawyer winced. "I don't think anyone's quite like Myrtle."

"Fair enough."

Later that evening, everyone had spread out, taking seats here and there across the sloping yard to wait for the fireworks to begin. Thanks to the way the land rolled and the tree line fell, most of the fireworks displays from towns within thirty miles of Hazard were visible on a clear night from the vantage point on top of the mountain. Sawyer had stepped in the house to visit the restroom, and he met Sydney on his way out the door.

"Are you serious about next weekend?" she asked, leaning up against the newel post at the foot of the stairs, her hands clasped behind her.

"Unless you have a major objection, yeah."

She sighed. "It might be awkward if you decide you don't want to reject some of their advances."

Sawyer stepped closer to her. The only light came from a single lamp on the table beside the door. Even knowing there were thirty people around the house, it felt like they were the only two in the world.

"I won't. You have my word."

Amelia's daughter, Sadie, came rushing in. "'Scuse me, gotta go!" she said, passing between them on her way to the bathroom.

"I'd feel a bit out of place," Sydney persisted after she'd gone.

"If you're really uncomfortable, I won't make you go. But after seeing the way you handled the Grainger project, I think you'd like it."

"I've never carried a badge and gun."

"You won't be the only one there who hasn't. Say yes."

She glanced down at her feet for a moment. "Okay. You can change your mind, though, if you decide you don't want me along."

"I won't."

Her lips curved in a half smile. "Go watch some fireworks, Boss."

Sawyer winked at her. "Yes, ma'am."

He didn't know when he'd looked more forward to a conference. And the reasons why? Not something he had any intention of examining too closely. Not even on a bet.

"Do you think they've caught on?" Rachel asked Amelia.

"No. Well, not really. I don't think Sawyer has, but Sydney's a little suspicious. Em?"

Emma nodded, resting back against Archer. "I'm not sure that she's suspicious so much as she's confused we're being so encouraging."

"Grandpa and Grandma sent them on a walk down to my house the other night," Noah said. He stretched his legs out in front of him. "I'm glad they've moved on to trying to matchmake for her. That means they're leaving me alone."

Molly came up behind him and tackled him, knocking him to the ground before scampering away with a laugh. She hurried around to the other side of the group, hands on her hips as she waited for Noah to get up. "Come on, chicken. Let's run."

He groaned and flopped back on the ground. "No. I'm tired. Go harass someone else."

"Spoilsport. What are you all talking about?" she asked, taking a seat on the blanket next to Amelia.

"Sawyer and Sydney," Amelia answered. She reached out and pushed a stray curl back off Molly's forehead. "But that's need-to-know only."

"You should have seen the way they were looking at each other last Friday. If I'd known he was at her house that night, I never would have gone."

Archer frowned. "He was at her house? How late?"

"Nine thirty? Ten?" Molly answered.

"He drove her home from the restaurant. I had an emergency I had to take care of," Danny put in. "I guess he stayed for coffee, from what Sydney said, but that's all it was."

"Hmmm. I'm not sure about this plan of ours," Archer said.

Emma patted his leg. "You're her father. Of course you're not sure about it."

"I have reservations, too," Danny said. "He's a good man, but he's not a permanent-setup kind of guy. And Sydney's not into flings."

"They hum when they're together," Amelia said softly. "If she could get past his defenses, I think they'd make each other very happy. From what I've seen, they could even be soul mates."

Rachel sighed. "Yeah, but that's the thing—she has to break down that stupid wall he's built around himself. It's a strong wall, too. He's had twenty-some years to perfect it."

The group was quiet for a couple of minutes, exchanging somber looks.

"Should we back off?" Rachel finally asked.

"No. Every instinct I have is yelling at me that they need to take this attraction and run with it," Amelia said. "Sydney keeps him on his toes, and he brings out that quirky happiness she hasn't had for years now. He enjoys baiting her and vice versa. Maybe if they do end up dating, if we show them support, he'll warm up to the idea."

"I hope you're right, Pip," Archer said, calling her by the nickname she'd had since childhood. "Because if this goes badly?"

"I know. I do know that, Archer. But I think we have to try for both their sakes."

CHAPTER TWENTY-FOUR

All week, Sydney kept expecting Sawyer to walk up to her desk and tell her he'd changed his mind about her going with him or that he'd just been kidding. But he didn't.

"I'd like to leave here about noon tomorrow, head down. That way we'll miss the rush-hour traffic in Knoxville," he told her Wednesday afternoon. "Is that okay?"

"That's fine. Which vehicle are we taking?"

"I figured we'd just take my truck."

She bit her lip. "Um, I can't drive a stick. So if we got down there and I needed to drive us anywhere... We can take my car. It's really comfortable on long trips."

Sawyer nodded. "Okay. If you're sure. I can just leave the truck here."

"Or you can bring it to my house and park it. It should be safer there, and between that and the lights on timers inside, people will think someone's home."

"That's a plan, then."

They closed up shop Thursday just before noon and headed to Sydney's house. She'd packed a lunch cooler, and she grabbed that and one of her two bags while he parked the truck.

Sawyer met her at the door. "Here, let me have those."

"Thanks. Trunk's unlocked, keys are in it," she said, going back to do one last look through the house. When she came out, the second bag was gone. Sawyer was leaned up against the bumper of the car, thumbing through his phone. He had on dark sunglasses, a close-fitting red polo shirt, and a pair of jeans so old they were soft. Between the way he looked and how good he smelled, she might just turn into a blathering idiot before they crossed the state line.

"Ready?" he asked. "I got your other bag."

"As ready as I'm going to be. Do you want to drive or do you want me to?"

"Entirely up to you," he said.

She handed him her keys. "Then I'll plan to kick back and relax for this leg of the trip." The truth was she loved watching him drive. When he'd driven her home the other night, the skill with which he'd handled the wheel had enthralled her. It was an utterly ridiculous aspect of the man to be attracted to, but there it was. Something about the way he used his hands on the steering wheel, the gearshift... It made her wonder just how skillful his hands would be set to other tasks.

For the first hour of the drive, they made small talk about work, going over current or upcoming projects. When they reached London, he suggested they stop at a popular state park for lunch.

"Okay. We used to go there with Aunt Pip and Logan and their kids, Nonny and Uncle Eli, the whole crew."

"You must miss them, Nonny and Eli."

Her smile was sad. "Every day. The ache never really disappears. I know they're better off, especially Nonny, but that doesn't stop the hurt."

"I don't even want to think about what it'll be like when something happens to Nan," he told her quietly. "She's healthy, she's spry, but she's also eighty-two."

"What happened to your grandfather?" Sydney asked as they took the exit that would get them to the park.

"He left when my mom was a kid. Died out in Texas when she was a teenager. Nan always said good riddance, but she never remarried, never even dated until she retired and moved to Florida."

"What did she do before she retired?"

"She was a school cook."

Sydney studied him. "She seems like she's a pistol from the few times I've spoken with her. You know we're fast becoming friends. We talk at least once a week now."

"I know. She says the same thing about you. If the two of you ever meet... God help us all." His grin was cheeky, relaxed, and it made Sydney laugh.

"What do your parents do?"

"You're full of questions today."

"And you're evading again."

"Ha! I'm not. I'm... stalling."

She shoved him lightly, barely budging him. "Stinker."

He didn't answer her question until they were walking down a path to one of the picnic shelters at the park.

"My dad's the son of a steel-mill owner. The old man sold it when things started going south in the industry, and Dad took over running the rest of his holdings. Mom's a housewife."

She slowed down, taking in the revelation that he came from wealth. "So when he got your mom pregnant..."

"It was quite a scandal," Sawyer admitted. "To say Nan wasn't happy is an understatement. She knew Mom wasn't completely innocent. She's very headstrong, my mother. But Dad was old enough to know better. And Nan made sure he took care of his responsibilities. She had the good sense not to push for them to get married right out of the gate."

Sydney couldn't believe he felt as casually about his parents as he tried to make out. "You said you have brothers?"

"Two. Frank and Matt. One's a lawyer, and the other's a dentist. Five nieces and nephews between them."

"Do you ever see them?" They reached an unoccupied

table. She started setting up the food, handing him containers.

"Every now and then. Once every year or so. It's better for all of us if we don't have too close an association, though things are a lot better now than they were in the past."

"What about Nan?"

"They all fly down every year and see her. That's enough for her, too."

"It sounds like a difficult relationship."

He shrugged. "It is what it is. When I was younger, I tried to fix things. I finally realized there wasn't anything to put back together. There never had been. It'd be like if your biological father was still in the picture and wasn't an asshole. You might have a relationship with him, but there's no way you could ever bring him into the Campbell-Gibson world. It would be a disaster waiting to happen. I'm not part of their world, and they're not part of mine."

She could only imagine. "Then you're lucky to have what you do."

They made a concerted effort after that to keep the conversation light, and the trip went by faster than Sydney expected it to. Before she knew it, they were in Gatlinburg, following the GPS's directions to their hotel. Instead of going downtown, though, they ended up taking a winding road to a remote group of cabins.

"This is... not what I was expecting," Sydney said as Sawyer brought the car to a stop in front of the small cabin designated "office." "I thought you had a suite booked."

"So did I. Lee made the reservation." Sawyer stared at the structure, then turned to her. "Um. Okay. The address matches what's on the paper he gave me."

"Well, let's go in and see if this is it."

Sure enough, it was. "You're in the third cabin down, which is the two-bedroom unit," the older lady behind the desk told them. She detailed some of the amenities.

"Someone's here twenty-four hours in case you need anything. You'll be checking out Sunday, right?"

"That's the plan," Sawyer said.

When they walked in the front door of the cabin, Sydney whistled. The view was breathtaking. The living room was on the opposite side of the house, the entire back wall comprised of two-story windows that showed off the incredible view of the forest beyond.

"Wow. This is spectacular," she said. "Let's see what the bedrooms are like." She dropped her bag and dashed for the nearest door, which led into the master suite. Also on the backside of the house, it was a large room, furnished with a king-sized bed and a...

"Is that a heart-shaped Jacuzzi?" she squeaked. "Oh, my gosh!"

"Are you serious?" Sawyer groaned from the doorway. "What is this, a honeymoon cabin?"

Sydney kicked her shoes off and got in the empty red tub, laughing. "This is unreal. I brought a bathing suit since I thought we were going to be staying at a hotel. We'll have to try this out." She lifted her legs, stretching, pretending to bathe. "You know you want to."

He put his hands on his hips and glowered at her. "No."

"Oh, come on. Are you chicken?"

"I am not getting in that tub."

She groaned. "You're too young to be so stodgy."

"Stodgy? I know you didn't just call me stodgy," he drawled, walking slowly across the room.

She hadn't meant to but clearly she'd issued a challenge. "Um, well... maybe?"

Sawyer leaned down, placing his hands on the edge of the tub. "You'd better watch yourself, Missy."

She raised up until her face was just a few inches from his. "Or what?"

His gaze dropped to her mouth, lingering there for what felt like days. "Let's see what else this place has to offer." He straightened, wicked satisfaction written all over his face when she gasped, and sauntered from the room. “I want to see this eighteen-foot-tall shower tower.”

She collapsed back into the tub with a muted groan. “Sadist.”

“I heard that.”

She couldn’t help but laugh. It was either that or cry from frustration, and she wasn’t quite to that point. Yet.

CHAPTER TWENTY-FIVE

IF WORKING WITH SYDNEY DAY in and day out without revealing his growing attraction to her was difficult, sleeping twenty feet away from her, separated by a single wall, was torture. Sawyer had dithered all week on whether he wanted to go through with the conference invitation or not, but every time he started to back out, something happened that stopped him.

So here he was, staring at the vaulted ceiling in the cabin's honeymoon suite, imagining what might happen if he were to go knock on Sydney's door and ask to share her bed.

"You're too old for this," he told himself, glancing down at the tented sheet with a wry grimace. A dozen offers in his inbox every day for this little blue pill or that little flame-logo'd ED helper reminded him he wasn't getting any younger. But since Sydney had started working for him? Achieving and maintaining an erection hadn't been a problem. No, getting the damned things to go away was the obstacle Sawyer was up against. He felt like a teenager again, and not in a good way.

"It could be worse. You might not have it when you need it," he mused. That would be a disaster, true. But this constant state of half or full arousal he was in? It was eroding his self-control and his judgment. He'd almost kissed her twice now. If he did and she returned his interest? There was no doubt in his mind they'd end up in bed.

At home, he'd go for a swim or walk around his property or simply take care of the problem with his hand. God knew he'd gotten plenty practice with that method in recent weeks. But that wasn't an option, not being so close to Sydney here and all. It felt too lecherous, too disrespectful.

"Maybe some fresh air will help." Throwing the covers back, he got up and padded to the door that led out onto the balcony. The nighttime world was quiet, warm, and the rising full moon illuminated the small yard and balcony with a silver glow. Bracing his hands on the rail, Sawyer lifted his head and closed his eyes, inhaling deeply.

He'd just started to get a handle on his arousal when he heard a door open. Every muscle in his body tensed as soft footsteps came up beside him, stopping a few feet away.

"You okay?" Sydney's voice was soft. The breeze lifted the scent of her perfume to his nose as though held up by taunting hands.

It was all he could do not to curse. "Yeah. Just having some trouble sleeping, that's all."

"So am I. New bed and all that, I guess. Plus I'm a little nervous about tomorrow."

"I promise you there's no need to be." He looked at her finally, his fears confirmed. She was gazing out into the yard, arms crossed. Hair down, tumbling around her shoulders in silky waves. Sleeveless, soft-looking nightgown that plunged to her navel and barely covered her shapely ass. Yep. For all the world, she looked like a woman who'd just crawled out of a man's bed. When she pushed her hair back, pulling it over her opposite shoulder to get it out of the way and then licked her lips, Sawyer broke.

"You shouldn't be out here."

Sydney blinked up at him, startled. "Why not? Oh, my gosh. You wanted to be alone. I'm so sorry." She turned to go back in, jumping a bit when he touched her arm with his hand. "I didn't mean to disturb you."

"You're so damned soft," he marveled, his fingers tracing the sensitive skin just above her elbow.

"W...what?"

"This is a bad idea," he whispered, stepping closer to her. "A very bad idea. You should go inside."

Sydney didn't move. Instead, she stared up at him, her soft lips parting on a puff of air. "I'd prefer to stay here."

Sawyer couldn't stand it another minute. Sliding his hand into her hair, he tipped her face up and kissed her.

He came awake with a jolt, sucking in lungfuls of air as he sat up in bed. Heart pounding, he was covered in sweat from head to toe. Cursing under his breath, he called himself everything except a milk cow, and for good measure, he cursed the convention, too. Kicking off the covers, he got up, furious with his frustration. The damned erection that stood straight out from his body didn't help any.

"Fuck this," he muttered, heading for the bathroom. He had to have a cold shower, the colder the better. And if the noise woke Sydney up? Too damned bad. After all, it was partly her fault he was wide awake and horny as hell at two a.m. It was only fair if she slept poorly, too.

When his phone alarm went off at six thirty, Sawyer came close to throwing it across the room. He'd finally managed to get to sleep around three after nearly freezing himself to death in the shower. Instead of committing mayhem against the hapless device, he dragged himself up and to the bathroom.

Sydney was in the kitchen when he came out of the bedroom. "Morning," she said.

"Hey."

"I've got toast, fruit, and eggs if you want them." She slid him a cup of coffee to the end of the kitchen island. "And the nectar of the gods, obviously."

"Thanks."

She eyed him as she poured her own cup. "You sleep okay?"

"Well enough," he hedged, taking a sip of coffee. "You?"

"Mm-hmmm. So what's on the schedule for today?" She came around the counter and took a seat in the breakfast nook. Somewhat reluctantly, Sawyer joined her with his own plate. He did a double take when he saw what she was eating.

"Peanut butter toast?"

She stopped, a slice halfway between her plate and her mouth. "Yeah. And?"

"Nothing."

"You have a problem with peanut butter toast?"

"No. It's just that I've never seen anyone over the age of twelve eat it."

Oh, he shouldn't have said that. He knew better as soon as the words came out of his mouth. But hell if he could drag them back or apologize.

"Who pissed in your Cheerios this morning?" she grumbled, taking a large bite of toast and chewing it noisily, her eyes challenging him to say another word about her breakfast choice. "Or are you normally so damned cheerful when you first get up?"

Sawyer didn't answer, instead pulling a sheet of paper from a folder in his briefcase. "Here's the itinerary. Let me know if anything looks interesting, and I'll see about getting you in."

She read through the schedule. "Which ones are you going to?"

He pointed to the talks. "These three. And there's a discussion panel late this afternoon. You should plan on hitting that one."

"Okay. Maybe my boss will have enough coffee in his system by then that he's bearable."

Sawyer sighed and sat back, crossing his arms. "Funny."

"True story. We're in my car, remember. I can leave you here if you aren't nice to me." She took her plate to the kitchen and rinsed it off. "What time are we leaving?"

"Whenever you're ready."

"Give me five minutes. I'm guessing paper and pens would be a good idea to take notes with?"

"Yes, ma'am."

"Okay." She left without a backward glance.

Sawyer rubbed his hands over his face. "Asshole."

He topped off his coffee and walked outside to the balcony to finish it off. The mountain air was cool, fog still lifting through the trees, and the calls of morning birds surrounded the cabin. Even though the Smokies were part of the same mountain chain that ran through Eastern Kentucky, they were significantly higher and had a different feel.

As in his dream the night before, Sydney came outside. Instead of the sexy nightgown he'd imagined, though, she was wearing a pretty blue blouse and khaki dress cargo pants. Smartly, she'd chosen comfortable, walking-friendly shoes. The hair that he itched to play with was neatly tucked away into a twist. And she didn't come all the way to the edge of the balcony but instead stopped just outside the door.

"Ready?"

"Sure. Isn't this view great?" Maybe he could offer a truce without actually having to apologize.

"Lovely, I'm sure." Her smile was tense as she looked down in the steep ravine, then away. "I'll be inside." She backed up, not turning her back on him until she was a few feet inside the house.

Frowning, Sawyer followed. "Are you okay?"

"I'm fine. I just don't much like heights." And she did look fine now that she was inside.

Sawyer glanced back over his shoulder. "This isn't much different from how the land lays at your grandparents' farm."

She quirked an eyebrow upward. "Not much different? It's a hundred times different. Way steeper and a lot farther to the bottom."

"How long have you been afraid of heights?" he asked as they started the drive down to Gatlinburg proper. He noticed then how she kept her eyes averted from the hill, which fell away from the road on her side of the car.

"Always." She chuckled nervously. "Daddy took me to Natural Bridge when I was five. He'd just lost his job at the Ford place and was getting ready to start where he is now, and he took a few days off in between. This was before he and Mom were married. Anyhow, he was so excited to show me the bridge, and all I could think about once we got up there was how big that hole was underneath it. He had to carry me down to the trail. I've not improved much since, no matter how hard I try."

Sawyer whistled. "That's tough. Heights don't bother me one bit. Being underground? That's a different story."

"I don't mind that so much. At least I can't fall if I'm in a hole."

Once they got to the convention hall and found a parking spot, Sawyer led her toward the registration table. They were stopped several times by people he knew.

"Is tomorrow the first time you've given one of the talks?" she asked as they stood in line to get their badges.

"I've sat in on a panel a few times."

"Are you nervous?"

He shrugged. "Not enough to cause a problem."

Since the conference catered to both law enforcement and private investigators, some of the talks covered bridging the gap between the two areas. Sawyer's session would discuss how to transition out of law enforcement and into the private sector.

"Sawyer Evans! You son of a buck, I was wondering when

you'd show up!" A balding man in a white button-down dress shirt was hurrying across the concourse to them.

"Gene, you bastard, how are you?" Sawyer greeted him, grinning wide. "Looks like it's hopping busy this year."

"It is. Attendance is up ten percent over last year. Who's this pretty lady?"

"Sydney Gibson, this is Gene Curry. Gene's the event coordinator. Sydney's my assistant. Since Lee had to stay and do court, she decided to tag along."

Sydney shook the man's proffered hand. "'Decided to tag along' translates into 'was brought to protect him from badge bunnies.' How do you do?"

Sawyer glowered at her, but she smiled sunnily, ignoring his dark look.

Gene laughed, looking from Sydney to him and back. "It is a real pleasure to meet you. How long have you been working for this donkey's ass?"

"About a month now, but I've known him for decades. He's friends with my family."

"Are you keeping him in line?" Gene asked, lowering his voice, a glint of humor in his eyes.

"I'm trying, but he's a bit stubborn," she said, matching his tone. "You may have noticed that."

Gene chuckled, slapping Sawyer on the shoulder. "I think it's been mentioned once or twice. She's got you pegged, doesn't she?"

"Hmmm, sure. I need a favor," Sawyer said, interrupting their glee. "She doesn't have a ticket. Think you can pull some strings for me?"

In answer, Gene reached into one of the pockets on his cargo pants and pulled out a pass. He handed it to Sydney. "That should do the trick. Just tell the ladies up here at the head of the line that I gave it to you. I'd better get back at it—you know how it is, a thousand and one things to do right now. We'll catch up later. Maybe dinner tonight? The usual place?"

"Sounds like fun. Just call me—you still have my number?" Sawyer asked.

"Yep. See you in a bit. Ma'am, nice to meet you." He tipped an invisible hat to Sydney and was gone.

"How long have you been coming to these things?" she asked, looking after Gene.

"Eight years? Ten? Something like that." A glimpse of a tall redhead walking through the crowd toward them caught his eye, and Sawyer groaned. "Oh, shit. This is just perfect."

"What?" Sydney stood on her tiptoes. "Who is it?"

"Grabby Charlene. Too late to hide. She sees me. Damn." He was in no mood to deal with the woman, whose entire face had lit up when she'd seen him. "I'd hoped she'd forgotten about me, or at the least, that she'd be too embarrassed to approach me."

"You really don't want her attention?"

Dead serious, he answered. "I really don't. Never did. Never will."

Sydney slipped her hand around his. "You'll owe me big time for this. Look at me."

When he did, she lifted her hand to her mouth and licked her thumb, then reached up and blotted at a spot next to his mouth on the opposite side of his face from where Charlene was approaching.

"How embarrassing is that?" she asked, trilling out a laugh. "My shade doesn't really work for you. Oh, hello."

Charlene, her smile dimmer than before, came to a stop beside them. "Hello. Sawyer. Who's your friend?"

He put his arm around Sydney's shoulders, playing along. "This is Sydney. She's my... assistant. Syd, this is Charlene. I'm sorry, what was your last name again?"

"Richards. I believe we spoke last week when I called Sawyer's office." She took in Sydney's appearance head-to-toe in a fast assessment. "I didn't know you two were involved, though."

"It isn't something we advertise," Sydney explained,

leaning into Sawyer's side. "At least, we haven't been. That's going to change now that he gave me this." She held her left hand out, displaying a large but tasteful diamond solitaire. "I'm so excited! Can you believe it?"

Sawyer pinched her side where Charlene couldn't see him. He was really going to have to have a talk with Sydney about what he'd meant when he'd asked for a chaperone. Her perky grin as she batted her lashes at him told him she was well aware of his discomfort.

"Minx."

"Congratulations," Charlene said, her voice tight. "You must be so happy."

"We are." Thankfully, the line had moved and they were at the registration table. "We'll see you around the conference, I guess," Sawyer told her.

"Sure. Nice meeting you," she said to Sydney.

Sydney didn't say a word other than to answer the questions the ladies manning the table asked. Once they had their badges, Sawyer drew her off to the side.

"Where'd you get the ring?"

"Department store. It's fake. It's a nice fake, though," she said, looking down at the jewelry. "Too much, Boss?"

Though she kept her voice light, he could tell she was a bit afraid she'd gone too far.

Sawyer shook his head. "Way over the top. You're definitely pushing it." But he was smiling when he spoke, and he couldn't keep a straight face. "If word of this 'engagement' gets back to Hazard and your father comes after me, I'm hiding behind you."

"You really think it will?"

He couldn't resist any longer. He had to touch her. Raising his hand, he brushed her bangs off to the side of her face. "It might. This is a pretty small community, all things considered. And there'll probably be at least a couple of guys here from our neck of the woods."

"Oh."

"Mmm, *oh.*"

She looked away, her cheeks heating, even as she laughed. "Where's our first lecture?"

He jerked his head. "West wing." They started walking. "Sorry I was such an ass this morning. I didn't sleep well last night."

"I figured. And thank you."

As they went into the room where the podium was set up, Sawyer let himself wonder what her family's reaction to a real engagement would be. He couldn't imagine they'd be pleased, that was for certain. And why he was even going down that road... The fact that the notion had even come into his mind was shocking. Shocking and potentially dangerous because being engaged to Sydney didn't sound as appalling as he'd expected it to.

CHAPTER TWENTY-SIX

"I HEAR CONGRATULATIONS ARE IN ORDER."

Sydney jumped, the man's low voice taking her by surprise as she sat in the back of the auditorium watching Sawyer's panel take questions.

"Lee! I thought you had court."

He took the seat beside hers. "The guy pled out, so I got sprung. Figured I had enough time to drive down here and catch some of the good stuff. How's it going?"

"It's fascinating. I think I have more questions now than when I first started working for Sawyer." She showed him her notepad, which was covered with writing.

"Glad you're enjoying it. Nice ring, by the way." He picked up her left hand and studied the fake diamond. "Have you set a date yet?"

Sydney took her hand back from him. "You know as well as I do this isn't real. How'd you hear about it?" she asked, keeping her voice low.

"My captain. He's here. He heard it from somewhere. How's the cabin?"

"Nice. Not the suite we were expecting."

He shifted in his seat. "It got uncomfortable last year, staying at the hotel with the rest of the gang. I figured the privacy would be nice."

"Mmm. So where are you staying?"

"Here at the hotel with the rest of the gang. Unless you want to let me sleep on your couch?"

She chuckled softly. "It does fold out."

"I'd hate to interrupt the happy couple, though."

"Oh, please." She rolled her eyes. "Don't be ridiculous."

"Sawyer might not appreciate my presence," he persisted. "You think I'm joking but he's territorial over you."

"Well, I'm not inviting you over to share my bed. And he's just protective. That's all."

"You keep telling yourself," Lee said. "I'll think about the offer."

"I figured you'd be happy to partake of the festivities, no offense. Since you're single and all."

That statement did make him uncomfortable.

"I tend to take the same path Sawyer does about that sort of thing. Easy pick-ups and flings... I just prefer to have something deeper, have at least a little respect for the person I'm with."

She tried to evaluate whether he was serious or not. "What about Rachel?"

Lee met her gaze head on. "What about her?"

"I guess I'm asking what your intentions are."

He rubbed his jaw. "I don't have any intentions other than to try to get to know her better. Not every man in uniform is looking for a notch on his gun belt, Ms. Gibson."

"No?"

Lee shook his head. "No. Some of us are looking for a mate. Not just a body to pass the night with."

She tipped her head to the side. "I think you mean that."

"I do." He took a sip of water from the bottle he carried. "That guy up there on stage? He's looking for a mate. He just doesn't know it. He's been hurt too much over the years."

Sydney turned to watch Sawyer as he fielded a question about gear. "I wish I believed that. Though I don't expect he'd ever..." When she realized what she'd been about to admit, she could have curled up and died.

"You don't expect he'd ever choose you?" Lee finished. "Why? Because you're younger than him?"

She didn't answer, couldn't. She was too embarrassed. But he persisted.

"Come on. Tell me."

"Because even if we got past the age difference and a myriad of other things, I want kids and he's convinced he can't have them."

"From what I understand, he can't," Lee countered.

"Not physically, no. But that's not the only way to have a family."

To her surprise, he smiled. "I knew I liked you for some reason. That's exactly what I told him the other day. Adoption isn't just for puppies and kittens, you know?" He blew out a breath. "I think if he let himself, he'd be all over you in a heartbeat. In the best kind of way," he hurried to reassure her when she turned wide eyes to him. "And if there's anything I can do to help, let me know. I'll be there."

They passed most of the rest of the lecture in silence, with Sydney lost in thought as she considered what he'd said. By the end of the session, she came away certain of two things—one, Lee was a damned nice guy. She was going to see what she could do to throw him and Rachel together, see what happened. And two, she'd never wanted someone to be right about another person's feelings so much in her whole life. She didn't think he was, but she couldn't help but wish Lee knew what he was talking about.

A quick trip to the bathroom ended up being more illuminating than Sydney was expecting, and definitely resulted in her hearing more than she wanted to hear. She'd just entered the stall and was rummaging through her purse when the outside door opened, admitting two women.

"Oh, my God, did you see him? He looks even better this year than he did. You don't know how much I was looking forward to this conference," the first woman said.

Her friend snickered. "I saw him. Did you see his fiancée? I can't believe he's engaged. She had her hands all over him this morning."

Ah, shit. She recognized that voice. It belonged to the tall redhead from the reception line. Charlene. Surely they weren't discussing her and Sawyer?

A snort and a sigh as two stalls down the row from Sydney opened, then closed. "I could have strangled her from across the room. And do you blame her? Hell, if I were engaged to Sawyer, I'd keep him locked in a bedroom. It's been three years and I'm still trying to find someone who knows how to do the things he did to me."

Yep, they were. Sydney cringed.

"Any luck?" Charlene asked.

"Not much, and believe me, I've tried. I should have just followed him back to Kentucky back then. I was so sure I'd be able to snag him again this year. Damn it."

"She's awfully young. He never struck me as the cradle-robber type. Think she's pregnant? She's definitely not his usual type—more kitten than tiger, if you know what I mean."

Sydney swallowed hard, closing her eyes. It was bad enough to be stuck in a bathroom stall, listening to women talk who, at least the one, had intimate knowledge of Sawyer. But the pregnancy speculation stung, as did their dissection of her. In light of his confession to being sterile, the mere thought of his child made her ache. Deciding she could wait or find another bathroom, she left the stall and the room, heading back to where she'd parted from Sawyer and Lee.

"At least I know now why they're so eager to chase him down. His reputation precedes him."

She also had something of an answer to her doubts

about Sawyer's willingness to have one-night stands. Presumably that's what had happened with the woman in the bathroom. Despite Lee's words to the contrary, casual sex was on Sawyer's menu.

"It's none of your business," she told herself as she wound her way through the crowd. "He's single. You shouldn't be offended by his sexuality."

But she was, at least a little. Not so much because he'd indulged in apparently knock-your-socks-off sex with the unknown woman, but—if she was being honest—because she knew she'd never get to experience the same for herself.

That evening, she didn't think twice about choosing the sexiest outfit in her arsenal to wear to dinner. She donned it with a battle-ready mindset. A one-shoulder, cleavage-baring ruched red dress that clung like a lover's breath to her curves, the garment was made from slinky fabric that allowed her to wear only the subtlest of lingerie beneath. The hem ended halfway down her thighs, ensuring that she had to be very careful how she moved in order to keep from revealing more than she wanted. Lace-topped thigh highs barely covered by the dress's hem, three-inch heels, dangling gold-hoop earrings, and three sparkling bracelets completed the ensemble.

Instead of the usual subtle makeup she wore for work, she used a heavier hand, going for smoky eyes. Blush highlighted her cheekbones, high arches she'd inherited from her mother and grandmother. And merlot-wine lipstick stained her mouth with a just-kissed look, matching the dress almost exactly. She finished with subtle touches of perfume at various pulse points.

"That should do very nicely," she told her reflection as she stood back, turning this way and that. The dress dipped down to her mid back, barely concealing the strapless bra she wore. She'd questioned her judgment when she'd packed the outfit but now she was glad she'd included it.

Even though the dress wouldn't do anything to Sawyer, she felt a hundred times sexier wearing it.

She didn't kid herself into thinking he might see her and fall head over heels into anything, not even lust. But she'd feel powerful tonight, more than a match for Sawyer or his women. He might not end up wanting her after tonight, but by God, there'd be no doubt in the man's mind that she was a woman. And in the end, she decided, that was what mattered.

CHAPTER TWENTY-SEVEN

WHEN SYDNEY CAME DOWNSTAIRS, READY to go to dinner, the only thing that kept Sawyer from dragging her back up to the nearest bed was Lee's presence. And from the grin on the other man's face, he knew it.

"Damn, but you clean up nice, Sydney. Not that you were a slouch to begin with, but damn." Lee kissed her on the cheek, taking her hand to twirl her around. "Isn't she gorgeous, Sawyer?"

Sawyer wanted to punch him. Instead, he gave a single nod. "You look very nice."

Sydney acknowledged the compliment with a regal inclination of her head. "You two don't look so bad yourselves."

They were wearing casual sports jackets with dress shirts and pants. Thank God, ties weren't required for the restaurant their reservations were at.

"We should go," Sawyer said. He'd been looking forward to the evening, but after seeing the way Sydney looked? He fully expected the next few hours to be an exercise in pure torture, especially considering that they had to pretend to be engaged.

Lee slapped him on the shoulder as he passed by where Sawyer stood on the way to the door. "This is going to be a fun dinner. Sydney, you'll get to hear all kinds of war stories tonight. Some of them are bound to be good blackmail material."

"Oh, I already got to hear some this afternoon," she said, casually twisting the bracelets she wore around on her wrist. "The woman from this morning? Charlene? She and a friend were in the bathroom, and they were expressing their regrets over Sawyer's being unavailable. Apparently, you left quite an impression one of them three years ago, lover boy." She breezed past him without a glance, leaving a trail of sultry perfume in her wake.

Lee grimaced at Sawyer as Sydney passed him. "Ouch."

"Oh, it's not a big deal. It isn't like we're really engaged," she said as she got in the car. "Though hearing my boss's prowess in the sack discussed so freely wasn't something I enjoyed."

Sawyer could have gone through the floor with shame. The second woman would be Monique, then. They'd flirted casually at several of the conventions, and in a moment of weakness, he'd taken her up on her offer. That had been the last time he'd had a one-night stand, and if he could go back and undo it to spare Sydney the embarrassment of hearing the conversation, he would have. He hated men who bragged about their bedroom conquests, and he'd always taken care to keep his professional life and personal life separate. He'd never expected something like this to happen.

Lee made a concerted effort to break the tension in the car as they drove down the hill. Sawyer was glad—he was too rattled to add much to the conversation. He mostly stayed quiet and let Lee and Sydney talk.

"So who all are we meeting?" Sydney asked as they reached the restaurant's parking lot.

"My old captain, Gene from this morning, a couple of other people probably. All in all, maybe ten? Twelve people?" Sawyer cringed as he realized Monique or Charlene might be some of those other people. He hadn't thought to ask

Gene who was coming, and the women had hung out with their group in the past.

Lee's smile was tense as he helped Sydney out of the car, and he shot Sawyer a look over her shoulder. He shrugged as though to ask what to do, and Sawyer gave a subtle shake of his head in response. He didn't have a clue.

"I'll head on in and see if our table's ready," Lee said as Sawyer came around the car.

Sawyer held his arm out, and after a brief hesitation, Sydney walked to his side.

"I'm sorry," he told her in a low voice. "If I'd had any idea... I'm sorry."

She studied him closely, evaluating him with a wariness he'd not seen from her before. "You don't have a thing to apologize for. Your sex life is none of my business."

He wanted to protest that it was her business, but she was right. As much as he was drawn to her, for all intents and purposes, they were just co-workers and very casual friends. And unless he wanted to make a formal offer to change that, he had to grin and bear the fallout from what she'd heard.

CHAPTER TWENTY-EIGHT

SYDNEY COULD TELL BY THE tension in Sawyer's body as they approached the group at the table that there was someone there he'd not wanted to see. Her money was on the attractive blonde whose eyes were shooting virtual daggers in her direction.

"Monique or Laurie?" she asked Sawyer under her breath, touching his chest while she spoke as though she were imparting a secret.

"Monique."

"Three-year girl?"

His lips compressed as he stared down at her, lost for words. After a second, he shook his head and slid a kiss across her temple. "I'm sorry," he whispered.

She couldn't help but feel bad for him. He was clearly embarrassed. She touched his chin. "I know."

They took seats on the outside of the table. There were nine other people in the group, and Sawyer made the introductions all around.

"This is Sydney. She's... um, we're engaged." His arm was around her shoulder, and his thumb brushed over the bare skin of her arm under the drape of fabric from the dress's single sleeve.

Sydney moved closer to him in the booth, clasping the hand he'd laid on the table with hers.

Dale Jameson, the man he'd introduced as his former captain, seemed skeptical. "When did this happen?"

"Honestly? On the way down here" she replied. She glanced up at Sawyer, then quickly away with a smile. "I wasn't expecting the proposal, but we stopped for lunch at a park in London, and he sprung it on me."

"You're kin to Rick Browning, am I right?" Jameson asked.

"I am. He's my mother's cousin."

"He never mentioned the two of you were seeing each other."

"How'd you meet?" Monique asked, no friendlier now than she'd been when they'd first walked up. Her gaze told Sydney she clearly found her lacking.

"Sydney's my assistant," Sawyer said. "But I've been friends with her family for a long time now."

Sydney laughed. "I think the first time we met was when I was six years old. Best I recall, I puked all over your shiny dress shoes. And you avoided me for about ten years after that."

Sawyer squeezed her arm gently, his body relaxing some. "I did. Until she stole her dad's car and drove halfway across the country when she was fifteen."

"I didn't know that," Lee said. He was beside Sydney in a chair at the table's corner. "What in the world possessed you?"

"That's a long story, and not worth getting into tonight."

"I almost arrested her when she was nineteen," Sawyer added.

"I was unaware of the laws pertaining to the carrying of concealed weapons," she protested. "That's all. I've been a good girl ever since."

"For the most part," he teased. Between the words and the heated look he gave her, there wasn't a person at the table who could doubt his meaning.

"Sawyer! Hush!" She covered her face with her hands, laughing softly as she peeked at him between her fingers.

He touched her cheek with the back of his hand, leaving it at that.

By the time dinner was over two hours later, Sydney was strung as tight as a bow. Between the jealous sniping coming at her across the table and Sawyer's attentiveness, she was ready to run screaming into the night.

From the careful eye Lee was keeping on her, she figured he was aware of her discomfort.

"Sawyer, can I borrow your girl for a dance or two?"

"I guess. If you want to," Sawyer said to Sydney.

"That'd be nice. I'm not used to sitting for so long."

Once they were out on the dance floor, she sighed. "Thanks for that. I was about to lose it."

"I was afraid of that. I could almost see steam coming out of your ears." He twirled her around absentmindedly. "You've done really well tonight. So well that Sawyer might find himself on the wrong side of your dad's shotgun when you get home."

She chuckled, truly amused. "I can see it now. And Daddy wouldn't use a shotgun. He'd use his hands, wrapped around Sawyer's throat. I guess I should send a text or two and let them know not to believe everything they hear."

Lee smiled. "I wish it were the truth. The two of you together... you're something else."

"You're building castles in the air, you closet romantic."

It was his turn to be amused. "Oh, I'm freely out and about with my romanticism. It's part of my charm."

"Don't take this the wrong way, but why couldn't we have fallen for each other?" she asked him wistfully. "It would be so easy, so uncomplicated."

"And so boring. As individuals, you and I are complex human beings. Put us together and we're quite pedestrian. You and Sawyer, however, you make the room spark. It's quite sickening, really." He crossed his eyes and batted his lashes, causing her to burst into laughter. "Oh, that drew us a nasty look. He'll be over here soon. Better run while we can. Chasing you will be good for him." And with that, he danced her to the opposite side of the room from where Sawyer was sitting.

The band was quite good, a smooth jazz trio that covered classics as well as modern hits. It was just the kind of place Sydney would have visited when she lived in Savannah.

Once they'd slowed back down to normal speed, she spoke. "Do you mind if I ask you a question?"

"Would it matter if I did? You're full of curiosity, and I don't think I could stop you."

She gave in to temptation and poked him in the shoulder. "Smart ass."

"Yeah, so? Ask away, madam."

"You have an odd turn of phrase here and there. I don't mean that as an insult. I'm just... curious. Where are you from?"

"I was born and raised in Letcher County, Kentucky."

Sydney peered up at him, not sure she believed him.

He grinned. "My father, however, is British. He teaches—don't laugh—English at a private school in Knott County."

"And your mother?"

"World-renowned quilter from Letcher County. They met while she was touring Ireland during summer break from college one year. He followed her here and you can guess the rest."

"Brothers, sisters?"

"Two older sisters who do their best to make sure I never see a moment's peace."

Sydney wasn't surprised. "I knew you'd have to be the baby."

He scowled down at her. "What's that mean?"

"Not a thing. You just have that air about you."

"You know, I've heard that before. And here comes a man who isn't the baby, unless I miss my guess."

He turned them so that Sydney could see Sawyer, who was weaving across the floor toward them.

"Green looks good on you," Lee told him. He kept Sydney in his embrace.

She happily stayed put for no other reason than it seemed to irritate Sawyer.

"Game's over, kids. We should head out."

"But we're having so much fun..." Sydney pouted. When his scowl intensified, she burst out laughing. "Oh, your face."

Sawyer held out his hand. "Come on."

Lee released her with a heartfelt sigh. "Well, so much for running away together."

Ooh, Sawyer really didn't like that. Sydney wondered what had happened at the table to turn his mood so sour. She took his hand.

"Are you okay?"

"Fine and dandy." He started back toward the door.

Sydney drew him to a stop, though, when the band started playing "Make You Feel My Love."

"Dance with a girl once?" she asked, her smile winsome.

For a moment, she thought he was going to refuse. "Sure. Why not?" he capitulated.

"I'll be in the bar," Lee said. "Call me if you can't find me."

"I thought we were trying to convince people we were engaged," Sawyer said as they started dancing. "You and Lee looked pretty cozy out here."

Sydney stared up at him, incredulous, and drew back. "Excuse me? I didn't sign up to be a sitting target for your damned girlfriend all evening, Sawyer. The more she drank, the worse she got. Lee saw that and got me out of there before I went across the table on her. Don't you dare snarl at me."

He pulled her back to him. "Sorry. I'm sorry. You're right."

After a few seconds, she relaxed into him. They didn't speak for the rest of the song, or during the song after that. Sydney was glad. The mood on the dance floor was intimate, heady, and being in Sawyer's arms... They were tucked as close together as they could get and still dance. With her head on his shoulder, nestled under his chin, she was in heaven and hell.

Sensations threatened to overwhelm her. When she felt the press of his lips on her bare shoulder, she gave a quiet gasp. She lifted her head to stare at him. "Who's watching?" she whispered.

"No one." His mouth brushed across hers lightly, then came back to settle warmly over hers in a deep, slow kiss.

Currents of electricity shot down her spine, running out in every direction, circling into her breasts and between her legs. Her hands curled into the fabric of his coat, clinging tightly as he drew back and pressed his forehead to hers.

"We should go find Lee. It's getting late." His voice was rough, full of emotion.

Sydney carefully uncurled her fingers, smoothing down the cotton where she'd wrinkled it. "Probably." But she didn't move.

Neither did he.

"He'll be looking for us," she whispered.

"Yeah. Damn it." Sawyer shook himself. He stepped back and drew in a breath. "It's probably a good thing he's with us tonight. Don't you think?"

"I suppose it depends on your perspective," she answered softly. "From the common sense side of things? Yes. From the risk-taking daredevil side? Not in the least."

"That's what I was afraid of." He touched her cheek. "Let's go."

Instead of pulling away from her as she'd expected, he kept her hand closely in his as they went to the bar and got Lee. And the whole drive back up the hill, they held hands in the front seat, out of sight.

When they got back to the cabin, she grabbed a bottle of water from the fridge. "I think I'm going to turn in," she said. "It's been a long day and I'm tired. What time are we leaving in the morning?"

"Seven thirty or eight," Sawyer said.

"Okay. See you both then. Goodnight."

"Night," they chorused.

She felt the weight of their gazes as she climbed the stairs. Once she was in her bedroom, she closed the door and leaned back against it.

Sawyer had kissed her. Honest-to-God kissed her. And it wasn't nearly enough.

Sydney didn't know what the kiss meant. She tried to convince herself it was an aberration because believing it was anything else would just lead to heartache down the road.

CHAPTER TWENTY-NINE

INSTEAD OF THE TEASING SAWYER was expecting from Lee, he found himself on the receiving end of a concerned assessment.

"What?" he asked. He stripped his jacket off and tossed it over a barstool as he headed to the fridge. "Beer?"

Lee took the proffered bottle. "You have feelings for her."

Sawyer didn't respond. He went out onto the balcony, the one Sydney was afraid of, and popped the top off his own beer.

Lee followed. "You know she's halfway in love with you."

"It's just a crush."

"No. I don't think so."

Sawyer studied the man he'd mentored ten years earlier. Lee mostly let life roll off his back like a duck would water. He took some flak from LEOs who didn't know him because of that attitude. So any time he grew serious, Sawyer listened.

"It would never work between us."

Lee shrugged. "That's what she said. Doesn't stop her from having feelings for you or you for her."

"No, I guess not." Sawyer sighed and sat down on one of the lounges. "Short of firing her and getting some distance between us, I don't know what to do."

Lee sat beside him on a second lounge. "Why not see where it goes? Remember that discussion we had the other day about puppies and kittens?"

Sawyer rolled the bottle between his hands. “It’s hard to adopt babies. And I’m almost fifty.”

When Lee handed him his cell phone, a website displayed on the screen, Sawyer frowned. “What’s this?”

“It’s called Google. You can find out all kinds of things by using it, like what sort of restrictions there are on couples wanting to adopt. As it happens, age isn’t as important as it used to be. What’s your next argument?”

“Let’s follow your ridiculous train of thought. Say I did end up in a relationship with—”

“Married to,” Lee interrupted.

Sawyer scowled. “Fine. Married to Sydney. Say that’s where we ended up. She might not want kids that aren’t hers. A lot of women don’t.”

“I’ve not seen anything about her that would lead me to think she’s like that. Have you?”

He wasn’t about to admit that Sydney might be more than open to the idea. “You’re putting the cart before the horse,” he told Lee instead.

“Somebody better get it ready to hitch up, the way you two were looking at each other tonight. I don’t mean to be pushy.”

Sawyer snorted. “Really?”

Lee grinned. “Okay, maybe I do. But you’re like a brother to me. And I know you’re struggling with how you feel about her. I just don’t think there’s any reason for you to fight it so hard, that’s all. Let what happens, happen. Life’s too short to waste playing it as safe as you do, Sawyer. You know that. What would you say if our situations were reversed?”

Any answer he gave would make him come across as a complete and total hypocrite, and Sawyer knew that. “What do you want me to say?”

“It isn’t what I want you to say. It’s what I want you to realize—that you have choices. With this woman, as it pertains to children… life doesn’t have to be as empty as you’ve made it.”

"Damn, Lee, what are you? Dr. Phil's off-screen partner?"

Lee smiled. "Nah. But I maybe had a couple of drinks while I was waiting on the two of you. I'm a bit snookered. You know how I get when I drink."

Sawyer shook his head. "You'd better watch it or you'll end up getting some of your own medicine."

"I can think of worse things than being loved by a beautiful woman," he said around a yawn. "I'm going to turn in. Thanks for the couch."

"Any time."

The night was warm, a pleasant breeze blowing across the hill. Even though he had to get an early start tomorrow, Sawyer couldn't bring himself to go inside. To climb up the stairs and bypass Sydney's bedroom, to lie on his own bed and stare at the ceiling for three hours until he drifted into a fitful sleep. If he was going to be awake, he might as well be out in the fresh air.

To his surprise, he started getting sleepy less than an hour after Lee had gone in. Hoping he could get some rest, he headed inside, taking care not to disturb Lee, who was snoring softly on the pull-out sofa bed. Upstairs, he'd just gotten stripped down and was pulling back the covers when his phone buzzed. Rachel's name showed on the display.

"What the heck?" It was almost midnight, not a time when she typically called him. A chill went down his spine. "Hello?"

"Sawyer? Are you with Sydney?" Rachel's voice was strained. He knew immediately something was very wrong.

"She's next door. What's going on?"

"It's Eli. He's been hurt. We don't know how bad yet, but it doesn't sound good. Noah... he saw him." She had to stop to clear her throat.

Sawyer closed his eyes. "Oh, God."

"Anyhow, Archer's calling Sydney now. This is going to hit her hard."

"I know. How are John and Zanny and your parents?" He

heard the muted ringing of Sydney's phone through the wall that separated their rooms. Grabbing his pajama bottoms, he tugged them on.

"Not good. John got in touch with his CO here in the states and the guy confirmed that Eli's been injured, but he couldn't tell them anything other than it was serious. They're flying him out of Afghanistan to Germany. John, Zanny, Noah, and Molly are on a plane to meet him there."

Sawyer cursed. "Sydney just got the call. I'd better go. Thanks for letting me know."

"Sawyer? Keep her safe."

"I will."

He hurried next door and knocked softly on her door.

"Come in."

She was sitting on the bed, her face reflecting her utter devastation as she listened to the call. Sawyer closed the door and crossed to sit beside her. She couldn't speak, couldn't even respond to her father, Sawyer saw. He gently took the phone from her and put his arm around her shoulder as he spoke to Archer.

"Hey. It's Sawyer. Rachel just called me."

Sydney got up, excusing herself to run into the bathroom, slamming the door behind her.

"Hey. We waited to call until we knew more. They confirmed it with his CO tonight about six and caught a ten o'clock flight out."

"That's what Rachel said." Sawyer walked over to the bathroom door, listening carefully. Sydney was crying, but that wasn't unexpected.

"Yeah. And unless there's bad news, we probably won't know any more until sometime tomorrow." Archer sighed. "We thought about not calling you all until the morning, but if something does happen..."

"I understand. What can we do?"

"Not a damned, fucking thing," Archer growled. "Sorry. Things are a little raw here."

"Don't apologize. Do we need to head home tonight?"

"I'd rather you wait until tomorrow. Try to get some rest if you can. Sydney texted earlier that it'd been a long day, and we don't need to worry about the two of you being on the road while you're tired. How is she?"

Sawyer laid his free hand on the door. "Upset. She's in the bathroom. God, Archer, I hate this."

The other man swallowed. "So do I. Take care of my little girl, you hear me?"

"Yeah. I will."

"If she needs to call, tell her to, no matter what time it is."

"Okay. Let us know if we can do anything."

Once he'd hung up, he tapped on the door. "Sydney?"

"I'll be out in a minute."

Sawyer paced to the window beside the bed, staring out into the night as he waited. After what felt like an hour, the door opened and she emerged. Her face was pale, though her eyes and the tip of her nose were red. She crossed her arms tightly over her chest.

"Tell me how I can help," Sawyer said.

She shrugged and tried to smile. "I don't know." But her smile melted as tears returned. "Oh, God, why?"

He wasted no time in getting to her, pulling her tightly into his arms as she sobbed. "I'm so sorry, Sydney. So damned sorry."

She was so fragile, he thought as he held her. Too fragile to hurt so much. He couldn't stand seeing her pain, but there wasn't a damned thing he could do to stop it.

When she started to lean into him heavily, he knew she was going down. Acting quickly, he caught her up in his arms and carried her to the bed, sitting down with her in his lap.

"D-daddy said N-Noah saw him," she whispered. "He saw him, Sawyer. You know what that means."

Sawyer was terrified he did. "I don't think his CO would

hold something like that back, though. And Rachel said the man would only confirm Eli was hurt. Maybe Noah saw him because they're brothers. It doesn't have to mean he's gone."

She sucked in a shuddering breath, trying to get a grip on her emotions. "I hope you're right."

"So do I." Sawyer picked up the box of Kleenex from the nightstand and put it beside his hip, handing her some of the tissues. "Here."

She wasn't wearing her glasses, and he gently blotted her eyes. His chest was damp from her tears, and when she used the tissues he'd given her to try to dry him off, Sawyer felt his heart break. He kissed her forehead.

"Nice sleep shirt," he said in an attempt to distract her.

She gave a bark of laughter and looked down at the sleeveless tunic-style oversized shirt that covered her from chest to knees. "You like Hello Kitty? I never would have guessed."

"Who doesn't? Ah, Sydney. What a fucking mess."

"I know. I don't know what to do." She tucked her face back into his shoulder, sniffling. Her fingers lightly touched his chest before curling into a fist under her chin. "Did Daddy want us to come home?"

"Not tonight. He wants us to wait, just to be safe. I figured we'd head out in the morning."

"What about your lecture?"

"Hang the lecture."

She sat up, drawing back to look at him. "No."

Sawyer lifted an eyebrow. "No?"

"You need to go through with it. We can leave after you're done. Whether we get on the road at eight o'clock or ten thirty, there's nothing we can do. Not for Eli or anyone else. You made a commitment. I won't let this interfere with it."

There were some strands of hair sticking to the side of her face, and he brushed them back, tucking them behind her ear. "Why don't we wait until morning to decide?"

She nodded. "If he doesn't make it... That would kill

Noah. With things the way they are between them..." Tears welled up in her eyes again, and she covered her mouth with her hand.

"Try to stay positive," he said, tightening his arms around her. "It might not be as bad as it sounds."

But Noah had seen Eli. That was something Sawyer couldn't discount. He knew the same thought weighed heavily on Sydney's mind.

They sat there for several minutes, Sawyer just holding her as the grief came in waves. A quiet knock sounded on the bedroom door, and Lee's voice came through.

"Everything okay?"

"Will you tell him?" Sydney whispered, getting to her feet.

"Sure." He ran a hand across her hair, then went to the door. When he opened it, Lee moved back, concern etched on his face. "Hey."

"She okay?" Lee asked.

"No." Sawyer explained the situation. "It doesn't sound good," he told the other man in a low voice. "She knows that. He's like a brother to her."

Lee rubbed a hand across his jaw. "That sucks. Is there anything I can do?"

"No. Just pray."

"Of course. Goes without saying. Let me know if you need anything. I'll head back downstairs."

"Sorry that we woke you."

He scowled. "Don't even go there. Holler if you need me."

"Thanks, Lee."

Sawyer leaned against the door briefly before going back inside. Sydney was standing by the window, her posture completely forlorn and lost. He walked up behind her.

"How can I help?"

She shook her head slowly. "You can't."

Taking a chance, he settled his hands on her shoulders

and lightly rubbed. “Do you want me to stay with you tonight?”

Her breath hitched as she turned around. She tilted her head. “I hate to ask you to do that.”

Sawyer cupped her face. “You aren’t asking.”

She dipped her chin, nuzzling into his palm. “Please?”

“Which side of the bed do you want?”

Her smile was tiny, but it was a smile. “I don’t care.”

As they settled in beside each other, Sawyer thought about his dreams from the night before. He couldn’t lie and say he wasn’t eager to feel Sydney’s body beside his, but his focus was entirely different now than it had been.

She turned the light off, then snuggled into the mattress with a sigh. “Thank you for staying,” she whispered.

“Is it okay if I hold you?”

“Yes.”

He rolled over and eased his arms around her, taking care not to move too fast. “Do you have your alarm set?”

“Six thirty. I doubt I’ll sleep, though.”

“I know.” Sawyer reached up and brushed her hair back, letting his fingers slide through the thick tresses.

“That feels nice.”

For a long time, he stroked her hair, the side of her face. He traced the shell of her ear and rubbed the spot where her neck met her shoulder, feeling her muscles slowly relax. The touch was comforting for him, too.

He didn’t know Eli that well, as he’d not had much to do with him when he and Noah were boys, and Eli had been gone from Hazard since he was eighteen or so. But he was a Campbell, and there was a connection there. The thought of losing him hurt, both personally and because of what it might mean for Sydney and Noah and the rest of the family.

After a while, Sydney sighed, her body relaxing fully. Sawyer didn’t stop caressing her for a few minutes, though, not until he was sure she was asleep. He hadn’t expected her to go to drift off so quickly, and he wondered then just how badly she'd slept the night before.

The warmth of her, the softness, was astounding. As fragile as she appeared, her muscles were strong, her body very real and solid against his. He realized as his eyes grew heavy that he'd been deluding himself by thinking he'd be able to keep his distance from her. No, his fate had been set in stone from the first moment he'd seen her at the Sunday dinner at the farm weeks earlier.

He couldn't think in terms of permanency. That sort of relationship wasn't in his lexicon anymore. But as soon as the crisis in her personal life straightened out, Sawyer was going to make his move. He'd ask her out for dinner, see where things went. He needed to be with her in a way he hadn't needed anyone for a long time.

CHAPTER THIRTY

SYDNEY WOKE UP AT FOUR. She was on her right side, her arm around Sawyer's waist. To her fascinated horror, her hand was flat on his belly, low, right above the waistband of his pajama bottoms. If she moved her hand just a bit lower… But she couldn't do that. She *wouldn't* do that. Instead, she eased her arm back to her side and rolled over. He barely moved, and she gave a quiet sigh of relief. She was feeling entirely too vulnerable to deal with an awake, sleep-tumbled Sawyer right now.

The clock on the nightstand slowly counted off time as she stared at the ceiling, glancing at it every couple of minutes and wishing time would move faster. She wanted to scream at the frustration of waiting for word on Eli. Having flown overseas with Adam a few times, she knew John and Zanny's flight would be a long one, and not to expect to hear anything before noon at the earliest. Lying here, not able to do anything, was threatening to drive her insane. She needed to *do* something. But here at the cabin there wasn't anything to do.

By four thirty, she knew if she didn't get up and move she was going to lose her mind. Carefully, she eased out of bed, doing her best not to wake Sawyer. She decided to use the bathroom in his room to keep from disturbing him, and put her glasses on, then grabbed her robe and headed for the door.

Once finished with that, she went on out to the balcony off his bedroom. It was much higher off the ground than she was typically comfortable going, but tonight, she felt reckless. She needed the adrenaline rush of standing on a surface that wasn't, to her phobic mind, solid. She needed to feel the fear to deal with the pain.

Some of her earliest memories included Eli and Noah. Until Molly came along when Sydney was five, they'd been the only three grandchildren. John and Zanny's house was only a couple of miles away from Sydney's, and the same lady had babysat the three of them in the afternoons and during the summer. As a result, Sydney was as close to them as she was her brothers, if not closer. She literally could not imagine life without them.

She didn't want to. And she was terrified she might end up having to.

Some time later, the sliding door opened behind her, and she turned to watch Sawyer walk outside.

"You okay?" he asked, his voice rough with sleep.

"Couldn't sleep. I tried not to wake you."

He rubbed his eyes with the heels of his hand and yawned. "I wasn't sleeping all that well, anyhow. I thought you were afraid of heights."

"I am. But I'm more afraid of other things tonight."

He came to stand beside her at the railing. Clad only in his low-riding pajama bottoms, he was a breathtaking sight to behold in the moonlight. Sydney'd seen twenty-year-old men who pampered their bodies to perfection but didn't have the muscles Sawyer did. And he wasn't bulked up, either, but lanky and lean, all long, hard lines.

"What exactly do you do to keep in shape like that?" she heard herself ask.

He glanced down at himself. "Swim a few miles every day. How long have you been out here?"

"I don't know. What time is it?"

"Five thirty."

She was shocked. "My mind must have really wandered. I got up an hour ago."

Now that he'd told her the time, she could feel fatigue setting into her body. Her muscles were stiff from the cool, damp air, and she realized her toes were numb.

Sawyer lightly touched her shoulder. "Think you can go back to sleep? Or even rest a little more?"

"Maybe. I'm a bit chilled, so at the very least, getting warm sounds like a good plan."

"Let's go in."

She let him lead her inside, through his room and into hers. They took care to move quietly so as not to disturb Lee. Once in the bedroom, she had a hard time untying the belt of the robe.

"Um, my hands are numb," she told Sawyer sheepishly. "I need a little help."

He brushed her fingers aside and undid the bow deftly, then eased the robe down her arms. As the material swished to the floor, awareness settled between them heavily.

Sydney was afraid to move, afraid to breathe as the moment stretched into time.

When he took her glasses off and folded them, setting them on the nightstand, she ducked her head shyly. His hands came back up to cup her face, sliding into her hair. He pressed his cheek to hers, the warmth of the man startling after the cool early morning air.

"You and I need to have a long talk one of these days," he whispered. "Preferably someplace private like this. But now isn't the time."

She had to swallow down her disappointment. "I know."

"Let's get you warm." He took her hand and drew her to the bed, getting in and holding the covers up for her to climb under. She joined him without hesitation.

"I'm glad you're here," she told him as he settled the covers around them. "As much as I hate what's happening, I'm glad you're here to... I'm just glad it's you."

He tensed for a moment, then relaxed as his arms came around her, pulling her back into him. "So am I."

After conferring with the family the next morning, they decided to stay and let Sawyer do his lecture. Lee stayed at Sydney's side, acting as a buffer between her and Monique, who was still fuming over Sawyer's being unavailable. As soon as the talk was finished and Sawyer had handled the post-lecture meet and greet, they were on the road.

To Sydney's surprise, Lee hugged them both before they left. "You two be careful, and please call me, let me know how things go. Okay?"

Sawyer saluted him. "We will. Thanks, man."

With Sawyer driving once again, as Sydney wasn't in the best of shape to be behind the wheel, they headed toward Knoxville and the interstate that would take them home.

"We should be hearing something any time now, right?" she asked as they hit I-75.

"Maybe. Do you know if they've made it to Germany yet?"

"Any minute now." She checked her phone for what felt like the thousandth time since they'd left Gatlinburg. "I'm scared."

"I know." Sawyer reached over the console, his fingers spread, and she gently placed her hand in his.

"Everything's changed now. Everything. You know in the back of your mind something like this could happen. You just never expect it to. It's always someone else's son or daughter, brother, sister, husband, wife. And then it happens to you."

"Same thought process applies in law enforcement. That's a big reason LEOs have such a high divorce rate. The stress of never knowing if your spouse is going to walk back in the door at the end of the day gets too heavy. That, and... well, I guess your badge bunnies is the nicest way to put it."

She gave him a half smile. "Not *my* badge bunnies, thank you very much." She watched him for a minute. "Do you think she would have stuck it out, your ex? If you'd had kids?"

"I don't know. Honestly? I doubt it. And after a while, knowing that took some of the sting out of it. Not a lot, but enough that it was measurable. Kind of an 'at least there's that,' you know?"

"I can understand that. I felt the same way about Adam." Her phone buzzed, and in her scramble to answer it, she dropped it on the floor. "Shit!"

When she finally got it in her hands, she saw that it was her mother calling, but she missed the call. While it was going to voice mail, Sydney called her back, putting the call on speaker. "Mom?"

"Hey, sweetie. I just heard from John. They're in Germany, and so is Eli. He's stable. He had to have surgery in the field, and he'll be going back in for another round soon now that he's in Germany. But he's stable. He's alive, Syd."

"Oh, thank God," she sobbed. For the second time in twelve hours, she had to give Sawyer her phone, too overcome with emotions to even hold on to the device.

"Emma, it's Sawyer. She has you on speaker. That's great news. Have they seen him yet?"

"No. They're on their way to the hospital now. They're hoping to get there before he goes in, but they might not." She sighed. "How about you all? Where are you?"

"Coming out of Knoxville. We should be in Hazard in just under three hours. Where is everyone? At the farm?"

"Yeah. We've thrown together a potluck. Pip and Logan are here, Ben and Ainsley. You know how we are—we gather together when someone's hurt."

"I know. It's part of what makes you all so unique. Here's Sydney." He handed the phone back to her.

Now that she was composed, Sydney could breathe again. "I'll head up there when we get home. How are Grandma and Grandpa taking this?"

"They're quiet, but they're okay. Getting word that he's stable has helped. How are you?"

"I'll be fine when we know he's going to make it. And Noah. What happened?"

Emma hesitated.

Sydney realized she probably didn't know that Sawyer was aware of Noah's abilities. "It's okay, Mom. Sawyer knows about Noah."

"You do?"

"Yes. I've known for a while now," Sawyer confirmed quietly. "Can you tell us what happened? Or tell Sydney if you aren't comfortable telling me."

Emma let out a watery, unhappy laugh. "I don't mind telling you both. It's just sad and scary, that's all. It's turned us all a bit upside down, in addition to what's going on with Eli. Noah was down at John's working on the yard and apparently, he just froze. Zanny said she'd never seen that look on his face, not in thirty-two years. Said he turned white as a sheet and fell to his knees. It was several minutes before he could tell them what was wrong. They were afraid he was having a heart attack or a stroke or something."

Sydney shook her head. "I don't understand how he saw Eli if Eli's still... not that I'm not glad he's alive. But how, Mom? What does Grandpa say?"

"He doesn't know what to think. From what Noah said while we were waiting for word from Eli's CO, he's never felt anything like it. He felt like he was there. Walked over to Eli, screamed at him and yelled that he'd better not be dead, told him to get his ass up and live and everything. But while he was out, Zanny said he didn't make a sound."

Sydney could tell her mother was almost as shaken by Noah's episode as she was by Eli's injury. "Poor guy. That had to be awful."

"You, miss, are the master of the understatement. Mom needs me, so I'd better go. You two be careful."

"We will. Love you, Mom. Give everyone a hug for me."

"Love you, too. And I will."

Sydney slid the phone into the console, then slumped back in her seat, drained.

Sawyer was visibly shaken as he took a long drink from his travel mug. "My God," he said quietly. "How in the hell does he live with something like that?"

"I don't know. But he manages, somehow. Hearing that, I can understand why he's reluctant to date. And I know he's long said he didn't want kids. His 'gift' is genetic and he doesn't want to pass it on."

"I think, if I were like Noah, I'd feel the same way. It's one thing to know you might hand down your eye color or the shape of your nose, but that? I'd be terrified of sentencing my children to that."

Sydney wondered how he'd feel if he knew the truth about her family, that Noah's ability wasn't by far the most strange, even though it seemed the most difficult to endure. "It's something that gives a person pause."

Sawyer's glance was speculative. "You said it was genetic, what he can do."

"It is. It comes through Zanny's line."

"But that's not the only 'gift' in your family, is it?" He tapped his fingers on the steering wheel.

As much as she trusted him, Sydney had to just about force herself to answer to the affirmative, the habit of protecting the truth was so deeply ingrained. "No, it isn't.

I told you Uncle John has a thing with numbers. I really meant he has a thing with numbers, not just that he's super smart or something. Ben can read plants and flowers. Pip is a Cupid—literally. Do you have any idea how many couples she's put together over the years?"

Sawyer laughed. "I did notice she seems to take an interest in pairing people up. What about you?"

"I can pick up health issues with some people, but not everyone. I can't read you, for example, or Grandpa or Noah. And there are other things, but they're not my secrets to reveal. Mom's the only normal one of us. Well, and Grandma. Even though most of the abilities we have seem to come from the Campbells, Grandpa does try to put some of the odder talents on her."

"I've read his books, your grandfather's."

Sydney was stunned. "I never would have guessed that."

He nodded. "They're good. Even for us big kids." This time his look was more assessing than speculative. "Interesting premise, a young boy who can shape-shift into a deer and his friends who can do the same."

Sydney looked out the window, trying not to react overtly. "Very interesting premise. He takes inspiration straight from Appalachian folklore."

"Hmmm. I did wonder."

He knew. She could tell he knew, or at the very least, he suspected. But like she'd told him, those weren't her secrets to reveal.

They moved on to other topics, but in the back of her mind she kept circling around and around the idea that he knew, and he hadn't demanded details or called her crazy. She didn't quite know what to make of that.

She'd never told Adam about her family's abilities. She'd held back that part of herself, not wanting him to think she was a lunatic at first. And then, there just didn't seem to be any need to tell him since they didn't plan to have kids straight away. In the end, keeping that secret had been the right decision.

But she couldn't help wonder how it would feel to be completely open and honest about who and what her family was with a man. With a partner. She couldn't imagine what that would be like, and she didn't know if she'd ever experience it, but she didn't try to pretend it wasn't something she didn't want, whether it was with Sawyer or someone else.

CHAPTER THIRTY-ONE

SYDNEY HAD FALLEN ASLEEP ON him a few miles shy of the Kentucky border, and she hadn't woken up until they'd reached the farm. Sawyer figured instead of disturbing her, he'd just borrow her car and take it back to her house to get his truck, or bum a ride with someone back to town.

Instead, he ended up staying at the farm for a while, having food and helping pass the time.

John had called shortly after they'd arrived at the farm to let the family know more about Eli's condition. "He was doing a test drive on a vehicle they were having problems with, and they wrecked. It flipped over on top of him. His left lower leg is crushed, and they don't know if they can save it. He's got several broken bones on top of that, a concussion... He's lucky to be alive."

"I guess they'll be gone a while," Sawyer said as they ate, "given the extent of Eli's injuries."

"Probably," Archer said from across the table. "That leg sounds like the worst of it."

Logan nodded. "They should know soon whether they can preserve it or not. Even if they can, though, I doubt he'll regain full use. Not with a crushing injury."

Logan's own career in the Army had ended after he'd been hurt during an explosion. From what Sawyer knew, he still had problems from time to time related to the wounds.

"What's being done about Fig?" Sydney asked. "If Noah's going to be gone for weeks, she's going to need someone to take her. Or move in his house for a while."

"I'd vote for the former versus the latter," Owen said. "As much as Noah would appreciate someone caring for her, I don't think he'd like the invasion of privacy."

Emma laughed. "Babysitting it is, then. I'd love to have her but with Carter's allergies..."

"I can take her," Sydney said. "I miss having cats."

Sawyer glanced at her. "You did have cats growing up, didn't you?"

"Mm-hmmm. Huff and Puff. Caleb gave them to us when I was five."

"We didn't even realize Carter was allergic, since he'd grown up around them," Emma said. "But after we lost them, while we were thinking about getting a couple of kittens, his allergies cleared up like you wouldn't believe. After seeing that, it was hard to justify bringing cats back in the house."

"As soon as he leaves for college, though, it's game on," Archer teased, causing her to roll her eyes at him as everyone laughed.

"I'll stop by his house and get her on the way home. He should have everything she needs down there," Sydney said.

"He does," Owen told her. "He said to let whoever ended up getting her know that he put her a bag together."

"Of course he did. That cat's like a child to him," Sarah said. "Sweet boy."

Sydney stood. "No offense to anyone, but I'm beat. I know Sawyer's probably itching to get back to his place. I think we'll head out, if that's okay with you," she told him.

"That's fine."

Sarah insisted on putting plates together for them. "Everyone's been stopping by. Once they heard about Eli, they wanted to help. We have more than enough food here, and you two are taking some of it."

By the time they left, they had a box of food to share

between them. The drive to Noah's took all of a minute, and when they went in, Fig met them at the door, meowing.

"She sounds worried," Sawyer said as Sydney picked her up and cuddled her.

"She probably is. He's never gone this long. Hey, sweetie. Your daddy's okay. He just had to take a trip. He'll be back, but in the meantime, how about you and I spend some time together?"

To his amazement, the cat was snuggling up to her much the same way he'd seen babies do to their mothers. "Wow. Look at that."

Sydney's smile was tense. "She's shaking under this purr. Oh, Fig, it'll be okay."

Finding the cat's bag was easy—it was a large backpack stuffed full, set up on the counter under the cabinet that held the marinara. Her carrier was beside it. A hastily scrawled note was attached, and Sawyer read it as Sydney comforted Fig. He chuckled.

"Looks like he had you all pegged. '*Syd, I figure you're the one who'll get her. I packed her enough food for two weeks. She gets a full can every day split into thirds. Yes, you have to refrigerate it. Warm it up just a bit and add water before you give it to her. No table scraps, but you can give her a little dry food in the evenings as a treat. Make sure she has fresh water and litter every day, please. I've listed the brand she likes, along with her vet's phone number for the office and for emergencies. Oh, and help yourself to the marinara and pesto. I'll owe you for this. N.*'"

"No, he won't."

Sawyer shook his head. "Stubborn, the lot of you. Do you want some marinara?"

"I'll come back for it if I do. I'd feel awful taking it now." She sat Fig down and headed toward a door across the room. "I'll get her box ready to go. Can you see if there are any trash bags under the sink? We'll just put it in one of those, part and parcel."

They got Fig and her belongings in the car. Halfway back to Hazard, Sydney's phone rang.

"It's Danny. Hey. Did you get my texts?" She listened to his response, nodding. "Yeah, we're on our way back to my house now. I have Fig with me. Okay. See you then."

"I'm surprised he wasn't at the farm," Sawyer said once she'd hung up.

"He was out there last night, and he would have been this morning, but he was tied up with a planning committee. He's going to swing by my house here in a bit." She let out a rough sigh. "I worry about him."

"How come?"

"You know why. Same reason I've always worried. He's struggling with whether or not to come out. I think he needs to from a personal perspective, but I'm scared to death it will destroy his career. I know a lot of churches in larger cities are okay with having gay pastors, but this is Hazard. Even if he has taken a vow of celibacy, it might not be enough to preserve his job."

"I don't envy him that decision," Sawyer said.

"Neither do I. I'm sorry we had to cut the conference short."

He scowled. "Stop right there."

She tilted her head to the side, her hair sliding over her shoulder with the movement. "What? I am. I could have driven home by myself."

They'd reached her house, and Sawyer pulled the car in beside his truck. When he shut the motor off, Fig piped up from the back. Sawyer glanced at her, then turned his attention back to Sydney.

"You Campbells are constantly telling me I'm part of the family. Do you honestly think I'd have let you come back here alone? Even if I wasn't close to you all, it'd be a lousy thing to do."

She shook her head, though her lips were turned up into a tiny smile. "Gibson, thank you, not Campbell. But point taken." When Fig meowed again, Sydney reached into the backseat. "I guess I'd better get her inside. Do you want to come in?"

"I'll help you get your stuff in."

"The good news here is that the house is mostly still vacant, so there won't be that much catproofing to do. The bad news? I'm sure she'll find something at three a.m. I should have put up."

Once her things were inside and Fig's box and food were set up, Sawyer knew he needed to go. But he didn't want to leave. He wanted to linger. He couldn't come up with a good excuse to stay, however.

"Let me know if there's any news?" he asked as they walked to the front door.

"I will." Sydney fiddled with the doorknob. "Thank you."

He had to shove his hands in his pockets to keep from grabbing her and kissing the life out of her. If Danny hadn't pulled up to the curb just then, he would have.

"See you Monday, then."

"Okay."

Walking away and getting in his truck was difficult. He had to tamp down the strong desire to go back in to Sydney. But Danny was with her, and she didn't need Sawyer anymore.

"You'd do well to remember that, old man. She's got more than enough people in her life to serve just about any role she needs. The two of you might pass the time on a trip, she might even flirt with you or end up in your bed, but that's all it will ever be. That's all you can let it be."

For the first time in years, he resented the restrictions he'd put on himself. Lee's words, as well as that damned kiss and holding Sydney close last night, were tearing through his reserve like well-aimed cannonballs. He might find himself in more trouble than he could handle if he wasn't careful, and no safe way out.

CHAPTER THIRTY-TWO

By Monday, Sawyer had managed to get enough emotional distance from Sydney to get a grip on his feelings. Thinking to get an early start, he headed to the office an hour ahead of time. As he drove, he couldn't help but think about how empty the passenger seat was.

The last thing he was expecting was to find Sydney already there, hard at work, when he walked in the door. He stopped, staring at her in blank confusion.

"What are you doing here?" he asked as he convinced his body to move and closed the door. He set his coffee and the bag containing his bear claw on her desk.

"Working. I couldn't sleep, and I needed to stay busy. There are only so many times I can clean my house. Daddy came and got Fig since he's off this week—he couldn't resist the allure of a temporary cat—so I was twiddling my thumbs."

"What about Carter's allergies?" Sawyer studied her closely. She looked tired, and he guessed she probably hadn't slept well since before they'd left Tennessee.

"Daddy gave him some antihistamines and dared him to sneeze. He really misses having cats. Said this would be a good trial run with Carter to see how he did." She yawned, her eyes watering as she covered her mouth. "Sorry."

Sawyer crossed his arms and donned his best stern face. "When did you get here?"

Sydney tried her best to look innocent, but she couldn't pull it off. "Um... early?"

"Sydney..."

"Six?"

"Six? This morning?" He was appalled.

Shamefaced, she nodded. "I couldn't sleep."

"When did you sleep last? Really sleep, I mean."

Her cheeks flushed, and she shrugged, looking at her computer instead of at him. "Before Tennessee."

Sawyer let out a half groan, half sigh. "Stubborn. Come on."

It was her turn to scowl. "Where are we going?"

He stopped by the edge of her desk, holding his hand out. "I'm putting you to bed. That's why the cot's here, in case I have to stay late or need a nap. Come on."

"Sawyer, you can't just put me to bed. I'm not a child," she protested, even as she yawned again, this time so widely her jaw popped.

He lifted his eyebrows and didn't say a word.

After a full minute, she rolled her eyes and stood. "Fine. I'll lie down, but I won't go to sleep."

"I'm sure you won't, but I'll feel better."

He followed her down the hall between the offices and the conference room to a small storage room located behind his office. It was just big enough for a table with a lamp, a cot, and a large wire shelf.

Sydney sat on the edge of the cot with a huff. "Okay. I'm in here. Scoot," she said, waving her hands toward him.

Instead, Sawyer crossed the room and turned the lamp on, then switched the overhead light off. "Glasses off, shoes off, feet up."

Once she'd complied, he unfolded the quilt at the foot of the cot and covered her with it.

"You call me stubborn," she said. "You should look in the mirror."

"I don't know what you're talking about," he said, laughing. "Do you need anything?"

"Not to be mother henned would be nice."

He ignored the complaint and pulled up a footstool, sitting. A lock of hair had fallen onto her cheek, and he pushed it back behind her ear. "I thought Eli was doing better, all things considered," he said softly.

"He is. Even with the loss of the leg, John said he's healing better than they'd hoped. Part of being a Campbell. But I worry about him psychologically. You know how Eli is—star athlete, mountain-climbing adrenaline junkie. What happens now?"

"I don't know. It's going to be up to him. If he's nearly as stubborn as the rest of you, though, he's got a damned good chance."

She laughed, even though tears were slipping from the corners of her eyes. Sawyer wanted to pull her into his arms and hold her until she was okay. He settled for wiping the dampness away with his thumb.

"Try to get some sleep," he whispered. "I'll be right out here if you need me."

"I'm going to remember this for when you get sick," she warned him softly as he went out the door.

"Yeah, yeah. I don't get sick."

"You just tempted fate. Hope you know that, buddy." Her eyelids were drooping, and he knew she'd be out as soon as he left her alone.

"Sleep, imp. Argue with me later." He pulled the door halfway closed and headed to his office. He'd get what he needed and work at Sydney's desk today, at least until she'd gotten some rest. And he'd do his damnedest to only check on her once an hour or so, instead of every ten minutes like he was tempted to do. Never mind his desire to watch over her while she slept or crawl in the cot with her. Those were urges he'd pretend didn't exist.

"You're getting awfully damned good at pretending

lately," he muttered to himself. But he didn't know what else he could do. Short of giving in to the urges, which he wasn't prepared for, he didn't have a lot of choice in the matter.

Emma came in around ten, her smile so sunny Sawyer knew she had good news.

"What is it?" he asked, laying his pen down on Sydney's desk.

"He's coming home late this week, they think. Well, back to the States, I should say. He'll go to Walter Reed for the rest of his recuperation." She was so happy, she clapped her hands. "Oh, thank God."

"That's great! Will he be able to have visitors?"

She nodded. "A whole convoy of Campbells. We'll have to stagger things, but yes. We'll be able to go see him."

"I'm so glad. That'll relieve a lot of minds," Sawyer said. He came to his feet and stretched. "I thought they closed Walter Reed."

"The old hospital, yes. There's a new facility, though, same name. Where's Syd?"

He directed her down the hall. "Sound asleep. I guess she came in at six this morning, and when I got here at eight, she was practically asleep at her desk. I made her come back here, and she's been out ever since." He stood back so Emma could ease the storage-room door open.

She watched Sydney for a minute, her lips compressed in a tight line, before pulling the door back around. Using her chin, she gestured back toward the office.

"She's had a rough few weeks, you know," she said once they were back in the reception area. "Even though not all of it's been bad. She loves this job, and she's happy to have met her brothers. But the rest of it? It's worked on her some."

"I know. I've tried to help as much as I could," he said.

He sat on the edge of Sydney's desk and picked up the paperweight she kept there just for him to play with. "I don't know what I'd do without her. John said I'd be saying that before long."

Emma smiled. "She's grown up quite nicely, I think. You always hope your kids will, and you do everything you can to walk that line between discipline and love. It's still a crapshoot sometimes."

"She's definitely not what I expected. And I don't mean that as an insult," he hurried to say. "Just... you and Archer should be proud of her."

"We are. I think if she can start dodging some of these punches life seems determined to throw at her, she'll be happy. And that's all we've ever wanted for her, to be happy. Like Daddy's fond of saying, it doesn't matter if our kids are world-famous photographers or if they're garbage collectors, as long as they're happy."

Sawyer chuckled. "I've heard Owen say that a time or two."

"I guess I'll head back to the shop. I wouldn't let her sleep much longer. She'll be ticked off if you do."

"I figured another hour, tops. Your daughter's got a mind of her own, in case you hadn't noticed. Thought I'd mention that," he said, tongue-in-cheek. "I'm sure it's never occurred to you before and you have no idea where she gets it from."

Emma's grin was both proud and sassy. "Comes from Archer. Have her call me when she's conscious. Thanks for looking out for her, Sawyer."

"Don't mention it."

After she left, he headed back down the hall to look in on Sydney again. She was still sleeping peacefully, not having moved from the spot he'd left her in hours earlier. He hated to disturb her, but he had to use the restroom, which was right next door to the storage room. Flushing the toilet would probably wake her up. That might not be a bad thing.

Even though he'd told Emma he planned to give her another hour, he figured earlier might be better. If she stayed asleep much longer, he'd be tempted to wake her with a kiss, and that simply would not do.

CHAPTER THIRTY-THREE

FRIDAY FOUND SYDNEY STILL TRYING to recover from her mortification at having slept for so long Monday morning. Coming into work when Sawyer would be taking the day off helped.

"We're caught up, and I'm supposed to be retired. I'm going to sit at home and do absolutely nothing," he'd told her Thursday afternoon. "You don't have to work tomorrow."

She'd glared at him without a word, and he'd shrugged. "Have fun, then."

Now, as it approached noon, she was running out of things to work on. A package had come that he'd been expecting. Since he'd told her to call him if it came in, she did.

"It's here, Boss," she said in a sing-song voice when he answered her call. "What shall I do with it?"

"Bring it out here. It's a part for this computer," he said.

"Okay. Where exactly is here? You're going to have to give me your address now," she told him with an evil cackle.

Sawyer snorted and told her the address. "Do you mind bringing it after lunch? Just shut the office down for the day."

"Fine. I'll see you in a bit, then. I'll grab something to eat and head that way. Do you want me to bring you anything?"

"Nope. I'm good."

As she called an order for a salad in to the bakery next

door, she couldn't deny the thrill of anticipation that went down her spine. She was going to get to see Sawyer's refuge, his home. Finally! Curiosity had been eating her alive.

He'd been very solicitous since Monday, not treating her with kid gloves exactly, but he'd made very sure she knew he was there for her if she needed him. It had taken more willpower than she'd known she possessed not to take him up on that offer.

"Begging the man to let me sleep in his bed so I can rest isn't exactly a great way to keep my job," she said to herself as she drove to the park to eat her lunch. "Although..."

She had to wonder. Sawyer hadn't been flirting with her, necessarily, but there was no disguising the heat that was building between them. And there was the kiss and dance to consider.

"That was probably an aberration due to proximity and distance from home." She'd told herself that a thousand times. She wasn't sure if she believed it or not.

With her lunch finished and his address programmed into her GPS, she hit the road. In fifteen minutes, she was easing along a narrow blacktop road looking for the gate he'd told her about. "I've seen driveways wider than this road," she muttered. "Good thing there isn't much traffic."

At last, she found it. The red metal gate was open, but there were prominent No Trespassing and Private Property signs posted all around the driveway.

"I hope I'm in the right place, or else I might end up getting myself shot. Here goes nothing."

The gravel driveway itself climbed slightly in elevation, winding around a shallow curve with a small creek running beside it. When she came out of the curve, a clearing opened ahead of her to a meadow of sorts. A rustic but well-kept log cabin was at the end of the driveway, a two-car attached garage on one side. She could just see the edges of a pond behind the house.

Parking in front of one of the garage stalls, she rolled

her windows down, then grabbed the package, her phone, her keys, and got out. Birds calling and squirrels chattering from the trees surrounding the clearing were the only sounds. The feel about the place was as peaceful as her grandparents' farm, and she tipped her face up to the sun, breathing in the clean air.

"What do you think?" Sawyer asked.

Sydney jumped, shrieking with surprise. She fumbled the package, but luckily, he was standing close enough that he caught it before it hit the ground.

"You scared me to death!" she scolded as he laughed, his eyes crinkling at the corners. "I'm gonna put a bell on you, I swear I am. Geez, Sawyer."

He grinned, completely unrepentant. "Come on in. I'll give you the tour."

Her heart was pounding, both from the fright and from the fact that the man was only wearing worn denim cut-offs. He was barefoot and a bit scruffy, having apparently decided to forego shaving that morning. And it was all she could do to keep her hands off of him.

As they walked through the cabin, she tried to focus on what he was showing her. "I can see Noah's touches here and there," she said. "He does good work. This is a very nice place."

"Yes, he does, and thanks. Here's the kitchen." Sawyer set the package down on the end of the counter. "And here's my patio." He held the french door open for her to pass through. "Pool's over there."

She looked to the right side of the stamped concrete pad. "A swim spa?"

"Yeah. It was an investment, but it was worth every penny. I'll probably try to enclose it this winter, though. Swimming in the snow and freezing temperatures lost its novelty pretty fast last year."

"I'd say. This is beautiful." She tried to take it all in. The valley the house sat in was wide, opening up more than one might have expected from the drive in. And the back of the house itself faced the meadow, which widened as it climbed toward the head of the hollow. A couple of hundred feet back from the house was the pond, complete with a long dock and a shady weeping willow tree. "I'd never leave if I lived here."

"I don't know about never. It gets a little close after a week or two," he teased.

"Do you fish out of the pond?"

"Nope. There're no fish in my pond."

She laughed. "That reminds me of a TV show Daddy loved to watch a few years back."

"Stargate, by chance?" he asked with a wink.

"Yes, as a matter of fact. He got me and Graydon hooked on it, too."

"I have the whole series on DVD."

"It's a good series."

They shared a smile.

"So why don't you stock it, if you don't mind my asking?" she said.

"What am I going to do with a pond full of fish? I won't eat them. The lack of fish doesn't stop me from dropping a line out there now and again. That's what I was getting ready to do, actually."

"Oh. I'll go, then. Guess I'll see you Monday?"

He stopped her with a hand on her arm. "I didn't mean it that way. You should stick around. Get some fresh air."

Sydney bit her lip, looking toward the pond. "I don't want to interrupt your day off."

"You aren't. What would you like to drink?" He listed several options.

"Tea's fine."

"Coming right up."

"Um, could I use the restroom?" she asked as they stepped back inside.

"Sure. I'll get your tea and take it outside, meet you out there."

As she washed her hands after she was done, she considered her outfit. Dressy navy-blue shorts, a sheer floral shirt over a tank top, and flip-flops. Discreet gold jewelry at her ears and neck and very little makeup.

"I doubt there's much chance he'll be throwing you down on the bed, more's the pity," she told her reflection as she took her hair down, shaking it out before repinning it. "But at least you're comfortable."

She was turning into the very person she had been afraid of becoming. The love-struck assistant in lust with her boss. If she didn't do something soon to alleviate her growing attraction to the man, she was going to embarrass herself beyond redemption.

"Asking him for a pity fuck definitely would be a bad idea, Syd. You'd end up jobless and no better off than you are now. Suck it up, girl."

Still, as she went through the house, she couldn't help but wonder what Sawyer's reaction would be if she went to his bedroom and stripped down, then crawled between his sheets. Part of her regretted that she was too chicken to find out. Part of her recklessly wanted to do it. And she was afraid the reckless part would soon overwhelm her sense of caution and reason, and then where would she be?

CHAPTER THIRTY-FOUR

SEDUCING YOUR HOUSEGUEST, WHO WAS only there to deliver a package, was not a good idea. Sawyer had to keep telling himself that as he waited for Sydney to join him on the dock. He hadn't been able to resist inviting her to stay. And he couldn't help but think about that promise he'd made her in Tennessee—that someday they'd have a long talk. In a private setting. Which his house most assuredly was.

God, he was in trouble.

He'd set up a second chair beside his on the wide leg of the dock that jutted out underneath the tree. The leaves and branches dipped down toward the water, providing a curtain of greenery that made the spot even more private, as well as creating a welcome shade from the hot early afternoon sun.

"It's warm out here today," Sydney said as she came up the dock toward him. "Feels good."

"Yeah, it does. We've been lucky so far this summer that we've not had much heat and humidity." He gave an inward cringe. They were talking about the weather. He hadn't thought he'd been out of the dating game *that* long.

She settled in beside him and stretched her legs out, sighing. "I don't know when I last took the time to sit down and do nothing. You may have to run me off later."

Sawyer laughed. "Nah. I'll just make you help me cook dinner."

"Pfft. That's nothing." She dropped her phone into the chair's cup holder and waved a hand lazily. "I could do that in my sleep."

"Your pole is beside your chair if you want to 'fish,'" he said.

"Maybe. You might have to show me what to do. It's been a few years since I did this."

For the next couple of hours, they passed the time chatting here and there, with comfortable silences falling between the conversation. When Sydney's line jerked, she nearly jumped out of her seat from shock.

"I thought you said there weren't any fish here." She stood up to get a better grip on the pole, whatever was on the other end pulling hard.

"There aren't," Sawyer insisted, coming to his feet. "Maybe it's a turtle."

"Well, it's definitely something. This is ridiculous." She was struggling to stay on her feet.

Sawyer lunged out to help her. But before he could reach her, she was yanked forward, stumbling... and went straight over the edge of the dock. She hung in midair for an endless moment, her arms and legs flailing, before plunging straight down into the pond with a huge splash.

"Oh, shit."

She surfaced almost immediately, her glasses half off her face, hair dripping down into her eyes. Gasping, she struggled to clear her face off as she treaded water.

"Are you okay?" Sawyer hunkered down beside her. He was doing his damnedest not to laugh, but his mind kept replaying that moment in time when she'd hung above the water. "I'm s-sorry," he stammered, covering his mouth with his hand.

"Don't you dare laugh! Oh, dear God, this water is cold. Eeeekkk!" Her screech was so loud, it echoed around the meadow. "Something touched my foot. Get me out of here!"

Through his laughter, Sawyer managed to reach down

and grab her upraised hands. Giving a mighty tug, he lifted her out of the water. But once she'd found her footing, he doubled over, overtaken by mirth.

Soaked to the skin, dripping with pond water, arms held out from her sides, Sydney stood glaring at him, her mouth open with shock. "You... you jackass. This is not funny."

"Oh, yes, it is," he snickered. He couldn't look at her. Every time he did, mirth hit him again. He apologized again, but he couldn't stop laughing.

"If I thought I could push you in there, buddy, you'd get a dunking. Damn it, I lost a shoe." She held up her remaining flip flop, gazing at it mournfully. "I haven't had those a month."

Sawyer finally got a handle on his amusement. "At least you didn't drown your phone."

She huffed out an aggravated breath and picked the device up from the chair. "There's that. Well, this was fun. You know how to show a girl a good time, I'll say that." She started past him.

That sobered him up. "Wait—what? You aren't leaving, are you? What about dinner?"

"Sawyer. Look at me. I'll have to borrow a couple of towels to get home."

He followed her up the dock. "I can find you something to wear. You can use my shower."

She shook her head. "I appreciate the offer, but no. I've done enough damage for one day. I'd hate to tempt fate."

This was not how he'd envisioned the day and evening going. The day that had seemed so perfect turned sour, leaving him disgruntled and bereft. But he wasn't going to beg her to stay, though, when she clearly was intent on leaving. However, that fate she'd been concerned about tempting stepped in to give him a reprieve. When she got to her car and tried to unlock the door with her key fob, it didn't work.

"Are you kidding me?" No matter how hard she pressed

the button, nothing. "At least I had the sense to leave the windows down. I've got a spare set in my purse. Do you mind getting it for me so I don't drip everywhere?"

Yes, he minded. He didn't want her to go. But he didn't say that, just reached in and snagged the bag's strap. "I'll get those towels. Are you sure you don't want to take a shower first?"

"I'm sure."

When he got back with the towels, she was leaning against the car, talking on the phone.

"No, Daddy, I understand. No, I don't want you to drive all the way back here. It's not that big a deal. Just wait until he's finished and have him call me. Hang on." She covered the phone and gave Sawyer a tense smile. "Graydon took my car down to the store at the mouth of the holler Sunday, and he used my spare keys. I can't find them, and he's in a ballgame in Virginia."

"Oh." Sawyer pressed his lips together trying to stop a smile from forming. "So you're stuck."

"It appears that I am."

"Guess you'll take that shower, huh?"

She narrowed her eyes. "You're enjoying this."

He shrugged, grinning. "Maybe a little."

She went back to the call, shaking her head. "Are you still there? Yeah, I'm okay. No, I told you, I'm at a friend's house. I promise you it isn't a big deal. Just have the critter call me when he's off the field. Okay, love you."

"I'd offer to give you a ride home," Sawyer said, turning to look at the garage, "but you parked behind me."

"Of course I did," she said with a tired laugh. "And there's no room for you to back out and turn. Lovely."

"You're going to give me a complex. Do you want to leave that badly?"

"No, it isn't that. I'm sorry—I didn't mean it that way. I feel like I'm imposing on your day off."

Sawyer stepped closer to her, pushing her glasses up on

her nose with a gentle finger. "You aren't. It's nice to have company. Now come on, let's get you in the shower and changed. Do you want to wash your clothes?"

She glanced down at herself. "If you don't mind. I'd at least like to rinse them out. I can probably do that in the tub or sink. I don't want to get your washer dirty."

"Okay. Come with me." He led her in the house to the bedroom, directing her into the bathroom. "I'll get you something to wear. Some running shorts and an Evans Investigations promotional T-shirt should do it. What size shirt do you want?"

"Large, please. Do you have a tank top I could wear underneath?"

He realized she was concerned about her breasts when she crossed her arms over her chest. "I don't. Sorry."

"It's okay."

He thought about telling her it was all right, that he wouldn't look, but he could neither keep that promise nor embarrass her by saying it. Instead, he pretended ignorance as he got the clothing.

"Here you go. Shampoo and soap are in the shower, towels are here," he said, placing them on the counter. "Yell if you need me."

"Thank you."

He headed to the kitchen while she got cleaned up, finally allowing his excitement to come through. Sydney's reluctance to stay tempered that somewhat, but if she really was only concerned about putting him out, he figured he could allay those fears with a little effort, and he knew just where to start. He opened a cabinet and pulled down one of the jars of marinara he'd bartered from Noah a couple of weeks earlier. There was a bottle of nice red wine in the small wine cellar cabinet in the back of his pantry that would pair up perfectly with the sauce. Sawyer'd been looking for an excuse to open it, and having Sydney stay for dinner would suit nicely.

As he built the dinner menu in his head, he tapped his fingers on the counter. The afternoon and evening would be the perfect opportunity for him to see if taking his relationship with Sydney to the next level—to his bedroom—was going to happen or not. He'd stopped in the local box superstore and picked up condoms just in case as his stash had some age on them. He didn't want to get ahead of himself, but neither did he want to be caught with his pants down.

"Guess we'll see," he said in the quiet kitchen as the shower shut off. He'd not been so nervous about a date in years, and at the same time, anticipation of what might happen was building. It was an odd mix of feelings, but it was better than what he'd been going through. One way or another, his gut was telling him there'd be resolution this evening. He could hardly wait.

CHAPTER THIRTY-FIVE

SYDNEY'S MORTIFICATION OVER NAPPING AT work was dwarfed by her humiliation at having fallen into Sawyer's pond. He'd been amused, obviously, but she'd wanted to sink through the deck and into the muck of the pond. And when her key didn't work, and she couldn't find the spare? She'd read romance novels with better intentional setups than this.

"What if he thinks I did it on purpose?" she muttered as she scrubbed her hair. She couldn't help but think about the disastrous kiss when she was nineteen, when she'd laid in wait for Sawyer in the parking lot of the state police post and kissed him. It had been a minor miracle no one had seen them.

The shower was hot, steamy, and she didn't want to get out. Not just because of her embarrassment, but because by using his body wash—who'd have thought the man used body wash?—and shampoo, she'd engulfed herself in a Sawyer-scented cloud. It was absolute torture to be so close to the man's belongings in such an intimate way.

Knowing she had to get out or else risk Sawyer thinking she was crazy, she turned the water off and reached for one of the thick towels he'd given her. She had to give herself a stern talking to in order to force herself to get out of the shower, to get dressed in the clothes he'd given her. The shorts were miles too large, even though they'd probably fit him rather snugly, but they had a drawstring waist so she was able to tighten them well enough. But the shirt... Sydney groaned.

"You'd think God would have given me a few more inches in height to balance these out," she whispered to her reflection as she studied the way the T-shirt draped over her breasts. Some women could go without a bra and no one would notice. Sydney was not one of those women. She was very lush on top, and to keep from looking too provocative, she had to wear something. If she and Sawyer were intimate, the sensual look would be a positive asset. But they weren't intimate.

"Nothing you can do about it," she told herself as she rinsed her bra and panties out in the sink. She wrapped them in the second towel and rolled it up to dry them, hoping against hope she could get enough dampness out to at least put the bra back on. But the cups were lightly padded, and if she wore the bra, she'd end up with two large wet splotches on the front of the shirt. She'd feel more exposed and ridiculous than she already did.

Resigned to the fact that she'd give Sawyer a bit of a show one way or another, she rinsed out her shorts and shirts and dried them the same way she'd done with the underwear. Finished, she wrapped the entire outfit in the least-damp towel and left the bathroom in search of Sawyer. She found him standing in the living room, looking out over the backyard. He'd put a shirt on, more was the pity.

"I'll need to borrow the towel," she told him.

"That's fine. Do you need anything else?" he asked as he turned.

"No. I'll put these in the car to dry."

"We can probably retrieve your shoe," he said. "I've got a net in the garage. I'll get it and see if I can fish the shoe out."

"Thank you."

By the time she came back in from the car, he was on his way to the house from the pond, a triumphant grin on his face. "Got it!" He held the flip flop up like a trophy, then handed it to her. "That should help."

Sydney couldn't hold on to her discomfort entirely in light of his pride in the accomplishment, and she smiled. "That does. Once again, I'm in your debt."

"So how long did Archer say it would be before Graydon's out of his game? Not that I'm trying to rush you off, but I'm curious."

"A couple of hours. It'd just started when I called."

It was just approaching four now.

"How hungry are you?" he asked.

She shrugged, keeping her arms carefully crossed. "I'm okay. I had a salad for lunch, nothing heavy. Why?"

"Because I'm starving. And I may have some marinara in there that came from Noah."

"You do?"

"Mm-hmmm. I kinda called him and ordered some after that first jar. It cost me a whole case of bear claws, but the sauce was worth it. And I might have some gourmet tortellini and crusty garlic bread to go with it."

Sydney's mouth was watering at the thought. "What are we waiting for?"

Sawyer laughed. "Not a thing."

In the kitchen, they worked side by side putting the meal together. Sawyer opened a bottle of wine and let it breathe, and Sydney gathered the ingredients for a salad. He'd given her carte blanche to pull whatever she wanted from the fridge.

"I've also got some unbelievable manchego in there," he told her as she was getting things together. "We could slice it. And there's mizithra to go on the pasta."

"Mizithra? Where in the world did you get that?" She was stunned by the eclectic and varied foods he had stocked.

"Lexington. I usually try to go down once a month and hit the bigger grocery stores. Just because I'm a vegetarian doesn't mean I like to eat boring food."

"I see that."

"There's deer salami in the deli drawer if you want some, and regular."

Sydney had to swallow her reaction down. Deer salami. Oh, God. "Have you ever had Rachel over for dinner?" she asked as she got the cheese out, leaving the meat behind.

"A time or two. Why?"

"Do me a favor. Don't ever offer her deer salami. Or deer anything."

Sawyer frowned. "Okay. Why?"

How in the world to explain? "She's pretty attached to the creatures. My whole family is, as far as that goes. Please tell me you don't hunt."

He laid his knife down and wiped his hands on a dish towel. "I don't. Never saw the sport in it. The whole family, huh?"

Sydney cleared her throat. "Yeah."

"Uh-huh. Okay. Because of Owen's books?"

"That's part of it," she said, focusing on the salad prep. She'd never been able to lie worth a damn, and she hoped he didn't come right out and ask her about shape-shifting. If he did, the gig was up.

"Makes sense, I suppose." He reached around her, his arm brushing hers, to take a piece of cheese. "Thanks for the warning. I'll have to mention it Lee. He does like to hunt on the rare occasion."

Sydney was horrified. "Oh, boy. Then he and Rachel definitely wouldn't make a good pair." She glanced at him. "He's really interested in her, too. Oh, I hate this."

"She's that opposed to hunting, that she'd not date someone who does? I knew she didn't like it, but that's all. Sounds like this goes a little deeper. Like maybe there's another reason behind the dislike. I can't imagine what that would be, though."

His tone was too casual. Sydney felt hot and cold all over. She'd not been faced with revealing this particular secret since she was a teenager and had confided in Danny. Scooping the cheese up into a row, she put in on the small plate Sawyer had given her, then faced him.

He was watching her, anticipation written all over his face.

"You can't imagine?" she asked dryly.

"Well, I could throw a couple of theories out there, but they might make me sound like a lunatic."

"Spit it out."

The timer beeped for the bread, causing her to jump. She cursed under her breath even as he chuckled and reached for the oven mitts.

"You can read people's medical conditions. Noah can see the dead. Your uncles have some interesting, if not spectacular, abilities. And your entire family has this wall of privacy up that very few people get behind. Who's the deer? Owen? Sarah?"

Sydney stared at him, biting her lip. "That isn't my secret to tell."

A wondrous grin spread across his face and he laughed. "Seriously? That's the secret? I can't believe it."

She spread her hands, admitting nothing. "You're right. You do sound like a lunatic."

But he wasn't deterred. "Son of a gun. I *knew* it was something like this. Ever since I found out about Noah, I've wondered."

He was getting way too big a kick out of his suppositions. Sydney sighed. "You're like a kid in a candy store."

"It isn't every day that you learn mythological creatures exist, and that you know some of them. Although maybe mythological isn't the right word. Creatures of lore might be better." He dipped the tortellini out into bowls, then covered it with sauce and handed it to Sydney to shower with shredded cheese.

"Grandpa's going to want to have a long talk with you," she told him. "Just so you know."

"To make sure I'm worthy of knowing? Or rather, what I suspect I know?"

"Something like that."

He nodded. "Makes sense. Grab the salad?" He picked up the plates and headed to the small table tucked into a nook of the kitchen.

With nothing else to do but go along, Sydney did. As they ate, she could tell he wanted to ask her more questions, but he held back. She was glad—part of her *wanted* to tell him about the family, to see the wonder in his eyes. But until Owen gave the all-clear, she couldn't.

Her phone rang just as they were finishing up, the display showing Carter's picture. "Hmm, okay. Hey. What's up?" she greeted him.

"Gray doesn't have your keys. I put them in your purse. He had his hands full of groceries. Where're you stuck at?"

"They're not in my purse, brat. And never mind where I'm stuck at." She didn't want to tell him, didn't want the family to know she was spending the day and evening at Sawyer's. She wanted to keep it private, close to her heart, at least for a little while.

"Syd, I put 'em in your purse. That ugly green bag hooked on the back of the seat? That's where they are. If you can't find 'em, it's not because of me."

"You... Carter, that's not my purse. That's my emergency bag. You dolt." She crossed her eyes and shook her head as Sawyer grinned from across the table. Standing, she nodded in the direction of the driveway. "Let me see if they're there. If they aren't, the cost for the locksmith is coming out of your allowance." She wasn't about to tell him she had free roadside assistance.

"Oh, come *on*, sis. That's not fair! I didn't do it on purpose."

"How could you think that backpack is a purse?"

"I dunno. I'm fifteen? What do I know about women's

purses?" His voice grew muted, and when the sound cleared, Archer was on the line.

"Syd? Did you find them?"

"I'm looking now." She'd reached the car and was digging through the bag. When her hand closed around the spare key, she gave a relieved sigh. "Got 'em."

Her father laughed. "So I guess you don't need me to call a locksmith? He's pacing, you know. He has plans for that allowance."

"I'm sure he does. No, I'm fine now." She clicked a button to make sure the spare worked, and her lights flashed cheerily. "Lucky for him and Gray, I have a sympathetic friend who fed me and didn't mind my staying later than anticipated."

"Which friend, Danny?"

"Um, no. Not Danny. Just a friend. I'd better go. Thanks, Daddy. How'd Gray do?"

"They lost. But he did well. Not well enough to pull the fat out of the fire, but I'm proud of him."

Sydney laughed. "You'd be proud of him regardless."

"True. Why don't you want me to know who your friend is?"

"I never said that. Gotta go. Love you guys! Be careful coming home." She hung up on him before he could respond, turning to meet Sawyer's speculative amusement.

"You don't want him to know you're here. Why?" He was leaning against the car, arms crossed. The late afternoon sunlight painted him with a gilded brush, highlighting the light-brown flecks in his eyes. The T-shirt he wore did nothing to disguise the muscles in his chest, his arms, his abdomen. If she'd had one of her mother's cameras, Sydney would have been clicking away.

"Partly because I like torturing my family, and speculation about where I am will definitely torture them. Painless torture, mind you. And partly because I'm a rebellious imp who doesn't like answering to authority." She reached into her purse and grabbed a hair tie, then did her hair up in a ponytail.

The other, unmentioned part was because she didn't want to set up any suspicion about her relationship with Sawyer and risk someone saying something to him.

"So are you going to rush off now, or do you want dessert?" he asked.

"Depends on whether you're tired of me or not," she quipped.

His expression sent chills down her spine, but not from fear. There was a lot of heat in that look, and every butterfly in her stomach took flight.

"I think I can put up with you a while longer. Let's go get some cheesecake. It might have to defrost, though."

Implying she'd be here for some time still. She didn't know if she could stand the anticipation.

CHAPTER THIRTY-SIX

In the kitchen, Sawyer got two servings of cheesecake from the freezer and set them out on plates to thaw. When he saw the quirky smile Sydney was watching him with, he shrugged. "What? You know how it is when you're single—either get single-sized portions or eat the whole thing in a sitting."

She snickered. "You don't strike me as the kind of guy who would sit down and eat a whole cheesecake at one time."

"No?" He grinned as he rinsed off some fresh strawberries and started slicing them to use as a topping. "I could do it without blinking. Same thing for ice cream. That's why I don't keep it in the house. What's your weakness?"

"You mean besides strawberry cupcakes? I have a deep-seated fondness for potato chips. Sour cream and cheddar, sour cream and onion... Mmm. Have you ever had crumbled potato chips on ice cream?" When he made a face, she laughed. "I'll take that as a no."

"Why would you do that to ice cream?" Sawyer shook his head and tickled the end of her nose. "That's cruel."

"Don't say that until you've tried it."

There was a little wine left in the bottle and he divided it between their glasses. "So what are we going to do while we wait for this to thaw?"

She glanced at the cheesecake, then at him, her eyes

full of mischief. “Now that I’m not awestruck by the sheer magnitude of being allowed in the sanctuary, I’m going to be nosy.” With a sassy flip of her ponytail, she headed for the living room.

Sawyer trailed behind, giving her room to explore as she ambled along, wineglass in hand, examining his belongings. While she was distracted, he took the opportunity to look his fill of her legs. For someone so short, they were a mile long. The image of those legs wrapped around him had him discreetly adjusting the fit of his pants.

“No music or books?” she said as she studied the painting hanging beside the entertainment center.

“They’re in the office.”

“Ahh... next!” She headed for the hall eagerly, leaving him to follow. “Nice TV, by the way.”

He looked at the fifty-two inch flat screen over his shoulder. “It does the job.”

“Ever watch any movies on it?” she asked, her head tilted to the side as she looked at the framed pictures on one of his bookshelves.

Sawyer bypassed her to sit on the edge of his desk. “Some. Usually in winter. I try to stay busy outside the rest of the year. There’s always something that needs doing on a property this size.” He finished off his wine and set the glass behind him.

“Oh, look at this,” Sydney said. She’d gotten to the picture of him and Nan the day he’d graduated from Kentucky’s trooper academy. “God, Sawyer, you were a baby. And she’s so proud of you. You can see it. I’ll bet she pinched your cheeks and everything.”

He smiled as he remembered the day. “She was pretty excited for me. It was a big deal. New chapter and all that.”

“I’m glad you were able to get a fresh start,” she told him seriously. “After what you went through, you needed one.”

“I can’t argue.”

She sighed, looking at the picture again. “Do you have

any idea how handsome you were in that uniform? Not that you aren't just as handsome now," she assured him cheekily, "but there's something about the uniform..."

Sawyer laughed, incredulous. "Sydney Gibson, you're a closet badge bunny."

Her cheeks were pink when she looked at him. "No. Aside from that one mortifying event when I was nineteen, I would never throw myself at you. I'd just admire you from afar. I still can't believe I did that. Did I ever apologize?"

"No, but none was necessary. I knew you regretted it as soon as it happened."

"That child was so impulsive... It's a miracle she didn't mess up her life more than she did."

She was close enough now that he could touch her and unable to resist the urge, he did. Reaching out, he tugged on her right hand, the hand that wasn't holding the wineglass, and pulled her to him.

"That girl had a lot going for her. She was just young and green. She also had more sense than you're giving her credit for."

"You remember her more fondly than I do, then." She set her glass down next to his, the move bringing them in full contact for a few seconds. "And that wine has loosened my tongue and my inhibitions."

"You've not had that much of it."

She scowled and nudged her glasses up her nose. "Of course I have. There's no other reason for my being so candid."

He grinned. "Have it your way, then. But I wouldn't be giving you a Breathalyzer based on how much you've put away tonight."

When she put her arms around his neck and buried her face in his shoulder, laughing, he was shocked. But he wasn't going to complain. Indeed, he brought his own hands up to her waist, drawing her closer to stand between his legs.

"Do you know what Neala calls a Breathalyzer?" she asked, snorting. "It has nothing to do with a device, everything to do with sucking instead of blowing, and from what she's said, it's gotten her out of several tickets. Oh, my God. I can't believe I told you that." She covered her mouth with her hand, but the mirth still leaked out from her eyes and through her laugh.

Sawyer drew in a sharp breath, every cell in his body becoming electrified as realization dawned. "I—I don't have words."

To his astonishment, instead of lowering her hand back to his chest, she brought it up and traced his lips with soft fingers. "So you've never let a girl out of a ticket by giving her a Breathalyzer?"

"No." He knew cops who had, though. "I'm not surprised Neala would employ that tactic. She's not my favorite person."

"I know."

When they were nineteen, Neala and Danny had gone to a party during summer break. Sydney, who'd had a job at the time and was working, hadn't been invited. Neala'd gotten Danny drunk with the intention of having sex with him despite knowing he was gay. Suffice it to say things hadn't gone well. Danny'd gotten his hands on a gun her step-father had left in his truck, and Neala'd barely managed to keep him from killing himself. She'd called Sydney, who'd rushed to the scene and talked him down.

As Danny hadn't been in any shape to go to his own home, Sydney'd taken him with her. Sawyer'd pulled her over just as a precaution, since it was close to three in the morning when he spotted her driving along. He hadn't expected to find a drunk, suicidal Danny in the car with her. He'd confiscated the gun, then escorted her home and stayed the rest of the night to help Archer and Emma sort through the mess.

"If it had been anyone else that night, we would have

been in a world of hurt. Did I ever say thank you?" she asked him now.

"A few times. I'm just glad it was me that night, not someone else. You would have been in real trouble."

Her smile carried a bit of sadness. "I know. Daddy actually put his foot down at that point, forbade me from having anything to do with her, even though I was an adult. I was happy to comply. I've still not forgiven her for that, even though Danny has. She has issues. Her childhood was rough, and she never has figured out that she has to let it go, that she has to choose not to be a victim any longer. I heard from her last week."

"What'd she want?"

"To reconnect, she said," her voice distracted as she followed the line of his jaw with her fingers. "You know, you kissed me in Tennessee."

"I did."

"When I kissed you all those years ago, it was terribly awkward. Tennessee... wasn't."

"No. I wouldn't use awkward to describe that kiss," he told her huskily.

"How would you describe it?" she asked boldly, her eyes meeting his for the first time since she'd stepped into his arms.

Sawyer reached up and removed her glasses, folding them carefully. He put them on the desk, then slid one hand into her hair, the other going back to her waist. "Tempting. Taunting, maybe. Entirely too short. And something that most definitely bears repeating." With that, he kissed her.

Unlike in Tennessee, where he'd had to be mindful of their audience, his only concern here was going too far, too fast for Sydney's taste. But as she met him more than halfway, immediately taking the kiss into the red-hot territory, he knew that wasn't an issue. Instead, they might burn the damned place down if they weren't careful.

The kiss went on and on, interrupted only when they

had to come up for air. Even then, his mouth only left her skin long enough to draw in a breath. Before long, it wasn't enough. When he felt her hands on the bare skin of his back, her nails lightly raking as she nibbled her way along his jaw, he groaned.

"This probably isn't a good idea. I'm your boss," he said.

She bit down harder, just a little, then soothed the sting with her tongue. "We aren't at work."

"I'm old enough to be your father."

"But you aren't. That role is more than filled, thank you very much." She pulled her face back, her hands coming to his chest to trail down past his abdomen to his waistband. "Any other objections?"

"Um... This won't turn into anything permanent?" His own hands were busy running over the smooth skin of her back, and he nuzzled the sensitive area beneath her ear with his mouth before sucking lightly.

Sydney's hands curled around the belt loops on his shorts, and she lifted onto her toes into his touch. "I know that," she finally gasped. "Doesn't mean we can't enjoy each other for a while, does it?"

It was Sawyer's turn to pull back, to study her flushed face. "No. It doesn't. I just don't want to hurt you."

"I'm a big girl. I'm responsible for my own feelings, just like you're responsible for yours. Maybe *I'll* be the one who hurts *you*."

"Maybe. Do you have any idea how much I want you in my bed?"

She gave a small whimper. "Some idea, yes. That desire thing works both ways."

He kissed her lightly as he brought his hands around, sliding up her ribcage to tease the undersides of her breasts. The warmth and soft fullness of her was beyond tempting, and he cupped her, his thumbs going to circle her nipples, which were already stiff and tight with longing.

"Oh, God, Sawyer. That's dangerous," she told him on a

moan, rubbing her cheek against his. Her hands came up to cover his, pressing him closer. "I think now's probably a good time for you to show me your bedroom."

"You do?" He was able to move his thumbs still, and he brushed them across the hardened tips. Her breath caught, and she turned her head. This time when she bit down on his neck, the nip was more aggressive.

That did it. If he didn't get her under him and fast, he was going to take her on the desk. Moving fast, he freed his hands and clasped one of hers, leading her out the office door and toward the bedroom. Once they were beside his bed, he used momentum to swing her around to stand in front of him. Without hesitation, he stripped his shirt off, then reached for the hem on hers.

Sydney was there ahead of him, whipping the T-shirt over her head so fast that it almost beat his to the floor. Her hands were on his waistband, fumbling with the button. Sawyer gently brushed them out of the way and undid them, letting them fall with his underwear to the floor. When she reached out to touch his erection, he grabbed her hands.

"Not this time."

"Hurry," she whispered as she dropped her own shorts, kicking them aside.

Thank God for condoms, he thought as he laid her on the bed, then opened the drawer to scramble for a foil packet. Not because he wanted a barrier between them, but because that barrier might dull the sensations enough that he didn't embarrass himself once he was inside her.

Sydney was waiting for him eagerly, her hips moving restlessly even as her legs were pressed tightly together, her knees bent. "It's been a while," she confessed shyly. "I want you but this might be a little rocky."

The words knocked a tiny bit of his urgent need down, and he forced himself to slow down, not to pounce on her. "Okay."

He climbed on the bed, putting his hands on her knees.

The skin was smooth, and later he'd spend time getting to know every inch of her body. But for right now? His focus was on the skin and wetness between her legs. He ran his hands down her legs to her hips, grateful when she opened for him. From there, he slid his right hand down to cup her, his thumb curving around to slide through her slick arousal.

Sydney arched up off the bed, gasping. Her hands clenched the bedspread beside her hips, and a deep flush covered her chest. "Now, please."

Sawyer couldn't speak. Kneeling between her legs, he used his left hand to guide himself to her entrance, not wanting to move his right hand from where it rested. He moved slowly but steadily, sliding inside her with a long, continuous stroke that left both of them gasping and breathless.

Letting his body down on top of hers, he was gratified to feel her legs come up, locking behind him as he withdrew and plunged back in. She was so tight around him, clenching so hard when he thrust, he could barely stand it, it felt so good. Setting a fast rhythm, he let his body take over.

When he felt her come apart, he followed her over the edge, burying his face in her neck as the climax overtook him.

Long minutes later, they'd come down enough to move. Her body was still clenching rhythmically around him, causing intense aftershocks to chase up his spine. He raised up enough that he could see her face.

"Okay?"

"Mmm, yes. You?"

"Oh, yeah." He moved to the side, taking some of his weight off her.

Sydney moved with him, keeping a leg around his hips. She didn't say anything, just snuggled up to him a bit as she ran her hands over his chest and abdomen.

Sawyer had never been a cuddler, but this, he didn't

mind. This was different. He cared for Sydney. The intimacy didn't bother him the way it might with someone else. He brushed her hair back, pressing kisses to her temple and her cheek as they recovered their energy.

Instead of the self-recrimination he'd feared, he felt an intense satisfaction. He wouldn't think about the repercussions right now. He was too busy feeling, too busy being in the moment.

CHAPTER THIRTY-SEVEN

SYDNEY COULD NOT MOVE. EVEN after Sawyer got up and went to the bathroom to dispose of the condom, she stayed on the bed trying to get her head to stop spinning. When he came back out and approached, running a hand up her leg, she stretched languidly.

"I hope you aren't going to throw me out now that you've had your way with me because I don't have a muscle or bone in my body."

"I'd have to turn in my man card if I threw you out." He trailed his fingers up over her hip, across her belly, and between her breasts to curve around her shoulder as he leaned down and kissed her. "But I am going to get something to drink. Want something?"

"Water'd be great. Please?"

"On its way." He snagged his boxers off the floor and tugged them on. She shamelessly watched him the whole time. When he noticed, he smiled. "What?"

"Just enjoying the view."

Sawyer laughed. "Yeah? I could say the same." He winked at her, but there was very real heat in his eyes as his gaze traveled from her head to her toes.

After he left, she forced herself to get up. Grabbing the T-shirt he'd had on, she pulled it over her head as she walked toward the bathroom. Her knees were weak and for a moment, she didn't think she was going to be able to make it across the room.

"That'd be bad—he comes back from the kitchen and you're collapsed in post-orgasmic tremors on the floor."

When she came out, he was setting the cheesecake down on the nightstand, along with two bottles of water.

"I thought you might appreciate these," he said as he handed her glasses to her.

"Absolutely. Thank you." She put them on, then accepted a bottle of water.

They eyed each other as they drank. The humor of the moment got to Sydney, and she had to swallow hastily or else risk choking. When a laugh sputtered out, Sawyer quirked his eyebrows.

"What's funny?"

"Nothing. Just us." She set the water down and closed the distance between them. "Thank you for today. For this evening. It's been fun."

Sawyer's hands came up under the edge of the shirt, resting on her bare hips as he pulled her into him. "It's been my pleasure. All of it, not just what happened here. And I'm glad you've had fun—I do try to throw all my guests into the pond at least once before they leave."

Sydney chuckled. Running her hands over his arms, shoulders, and upper chest, she let her body relax into his. "If that's the case, I wonder that you ever get lucky."

A peculiar stillness came over him, and his hands tightened just enough that she felt it. "I don't bring my dates here. I don't... I've always tried to keep that part of my life separate from everything else."

"Oh." She tilted her head. "Does it make you uncomfortable that I'm... that we've... that we were together here?" she finally settled on asking.

"No. Not at all. I didn't mean it that way." He rested his forehead against hers. "And this *has* been fun. Not that I want the evening to end now, mind you. I just wanted to let you know that I've enjoyed today, too."

Sydney sent him a quirky smile. "Of course it can't end yet. We've not had the cheesecake."

When she turned to reach for one of the plates, Sawyer used her momentum to whip her around, pressing her back to his front as he lowered his head to the curve of her neck and nipped.

"Cheesecake is not what I was thinking about when I said 'fun'," he said, his voice husky as his right hand slid across her hip and dipped between her thighs to cup her, his fingers probing with a sure-handed confidence that left her gasping. At the same time, he brought her left hand around behind her with his to press into his erection. He was so big her hand barely fit around him, and the memory of how he'd felt inside her as well as the movement of his fingers between her legs now, made her moan.

"No?" she managed to whisper.

"No. Want to guess what I have in mind?"

Sydney shivered, desire coursing through her. "Maybe you should show me."

He did. The cheesecake sat forgotten for well over an hour after that, and Sydney couldn't have cared less.

CHAPTER THIRTY-EIGHT

Sawyer found himself wrapped around Sydney, his thigh between her legs, the next morning. Thanks to the blackout curtains, the bedroom was still mostly dark, though daylight was visible around the edges of the windows and from the hall. He hadn't had time to wake up fully, much less roll over, when her phone rang.

"Ugh, what time is it?" she groaned, reaching out blindly to the nightstand. She grabbed the phone. "Hello?"

"Syd? Did I wake you?"

Sawyer could hear Danny clearly on the other end of the call as he was still snuggled close to Sydney.

"Of course you woke me. What time is it?"

"Um... Nine fifteen?"

"Nine... What? You're kidding."

That woke her up. She sat halfway up, dislodging Sawyer as she pushed her hair out of her face and held the phone away from her ear to look at the display.

"Oh, my gosh. Oh, Danny, I'm sorry. I forgot about you!"

The other man laughed. "Well, get up and come let me in. I brought coffee."

She sat up fully, and there was just enough light that Sawyer could make out the outline of her biting her lip. "I would do that, but I'm... I'm not home."

There was a long pause. "You're not home?"

"No."

Danny cleared his throat. "But you're still in bed?"

"Yes?"

"Not your bed."

"We've already established that," she said, rubbing her forehead with her free hand. "I'm, um, at a friend's."

Another pause, this one shorter, then a snort. "Oh, my God. You're not alone, are you?" Danny's laughter rang out. "You're not!"

Sydney fell back onto the bed with a mangled groan, the hand holding the phone falling into her lap. "He's enjoying this way too much."

Sawyer grinned. He kissed her bare shoulder and slid out of bed. "Morning, sunshine."

When he came out of the bathroom a few minutes later, she was still in bed, though she was sitting up.

"You two were going to do something?" he asked.

"Just hang out some, maybe do some shopping or whatever. He, um, he knows it's you. That I spent the night with, I mean."

"Okay. Did you tell him or did he guess?"

"He guessed." She ran her hands through her hair, gathering it into an unfastened ponytail. "I'm sorry. I figured he'd probably know eventually—he *is* my best friend and yes, we do gossip about things—but I wanted to talk to you first."

Sawyer sat on the edge of the bed beside her. "I'm not surprised he guessed. And it's okay. I'm not ashamed of what we did."

"I'm not, either," she said, reaching out to clasp his hand. "But that said, the fewer people who know about us, the better I think we'll be. Especially people in my family. Once we... once things are not like this," she said, gesturing to the bed, "I don't want to damage your relationship with the family. There's no reason for them to know. This is between us."

He didn't know how he felt about that. "Oh."

She looked down at their hands. “If the family knows, they might put well-intentioned pressure on us to make things more permanent than we’re comfortable with. And I don’t want that for either of us. What we did here, assuming we don’t just write this off as a night out of time, it shouldn’t be tempered by imaginary or implied expectations.”

“What about exclusivity?” He had to ask. He had a pretty damned good idea what her answer would be, but then again, she’d kind of floored him with her logical view of what they’d done. “I’m not much on long-term commitments, but I won’t be with anyone else while we’re together.”

Sydney lifted the back of his hand to her mouth and pressed a hard kiss there. “Good. I feel the same. I promise. Is that... are we okay then?”

“Yeah.” He kissed her forehead, sliding his mouth down to her temple. “We’re good.”

She laughed and tickled his belly. “I thought so.”

“Imp.” He fell back on the bed, drawing her with him so that she was draped across him. “So are you meeting Danny later?”

“Mmm, this afternoon,” she said as she traced the light smattering of hair on his chest and stomach.

When her hands went further, cupping his erection, Sawyer drew in a breath.

“You hold that thought,” she murmured even as she brushed a kiss across his belly button. “I’ll be right back.” She jumped up and dashed to the bathroom.

He didn’t exhale fully until the door closed behind her. No, he didn’t want anything permanent and serious with Sydney. But with her being so reasonable about the direction of their relationship, damned if he didn’t feel almost like he’d lost something.

CHAPTER THIRTY-NINE

EVEN THOUGH SYDNEY DIDN'T SPEAK a word of where she'd been Friday night, people were starting to ask questions. The family was at the farm for Sunday dinner, and in the kitchen before the meal, Sarah commented on Sydney's demeanor.

"You can't stop smiling, young lady. I know you're happy Eli's back in the country and doing better, and that Noah and Molly are home safely, but something tells me there's more to your attitude than that. Who is he?"

"A girl can't just be happy, Grandma?" Sydney teased, planting a kiss on Sarah's cheek.

Sarah tugged on her ponytail. "Of course she can. But I've known you since you were born. Out with it. Dish."

Sydney laughed, even as her cheeks flushed at the idea of admitting she was having an affair. "He's... we're just... it isn't a relationship. We're just playing. Just having fun."

"Do we know him?" Emma asked, her eyes alight with curiosity. She leaned in across the counter. "Where'd you meet? She was all mysterious with her Daddy Friday, and he just about drove me nuts trying to find out what I know, which is exactly nothing. I'm supposed to grill you today."

Sydney stuck her tongue out at Emma. "You've met him, and how we got involved isn't important. Like I said, we're just playing. And I love you all dearly," she said, looking around the kitchen at her mother, grandmother, and Rachel. "But this is private."

She took a dish of mashed potatoes through to the dining room, catcalls following her through the door. No way they'd let it go, she thought, even though she really hoped they would. But to her surprise, though she endured a little more teasing throughout the meal, they didn't ask again. She thought she'd gotten away without having to face an inquisition, but when she got ready to leave late that afternoon, Rachel got up, too.

"I'll head out with you."

"Okay. Is Easton excited about going back to school in a few weeks?" Sydney asked as they walked.

"Yes. He's trying to pretend he's an old hand at it now, since this is his second year and all, but he's got a bit of a kid-in-a-candy-store air about him. Are you sleeping with Sawyer?"

Sydney came to a dead stop, staring at Rachel in shock as she tried to figure out how to answer. "What?"

"I know you're an adult. I know it's private. But Syd, he's... He doesn't do forever after."

"Are you warning me off because you're worried about me or concerned about what it would mean for you—if I *were* sleeping with him, I mean?"

Rachel sent her an exasperated look. "Please. You know we're only friends, always have been. I don't want to see either of you get hurt. Is it him?"

Sydney crossed her arms and looked down the driveway. "I don't expect forever after with him, Aunt Rachel. I'll settle for a short period of happiness. I'm not sure I'm looking for something permanent either, as far as that goes. I don't know if I can ever trust someone enough to yield that much control to them again."

Rachel didn't say anything for a long minute, just studied her. "He's a good man. And the two of you bring something out in each other I've not seen anyone else do. No, not even

Adam," she said before Sydney could ask. "Especially not Adam. I won't say anything to the rest of the family. But if you need me, if you need to talk or need me to kick his ass for you? I'll be there. Okay?"

"Okay." Sydney hugged her. "Thank you. I don't want anyone to know because when it does end, it'll be awkward enough. He shouldn't lose the family just because we spent some time together off the books. And if everyone knows... You understand?"

"I do."

As she drove home, Sydney wondered if she could continue being so damned mature about things. Sawyer had turned her inside out and upside down Friday night. He was a demanding lover, taking as much as he gave and not letting her hardly catch her breath.

"I can see why Monique was so eager to renew their fling," she admitted. She was still pleasantly sore from everything they'd done and it'd been more than twenty-four hours since she'd left him. At the same time, she was half tempted to drive to his house for round two instead of going home and taking care of her chores like she needed to do.

She resisted, though. "No point in burning out faster, Syd. Stretch it out, make it last. Make some memories."

It wouldn't last. It couldn't. She knew that. And she wouldn't ask him for anything more than what he was prepared to give. She might not have too much pride to accept whatever affection Sawyer was willing to give for as long as he was willing to give it, but she sure as hell had too much pride to beg him for more.

CHAPTER FORTY

THURSDAY AFTERNOON, SAWYER WAS SITTING in his office on a call, his feet on his desk. He was watching Sydney work, and he was giving serious contemplation to the thought of seducing her in the storage room despite her moratorium on any romantic activities at work. Even though she'd spent two nights this week at his house, his hunger for her was not diminished. Those thoughts were derailed, however, when the outer door opened.

"Is he in?" he heard Rachel ask.

"Yeah, but he's on a call...." Sydney's voice trailed off as Rachel stormed into his office and slammed the door.

"Let me call you back," he told the man he was talking to. He hung up, lowering his feet to the floor without taking his eyes off Rachel. "Something I can help you with?"

She was seething, her cheeks flushed, breath coming between her teeth in a hiss. "You—you jackass! This is *your* fault!" She paced back and forth in front of his desk, hands on her hips.

Sure she was talking about Sydney, he tried to keep his poker face on. "It is?"

"Yes, it is! He's your protégé! What the hell, Sawyer? He kissed me. *Kissed*! On the mouth! Impertinent asshole."

Realization dawned. Lee.

Sawyer sat back, relieved, and grinned widely. "On the mouth, huh?"

"Don't you dare laugh," she warned even as his chuckles were building. "He kissed me in the driveway at my house where anyone, including my *son*, could have seen. How the hell would I explain that to Easton? Huh?"

He spread his hands. "If you mean to tell me you've not had that little birds and bees talk with him yet, I don't know what to say. I would have thought that happened years ago."

She put her hands on his desk with an exasperated growl. "He's a cop. He's young enough to be my child, damn it. This is not funny."

If he hadn't seen the real fear and dejection in her eyes, he would have teased her more. But Rachel was scared. And he could count on one hand the number of times through the years he'd seen her afraid. He leaned forward, matching her posture.

"He's a good guy. He's been crushing on you for weeks now. He isn't like Bear, Rach. He doesn't see women and the bedroom as a power play. I swear to you he doesn't."

She bowed her head. As far as he knew, she'd told him things about her relationship with her ex-husband that she'd never told anyone—about the abuse, both verbal and physical, that she'd endured at Bear's hands when their marriage had gone south. It hadn't been long-standing, that abuse, but it had caused Rachel to stop trusting in the good inside people. That, as well as Bear's affair with a younger woman, a relationship that had resulted in a child.

"I don't need a man in my life," she told him quietly. "I'm perfectly content as I am."

"Really? *Content*? That's what you're willing to settle for? You deserve to be happy."

"And what about you, huh? What do you deserve?" She looked straight in his eyes, defiant. "Short-term affairs with good women who would make you blissfully happy if you weren't so damned stubborn and would give them half a chance?"

She knew. Some of the anger in her eyes was directed at him because of Sydney.

Sawyer didn't try to pretend not to know what she was talking about. "She told you?"

"Reluctantly. Swore me to secrecy. She's willing to *settle* for what you have now. Her words, not mine. She's convinced herself she doesn't want a happily ever after, even though she deserves it more than just about anyone I know. She isn't expecting one with you. And if you dare tell her about this part of our conversation? I'll beat you to death."

He smiled at the thought of her trying, even though he felt a little sick. As much as he'd been trying to ignore his guilt over being with Sydney, it was still there. He'd suppressed most of it by reminding himself she was an adult who knew their relationship had limitations.

"What do you want me to say?" The irony that he'd asked Lee that same question a couple of weeks ago wasn't lost on him.

"That if you end up feeling more for her than you expect to, that if you find yourself falling in love, you won't turn away. That you'll fight for her."

"I could say the same thing to you," he told her quietly.

She blew out a long breath. "I know you could. I'm hoping you won't. What the hell was he *thinking*, Sawyer? He can't seriously be attracted to me."

This time when he smiled, Sawyer meant it. "Rachel, he's taken weeks to work up the courage to do more than say hi across the fence. I've not seen him so awkward, well, ever. He's usually pretty straightforward. And he kissed you? I didn't think you two had done much more than say hello."

She shook her head and straightened up. "We haven't. I mean, he and Easton have been hanging out, and after Eli was hurt... I may have cried on his shoulder a bit. Just a bit," she insisted as he grinned. "And then today he just walked up to me and kissed me."

"What were you doing before that?"

"I dropped a file with some papers and they went everywhere. He helped me pick them up. Damn it, Sawyer. I slapped him."

That did it. He laughed. And once he started, he couldn't stop. "You slapped him? How hard?"

She winced. "Not hard enough to bruise, thank God. I apologized as soon as it happened. He took me by surprise, and… I didn't handle it well."

"No kidding. What did he say?"

Poor Lee. Sawyer'd have to call him as soon as he had a chance.

"He apologized for kissing me. And he went home. I feel like I kicked a damned puppy."

Sawyer stood. "I understand why you're afraid, but Rachel… He's a good guy. Now, he does like to hunt. The uh, the discussion came up Friday with Sydney that your entire family is very fond of deer. So I should probably warn you now that if you do apologize in a more personal way, there's that."

It was Rachel's turn to stare at him, lost for words. "Discussion? What kind of discussion?"

He shrugged. "That I need to have a talk with your father. That… his books might be more biographical than I ever suspected they were."

She swallowed audibly. "Oh. In that case, it's probably a good idea that you two talk, I mean. And I knew Lee hunted—Easton warned me."

"Easton likes him?"

He could tell it pained her to admit it, but she did finally nod. "He does. He's full of 'Lee said this' and 'Lee said that.'"

"I've always thought he was a smart kid. And he has a smart mom, too. I'll tell you what. I'll make you a deal. I'll give your words strong consideration if you make an effort to make things right with Lee. Make him dinner or something. I happen to know he's fond of lasagna."

She crossed her arms as he came around the desk.

"And you know I make a kick-ass lasagna. How strong of a consideration are we talking about?"

"Strong enough that I'm more than a little uncomfortable with the notion."

After a minute, she nodded. "Deal." She held out her hand.

Sawyer lifted an eyebrow. "Really? You're going to make me shake on it?"

"Abso-freaking-lutely, buddy." Her grin was saucy, even though her eyes were serious.

He felt a bit like he'd been played by a master. If he hadn't been so certain Rachel was scared to death about Lee, he'd think the whole thing had been a setup. Regardless, he'd keep his word. He was already halfway there.

CHAPTER FORTY-ONE

Sydney was on pins and needles in the reception area as she waited for Rachel and Sawyer to come out of his office. At first, she'd thought her aunt was going after him because of what she'd admitted Sunday, but then she'd heard Rachel's proclamation about the kiss. Since there was no one looking, Sydney'd done a dance in her chair.

"Finally!" she muttered. Vastly relieved not to be the one in the hot seat, she couldn't help being amused at Rachel's discomfort. "Someone's needed to shake her up for a long time."

When they finally came out, Sydney assessed them both. "Everything okay?"

Rachel's face was red. "Fine. Sorry about that. I'll see you soon, sweetie. I need some air right now. Sawyer, I'll talk to Daddy for you, set you up. Maybe this weekend?"

"Sounds fine. Let me know what time."

After she'd left, Sydney got to her feet. "Is everything really okay? Did I hear right—Lee kissed her?"

Sawyer crossed his arms, pensive. "Yeah. It didn't go that well."

"Oh." She fiddled with her pen. "You told her about our deer talk?"

"It came up." He sighed. "Do you think Owen will take the news well?"

She crossed to him and laid a hand on his arm, squeezing tightly. "I'm surprised he hasn't told you already. If he didn't trust you, you never would have been invited to the farm as much as you've been over the years."

He unbent enough to capture her hand, lacing their fingers together. "No?"

"No." Something else was bothering him, though, she could tell. "Are you okay?"

"Fine. Maybe a bit concerned about Rachel and Lee. They'll figure it out, though."

"I hope so. He'd be good for her." She tightened her hand a little, then let go and walked to the window beside her desk. "I hate to add to your concern, but I need to hire you."

"Okay. That's a bit disconcerting." He walked over to stand behind her, not touching but close enough that she could feel his warmth. "Care to explain?"

Sydney hugged herself. "Danny's worried about Neala. You know I mentioned she'd called me last week, right? Well, she called him, too. And he said she sounded... not herself. You know she has a baby now. Danny worries that she's going to get into a mess and not be able to get out of it. We'd like to have you do a quick check on her."

"Actually, I didn't know she had a baby. Since when? It's been a couple of years since I've seen her."

"He's about six months old, I guess. She's in Louisville. Danny drove up when she had the baby. He's named after him," she told him, throwing a tiny smile over her shoulder. "I guess the father's not in the picture."

Sawyer touched her, letting his hand rest on the small of her back. "I didn't think the two of you were particularly close, not after what happened when you were nineteen."

She shrugged and leaned into his touch. "We reconnected a couple of years ago online. Maybe three. Not long after the divorce. She's grown up some, but like I said the other night, she still has a ways to go. And we're not that close, more like casual acquaintances. Anyhow, we just want to make sure she's not in trouble. No arrests, that sort of thing."

"Okay. I'll get started on it today or tomorrow."

Tomorrow. Friday. His day off. "Sawyer, no. You don't have to do that."

"Hush." He stepped closer and slid his arm around her hips for a brief hug, then let go. "Are you excited about this weekend?"

She smiled as she turned around. "Some. And I'm scared. I don't want to fumble and hurt Eli. You know?"

He tapped her chin. "You'll be fine. You'll aggravate the snot out of him and make him smile just like you told me you'd planned."

"I hope so." She, Archer, Emma, and Molly were heading to Washington tomorrow to see Eli. They'd be taking her car, John and Zanny's, and Molly's. "I wish Grandma and Grandpa felt up to going."

"It's a long trip, and you all are dashing out and dashing back. Besides, aren't they planning to go next week with Amelia and Logan when they can take their time?"

"Yes. That's why our birthday dinner's getting pushed back to the weekend after next. They won't be back in time." When he smiled, she tilted her head. "What?"

"It must be interesting, sharing a birthday with your mother and uncle."

Sydney chuckled. "It created a few problems growing up, yes. I got jealous for a couple of years that I didn't have my own day, so they started doing something special just for me. Mom and Ben never knew what it was like to have a birthday on their own, since they're twins, but I guess they went through the same thing when they were teenagers. Grandma would have a party for Mom one weekend and one for Ben the next."

"How'd they decide that?" he asked. He tucked a stray lock of hair behind her ear, causing a shiver of awareness to trace her spine.

"Coin toss."

"So are you still planning to come out to the house tonight?" Instead of moving back, he'd stepped closer.

Sydney gently pushed on his chest, backing him up so that there was a safe distance between them. "If you still want me there."

"I was thinking about taking the rest of the day off, actually." He grinned and waggled his eyebrows.

She laughed. "You were not. We have too much work to do."

"Yeah, and I might not make it until tonight. You might have to revive me."

"Uh-huh. I'm not unsympathetic to your plight, Boss, but that's not happening here." She went around her desk and sat down.

Sawyer let out a long-suffering sigh. "You are so cruel to me."

"Mmm, that's not what you said last night."

If anyone had been looking at his face right then, they'd have known without having to ask what was going on between her and Sawyer. The most self-satisfied grin she thought she'd ever seen spread across his face.

"There is that. Get me Neala's information and I'll get started on a check."

"Thank you. Take the cost out of my pay this week."

Defiantly, he came around the desk and planted a kiss soundly on her mouth. "You're cooking supper tonight. That's payment enough. Maybe some biscuits?"

Sydney bit her lip and touched his cheek near the corner of his mouth. "Deal."

It took her several minutes after he'd gone in his office before she could focus on her work. Instead of being less distracting now that they were sleeping together, he was more dangerous than ever. Now she knew what he was capable of, both as a lover and as a considerate beau of sorts, her mind tended to wander in that direction.

More than once since she'd imposed the ban on office intimacy, she cursed her levelheadedness. She knew she had to stick to her guns, but oh, she didn't want to. No, she wanted to lock the door and go to his office, strip naked, and have her way with him. Over and over and over again.

"And that's just not an option, girl. Get that out of your head."

Keeping that line uncrossed, from the bedroom to the office, was vital. Once things were over between them, she didn't know if she would be able to keep her job or not. But just in case she was, she had to do what was necessary to protect herself. No matter how much she wanted to give in and play.

CHAPTER FORTY-TWO

THE CALL FROM OWEN CAME Friday morning. Sawyer'd just come in from cutting the grass and barely managed to catch the phone before it went to voice mail.

"Hello?"

"I hear you have some questions about my books," Owen said by way of greeting.

"A few, yeah."

"Hmmm. Have plans for dinner this evening?"

Sawyer toed his shoes off and wiped his brow with his forearm. "No, sir."

"Why don't you come up to the farm, then. Say around four? That'll give us time to talk before we sit down to eat."

"I'll be there. Want me to bring anything?"

Owen chuckled. "I think we have it. See you then."

After he got cleaned up, he grabbed a sandwich and went to his home office. He'd not gotten as far as he'd wanted to on his background check on Neala yesterday, and he had plenty time to finish it now. So far, he wasn't seeing anything that was setting off alarm bells, and he'd run the usual, thorough report. Because Sydney had asked, he'd dig deeper than he typically went for clients.

He'd be lying if he said he wasn't nervous about the meeting this afternoon with Owen. He didn't know what to expect. Given what he knew about Noah's abilities, the conversation could literally lead anywhere.

"What do you think he knows?" Sarah asked as Owen hung up.

"I don't know. Rachel was a bit shaken when she called. All she knows is that part of the secret's out of the bag, and apparently it came out through Sydney." He traced a pattern on the arm of the couch as he studied her. "You think that was part of a regular conversation and he picked up on something, or...?"

Sarah, who was resting on the other end of the couch, stretched her legs out toward him. "I imagine it came out during their date Friday." She gave a happy hum as he took one of her feet in his hands and started gently massaging.

"She admitted she was with him?"

"No. That's me guessing."

Owen scowled. "I don't like that they're hiding. It doesn't bode well for the future."

"I didn't expect they'd bring it out in the open," she countered. When he looked at her, surprised, she smiled. "Honey, he's very careful about his romantic life. I'm counting on our granddaughter's sweetness and Sawyer's own innate goodness to do its magic. They've kindled the fire. Now we have to hope it takes hold and burns."

"From the sounds of things, it's burning quite well," he replied grumpily.

She laughed. "I hope so."

"Should I give him a nudge?"

As she withdrew her right foot and extended her left, she laid back, her arm behind her head, and stared at the ceiling, thinking. "I don't know," she finally said. "How much are you going to tell him? About the family, I mean."

"As much as he can handle. I trust Sawyer. He's a good man. He's kept Noah's secret well for a decade. Shoot, I didn't know he was aware of Noah's abilities for a year or so after he learned about them, and then it was only because Noah mentioned it in passing." He sighed. "I'll play it by ear. Think he's going to want a demonstration?"

Sarah smiled. "Want me to call Rachel, have her come up for dinner?"

"Probably wouldn't be a bad idea."

Now that he was older, changing into the deer or wolf took a lot out of him. He could still do it, but it wasn't the pleasant, cleansing metamorphosis it had been when he was younger. Thankfully, the compulsion to shift had died down over the last decade or so.

"I think we should pretend ignorance as far as his being with Sydney goes," Sarah said as he handed her the phone. "After all, we could be wrong."

"Do you really think we are?" he asked, sliding his hand up to her calf where he knew her muscles tended to tighten up into painful knots.

"I don't think so, no. Or maybe that's just my optimism talking."

"I love your optimism, woman. Nothing wrong with it," he said, easing over to lean down and kiss her. "I'll see what I can find out. Subtly, of course, but I should be able to ferret out some information."

"Good. And then we can decide when to push." When he went to sit back up, she grabbed his shirt and tugged. "More, please."

Owen laughed and lowered himself back down, bracing his weight on the couch as he dipped his head to kiss her again. "Yes, ma'am."

CHAPTER FORTY-THREE

When Sawyer got to the farm five minutes before four, Owen was standing on the porch with Noah. They came down the steps as he parked and met him at his truck.

"Why don't we walk?" Owen suggested. "It's a good day for it."

Even though it was late July, as high up on the mountain as they were, a good breeze was blowing. Unlike the steamy misery in the valleys, the air was comfortable and pleasant up top.

"Sure. Where're we heading?"

"Down to my house," Noah said.

Sawyer looked at Owen, remembering the grimace from a few weeks ago. "You sure about that?"

Owen winked and slapped him on the shoulder. "I'm not as decrepit as you think. Let's go." He started out, walking briskly and with a surefooted stride of a man twenty years younger.

Noah grinned at Sawyer's surprise. "Come on before he beats us down there."

"How's Eli?" Sawyer asked as they caught up to Owen.

"Better," Noah said. "They had him up walking on crutches before we left Germany, and Mom said he's fighting mad to get out of the hospital here. If everything goes as planned, he'll probably go to rehab Monday or Tuesday. And he could come home a couple of weeks after that."

Sawyer was stunned. "That soon?"

Owen smiled. "That soon. He's a Campbell. A lot of us heal faster than the average bear."

As much as he wanted to delve into that little tidbit of information, Sawyer had something else on his mind.

"How are *you* doing?" he asked Noah, who was slightly ahead of them on the wide path.

The younger man shrugged. He looked wearier than Sawyer had ever seen him. "Now that I'm home, I'm good. There's less... How do I say this? Hospitals aren't the best place for someone like me. There's a lot of suffering that goes on, especially in the kinds of hospitals Eli's been in. A lot of people don't walk away from those places."

Sawyer exchanged a look with Owen. Noah was talking about the dead.

"Hopefully you won't have to go back there," Owen said. "He'll be home soon."

"Yeah. I hope we can get things sorted out between us once he is home. He's stubborn, though. Gets that from the Campbells, too." Noah turned and walked backward to grin at his grandfather. It was a startling reflection of what Owen must have looked like fifty years earlier. The smile was Zanny's, but everything else was pure Campbell.

In that moment, Sawyer couldn't help but wonder what a child of his and Sydney's might look like. He ruthlessly tamped down that train of thought, knowing from painful experience that it would only lead to heartache.

"So what else runs in the Campbell family?" Sawyer asked. They'd reached the edge of the clearing where Noah lived. In the bright sunshine, he could see even more details of the magical setting.

"That's why we brought you here," Owen answered. He heaved out a sigh, eyeing Sawyer carefully. "You've kept Noah's secrets well. And what we're getting ready to discuss here, it's vitally important you keep those secrets, too. If word got out about this, it could be disastrous for our family. Do you understand that?"

Owen was as serious as Sawyer had ever seen him. He nodded. "Yes, sir. I think I do."

After a minute, Owen accepted the words. "Okay, then. How much do you know?"

"I know that when I offered Sydney some deer salami, she turned white as a sheet. And she told me not to ever offer anyone else in the family anything made of deer. She had that sick look on her face the two of you have right now. Between that and reading your books, I'm guessing what Noah can do is just the tip of the iceberg."

Owen exchanged a look with Noah. The younger man shrugged. "Might as well."

"Come with me. Noah, you get our... demonstration ready."

Sawyer followed Owen to a shady corner of the garden, far removed from the house. A round table was situated under an arching maple tree, comfortable-looking chairs arranged around its perimeter. On the edge of the area was the carved statue of a young buck, a cluster of daisies in his mouth as he looked up, startled. The sight made Sawyer laugh.

"That's so lifelike. Noah has so much talent. You can tell that guy's shocked to have been discovered eating those flowers."

Owen grinned. "Sarah snapped a picture of me while I was grazing in her flower bed one day about oh, thirty years ago. Those daisies were too tempting to resist. Almost as good as sliced apple. Noah took the picture and made this. Said it appealed to his sense of whimsy."

It took a few seconds for the meaning behind the words to sink in. "Excuse me?" Sawyer asked faintly. He eased down into one of the chairs, not taking his eyes off Owen.

Instead of answering directly, Owen moved on to a

beautiful wolf, caught in a playful pose as it nipped at the tail of a seated mountain lion who, Sawyer swore, was watching it with indulgent resignation. Owen rested his hand on the wolf's head. "You'd never know it by talking to her, but this is Amelia. I can change into either a wolf or a deer depending on how I feel. I've never been entirely comfortable as the wolf. That's usually reserved for when I'm in a dark place mentally. But my baby girl, she takes *such* joy in becoming that animal."

He touched the mountain lion's ear. "Logan, bless his patient soul, endures all kinds of teasing from her when she's in her wolf form. She likes to chew on his tail. Not hard, mind you. Just enough to remind him she's there."

Sawyer couldn't have spoken or moved then if his life depended on it. Fortunately, Owen saw that, and he moved down the line to the mountain lion who was reclining on its side, one paw raised as he licked at it. His eyes were half closed, and Sawyer would have sworn he could see satisfaction in the cat's face. Two cubs with chunky feet and curious expressions were climbing over the lion's back.

"Archer and the boys. Shifting tends to run in the family, you see. He lost his cat for a few years after he was shot, back before he met Emma. Remember when that bullet fragment shifted and we almost lost him? Not long after they were married?"

Sawyer nodded slowly. "Yeah."

"He got the cat back then. Didn't know it for a few weeks after surgery. Emma woke up one morning to find a cat in her bed, and not Huff and Puff." Owen chuckled. "She was pregnant with Graydon, just starting to show. Called me, told me to expect her with a cat, and came out here so fast she didn't even let Sydney get dressed. Just pulled her robe on over her pajamas. Sarah and I thought she was bringing us a kitten or something."

"But it was Archer?" Sawyer managed.

"Yep. As soon as she parked, she got out and held the

door open. He ran and ran and ran that day. Hadn't been able to shift for close to ten years at that point. Emma just sat on the porch and cried, she was so happy."

"And both their sons..."

"Are mountain lions. Carter's been able to shift since he was little. Graydon only figured it out when he was twelve."

It was so much more to take in than Sawyer had ever imagined. "Emma's the only normal one, Sydney said. And Sarah."

Owen sat beside him as Noah came out, a tray with tall glasses and a jug of lemonade on it. There was also a small bowl of sliced apples. Noah dished some out and handed them to Owen, then offered some to Sawyer, who shook his head.

Owen took a drink of lemonade. "Ah, there's my boy. Thank you. Emma's so stubborn she more than makes up for being normal. And Sarah... she might not be a shifter or have the abilities some of our offspring have, but I think there's something there. Several talents popped up in our progeny that didn't come from the Campbells."

"What about Rachel? Easton? Eli? Amelia and Logan's kids?"

Noah sat down across from Sawyer and poured himself a glass. "Easton's normal. Eli has Dad's gift for patterns, maybe even stronger than Dad. Two of Pip's kids are shifters—one cat and one wolf. I'm working on their statues now. As for Rachel... if she'd ever come out, you could see for yourself," he said, raising his voice and looking toward the house. "He's not freaking out. Come on. Stop being nervous. I have apples."

After a minute, soft footfalls sounded in the grass and a wary deer poked its head around a shrub. It studied Sawyer for a long time, assessing him, before stepping forward. A doe, it eased toward the table carefully. Once she saw he wasn't going to react violently, she relaxed and came up to Noah, who fed her sliced apples.

"Oh, my God." Sawyer was afraid to breathe. He gathered he was supposed to believe the deer was Rachel, but he couldn't accept that. It was too fantastical. That said, the magic of a deer who was so tame was mind blowing. "How'd you get it to come in the yard?"

"It? Um, *she* volunteered to show you the deer," Noah said, handing him some apple. "She changed in the house."

Sawyer chuckled. "Okay. If you say so." He held the fruit out in his palm.

The deer took it, but before she pulled back, she snorted mightily as though offended.

"It's a lot to take in," Owen said. "But that's Rachel."

"Sure it is. No offense. This is a really charming fairytale you two have woven here. But I can't... no. I could believe one of you. But so many of you?" He shrugged, shaking on the inside. He didn't believe it. He couldn't. Could he? "So where's 'Rachel's' statue?"

"In the workshop. A limb fell and knocked her ear off," Noah said. The deer snorted again, nudging him in the side hard enough to shift his chair. "What? I'm sorry. It wasn't my fault. I'll make it as good as new."

As he looked from the deer to Noah to Owen, Sawyer didn't see the hint of a laugh or a smile that might indicate they were joking, only indulgent tolerance. Though he'd been expecting something, he sure as hell hadn't been expecting this.

"Why don't you follow her back to the house, Sawyer?" Owen suggested. "She'll change back and answer your questions."

"Okay." He still didn't believe what he was seeing, but he was at a loss as to what else to do. Without an argument to the contrary, he stood. The deer turned and led the way back to the house.

By the time they reached the deck, Sawyer was on his way to being able to accept what he'd been told. The deer hadn't just wandered a path and ended up at the house. She moved with purpose.

When they got to the door, she looked over her shoulder at him as though asking him to open it. He did.

"What, you can't turn the knob?" he asked as he twisted it.

She shook her head and butted the door gently, opening it wide enough that she could walk through. Astonished, Sawyer followed and closed it. He watched as she went to the bathroom and closed the door with her nose.

Fig meowed at him from the loft above the living room, causing him to jump.

"Cat, you scared me to death. What do you think about a deer being in your house?" he asked as she bunny-hopped downstairs and scampered over to where he was standing next to the bar. She didn't answer him, but by this point, he wouldn't have been surprised if she'd spoken.

Two minutes after the door had closed, it opened. And instead of the deer, out came Rachel, fully dressed.

"You want to check and make sure there's no way out?" she asked as she crossed to the kitchen.

He didn't respond, just hurried to the bathroom to look. No deer, no window or door to the outside of the house. His knees were weak as he turned to face Rachel, who was sipping on some water.

"You okay?" she asked.

Sawyer shook his head, an incredulous huff escaping as he grasped the doorframe to keep from falling. "You, you... How? I can't... I need to sit down."

He was still on the couch several minutes later when Noah and Owen came in. Rachel, seated beside him, was rubbing his shoulder. Head in his hands, he lifted his face briefly to look at the men, then lowered it back.

"He's okay," she told them. "It's just taking a little time for everything to sink in. Knowing and *knowing* are different cats entirely."

"You must have questions," Owen said, taking a seat in the recliner next to the couch. "When you're ready, we'll answer them. There's no rush."

Sawyer didn't even know where to begin. He looked at Rachel, studying her as though he'd never seen her before. "Sydney wouldn't tell me what the secret was. Just that I needed to talk to you," he said to Owen, "and that it wasn't her secret to tell."

"That's my girl. It says a lot about how much she trusts you that she'd even say that much to you."

"Just how *did* that conversation come up?" Rachel asked. There was a bit of a challenge in her tone, but it was teasing, not adversarial.

"He offered her some deer salami," Noah said when Sawyer hesitated.

Rachel sucked in a breath. "Oh. What the hell were you doing with that? You're a vegetarian."

"A friend gave it to me. I have omnivores over from time to time. No point in throwing it away. Well, there wasn't. Damn, I've never been so glad I don't eat meat. I'll dispose of it as soon as I get home." He felt sick, thinking about Rachel being caught outside the safety of Owen's property by hunters. "That's why this property's so big."

Owen nodded. "At first, I wanted to protect my privacy. And then when I met Sarah and we started having kids, it became about making sure they had a safe place to change, to grow up."

"Speaking of Grandma, we'd better head back up to the house," Noah said. "She'll be wondering what happened to us."

All through dinner, Sawyer kept trying to figure out if he was dreaming or if the last few hours had really happened. He wished Sydney was there to guide him through the maze he felt like he was lost in. She had a unique perspective on the world, a way of viewing life that was very different from how he interpreted things, but somehow, her vision complemented his.

When he realized what he was thinking—that he was starting to turn to her for emotional support in ways he'd not done with anyone in years—it rocked him more than any revelations Owen had made.

She was sneaking in behind the wall he'd built, and he didn't know how in the world he was going to get her out, or even if he wanted to get her out. He'd dealt with enough today already without having to figure out his suddenly complicated feelings. There'd be time enough to deal with that once she got home.

CHAPTER FORTY-FOUR

BY NOON ON MONDAY, SAWYER was pacing the office, waiting anxiously for Sydney's return. She'd been delayed leaving Virginia, and when she'd texted him at ten Sunday night, she'd guessed it would be at least three a.m. before they got in. He'd texted her back, insisting she not come in until noon if she felt like coming in at all. His phone rang a few seconds later.

"Don't be ridiculous. Of course I'll feel like coming in. How are things there?"

"Quiet. Boring. Lonely. Did you have a good visit?" he asked, stretching out on the bed.

"We did. I'll tell you more when I see you. I can't talk long tonight. Daddy and I stopped at a rest area for a few minutes. He's lost without Mom, even though she's only going to be out there a week." Emma was staying to give John and Zanny a break.

Sawyer knew how Archer felt, he thought uncomfortably. "How far out are you?"

"About an hour from Roanoke on the Washington side. I wish we were home."

Unspoken was that she wished she were there with him. "I know. I wish you were, too." He hadn't meant to say that. It just slipped out. But he didn't try to clarify, didn't try to call it back. Instead, he let it stand on its own.

"I'd better go. I don't want Daddy to think I've been abducted or something."

"Hey, don't even joke about that. Rest stops are dangerous places. Text me when you're back in the car to let me know you're okay?"

"I will. See you soon."

After they hung up, he stared at the ceiling for a long time, his mind going round and round in circles. The beginning of the circle was his inability to have children, followed by his age, with the end being that Sydney was different. The way she made him feel was different.

Now, as he waited for her to come up the stairs, he tried to shove that circle of thoughts aside. When he heard steps outside, he rushed to sit on the edge of her desk. He didn't want to appear overly eager to see her, after all. But Sydney wasn't the woman who walked through the door. Instead, it was Neala, and she had her baby with her.

"Sawyer, hi! Look at you, all out of uniform and everything. Is Syd here? I'm supposed to meet her."

"No. She hasn't made it in yet, but she should be shortly." He hadn't been able to find anything on Neala that gave him reason for concern, and looking her over, he had to admit she looked worlds healthier than the last time they'd crossed paths. "Is this your son?"

The baby was perched on her hip, babbling away happily as he took in his surroundings. His hair stood straight up on his head in a wispy black spike, and he looked clean and well cared for.

"This is Daniel. Want to say hi?"

Before Sawyer could protest, she'd handed the baby over. Awkwardly, he held on to him, scowling at Neala as he tried to figure out where to put his hands. "Um, you'd better take him back. I might drop him."

"I can't. I have to run. Syd was supposed to be here. I'm sorry—she's on her way, right?" She set the baby's bag down on the floor beside Sydney's desk and started backing away.

"Tell her I'll call her as soon as I can, and that I appreciate this. I really have to run. Thank you!"

She was gone before he could stop her.

With his jaw on the floor with shock and outrage, Sawyer stared at the empty doorway, then down at the baby, who gurgled up at him. He had to move fast to avoid a swipe of the little guy's wet hand.

"What the ever-loving hell am I going to do with you?" He tried to reach for his phone, but as soon as he took his hand off the baby, he started whimpering. "Okay, okay. We'll give her a minute."

But the damage was done. Daniel's lip started quivering as his eyes filled with tears, as though he'd finally realized his mother was gone and had left him with a total stranger who knew nothing about babies.

"Oh, shit. Now what?"

Very carefully, he tucked the baby closer to his body and, trying to remember what he'd seen parents do, he patted his back.

"Now you have to stay calm," he said. "Because the closest help I can get for us right now is Myrtle downstairs, and buddy, you and I *don't* want to go there. She'd eat us alive." He didn't know if it was the talking or the patting that was working, but Daniel had stopped the lip-quivering and tearing up. Sawyer kept his voice soft. "God, Sydney, please get here. Where the hell are you?"

Even though it was only a couple of minutes, it felt like hours before Sydney came in, coffee in one hand. Archer was behind her. She stopped so fast, he almost ran over her.

"Um. Sawyer?"

Scowling so hard his face hurt, he growled. "Neala was here. She left something for you." He started to hand the baby over, but Daniel had a tight grip on the front of his shirt. When Sawyer moved to give him to Sydney, he let out a screech fit to wake the dead and tightened his hands.

"Son of a bitch," Sawyer cursed as quietly as he could. He moved the baby back to his shoulder, rubbing at what he suspected was now a raw patch of hairless skin on his chest.

"Did he get your hair?" Archer asked with a grin, stepping closer to get a look at the baby. "I take it this is Daniel?"

"Yes. And yes. She said you'd agreed to keep him," Sawyer told Sydney.

She shook her head, her eyes wide, and set the coffee and her purse down on her desk. "She told me she might swing by today when she came through. She didn't say a word about Daniel." Moving closer, she bent her head and touched the baby, who hid his face against Sawyer's shoulder. "He's adorable. Look at that hair."

"I'll bet it won't lay down," Archer said quietly. "Carter's was like that. Stood straight up for the first eighteen months. What did Neala say, exactly? How long is she going to be gone?"

Sawyer blew out a tense breath. "She didn't say. She gave the impression that Sydney knew about this." When he felt the baby relax, he looked down. He'd drifted off, his eyes closed as he sucked on a thumb, drool dampening his chin and Sawyer's shirt. A sharp pain of regret stabbed at Sawyer, and his jaw tightened. "Maybe you'd better try to call her."

Sydney nodded. "Yeah. How long ago was she here?" she asked as she dug into her purse for her phone.

"Ten minutes? Fifteen? An hour or two? I don't know. Feels like forever." Sawyer eased into the chair in front of her desk, taking care not to wake Daniel.

"Is that the first time you've ever held a baby?" Archer

asked. He hunkered down beside the chair and ran a hand over Daniel's hair. "Want me to take him?"

Sawyer gave an instant's thought to trying to transfer the baby to Archer, but something held him back. "Pretty much. I've tried to stay away from kids through the years. And no, he's quiet here. He can stay."

From the look Archer gave him, Sawyer figured he knew about the sterility. It certainly wasn't anything they'd ever discussed, but neither was it something he kept secret.

"She's not answering," Sydney said, muttering a curse under her breath. "I'm calling Danny. Hopefully he'll—hey, are you busy? We've got a bit of a situation here. Have you heard from Neala?"

While she told Danny what was going on, Archer straightened and went to the baby's bag. He set it on Sydney's desk and started going through it. As Sawyer watched, his face grew more and more serious.

"There's quite a bit of stuff in here," Archer said when Sydney hung up. "And notes on what to feed him, when to feed him, allergies, that sort of thing. What'd Danny say?"

"He's on his way. She didn't tell him about this, either." Sydney crossed her arms and stared at the baby pensively. "Surely to God she didn't just leave him here for good," she whispered.

Sawyer exchanged a look with Archer. That was exactly what he was wondering, and Archer, as well, if he was reading the other man correctly.

"Let's see what Danny knows when he gets here. Maybe he'll have some answers." Sawyer carefully adjusted the baby so that his arm wasn't in an awkward position.

"I hope so," Archer said. "I'd hate to see you have to involve CPS in this. Neala's always had a loose definition of responsibility, but I thought that had changed since she had him."

"Did you find out anything in her background check?" Sydney asked, then explained to Archer, "Danny and I had him run one. Danny had a gut feeling that something was going on with her."

"Nothing. She works two jobs, seems to be living a straight, if modest, life."

But he couldn't help thinking about how she'd run out of the office as though she were escaping. And too many times, he'd seen people running who never had any intention of coming back to what they were leaving. He just hoped that wasn't the case with Daniel.

CHAPTER FORTY-FIVE

Two hours later, Sydney was head-over-heels in love. Simultaneously, she was ready to strangle Neala. "I don't understand how she could just drop him off like that," she told Danny as she fed the baby.

"She said she didn't have a choice when we talked," he reminded her quietly. He handed her a soft cloth to wipe Daniel's mouth with, and he sighed. "Sawyer took it pretty well."

Sydney's mouth tightened as she raised an eyebrow. "He didn't have a lot of say in the matter, did he? It hurt him, Danny. I could see it."

"So could I. I'm sorry."

She shook her head. "Nothing to be done for it." She sat back in the rocking chair, adjusting Daniel a bit. "What the hell am I going to do with a baby?"

Danny smiled. "Enjoy him. Practice. I'll help."

"Thank God for you. And at least Neala had the sense to drop the rest of his belongings off at Mom's shop."

Sam, her mother's assistant manager, had called a few minutes after Danny arrived, letting them know that Neala had left several things at the shop for Sydney. A suitcase full of clothes and formula, his car seat, and a playpen to be exact. Since she couldn't exactly work with a baby in the office, she'd come home.

"Do you think she'll pick him up this weekend like she

said she would?" She handed Danny the bottle, which the baby had made short work of, and looked to him for instruction. "Now what?"

"That depends on him. What does he want to do?"

"Seriously? He's a baby. I can't just ask him," she said, pressing a kiss to the soft skin of his forehead. Daniel gurgled and babbled at her, blowing milk bubbles. "I thought they went to sleep when you fed them."

"Not always. Here, let me have him." Danny picked him up like a pro, making funny faces. The baby squealed and watched him, fascinated.

"Good thing you have nieces and nephews." Sydney felt like crying. "You're moving in here for a few days. No way you're leaving me alone with him."

"You know I won't leave you high and dry. And you're doing just fine."

"Daddy was ready to take him home. Maybe I should have let him. If he didn't have to work, I would have. How the hell do parents learn this stuff, Dan?" She stood and went to the baby's bag, sorting through it for the fourth or fifth time. She held up a pair of striped socks that fit in the palm of her hand. "Look at these. They're so tiny."

"You're hurting as much as Sawyer is. I'm as angry with Neala about that as I am about her leaving this guy alone. If I didn't really think she was a good mother, I'd call CPS myself."

Sydney put the socks back in the bag. "I've tried not to let myself think about anything permanent with Sawyer. There's no point to it. But when I walked in earlier and found him cradling that little guy so close, looking like he was ready to do battle for him, it almost killed me. He wants children. Not with me, I don't think, but if he had half a chance to be a father, he'd take it."

Danny was quiet as he gave the baby a pacifier. When he did speak, it was with hesitation. "I've known Sawyer for a while now. And when you started working for him, I worried.

I figured you'd end up with a crush on him or even more, that you'd fall in love and he wouldn't love you back. I know you're a big girl," he said when she started to speak. "But the heart wants what the heart wants, Syd. You know that as well as I do."

"I guess so."

"When the two of you started dancing around each other, when you told me about the kiss, I wondered what that meant. But seeing the way he looked at you today? I wouldn't be so sure his feelings aren't engaged."

"Of course his feelings are engaged. He cares for me, Dan. I know that. But caring and wanting to spend your life with someone aren't the same thing. I'd be naive to think they are. Naive and setting myself up for heartache."

She couldn't let herself go down that road. She wouldn't.

Danny changed the subject. "If you need to work, I can watch him during the day. It won't be a problem at all. I'll set him up in my office and we'll keep each other company. Won't we, big guy?"

The baby gave a long, loud squeal that sounded very much like an agreement.

Sydney couldn't help but be amused by their interactions. "Your mother might think he's yours."

Danny winked at her. "Might do my reputation some good. It's terrible of me to say I'm looking forward to how perturbed she'll be when she meets him, but I am. Especially when she learns who his mother is and who he's named after."

"You go right ahead and tug on that tiger's tail, buddy. I'm steering clear of Miriam."

"Ah, it gives her purpose, trying to figure me out. Keeps her off Dad's back and the brothers appreciate the reprieve."

She pushed a hank of wheat-blond hair back off his forehead. "Just as long as they return the favor." She was still worried about Danny. That hadn't changed. "Any decision yet?"

"I'm waiting for a good time to break the news. I'm tired of hiding it from the family. But I'm not coming out to the general public. My sexual orientation isn't fodder for gossip, and it's nobody's business but mine."

"Does it make me paranoid to worry that Miriam might out you to the church?"

He shook his head. "Nope. I've had the same concern. My mentor knows, and so do his bosses. If it comes out, I'll deal with it." There was a resolve in his voice she hadn't heard before.

"What changed?"

"Watching my parishioners battle to keep food on the table as the coal industry dies, watching them lose spouses, Eli's accident, you coming home. I guess I finally decided that I just don't care anymore if people know, if they pass judgment on me. Maybe I've accepted myself." He shrugged.

Sydney slid her arm around his waist and hugged him. "I adore you, you know that? You're one of the strongest people I know, and I'm glad you're in my life."

"Ah, heck, Syd. Don't get all mushy on me," he said softly, bussing the top of her head. "And back at you. Now if we can just get you and Sawyer married off, we'll start working on the rest of the world's problems."

She laughed. "You're such an optimist. Love you, Dan."

"Back at ya, kid."

She still didn't think she and Sawyer were meant for anything permanent, not with each other. But hearing Danny's calm resolution, she felt a lot better about going forward, wherever that path led.

Sawyer chided himself during the drive to Sydney's that evening. "You should go home. Peace, quiet, no babies crying, diapers needing to be changed. No dreams you can't fulfill being shattered." But still he drove on.

The office wasn't far from her house, only about ten minutes in heavy traffic. Not nearly long enough of a drive for his common sense to kick in and turn him around. No, here he was, walking up to the door, ringing the bell. Volunteering to go face to face with what he couldn't have.

Danny opened the door. "Hey, come on in."

"I thought I'd swing by, see how things are going."

The younger man grinned. "Syd's cursing baby boys and their ability to shoot pee across the room."

Sawyer blinked. "Across the room?"

"Maybe I should have let you discover that for yourself, huh?"

"Uh, I could come back."

Danny's knowing look stopped his backward steps.

"Or I could come in. Any word from Neala?"

"Just that she'll be back at the end of the week to get him. She's apparently trying to work things out with his father." There was deep sarcasm in Danny's voice as he led Sawyer down the hall to the kitchen. "Doing okay in here?"

Sydney looked up, frowning, and used her suds-covered hand to push her glasses up on her nose. "Fine and dandy. As long as the air doesn't hit his hoo-ha, he's good. Hey," she said to Sawyer.

"Hoo-ha? Okay then. You're looking good there," he said, not hiding his grin.

She was a mess. Her hair was half down from its ponytail, her shirt was soaked with wet and bubbles, and so were the front of her shorts. Daniel was taking a bath in the sink, splashing the water as he chortled.

She used the hand that wasn't supporting the baby to flip him off. "You don't know how much trouble someone who can't walk, crawl, or talk can cause. I know why babies are so cute now. If they weren't, no one would have them." She winced and looked down at Daniel.

"I'm not glass, Sydney. I won't break," Sawyer said softly.

"I know that." But she wouldn't meet his eyes.

"Okay, you know how to change his diaper. He's not going to need food for at least another hour or two," Danny said. "Be careful when you lift him out of there, as he'll be slippery as an eel. And make sure you rinse all the soap off. Then lotion him up with this." He set a bottle of baby lotion down on the counter. "Keep him warm, too."

Pure panic filled Sydney's eyes. "Where are you going?"

"To get a bag together for a few nights. I'm not leaving you alone. Sawyer's here. The two of you can figure this out." He patted her shoulder, winked at Sawyer, and headed for the hall. "Call if you need me."

"Danny, don't you dare walk out that door!" she hollered. "Sawyer, stop him. I can't do this."

But Danny was gone.

Sawyer walked over to the sink, holding his hand out to the baby, who slapped it. "He'll be back soon enough. We have this."

Sydney stared up at him, doubt clear on her face. "Sure we do."

She looked so worried he had to do something, so he kissed her. He didn't stop until he felt her start to relax.

"Welcome home," he whispered when he pulled back.

She buried her face in his shoulder. "I'm so scared I'll break him."

"Nah. He's durable." He gently scooted her out of the way and put his hands around the baby. "He's also going to sleep. Let's get him out of the water before he does."

Together, they got Daniel dried off, lotioned, and dressed.

"Want me to take him?" she asked as they headed to the living room.

"I have him." He didn't even try to pretend he didn't want to hold the baby. They settled in on the couch, and Sawyer felt part of his heart right itself when Sydney snuggled up next to him.

In just a few minutes, the baby was out.

Sydney rubbed her face against Sawyer's shoulder. "You know you can put him in the pen whenever you want, right?"

"Yeah. I know."

Her breath shuddered out. "I can't stand it," she admitted.

Sawyer carefully freed one of his hands and put his arm around her, pulling her close. "I know that, too."

They stayed like that for some time, not speaking. When the slam of a car door sounded from just outside, Sydney straightened away from him and stood.

"That's either Danny or Daddy and the boys."

"Here. Better put him in the pen." He let Sydney have the baby, running a hand over his head as she took him.

"Yeah, and then I'd better change clothes. I'm a mess."

It was true, she was. But she appealed to Sawyer on a level that he'd never expected she would before. He could too easily imagine her as a mother now, and on top of everything else the last few weeks had wrought, that almost sent him running out the door.

Before he could flee, however, Sydney had let her father in.

"Where are the boys?" she asked.

"Home. For some reason, they weren't excited to see the baby. Where is he?" Archer came into the living room, anticipation on his face. He had a furry, stuffed yellow duck in one hand. "Hi, Sawyer."

"Hi."

"He's asleep. Just went down for a nap," Sydney said. She took the duck, shaking her head. "You're going to have him spoiled by the time Neala gets home, aren't you?"

Archer hugged her. "I'm going to do my damnedest. So what's the scoop?"

Sydney filled him in on what they knew. By the time she'd finished, Danny was back.

"I brought pizza," he said, holding up two white boxes. "Sausage pepperoni and veggie lovers."

When they were settled around the dining room table, eating, Archer startled Sawyer by bringing up one of the topics that had been on Sawyer's mind all weekend.

"I hear you had quite the revelatory adventure Friday. How're you doing with that?"

Sawyer's hand tightened around his glass as he glanced from Archer to Danny. "I beg your pardon?"

"He knows. Sydney told him when they were teenagers," Archer said.

"Oh." Sawyer shrugged. "I'm okay. It's still a bit... fantastical, I guess, but it's sinking in." He eyed the other man carefully, trying to gauge Archer's mood.

Archer smiled. "I imagine you have questions."

"I do. But I also don't want to trample on your privacy."

"How long have we known each other? Twenty years now? Long enough that you know I'm hard to offend. Ask away. If I don't want to answer, I'll say so bluntly."

For the rest of the meal, Sawyer did just that. He was more comfortable talking to Archer about shifting than he'd been discussing it with Owen. They were contemporaries, he and Sydney's father, after all.

"So what about you?" he asked Sydney. "I know you said you could feel certain things with people health wise. Is that really all?"

She looked up at him warily, then at her father, and shrugged. "Mostly."

Archer frowned. "Mostly? What does that mean?"

"I don't know." She shot Sawyer an irritated glance. "I guess it means I think there's more to it. That in certain cases under special circumstances that maybe I can do more than sense a person's health. Sometimes I can... enhance it, I guess."

Archer was dead quiet as he stared at her. "You mean heal," he finally said. "You think you can heal people."

"Not intentionally. I can't control it. It just happens. And I don't even know I'm doing it until it's done. What?"

Archer was staring at her, slowly shaking his head. "I didn't know you knew about that."

She scowled. "Of course I knew about it. Don't tell me you did."

He sighed and rubbed a hand over his face. "Your mother has long suspected it was part of your abilities, yes. She didn't want to say anything to you. Didn't want to put pressure on you."

Sydney touched his arm. "Daddy... You two are something else."

"When did you figure it out?"

She smiled. "After Zanny got sick. You all tried so hard to protect us, but we knew things were worse than you were letting on. And I overheard you and Mom one night after she had more tests run in Lexington. She was better than she'd been when she was diagnosed, and that was before the doctors did anything." She shrugged again. "Like I said, it isn't something I can do at will. It either happens or it doesn't. I learned a long time ago not to try to control it. If I did try, it would drive me mad. There've been a lot of people through the years I've wanted to help but couldn't."

Archer hugged her. "I know. I'm sorry."

"There've been a lot of people through the years you have helped, too," Danny said quietly. "Don't even think there aren't."

She nodded. "I know."

After dinner, Archer stayed for a while to play with the baby. Sawyer was hoping he would leave first, so that he could figure out whether or not Sydney wanted him to stay, but it didn't look like that was going to happen. Reluctantly, he gave in first.

"I'll head out. Are you planning to stay home tomorrow?" he asked Sydney as he got to his feet.

"No. Danny's going to babysit. I'll try to be in at the normal time."

"Okay."

Archer was frowning. "How much of an inconvenience would it be for you to stay here tonight, Sawyer?"

That was the last thing he'd been expecting to hear. "Excuse me?"

"Not that I don't think Danny and Sydney can protect themselves, but I'd feel a lot more comfortable if you could stay. If something happens, if Neala comes back... You know how to defuse the situation and who to call first if it gets out of hand. I'm assuming you carry."

"I do." Sawyer didn't know what to think, and if the look on her face was any indication, Sydney was just as surprised as he was. "You don't trust Neala?"

"Not as far as I can throw her," Archer replied, dead serious. "And while she may have cleaned her act up in recent years, she used to run with a pretty rough crowd. If I didn't have to worry about the boys being home alone, I'd stay. Syd? What do you think?"

She spread her hands, her eyes wide as she struggled for words. "I... uh, I don't know. It's up to Sawyer."

"I don't have a problem staying if you don't have a problem having me," he said.

Archer grinned. "Good. I'll sleep a lot better tonight knowing you're here. Well, guess I'd better run. Holler if you need me." He hugged Sydney and was gone before anyone in the living room could say much more than good-bye.

Sawyer stared after him, then turned back to Sydney and Danny. "Do you get the feeling we just got set up?"

"By a pro," she said, nodding. "But... Okay. I won't argue. He does have a point."

Danny agreed. "So I'm upstairs in the guest room. Are you keeping this guy with you in your room?" He raised Daniel over his head, making him squeal with delight.

"I guess so."

"Then that leaves me the couch. All right. This is... yeah. This will work," Sawyer said. He sat back down as Danny snorted. "What?"

"You'll take the couch. Really? Got a bridge you want to sell me?"

Sawyer scowled even as Sydney snickered. He was mortified to feel himself blush.

"If you want to stay on the couch, feel free," Sydney said. "Wherever you're comfortable."

He didn't even try to get them to stop their teasing. They all knew where he'd be sleeping.

"Do you think he knows about us?" Sawyer asked Sydney when Danny excused himself for a few minutes. "Your father, I mean?"

"I don't know," she replied pensively. She was lying on the rug, the baby propped up against her on a blanket, playing with his toys. He'd not let go of the duck since he'd laid eyes on it. "I don't think he does. Do you?"

"I don't know."

But Sawyer was starting to wonder. He knew the old adage, that a person only saw what they wanted to see, what they expected to see. And he was starting to think that he hadn't seen a lot as it pertained to Sydney's family. After all, he never would have imagined they'd support a romantic relationship between him and Sydney, as they knew it wouldn't go anywhere. But he got the impression they knew a lot more than they were admitting to.

"I wonder if they haven't set us up all along," he slowly admitted. "But..." He'd started to ask "to what end?" but that might not be the best question to ask her. It could start a discussion he was in no way prepared to take on, much less finish, at the moment.

She bit her lip. "They *are* a nosy bunch of matchmakers."

"Who are?" Danny asked as he came back in.

"My family. We're trying to figure out if they know about

us. Sawyer was asking if they might not have set us up from the get go. Have they said anything to you?"

Danny almost choked on his soda. "Huh? To me? Why would they say anything to me?"

She groaned and fell back, taking care to keep Daniel upright. "Oh, God. They have. How bad is it?"

Danny sent Sawyer an apologetic look, then Sydney. "They're in it up to their eyeballs. Sorry, kids."

Sawyer laughed. "Of course they are. Shit." He was stunned, but at the same time, it fit. He rubbed his forehead.

"I'm sorry," Sydney told him. Regret and wary concern filled her eyes. "That's the last thing I wanted."

"I know. But we should have expected it. God bless 'em." He shook his head, chuckling.

She sat up, her brow furrowed with confusion. "You're not mad?"

"Would it do any good for me to be?"

"I don't know." She growled and tugged on her hair. "Is everyone trying to matchmake us?" she asked Danny.

"Everyone except Noah."

Sawyer scowled. "What's his objection?"

"Nothing specific. He just worries," Danny said.

Sydney nodded. "That's kind of what Noah does—worries. It's nothing personal."

He blew out an amused sigh. "Well, at least the last few weeks haven't been boring, right?"

She laid back down. "Tell me about it."

Sawyer and Danny exchanged a look. She seemed more perturbed about the meddling than Sawyer was, but he didn't understand why. Now wasn't the time to get into it, though.

And as to why he wasn't more upset? That was something else he dwell on later.

CHAPTER FORTY-SIX

SYDNEY HADN'T BEEN AT WORK long Thursday morning when Neala called.

"We'll be back in town this afternoon, probably around two. I talked to Danny. He said he'd meet me at your house with Daniel so we can get his things."

"So you're taking him today?"

"Yep. I've missed him so much, but I had to do this. Kyle's with me. He's never met Daniel. He's so excited."

Sydney wanted to scream that he'd never meet him, that she'd take the baby and Neala would be shit out of luck. But she couldn't.

"I'll see you around two then, I guess." She didn't wait for a response, just ended the call, staring into space numbly. It shouldn't hurt so much, the thought of letting the baby go after she'd only had him for a few days. But she felt like her heart was being ripped from her chest.

When she could breathe again, she stood and went to Sawyer's door. He turned the radio down as he looked over.

"What's up?"

"That was Neala."

He frowned. "She's coming?"

"Today at two." Sydney picked at the doorframe. "I'll call Danny, see what he wants to do."

Sawyer's chair creaked as he sat back. "Where're you meeting her? I'd like to be there."

The line of his jaw was hard, his eyes shuttered, as he turned his pen end over end. He had grown just as attached to Daniel as she had, something that made Sydney even angrier. She wasn't the only one losing the baby today.

"The house."

He nodded. "What time do you want to go?"

She took her glasses off and cleaned them on her shirttail. "Maybe around eleven? That'll give me time to get his things together, feed him before he goes."

"Okay. How do you want to handle the transfer?"

"Honestly? I'd like to punch her. That's not really an option, I know, but it would make me feel better. At least for a few minutes." She sighed roughly. "I don't want to see her. She hasn't even said thanks yet, you know?"

"I know. I have quite a bit to say to her before she takes him. She probably won't appreciate most of it, but I don't give a fuck how she feels at this point."

Sydney gave a quick laugh, even though she felt like crying. "Her 'baby daddy' is with her. Kyle, she said his name was. I guess things went well for her. She said he's all excited to meet Daniel. I don't want to give him back."

"You don't have a choice. And I can see you calculating how far you could get in five hours' time," he said, standing and coming around his desk. He pulled her straight into his arms with a sigh. "I'm sorry."

Sydney clung to him, slow tears tracking down her cheeks. "It isn't fair."

"No, it isn't."

There wasn't anything else to say. Nothing would fix the loss—Daniel would go home with Neala, Sydney would be with Sawyer for however long their fling lasted, and then she'd be alone again. She'd come to realize over the last few days that while she'd been prepared to lose him at the end of their run and was able to face that reality, adding the baby to the mix had changed things. Now she saw exactly what it would be like to have a family with Sawyer. He'd make a spectacular father. And she couldn't erase the images of him with Daniel from her mind. They already haunted her.

The dynamic between them had changed, as well. It felt more like a real relationship, not a casual, fun, lighthearted affair. And Sydney wasn't comfortable in that skin, not as long as she knew it would end sooner rather than later. She knew Sawyer was worried about her, as he'd asked her several times this past week what was wrong. She'd gotten quiet, and being a smart man, he'd picked up on that. She kept insisting nothing was the matter, but he didn't believe her. She knew that, too.

When her phone rang, she pulled away from him. "That's probably Danny."

"Okay. I'll wrap things up here so we can leave at eleven."

"Thanks. I think I'm going to take a walk, very brief, and get some air. I'll be back in a few minutes."

"Take your time."

She felt the weight of his gaze on her back as she grabbed her phone and wallet. She couldn't turn around and support him, though. Not right this moment. Right now, it was all she could do to keep herself together, much less anyone else.

As Sydney left the office, Sawyer growled out his frustration in a long string of curses that were less than flattering to Neala and her errant boyfriend. The week had been both tremendously long and unbelievably short. He'd still been reeling Monday from the weekend's blows as he struggled to deal with everything he'd learned, everything he was starting to feel for Sydney. With the baby thrown in the mix... He felt like his entire life had been turned upside down, all the neat, logical pieces scattered across the ground so far out of reach, he'd never find all of them.

He was terrified he was falling in love with Sydney. Hell, if he was being honest, "falling" wasn't even close. "Had fallen" was more like it. Head-over-heels, through-and-through in love.

And she was withdrawing from him faster than he could run to catch her.

After Danny's revelation that her family was on to them, had been in on the whole thing since before Sawyer had ever made his first move, they'd talked about what to do.

"Should we let them know that we know?" Sawyer'd asked as they got ready for bed that night.

"I don't think so," Sydney said. "Maybe it's petty of me, but I intend to play dumb if for no other reason than to get Daddy's goat."

Sawyer slid his arms around her waist, pulling her back into him as he laughed. "You're liable to get us in trouble."

"Nah. But maybe it'll back them off Noah a little. They need to learn they can't play Cupid like that and get away with it. Unintended consequences and the like."

The baby had cried then, and Sawyer hadn't been able to ask her what she'd meant. But her withdrawal had been blatantly obvious as the week had gone on. Danny had even noticed and commented on it.

"Is she mad at you for some reason?"

"I don't know what's going on." Until he had a better idea of his own feelings, he wasn't about to ask, either.

The insecure side of him wondered if her stepping back was because of his sterility. If, by seeing what life with a baby was like, she was regretting the decision to start a relationship with Sawyer. If she was thinking about moving on to someone who could give her a child.

He knew Sydney wouldn't cheat on him. And since they were in what they'd both defined as a casual relationship, it wasn't like there'd be a big, dramatic breakup when they went their separate ways. But he'd seen what the desire to be a mother could do to a woman, and he knew having a lover would be a deterrent to the end goal of motherhood for someone like Sydney, no matter how much she cared for him as a person.

After twenty years of being single, he had never expected to find himself being the one who wasn't ready for a relationship to end, but there it was. He didn't want to let Sydney go. He admitted to himself that he wanted to see what would happen if they had a chance to build on what they'd started. And knowing they'd almost certainly never get the opportunity to do that was tearing him apart.

CHAPTER FORTY-SEVEN

SYDNEY DROVE SEPARATELY FROM SAWYER, arriving at the house a few minutes before he or Danny got there. She was glad—she needed the time to herself. When she went in, she stood in the hall from the garage for a bit, listening to how quiet and empty the house sounded.

"You're being ridiculous, Syd," she told herself, shaking off the emotions that threatened to overwhelm her. "Get his things ready to go so you can spend the rest of the time with him once he gets here. And let it go."

"It" being the yearning and longing she felt for a future and a family with Sawyer.

She forced herself to move quickly and as mechanically as possible as she gathered the baby's things. It was hard to believe he had so much stuff, she thought as she folded his clean clothes from the dryer. Archer'd been bringing him gifts every evening after work.

"Daddy… Oh, geez." There was another man whose heart had been captured by the fifteen-pound bundle of cuteness that had dropped into their lives Monday. She should call and let him know that Neala was on the way. He'd want to swing by during lunch and say good-bye.

When Danny showed up, an underlying sadness was etched on his face. "I think we should keep him. She can have another," he told Sydney. "And between you, me, Sawyer, and your dad, he'll not want for anything ever."

Sydney kissed Daniel's cheek as she lifted him from his carrier. "You know that would never work."

"The hell it wouldn't." His ferocity surprised her. "She needs to know she can't just do this. Not to him, not to us."

Tucking the baby on her hip, she put her arm around Danny's waist and hugged him. "Sawyer's planning to have words with her."

"Good. He'll ream her a new one. She's always been a little afraid of him, you know. Maybe he'll make a positive impact."

"Neala, afraid of Sawyer? Really?" Sydney laughed. "I always thought she had a bit of a crush on him."

"I never said she didn't have good taste," he protested, causing her to snort with the first true laughter she'd felt all day. "But you didn't see the way he lit into her after you left here when you were nineteen. You know how when some people get mad, they get cold?"

"Like Daddy and Grandpa? Yeah. It's scary as hell."

"Sawyer can give them a run for their money any day," Danny said as the man himself came in the door.

"Give who a run doing what? How's my big guy?" He headed straight for the baby, who'd leaned toward him so fast, Sydney almost dropped him. Taking him like he'd held babies his whole life, he planted a noisy raspberry on Daniel's belly. "So who am I running against?"

"Daddy and Grandpa and their tempers," Sydney said.

Danny shook his head as he watched Sawyer play with the baby. He crossed his arms, and Sydney could practically see the steam building in his head. "It isn't too late to call CPS."

"Yeah, it is," Sawyer said. "There's nothing I could find that indicates she's not a good mother. If there was, they'd have been called that first day, and this guy would be ours for a while." He seemed to realize what he'd said, his eyes darting to Sydney, then away. "Did you call Archer?"

"He'll be here shortly," she said. "I'll make a run through

and make sure all his things are together." She had to get out of the living room or else she'd break down in a bawling, sobbing mess on the floor.

Danny tapped on the bedroom door a few minutes later. "You okay?"

She jerked, not having heard him approach. "Fine as frog's hair. You?"

He closed the door and stared at her, silently daring her to lie to him again.

"I can't do this now. Not until it's over."

"Okay. But it's coming. You know that."

"I do." She blew out a breath. "Help me with this stuff?"

Archer was just coming in when they got back to the living room. Much as Sawyer had, he made a beeline for Daniel.

"Good thing Mom isn't home or you'd be trying for more babies of your own," Sydney joked as he cooed and babbled at the baby.

Archer grinned. "Nah. We're past that stage. It's time to start enjoying our grandkids now."

"Um, aren't Graydon and Carter just a teeny bit young, Daddy?"

He scowled fiercely. "Don't even joke about that. I have nightmares about those two. I know what it's like to be a boy that age," he said as everyone snickered. "No, I was thinking more about you. There's a new guy at the garage—nice, young, exceptionally reliable. Maybe I'll invite him up to the farm for dinner Sunday."

Sydney didn't think there was a square inch of air in the room after the breaths that got sucked in following that pronouncement.

"Daddy, I'm seeing someone."

"Pfft, you told your mother you were just playing. And where's he been? Am I right, big guy?" he asked the baby in a funny voice. "I mean, you've spent the week with Sawyer and Danny here. Not much of a man if he lets you get away with that without getting jealous. Is he, Sawyer?"

Sawyer was struck speechless, Danny's face turned ten shades of red as he struggled not to laugh, and Sydney...

"You...I... Oooh! *Men*," she hissed. "The lot of you can go to hell." Stalking to Archer, she took the baby. "Except this one. He's not learned how to be an ass just yet. We're going to the kitchen to get some lunch. Excuse me."

Silence followed her out of the room.

The jab, though delivered with a soft hand, had been pointed and direct. Aimed not just at Sawyer but at her as well, it had slipped in and found a soft spot with deadly accuracy.

Once Neala picked Daniel up, Sydney might just get in her car and drive. She could go visit Eli, or she could go spend some time with Ben and Ainsley in Lexington. Her brothers Grant and Cade had invited her to Charleston. Or she could go somewhere completely devoid of family for some peace and quiet.

"That sounds like a damned fine idea, don't you think?" she asked the baby as she got his mushed peas and carrots ready. "I could use a vacation from the madness."

Normally, she'd never consider running. But she couldn't call the last few weeks normal by any stretch of the imagination, and right about now, going far and fast held a lot more appeal than staying to face the heartache.

CHAPTER FORTY-EIGHT

SAWYER WAITED UNTIL SYDNEY WAS in the kitchen before he approached her father.

"She doesn't need this right now," he said in a low voice.

Archer raised his eyebrows, propping his hands on his hips. "Excuse me? You're telling me what my daughter needs?"

"Yes, I am. Archer, she's hurting. Leave her be. Don't push her."

"You sure it's Sydney you're concerned about being pushed? Or is it you?" Archer asked softly. "Maybe this little game isn't all carefree fun like you'd planned, huh?"

"I have tremendous respect for you, always have, but I'm not discussing her with you. Not like this." Sawyer met Archer's gaze head-on, not blinking. "You know it isn't as simple as you're making it out to be."

"You honestly expect me to believe that if that baby was free and clear, you wouldn't love him like he was yours?" Archer's voice was low and tight. "Because I'm not buying that. I see how you are with him. Your excuse that you can't have kids doesn't hold water anymore, buddy."

"If you want to have this discussion, fine. We'll do it later. But not here, not now. Not today. Sydney doesn't need tension between us on top of everything else." Sawyer waited a beat, then headed to the kitchen. He was fairly certain Archer was testing him, which was fine. But he was dead serious about protecting her today. She was ready to break, and Sawyer'd do whatever he had to do to protect her from any more hurt.

"That was subtle as a brick bat," Danny drawled as they watched him go.

Archer shrugged, feeling out of sorts and testy. "I didn't intend it to be subtle. I wanted to test his mettle."

"Seemed pretty solid to me."

"Yeah. He always has been." He sighed. "I probably pushed too hard."

Danny, usually the diplomat, didn't try to smooth it over. "You'll catch hell when Emma hears about this. And don't think she won't. Sydney will be more than happy to hang you out to dry after this fiasco. They know, by the way, that you all played a hand in getting them together. Even before this display of fatherly interference. And Syd's pissed."

Archer growled, running a hand through his hair. "Do you think I'm wrong?"

"Wrong about them? No. Wrong to push right now? Yeah, I do. I think he's done running, but she's just getting ready to start. Archer, she's scared to death. She's convinced herself he'll never want her permanently. And it isn't because of anything he's done," he said, holding his hands up to stop Archer's outrage before it flared. "Her ability to hope is still crushed from what Adam did."

"I should have castrated the bastard."

"Wouldn't have done any good. The damage was done. You know that." Danny shrugged. "Sawyer can undo it. Seeing them together the last few days, it's been enlightening. I never would have thought the man had it in him. But she brings something out in him I've not seen before. The problem is, she's so convinced it's temporary he's going to have a hell of a time making her believe he wants forever. He's just figured it out himself, I think. It's not a comfortable time for either of them."

Archer sighed. As much as he hated to admit it, Danny was right. "Do you think she'll run?"

He grimaced. "Probably. But he'll follow. *If* he can figure out where she runs to."

"We can help with that. She won't go anywhere without telling someone where she's headed."

Danny nodded. "Unless she tells Noah. He's a clam. Then we might have a problem."

Archer squeezed Danny's shoulder in a quick hug. "Even clams can be pried open. Let's hope it doesn't come to that." But being Sydney's father and knowing her as well as he did, he had a feeling it would.

CHAPTER FORTY-NINE

SAWYER WAS IN NO WAY ready to turn the baby over by the time Neala showed up with Daniel's father. After the mess in the living room, he, Danny, Archer, and Sydney had skirted around any serious conversation as they took turns coddling the baby. Sawyer had him when the doorbell rang, and he unconsciously tightened his grip. Daniel was drowsy, almost asleep on his shoulder, and for a few seconds, Sawyer cursed his decision not to let Sydney run with the baby.

Archer had stayed after lunch, having taken the rest of the day off in case he was needed. "I'll get the door."

A few seconds later, Neala and a tall, skinny young man who barely looked old enough to vote were following Archer into the living room.

Daniel didn't stir, having fallen sound asleep.

"There's my baby. Oh, Danny Boy, come to Mommy. I've missed you so." Neala held her hands out, but Sawyer took a step back, turning so that the baby was on the opposite side of his body.

"Not so fast. We're going to have a discussion before you lay hands on him. Sydney?"

She stepped up and took Daniel even as Neala sputtered with outrage.

"You can't do that. He's my son."

Sawyer moved so that he towered over her. The kid she

was with puffed his chest up but a stony glare stopped him in his tracks. Once he was contained, Sawyer focused again on Neala.

"You dropped him off and left him with people you hadn't seen in years without a second thought," he growled. "You had no idea if we were willing or able to take care of him. You've not seen Sydney or me in years. For all you knew, we were fucking drug addicts or into kiddie porn. You dashed in and out without a care in the world about that little boy. And if you think there aren't consequences from that, you're out of your goddamned mind."

Her cheeks were bright red flags of embarrassment, but Sawyer didn't stop.

"Here's how this is going to go. He," he said, pointing at Kyle, "is going to give me his driver's license and social security number. I'm going to keep a very close eye on you both until I'm one-hundred percent certain that baby doesn't need me anymore. And if I *ever* see anything at all that raises a red flag? I'll be on your doorstep demanding answers. You gave him to me to watch. What you didn't realize at the time was what you were getting yourself into. I take my responsibilities very seriously, Neala. And when you left him with me, you made him my responsibility. You've known me too long to take that lightly, I hope."

She looked around the room, trying to gauge whether or not she had any allies, Sawyer figured. But everyone, save Kyle, met her gaze with a stony glare. Still, she tried.

"You're not a cop anymore. You can't do jack shit to me."

Sawyer abhorred men who used their strength to browbeat their way through life, especially against women. The closest he came to pushing a woman in that way was what he'd done a moment ago, using his height and mass to get his point across. He wouldn't have done that much if the baby hadn't been involved. But if he'd been a different kind of man, he would have slapped Neala.

He leaned in closer to her. "Try me."

Archer cleared his throat. "You aren't stupid, Neala. We're only concerned for the baby, and for you, too. We want to help."

"How is threatening me help?" she asked, tears forming in her eyes. "I had to leave him. I didn't have a choice. Kyle, tell them."

The guy shrugged. "I got out of the Army and she came to get me. It was the only place she knew where to find me."

Sawyer growled at him. "That's as responsible as hell—mother of your child not having any way of getting in touch with you in case he needed something. How are you going to support them?"

"My old man's got a construction job waiting for me. Sheesh, buddy, you got a stick up your ass or what? Just let us have the kid and we'll go."

"You aren't helping," Neala hissed. "And he isn't just a kid. He's your son."

"Fine, fine. Whatever."

To her credit, she appeared as disgusted as Sawyer felt. That, as well as the anxiety on her face, made him relent.

"When you take him, where are you going?" he asked.

"Back to Louisville. I have to get back to work Monday."

"Who's been watching Daniel while you work?" Sydney asked quietly.

"My aunt Joanie. We live in an apartment over her garage."

Sawyer watched Neala carefully for a minute, then sighed. He pulled a business card out of his wallet. "I won't let you go until you promise me that if he needs me, if *you* need me, you'll call. No judgments. You have my word."

More somber than she'd been since she walked in the door, Neala nodded. "Okay. I promise." She looked at Sydney. "Could I please have my son now?" she whispered.

Sydney looked at Sawyer, who inclined his head slightly. She kissed Daniel's cheek, and when Neala held her hands out, Sydney gave her the baby. With one last touch on his head and across his back, it was done.

"Excuse me." She left the room nearly running.

Sawyer looked at Archer.

"Go. We have this."

"Okay." He laid his hand briefly on Daniel, then went after Sydney. She wasn't in the bedroom as he'd expected, but instead in the backyard. Arms crossed tight, she was pacing back and forth near the back fence. When she looked up and saw him, her face was so full of anguish it nearly brought him to his knees.

He didn't say anything, just went to her and pulled her into his arms.

Unlike in the office where her tears had been silent, here they were noisy, messy, and painfully hard.

"He'll be okay," he promised her. "We'll make sure of that. I swear to you we will."

"But what about us? What happens to us without him?"

"We just have to hold on tighter and not let go."

CHAPTER FIFTY

After Daniel was gone, Sydney didn't have the strength to feel anything other than hurt. The blow of losing the baby had pushed her over the edge and into a chasm of self-preservation.

Sawyer walked her inside after her tears had died down, leading her to the bathroom. "Let's get your face washed," he said softly.

She stood perfectly still as he wet the washcloth, then took her glasses off and carefully set them aside. When he started gently blotting her face, she stopped him. His kindness was killing her.

"This isn't working for me," she rasped. She laid the cloth aside and reached instead for the tissues. Once her nose was clean, she ran water and splashed her face, aware of Sawyer's tension as she delayed.

"You're going to have to be more specific," he said. "What isn't working?"

"All of this. Us."

She kept her eyes on the sink, the water playing over her hands.

Sawyer reached out and turned it off. "Look at me."

"There's nothing to say," she protested, pulling back when he reached for her. "Do we have to make a big deal over this? I thought we agreed that wouldn't happen."

He blew out a breath. She could tell he was struggling to

maintain his calm. “Okay. I’ll back off for now. But we are going to talk.” Moving fast, he sneaked in a hard, desperate kiss.

Before she could do more than gasp, he was gone.

A couple of minutes later, her father was knocking on the door. “Sydney?”

“I’ll be right out.”

She put her glasses on, avoiding her reflection in the mirror, and opened the door. Archer was leaning against the opposite wall, arms crossed.

“Are they gone?” she asked.

“It’s just you and me, kid.” He eyed her with concern. “What do you want me to do?”

She shook her head. “I don’t know. Make everything okay?”

He held his arms open, and she walked in for a hug. “I wish I could. Want to go home with me? I’ll make you pancakes and we can watch TV.”

Sydney tightened her grip, hugging him so hard that he grunted. “I appreciate the offer, but I think I need some time alone.”

“If you change your mind, you know where to find me.”

“Love you, Daddy. Thanks for understanding.”

Archer kissed her forehead. “Love you, too, sweetheart.”

After he left, she locked the house down and went back to the bedroom. She was utterly exhausted. Stripping down, she crawled in bed and waited for the oblivion of sleep to claim her.

With Sydney clearly needing space, Sawyer didn’t have much choice but to leave. He stopped to have a brief word with Danny and Archer on his way out.

“If she needs anything, will one of you let me know?”

Archer nodded. "I'm sorry for whatever role I played in... I shouldn't have pushed."

"This isn't about today," Sawyer admitted. "It's a culmination of things. Just take care of her?"

"We will."

Needing some space himself, he headed home. Several miles of swimming would at least burn off some of his anger and frustration, he hoped.

By bedtime that night, he'd exhausted himself to the point that he thought he could sleep. He wanted to go to Sydney, but that wasn't an option. If he ever wanted it to happen again, he knew he had to keep his distance.

Whatever Gods existed in the universe were laughing at him. He knew that. If he weren't hurting so much, he'd be laughing, too.

He had an appointment tomorrow in Lexington he had to keep. He'd use that time, and maybe the weekend, as well, to let things calm down between him and Sydney. But if he hadn't heard from her come Monday, he'd reach out. There was no way he was willing to let her go as easily as she seemed to think he would. Not until she told him in plain words why it was over, and maybe not even then.

CHAPTER FIFTY-ONE

KNOWING SAWYER WOULD BE AWAY Friday, Sydney went into the office. She made a couple of circles around the block first to make sure he wasn't in town. When she didn't see his truck, she parked and went to work.

A lot of tasks had gotten pushed aside through the week, as well as the week before, thanks to everything that had happened. And while she figured she probably wouldn't have a job much longer, until he told her she was fired, she had things that she needed to do. Besides, the busywork would keep her mind off the state of her personal life.

By the time four o'clock rolled around, she'd plowed through a great deal of the paperwork that had built up. She stacked the finished work on Sawyer's desk and locked the place down. Danny had called earlier to ask her to dinner, the invitation a thinly veiled command.

"We need to talk," he said.

"I know. I'd appreciate a shoulder to cry on, to tell the truth. A sounding board. When and where do you want to meet?"

They'd decided on his small apartment at the church and set the time.

She stopped by the house to change into comfortable clothes, then made the drive, using the time to clear her mind.

When she got to the church, Danny was out back,

watering his small garden patch. In khaki shorts and a ratty T-shirt that she remembered him wearing new when they were teenagers, the familiar sight of him nearly made her cry.

"Feeling better today?" he asked.

"Some. I went in to work."

He turned off the water hose. "With Sawyer? How'd that go?"

"He's in Lexington today. He didn't know I was there."

"Ah." He pursed his lips as he rolled the hose up. "Are you quitting your job or do you plan to try to stay on?"

"I don't know. What do you think I should do?"

"I think you need to talk to him. Tell him you're in love with him."

She walked over to a healthy pot of basil and bent down to sniff its fragrant leaves. "I'd rather not do that."

He shrugged. "I hate spinach but I eat it."

Sydney threw him a dirty look over her shoulder. "Smart ass."

"Yeah. What's your point?"

"I don't think I'm strong enough to have that conversation, Dan."

"Maybe not. You might not get a choice. Monday will be here before you know it."

"I am very aware of that. I hope I have a plan by then."

But she didn't. All weekend, she dithered, going back and forth between wanting to run and wanting to stay and have it out with Sawyer. Tired of her own indecision, she texted him Sunday night.

"*Do I still have a job, or am I fired?*"

His response didn't come for several minutes, long enough that she was starting to wonder whether he'd received the message or not.

"*Up to you. Ready to talk yet?*"

"*No.*"

"*Okay, then. See you at nine,*" he texted back.

Sydney fell back on the bed with a sigh. "At least there's that," she told the ceiling.

Incredibly awkward didn't begin to describe the mood in the office Monday morning. Sawyer was there before she was, going through papers in the reception area. He looked up warily as she came in.

"Hey," Sydney said, watching him. He looked tired, a little worn, and she felt guilty for that.

"Hey. You worked this weekend?" He held up one of the reports she'd finished Friday.

"Yeah. I needed to catch up."

"Okay." He looked down at the papers in his hand. "I'll be in the office, then."

By lunchtime, some of the tension had faded, but it was still less than ideal. Sydney figured it would be until after they talked. She was trying to gather her courage to suggest they do just that when he came out of the office to make some copies. Before she could speak, his cell phone rang. He frowned when he pulled it from its case and saw the caller's name.

"Hello? Hey, Frank. What's going on?" He went still, so much so that Sydney knew something was very wrong. "When? Ah, geez. No, okay. I'm sorry. I... Yeah. Have you called Nan?" He closed his eyes and sighed. "I will. I'll have to let you know. How's Mom?"

Sydney got to her feet, gripping her pen so tightly in her hand it would leave an imprint as she waited for him to end the call.

"Tell her I'm sorry. I'll call Nan right away, and I'll be in touch." He ended the call, staring at his phone as though it were an alien device.

"Sawyer?"

"My father's dead." His voice was flat. "I have to call Nan. Excuse me." He turned and went into his office, closing the door.

"What? No," she said, following him. When she opened the door, he turned, a fiercely angry scowl on his face.

"Do you know what that door being closed means?" he growled.

"Yes, I do. But you can't say something like that and just walk away. What happened?"

For a moment, she thought he was going to tell her off. Instead, he ignored her and made a call as he paced behind the desk. "Nan? Hey. You busy?"

Much the same way he was wont to do with her, Sydney perched on the edge of his desk and listened to the conversation. The nasty looks he was giving her didn't sway her in the least.

"Frank just called. I have some bad news. Dad's gone. I guess he had a heart attack."

Sydney could hear Nan's muted reaction, and though she couldn't understand the words, she picked up the nuances.

"I'll drive up tomorrow if you're sure you're up to flying alone. Okay. No, he said Mom's sedated. She's at home. He and Jana are there with her. Matt's on his way in."

When he hung up, he stared at a poster on the wall. "I need you to cancel everything for the rest of the week. And we might have to work late tonight to get things done."

"Okay. I'll get started on that right now." She waited for another minute, but he didn't say anything else, so she went out, closing the door behind her. She leaned against it, her heart breaking for him. There was never a good time to get the kind of news he'd just received, but to have gotten it on top of all the turmoil from everything else?

"It just isn't fair," she whispered under her breath. "Why'd you have to do this to him now?" She wasn't sure if she was asking that of God or herself. She knew if she hadn't pushed him away, she might be able to help ease the burden he'd be carrying in the coming days. But she couldn't go back, as much as she regretted how she'd acted.

She'd have to try to help from a distance, instead, and hope it was enough.

An hour later, Nan called her cell phone. "Can you talk?"

Sydney glanced at the door. "Give me just a couple of minutes and I'll call you back. I don't want him to overhear."

"Okay."

She grabbed her wallet and phone, then went to the door and tapped.

"Come in." When she opened the door, Sawyer was sorting through papers, his phone tucked between his shoulder and ear. "Yeah?"

"I'm going to grab something to eat. Can I get you anything?"

"No. I'm fine, thanks." He looked away, dismissing her.

Sydney took the hint and closed the door, then left. She called Nan back once she'd reached her car.

"Hey. Sorry about that. I wanted to get someplace private. How are you?"

Sawyer's grandmother let out a huffing breath. "Worried about my boy. How is he? I know you two are having problems. I'm assuming from your remark about him overhearing that you're at work?"

"Yes. He's... I don't know how he is. He shut me out as soon as the call came in, not that I blame him given how things have been the last few days. How much do you know?"

"I know about the baby, but why don't you fill me in?"

Sydney did. Over the weeks she'd been working with Sawyer, she'd gotten to know Nan fairly well, and they'd struck up a friendship. They usually talked on the phone at least once a week now.

"So that's where we're at. I was shocked when he didn't object to me coming in this morning," she finished.

"Hmmm. I'm not. The boy has some common sense, after all. He's a stubborn Evans, and he gets a fair amount from the Carsons, God knows, but he's smart for all that obstinance. You realize this is going to hit him hard, right?"

"Yeah, I do. And if I hadn't been so damned obstinate myself, I'd be able to help him. What should I do, Nan?"

"Don't let him head north by himself. Go with him. He won't like it, but I have faith in you. You can figure out how to get him to let you ride along."

"He said something about you flying in?"

"I'll be on a plane late this evening. Matty is going to meet me at the airport." She sighed. "I've wanted to meet you, but sure as hell not under these circumstances."

"Me, too. Are you sure I should force his hand?"

Nan gave a short laugh. "Absolutely. I can't promise it won't get ugly, though."

Sydney grimaced. "Oh, I can almost guarantee you it will. I have an idea of how to approach him, but I don't know if it will work or not."

"Like I said, I have faith in you, girl. You two be careful on the road, hear me?"

"Wish me luck."

She could hear the smile in Nan's voice. "You have it."

After she hung up, Sydney closed her eyes and leaned back, praying for strength. As long as Sawyer stuck to his plan to head out in the morning, she could pull this off. They'd be working late, and as soon as she got off, she'd head home and pack, then drive to his house.

"God, what if he isn't alone?" she whispered. "What if we're all misreading this and he's not as broken up over us as we think?"

Learning that was the case would do her in, but she'd promised Nan she'd pull a rabbit out of her hat. She had to try. She just hoped her fears were unfounded.

CHAPTER FIFTY-TWO

SAWYER GOT HOME THAT EVENING after nine, tired, hurting, and entirely out of sorts. He'd not slept well since Wednesday night, and he was at his emotional breaking point.

"Guess we're taking turns," he said to the empty bedroom. He pulled his clothes off and angrily tossed them into the hamper, then hit the pool hard. He swam for close to an hour before he finally felt like he'd exhausted his pent-up anger enough to get out. He'd just gotten showered and dressed and had sat down with a sandwich in his office when headlights flashed through the house.

"Who in the world?" It was after ten. Grabbing a gun from his desk drawer, he tucked it into his waistband at the small of his back and went to the door. A glance through the peephole showed Sydney coming up the walk, a small overnight bag in her hand.

"What are you doing here?" he asked as he jerked the door open.

"I'm going with you tomorrow," she told him through the screen door.

Sawyer glared at her, his head warring with his heart and his emotions. "You're what?"

"Going with you. We can take my car. Nan made me promise. Are you going to let me in, or am I going to have to stand out here all night?"

"How about you go home? How's that sound? I like that idea a hell of a lot better."

She raised her chin stubbornly. "I'm sure you do. It isn't happening."

"You're the one who told me we weren't working. What is this, then?"

"This is you being a stubborn ass who wants an argument. We don't need to go down that road right now and you know it. Let me in. I'll sleep on the couch. For the next few days, just think of me as a pesky co-worker. All right?"

With an aggravated growl, he flipped the latch and let her in. "Take the bed. I'm on the couch." That was part of the reason he wasn't sleeping well—he'd been on the couch since he came home from her house. The empty bed was too much of a reminder that she wasn't there.

"Do you have your bags packed?" she asked as she set her own down at the end of the couch.

"Not yet. I needed to decompress first."

"Want some help with that? The packing, not the decompressing," she clarified when he shot her an incredulous look. He was gratified to see her cheeks flush and was half tempted to push her just for the sake of being contrary.

"Whatever floats your boat," he said instead. He headed to the office for his food, leaving her to follow or not. She did, but she stopped in the doorway.

"Where's your luggage? The closet?"

"Yeah. I'll have to get it down."

There wasn't much conversation as she supervised the packing. Instead of the throw it in and make it fit method he preferred, she was neat and orderly.

"Which suits are you taking?" she asked, walking into the closet.

He chose two, a medium-gray and a darker charcoal-gray, along with four white dress shirts. Sydney picked out several ties, holding them up for his inspection, and he nodded.

"Those are fine."

As he zipped the dress clothes into their hanging bag, the idea that his father was gone caught him off guard. His hands tightened on the vinyl of the bag, and he had to blow out a slow breath to retain his focus.

"What time are we leaving?" Sydney asked quietly as she dug dark-colored socks out of his dresser.

"I'd like to be on the road by six. How much gas is in the car?"

"Full tank. I stopped on the way here and filled up."

"Does your family know you're going with me?" He hung the bag up on the closet door, straightening it with precision just to give his hands something to do besides reach for her.

"Of course. They send their condolences, by the way, and if you need anything, you're to just ask."

"Yeah. Rachel called. So did Lee. He'll be out tomorrow to get the perishables from the fridge." It was after eleven now, and he knew he wouldn't see a bit of sleep tonight. Regardless, morning would come early. "I'll get out of here, let you get some rest."

Sydney nodded. "Holler if you need me."

He gently closed the door as he left the bedroom, then made his way through the rest of the rooms, shutting the house down. By the time he settled in on the couch, he could hardly hold his eyes open. Within minutes, he was out.

Soft hands woke him some time later. "Shhh, Sawyer, it's okay. It's just a dream. Come on, wake up."

He sat up with a start, his heart pounding. Drenched in sweat, all he could do was stare at Sydney. She'd turned the small lamp on just outside the bedroom, and it didn't do much to take away the gloom in the living room. He could make out that she was wearing the Hello Kitty sleep shirt and that she didn't have her glasses on. Her eyes were filled with concern.

"You were dreaming," she told him softly as she touched his cheek. His wet cheek.

He remembered then what the nightmare had been about. Instead of getting ready to attend his father's funeral, he'd been preparing for hers. He swallowed roughly, closing his eyes as he nuzzled her hand.

"What time is it?" he rasped.

"Just after midnight. Here, have some water." She placed a cold bottle in his hand, and he opened it, greedily sucking it down. "Better?"

He nodded. "Sorry."

"You're fine." Gentle fingers pressed against his lips. When those fingers disappeared, replaced with her lips, he gasped.

"What happened to being co-workers?"

"Hush." She moved back in to kiss him more fully. Sawyer could have stopped her, and he probably should have. But the week had been filled with too much hurt and pain. Pain he needed to make go away.

In seconds, he was on fire, desperate to feel her, to kiss her. He shoved back the quilt he'd covered up with and pulled her on down top of him, whipping the gown over her head. He'd been naked under the quilt, and the feel of her bare skin against his was too intense for words. Sliding his hands down her back, he cupped her behind for a moment, then curved his fingers down between her thighs. When he reached her wet core, she cried out quietly.

"No. Not yet."

Backing away, she settled between his legs, the brush of her hair against his thighs the only warning he had before her warm, hot mouth settled over the head of his erection, sucking him down with an intensity that had his hips lifting off the couch.

His hands came to her head, locking her in place even

though she didn't offer to withdraw. Without a condom, the sensations were overwhelming, and it didn't take long before he was reaching the point of no return.

"Sydney," he gasped, trying to warn her.

She pulled back, and even in the dim light, he could see her lips glistening. Her chest heaving, she ran her hands up and down his thighs as he fell back from the precipice.

"Don't you dare think you're going over without me," she told him huskily as she straddled him, her wetness sliding against his length, making them both moan.

Sawyer reached down, using his hand to guide his cock to her entrance. She obliged him by sinking down, not stopping until they were sealed together fully. He let her take over and set the pace, rising slowly only to fall back down with a gratifying urgency.

She grasped his hands, placing them over her breasts as she rode him. When he'd learned how sensitive they were, he'd taken full advantage of that to drive her to distraction when they made love. Now, he used that knowledge with a vengeance. Sitting up, he cupped her breast and sucked one of her nipples into his mouth, biting down just hard enough to cause a spike of pleasure-pain to shoot through her. With his other hand, he pinched the nubbin of flesh between her thighs. She cried out, her intimate muscles clamping down on him rhythmically as she came apart.

It wasn't enough. He needed more. He needed to come inside her with a fierceness that punished him as much as it pleasured him. Withdrawing, he raised her up so that he could slide out from under her, then turned her so that she was facing the back of the couch. Using his knee, he spread her legs as he slid an arm around her hips, pulling her back toward him as he penetrated her from behind.

"Hold on," he told her, gathering her hair in one hand as he bit down lightly on her shoulder. He used her roughly, holding on to her hips as he drove into her. Far from rejecting him, as he'd half feared she would, she instead pressed back into his thrusts, driving his desire up into the inferno range.

Taking one of her hands from the couch, he pressed it between her legs. "Do it," he growled. "Make yourself come."

But she was already there, her hand turning to clasp his as she screamed with pleasure. Feeling the contractions that rippled through her pushed him over the edge, and with a hoarse shout, he buried himself to the hilt inside her and let himself come. The orgasm lasted forever, it seemed. By the time he was done, Sawyer felt like he'd emptied every bit of his soul into her.

Limbs shaking, he managed to brace himself on the couch, curled around her trembling, sweat-covered body.

Sydney's breath was coming in shuddering gasps, and her hand, still around his, was squeezing so tightly it hurt. He didn't care.

"I can see why women are willing to follow you from other states," she surprised him by saying. "Oh, my God."

A startled laugh escaped him as he cradled her close. Once it started, he couldn't stop. Before long the laughter had turned to tears, and he buried his face in her neck as he cried.

CHAPTER FIFTY-THREE

When she'd come out of the bedroom to check on Sawyer, Sydney had never expected to end up wrapped in his arms, naked and trying to recover from mind-blowing sex while he cried. However, aside from cursing her stupid tongue for the other women comment, she didn't have a single regret.

Positioned as they were, she couldn't turn around and hold him, so instead she tightened her hands over his and held on.

His tears didn't last long, but she had a gut feeling that for a man like Sawyer, crying was something he'd probably only done a handful of times as an adult. Once he was down to the occasional sniffle, he slowly unlocked their hands and moved back. He didn't go far, just swung around to sit on the blanket.

Sydney had to move fast to get her hands on the nightshirt, which she stuffed between her thighs.

"Good thing the couch is leather," he said quietly. "Are you okay?"

"I think so. I might not be able to stand up, though," she said as she got to her feet. She was a bit wobbly at first, but her legs held. "I need to, um, excuse myself, I guess."

He didn't protest, just buried his head in his hands. He looked utterly dejected, and Sydney didn't know what to think. She settled for placing a kiss on his head and making her way to the master bathroom.

Sawyer came in, still naked, a couple of minutes later. "I need a shower," he said apologetically.

"So do I. Mind if we share?"

He shook his head. "Not at all."

Though he touched her and vice versa while they got clean, the caresses were less sexual than loving, if she dared to even think that way. Once they were out and dried off, Sydney held her hand out.

"Come to bed?"

"If you're sure."

"I am."

In mere minutes, with Sawyer pressed tight against her, Sydney was sound asleep.

They slept through the alarm the next morning. Sydney was the first to wake up, and when she glanced at the clock and saw it was nearly eight, she gasped.

"Oh, crap. Sawyer, we're late." She jumped out of bed as he rolled over. Grabbing her bag, she headed for the bathroom. Her hair was a wild tangle around her head, but she managed to tame it enough to put it in a loose twist. She'd just finished getting dressed when he came in.

"I can't believe we slept that late," he said, moving to the sink to brush his teeth.

"I'm sorry. I feel like it's my fault. I know you wanted to get an early start."

He rinsed his mouth out and set the toothbrush down, then cupped her face. "Hush," he said, right before he kissed her.

Sydney clung to him. "I'm not sorry about what happened."

He searched her face. "No?"

She shook her head. "No."

"Good."

They were on the road a short time later. Sydney took

the first leg of the driving, and they didn't say very much for a while. Sawyer seemed lost in thought, and Sydney was happy to let him stay there. Too much conversation might break the spell that seemed to have captured them.

When they were a few miles outside Morgantown, West Virginia, though, curiosity was starting to set in.

"Tell me what we're walking into?" she asked. They'd switched places a short time earlier, with him taking the wheel as they prepared to enter his old stomping grounds.

"What do you want to know?"

"Who are we liable to see, what protocols should I observe, what toes do I avoid stepping on unintentionally, that sort of thing."

"As far as protocol goes, you know what to do. Be yourself. Who we'll see?" He rubbed a hand over his hair. "Frank and Jana, my next oldest brother and his wife. Matt and Leslie, the baby brother and his wife. Their kids." He listed them. "Mom, Nan, a few cousins on Dad's side probably. Business associates, people from the community... a pretty high-flying crowd in all likelihood, so prepare for that. And uh, we might run into my ex."

Sydney paused in getting a sip of water. "Your ex-wife? She's still around?"

He tried to give her a casual smile, but he couldn't quite pull it off. "Remember I told you she'd remarried, had her first kid before a year was up?"

"Yes."

"The guy she married was my best friend since grade school. They got hitched about two weeks after our divorce was final. And he works in one of the companies the family has an interest in. He's a VP there. So she's never really lost touch with the family."

Sydney had to take a deep breath to calm down. "What's her name?"

"Christie."

"She sounds blond."

Sawyer laughed so hard he snorted. "She is."

"Your *best friend*?"

He shrugged. "I guess it had been building for a while. He had a couple of kids by a former wife, so she knew he was fertile. Match made in heaven."

Sydney had a few choice words to describe what she thought of that, and none of them would have been allowed in a church.

"So she'll just be there? And you have to put up with her?"

"Probably, yes. My parents were always closer to her than they were to me. I'm sorry."

She shook her head, outraged on his behalf. "I hate people. They're so ridiculous. And I'm the one who should be saying sorry. I wish you didn't have to go through this, especially not right now."

In response, he held his hand out. She gladly took it.

For the rest of the drive, he told her about where he'd grown up, the small trailer park he and Nan had called home. "The house we're going to, though... I imagine it's a lot closer to what you were used to with your in-laws," he said.

"Good thing I brought my good dress, then." She squeezed his hand. "Are we staying there?"

He shot her a disbelieving look. "No. I figured we'd get a room close by."

"Why don't I go ahead and do that? Give me the address."

By the time they reached Pittsburgh, she'd made reservations in a good hotel near his parents' house. Sawyer'd given her a side look when she asked for a suite, and she'd held up a finger. "I'll explain in a second," she told him.

"So what's with the suite?" he asked as he made the turns that would get them to their destination. "Not that I don't think it's fine if you want your own room."

"I don't particularly want my own room, thank you very

much," she chided softly. "But with a suite, if someone wants to come over and visit away from the house, they can. It makes a big difference during times like these, believe me. I learned that when Eli's wife died."

Once they were checked in and had their luggage in the room, Sydney took a few minutes to freshen up. Now that she had an idea of what they'd be facing, she wanted to make sure she looked her best. If her worst expectations came to fruition, she knew her appearance would serve as a kind of armor.

"Sure do hope I'm wrong," she told her reflection. She'd changed out of the comfortable jeans and loose top she'd been wearing into the more formal casual wear of slacks, a dressier blouse, and high-heeled sandals. Gold-knot earrings gleamed at her ears, and a tasteful gold watch adorned her wrist. The effect was one of understated elegance, something she'd learned from both her mother and Adam's.

A casual stranger wouldn't understand the message behind the ensemble, but they'd come away thinking she was well put together. But someone from that world, someone who was used to assessing a person from head to toe in ten seconds and tallying their net worth to within a few thousand dollars, would look at Sydney and know very quickly that she was at the very least on their same societal level. That was exactly the image she wanted to project.

When she went back to the suite's living room, Sawyer was standing at the window, gazing out across the city. She moved behind him, sliding her arms around his waist.

"You okay?"

"No. But I will be. Thanks for being here."

She tightened her arms. "Thanks for letting me come with. Um, not to bring up an indelicate subject, but how in the world are you planning to introduce me?"

He turned to embrace her, taking a moment to look at the changes she'd made. "Snazzy outfit."

"Thanks. I know I'll be on inspection. I want to pass."

"Sydney, you'd pass if you were wearing that silly Hello Kitty gown thing," he told her with a cheeky grin.

She goosed him. "I'd pass *your* inspection, yeah. I never thought of that thing as a negligee before last night. And you didn't answer the question."

He sighed. "I guess I'll introduce you as Sydney. And when people ask who you are, I'll say you're with me. If they can't make the deduction past that, they have bigger problems."

"Are you planning to tell them I work for you?"

"Well, I'm not ashamed of that, if that's what you're getting at. Though I do feel a bit like a cliché, if you want the truth. Not unhappily, but I never thought I'd be a stereotype."

She ducked her head, amused and embarrassed at the same time. "Neither did I. Think that about myself, I mean."

He drew her close, holding on for a few moments. "I don't want to go."

"I know. I'm sorry."

She could feel the tension in his muscles, and thinking about what had worked so well last night, she reached for his belt at the same time as she rose up on her tiptoes.

"Did I ever mention to you the fact that I love how it feels when you use my mouth?" she whispered as she lowered his zipper. "The way you hold my head like you're never going to let go, like you can't get inside me deep enough? The way you taste when you come?"

A dark flush spread across his cheeks and his lips parted. She closed the distance between them to nip sharply at his lower lip, then took her glasses off and set them aside. While he was still struggling for breath to respond, she went to her knees and pushed his pants and briefs out of the way.

Loving him like this wouldn't fix the pain of the loss, but it wouldn't hurt, either. After all, this was a different sort of armor for a different sort of battle. On top of him losing his father, he'd likely be coming face to face with the woman who'd destroyed his heart and dented his manhood because of his sterility. Taking him this way now would hopefully stave off any self-doubt he had, and it wouldn't be terrible for Sydney's ego, either. After all, she told herself, it would be hard to feel insecure when facing his ex if she still had the taste of him in her mouth.

CHAPTER FIFTY-FOUR

ONCE THEY WERE IN THE car and driving to his parents' house, all the emotions Sawyer had been pushing back since he'd received the call from Frank threatened to rise up and overwhelm him.

"You okay?" Sydney asked.

He blew out a breath. "Working on it."

The feel of her hand tucked securely in his helped, as did the memory of what had transpired before they'd left the hotel. He knew that had been part of her intention all along.

"How long has it been since you've been home?" she asked quietly as they drove slowly down the oak-lined avenues near the house.

"Three years. I saw everybody last winter in Florida. Dad had had some issues then, but nothing major, I didn't think. I guess I should have asked more questions."

"Was it a good visit?"

He considered the question. "Yeah, it was. As much as my relationship with them has never been all warm and fuzzy, I have to say that last year, we had fun. Mom's going to be devastated without him. He's been her life since she was just a girl."

"So despite their... somewhat salacious start, I guess you could say, they loved each other?"

"They did. Deeply."

They'd reached the house, and Sawyer pulled the car

into the driveway slowly. There were six or seven other vehicles there, and he parked behind one of the large SUVs.

"This is it."

Sydney let out a silent whistle. "This is beautiful."

He couldn't disagree. Set far back off the street, the property encompassed just over two acres and was surrounded by a tall wrought-iron fence. With stately oaks, landscaped flower beds, and a brick-paved driveway, the scene was set for the house itself.

"How big is it?" she asked as they got out.

"Just under five thousand square feet, best I recall," he said as they met at the front of the car. The sandstone three-story mansion was stunning, welcoming for all it's size. "This place scared the hell out of me when I was a kid. Coming from a three-bedroom trailer that had seen better days, I was always terrified I'd put a foot wrong or use the wrong fork or something."

"Would they have cared if you did?" Sydney asked as she slid an arm around his waist.

"Nah. Not until my brothers got old enough to be embarrassed by me. Then it got hard to explain to friends how I was their brother but didn't live here. I stayed away most of the time after that started happening. Mom and Dad came to see me at Nan's. Things got better between us all after we were older and living in different states. Here's Frank now."

A tall, dark-haired man just a couple of inches shorter than him was coming down the wide steps to meet them. He held his arms open and Sawyer stepped up for a hug. It was tight and hard and full of emotion.

"Glad you're here," Frank said as he pulled back, looking Sawyer over from head to toe. "Good Lord, you're in even better shape than you were in Florida. Didn't you get the memo that you're supposed to be getting paunchy and bald by now?" he said with a half grin.

Sawyer smiled. "That one must have slipped by my desk.

You aren't looking half bad, yourself." It was true. There were some good genes in the family pool, Sawyer thought.

"Thanks. You'll have to tell me what you do to keep those muscles toned, though." Frank squeezed his arm. "You must be Sydney. You don't look half bad for someone who rode from Kentucky in the trunk of a car. I'm Frank, this lug's brother."

She shook hands with him, a puzzled frown on her face. "Nice to meet you. But what in the world are you talking about, the trunk of the car?"

Frank winked at her. "When he called a few hours ago to let us know you'd been delayed, Nan asked about you. He told her he'd tied you up in the trunk."

Sydney's mouth dropped open and she smacked Sawyer's arm. "That's what you were laughing about. Turkey." Her cheeks flushed. "I can't believe you said that. They're going to think I'm awful."

Sawyer grinned at her discomfort. "I couldn't resist." His amusement didn't last, however, as they approached the front door. "How's Mom?"

Frank shook his head. "Lost. Stunned. She went up for a nap a while ago. I think she's still waiting to wake up from the nightmare. Hell, we all are. Come on in."

His mother was coming down the steps as they entered the foyer. She gasped, tears forming in her eyes, and hurried down to meet them.

"Oh, my baby boy. Oh, Sawyer. Thank God."

He enveloped her in a tight hug. "Mom." Out of the corner of his eye, he saw Nan come out of the living room. She nodded at him but went to Sydney, giving him a moment alone with his mother.

"Let me look at you," Elise Evans said, pulling back as she swiped at her cheeks. "Such a handsome boy. You look so much like him."

"Hardly a boy anymore," he said with a sad smile. "I'm sorry, Mom. So damned sorry."

"So am I. It was so *fast*, Sawyer. He was happy, smiling and laughing, telling me one of those awful jokes. And then he was just gone. I can't believe he's gone," she whispered.

Sawyer tucked her under his chin, closing his eyes as she cried. "Neither can I."

As harshly as she'd thought of Sawyer's parents after learning how they'd practically abandoned him, Sydney's heart broke as she watched him console his mother. The raw grief on her face spoke loudly to the depth of her feelings for the man who was gone. It reminded Sydney that people were never one-dimensional, but were multifaceted and complex, good and bad simultaneously. Even something that seemed so black-and-white as Sawyer's childhood had shades of gray thrown in the mix.

"Well, look at you. I expected you to be taller," a trim woman with short gray hair and Sawyer's eyes said as she approached. "And you're just as cute as a damned button. Sawyer has good taste. I'm Nan."

Sydney smiled as she hugged the woman who wasn't any taller than her. "I'm so happy to meet you. And I thought you'd be taller, too."

"I told her she looks pretty good for someone who's been locked in the trunk for hours," Frank said in a low voice. "Come on in the living room and I'll introduce you to everyone."

"We'll be right in, Frank." Nan linked their arms together as they followed him. "Word of warning—Christie's here. That's Sawyer's ex-wife. I'm sorry."

"He mentioned she probably would be," Sydney assured her. "I'm a big girl. I can handle her."

"I'm looking forward to seeing that," Nan said quietly.

"He's never brought anyone home with him before. That has her panties in something of a twist."

"Well, it wasn't like he volunteered to bring me, exactly."

"She doesn't know that." Nan leveled a knowing look on her. "So you're still not on speaking terms, is that what you're trying to tell me?"

The heat in Sydney's cheeks was answer enough for Nan, who grinned. "That's my boy." She patted Sydney's hand. "Let's stir 'em up a little."

"God help us." Sydney cast a glance over her shoulder at Sawyer. "I didn't expect to feel sorry for her. I suppose that's an awful thing to say to you, given that she's your daughter. But once he told me about his childhood... Thank God he had you."

Nan was studying her closely. "You love him, don't you?"

Sydney pressed her lips together and nodded. "Too much, it feels like. And at the same time, that's not enough. Does that make sense?"

"Oh, more than you know."

They went on in the living room and Frank made the introductions.

"My wife, Jana. Our oldest daughter, Samantha. My brother Matt, the baby, and his wife Leslie. And this is Christie Denton. She's a uh, a friend of the family from way back."

"I'm aware," Sydney said, meeting the cool blonde's gaze head on with a regal nod.

"So just who are you exactly?" Matt asked, not unkindly. "Nan's been insinuating all sorts of juicy things." Although he resembled Sawyer and Frank enough that one could tell they were related, he was softer, more of a cherub version of his older brothers.

"I don't even know you're last name," Frank said, embarrassed. "That's awful. I'm so sorry."

Sydney smiled. "It's Gibson."

"Don't let her kid you," Sawyer said from behind her. He

touched her shoulder. “It’s Trouble, capital T. Mom, this is Sydney. Sydney, my mother, Elise.”

“Sawyer told me you were special,” Elise said in Sydney’s ear when they hugged. “I’m so pleased to meet you.”

“Likewise, though I’m sorry it’s under these circumstances. I’m very sorry for your loss.”

Elise nodded. “Thank you. Come sit down, you two. How was the trip up?”

“Uneventful,” Sawyer told her as they sat down on a short couch. He stretched his arm out behind Sydney casually, as though he’d done it a thousand times. She didn’t know if the move was calculated or not, nor did she care, but it sent a clear message they were more than friends. Especially when she leaned into him just a bit, needing to feel the solidness of him against her.

“I didn’t know you were coming,” Elise told her apologetically. “All the guest rooms are taken.”

“I’m sure she can find a nice hotel room not far from here,” Christie said with a gracious smile. “I wouldn’t worry too much about that, Elise. I’m sure Cindy understands, don’t you?”

As an opening sally, Sydney had to admit it was a pretty good one. Bold, worked straight to the point at setting the tone. If the situation had been less serious, she would have applauded.

“It’s Sydney. And actually, we already have a room,” Sawyer said. “No offense, Mom.”

Elise frowned, concerned. “Are you sure?”

Sydney touched Sawyer’s side with her hand. “It’s fine. I promise.” She thought about calling Sawyer’s ex Cathy, but she didn’t want to lower herself to that level. Instead, she just ignored her.

“Well, at least say you’ll have meals with us,” Elise said worriedly. “I don’t want either of you to feel like you’re not welcome here.”

"Absolutely, we'll eat here," Sawyer assured her, glancing at Sydney, who nodded.

"So not to be nosy," Matt said, causing his wife to jab him in the ribs and roll her eyes, "but I am. How'd you meet?"

Sydney looked at Sawyer, whose lips were twitching. "Oh, no. Not there."

"It's the beginning," he said with a shrug as she groaned and ducked her face against his shoulder. "She threw up on me."

"I was six! I couldn't help it. Besides, you should have moved faster."

He gently pinched her arm. "Moved faster? There was no warning. Just blaaaaahh," he said, making a flowing gesture from his mouth with his hand to add to the effect.

"Love at first sight, huh?" Frank grinned at them.

Sydney hid her face behind her hands, shaking her head. "I did have the most awful crush on him after that."

Christie's lip curled up. "Bonding over vomit. How romantic. So this is long-standing, your relationship, I mean."

"Not really," Sydney said, watching Sawyer. "He's been a family friend for years. After that, he pretty much avoided me, and I can't say that I blame him. But then when I came home a couple of months ago, my father mentioned that Sawyer needed an assistant."

"I didn't want to hire her," he admitted. "She kissed me when she was nineteen, you see. Just about embarrassed the both of us to death. And I hadn't seen her since."

Sydney poked him in the ribs. "Are you *trying* to make them think I'm awful? You keep this up and you might end up needing that room here, after all."

Even his mother chuckled at that.

"What? It's the truth," he said, laughing softly. "Ten years from now when the kids are asking us how we met, they'll cackle about how you got sick all over me. But if we have daughters, we won't mention the kiss. Not until *they're* married. I'd hate to give them ideas."

He stared at her, his gaze challenging, but Sydney was dumbstruck. She couldn't have responded right then if she were on fire.

"Kids? You have children?" Christie asked.

The unholy glee in the woman's face lit Sydney's temper. "Not yet, we don't." If it wouldn't have embarrassed Sawyer terribly and potentially caused his family pain, she would have told the bitch to fuck off.

"Sydney assures me that adoption isn't just for puppies and kittens," he said, giving her a wink.

"Aren't you getting too old for that?" Christie said, taking a sip of her drink. Judging from the color of the liquid and the shape of the glass, Sydney felt safe in assuming it wasn't sweet tea or cola.

"I'm not." Sawyer stared at Christie pointedly. "Anything else you'd like to ask?"

She turned away, staring out the window. Sydney thought she would have been frowning if her face hadn't been so tight from having been tugged and pulled this way and that.

"I'm glad you've finally come to your senses," Nan put in from beside Sydney, her tone smug with satisfaction. "I've been waiting years for him to figure that out, you know, about puppies and kittens. Looks like he just needed a certain kind of push."

"Or a certain person to do the pushing," Sawyer said. He sat forward, sighing. "Mom mentioned that there's food. We didn't stop to eat. I could use some calories."

Sydney nodded, following his lead. "If it isn't too much trouble."

"Not at all," Elise said, standing. "There's a buffet in the dining room. We're expecting a full house, so we'll probably keep food going for the next few days."

"If you're feeding them, you'd better eat, too," Matt told

her as several people got to their feet. "She hasn't been eating."

"I'm not hungry. And I ate a little breakfast this morning," she told him as he kissed her cheek. "Come on, you two. Let's get you fed."

"Actually, I need the restroom first," Sydney said.

"I'll show you where it is." Sawyer held his hand out and she took it. "I need to wash up, too."

"We'll see you in the dining room, then," Nan said. "Take your time. We'll just be grazing."

They left the living room, Sawyer leading her down the hall to the left.

"Bathroom's here under the stairs," he said. But he kept going.

Sydney, her hand still in his, followed. "Okay. Where are you taking me?"

"In here." He went through a door that opened into a study, closing it behind them by backing Sydney into it. "I'm sorry. I didn't mean to say all that. It just slipped out."

She flattened her hands against his chest, trying to hide her disappointment. "So you didn't mean it."

"I didn't say that." He braced his hands on either side of her head, leaning in to steal a kiss. "I didn't say that at all."

By the time he raised his head, she was breathless and flushed. Her emotions were roiling through her, confusion warring with hope.

"You didn't seem to object too heavily to what I was saying," he said, his voice low as he traced her lips with his thumb.

Sydney nipped him, capturing the digit between her teeth. "You, sir, are trying to start two things we cannot and will not finish here," she warned. "And I didn't hear anything I disagreed with out there."

"No?"

She shook her head.

"You'd really have kids with me?" He asked the question

solemnly, his eyes sober, with a tiny furrow of concern appearing between his brows.

Sydney reached up and touched his cheek. “I really would.”

“Even if they were adopted?”

“Well, unless you know of some other way, they’d have to be,” she chided softly. “Silly man.”

To her surprise, he ducked his head, his cheeks flushing as he pressed a hand low on her belly. “I’d like to see you pregnant. Maybe we could… maybe Danny would provide… or a clinic… I don’t know.”

“Sawyer…” she whispered, stunned. “You’re serious?”

He lifted his head. “I love you. And yeah, I’m serious.”

She felt like she’d been sucker punched, like all the air in the room had been sucked out. “You love me?”

“With everything in me.” He removed her glasses and stuck them in the pocket of his dress shirt, then wiped away the tears she hadn’t even been aware of shedding.

“Since when?”

He shrugged. “Tennessee, maybe. Maybe before that. I don’t know. I figured it out last week. Your dad and Danny knew it, too. It was all they could do not to laugh at me, especially Archer. After seeing me swear off love and marriage for so many years, I guess he’s—”

Sydney’s kiss cut his words off. She didn’t give a damn what her father thought. All she cared about was somehow convincing herself she hadn’t imagined the last few minutes.

“You have hellacious timing, did you know that?” she whispered when she pulled back. “You meant what you said? You aren’t just teasing me?”

He threaded his fingers into her hair carefully. “I meant every word. I love you. I want to marry you, have a family… or not. Depending on what you want.”

“I want you. Anything or anyone else would just be a bonus,” she rasped through her tears. “I love you so much.”

Sawyer drew her to him, holding her tight. “Thank God.”

A knock at the door interrupted them a minute later. "You okay in there, kids?" Nan asked.

"Just fine," Sawyer told her, opening the door. "We just had a little air to clear."

She raised an eyebrow, glancing from his happy grin to Sydney's tearstained, smiling face. "I see. Good to know. Come get some food."

"I still need the restroom," Sydney said, putting her glasses on as they went back down the hall. "I'll be in there in just a second."

Once she was closeted alone in the bathroom, she let her body sag against the door, too weak with emotions to move for a few seconds. She couldn't believe it—Sawyer loved her. Moreover, he wasn't rejecting her and that love. He was embracing it. Of all the results she'd expected when she'd started working for him, this hadn't even been on the list. She half worried she'd lost her mind.

She had to pull herself together now, though. Later there'd be time to sift back through the day, analyze his words, her emotions. She wasn't sure she hadn't dreamed the whole thing.

"Time," she murmured as she straightened her hair. "Just take things slowly and carefully. You have all the time in the world, and even if you don't, you need to take it."

She wouldn't start believing this was real until she woke up tomorrow morning in Sawyer's arms and heard him say the words again. And even then, she might still doubt her sanity. But if she was going crazy, she had to admit, insanity seemed a lot nicer than what she'd been led to believe.

CHAPTER FIFTY-FIVE

SAWYER WAS CERTAIN HE'D SCREWED up things between him and Sydney forever by opening his big mouth and joking about adoption. And he hadn't intended to lock himself in a room with her at his parents' house and pour out his feelings. But that's what he'd ended up doing.

By the sheer grace of God, he figured, he hadn't ended up with egg all over his face.

She'd been so stunned, he could tell she was having a hard time getting her head around the concept that he was in love with her. And he didn't expect that now that the cat was out of the bag, things would go smoothly.

In addition to calling his brother earlier when they'd stopped for gas, he'd received a call from Danny.

"I'm sorry about your father," the younger man had started out by saying. "Is there anything I can do?"

"No. But I appreciate the words."

"Sydney's with you?" Danny asked.

Sawyer glanced over his shoulder to make sure she wasn't within earshot. "She is. We've stopped for gas. Why?"

"She's scared, that's why. And I'm afraid she'll buck up and run before you two work things out."

"We've made a good start at that, I think," he said, not wanting to tell the other man about his and Sydney's intimacy the night before.

"Have you told her you love her yet?"

Sawyer winced. "No."

"Well, when you do, don't be surprised if she doesn't believe you. I don't think you have any idea of just how shattered she was after Adam. She doesn't trust in happily ever after anymore."

"Okay." He pinched the bridge of his nose. "What do you suggest?"

"Be patient with her. Once you tell her you love her, it's going to hit her hard. You'll have to be persistent and patient."

Sydney'd stepped up to the counter inside, he saw. "I'd better go. She's getting ready to come out. I appreciate the call. Seriously."

"Just let me know if I can do anything. I think you can make her happy, and I think she can do the same for you. I'll help facilitate that however I can."

Now, as they grabbed a bite to eat with his family, he kept an eye on her. She seemed to be fitting in nicely, not that he'd expected her not to. But he'd particularly worried about how she'd stand up against Christie. His ex-wife could be vicious, and he'd figured her feathers would be ruffled by the fact that he'd brought a woman home.

As far as Christie went, he knew better than to think she'd be satisfied with the barbs she'd gotten in. She'd find a way to hit out at him sometime during the next few days, of that he was certain. He just didn't know when exactly she'd strike. All he could do was hope she went after him and not Sydney. Because if she attacked Sydney? As much stress and pressure as they'd been under the last few weeks, he'd snap.

Christie always brought the worst out in him and he had a hard time holding back under ideal circumstances. They'd only seen each other a handful of times in the last twenty-four years, and that was the only thing that had kept the peace. The last thing the family needed now was to have to mediate a fight between Sawyer and Christie, but if she tried to sharpen her claws on Sydney, a fight's exactly what they'd get.

By the day of the funeral, Sawyer's nerves were stretched tight. Even with Sydney at his side, his stress level had shot through the roof. Christie had sniped at them a few more times, but nothing major. He worried about leaving Sydney alone while he performed his duties as one of his father's pallbearers, but Nan was with her. Besides, Sydney could stand up for herself.

He just didn't want her to have to.

So when, after the funeral, he was upstairs changing out of his suit, he overheard Christie's voice in the next room, talking to Sydney, his hackles rose. He edged closer to the bathroom door so he could hear better.

"You've settled in here nicely with the family," Christie said. "Made yourself right at home. I'm surprised you haven't moved in."

"Are you? Well, maybe I will move in. Elise did ask us to stay for a while."

"How'd you hook him?"

"With my feminine wiles, of course. Low-cut blouses, skin-tight skirts, blow jobs under the desk. The usual. Why? Looking for pointers?" Sydney asked dryly.

He should have expected Sydney to turn the tables on his ex. It was all he could do not to laugh out loud. He wished he could see Sydney's face. None of it was true, of course. Her work wardrobe was perfectly respectable, if attractive, and as to the other… He'd remind her of that later.

"He won't marry you. Sawyer's the ultimate confirmed bachelor. He never got over me. Why do you think he's stayed single for so long?"

Sydney sighed. "Having met you, I figured it had

something to do with the shit-ass skid marks you left on his heart and a healthy dose of common sense. Do you want him back? Because frankly, I'm getting really tired of all that sex. You were married to him—you know how it is. The huge cock—seriously, what is it, a summer sausage? I'd much prefer a hot dog sometimes. Makes walking the next day easier. Then there's the flipping you over this couch here, bending you over that desk there, the constant orgasms... Sometimes I just want to curl up on the couch and watch TV. Eat ice cream. Fart."

He had to bite his hand. That's exactly what they'd done the last two nights at the hotel. It had been bliss. Well, maybe not the farting. But the rest had been a godsend, a bit of tranquility in the mess surrounding his father's death.

"You don't take much of anything seriously, do you?" Christie said, nastiness rising in her voice. "If you think he doesn't see you for the gold-digging whore you are, think again. He may be letting you lead him around by his dick right now, but he's not stupid."

"Are you frowning or smiling? I can't tell. You really might want to consider switching plastic surgeons," Sydney said. Her voice moved closer to the door. "Nice job on the tits, though. Are you finished?" she said, swinging the door open, an annoyed frown on her face when she saw him standing there. "Get a good earful?"

"More than," he told her with a grin. He leaned around the frame to look at Christie. "Weren't you going to go fuck yourself or something? She's got to perform her thrice-daily blow job now. Unless you'd like to stay and watch."

"I might get performance anxiety," Sydney protested as Christie stormed out the door, cursing. "Is that a no?" she hollered after her.

Sawyer couldn't contain his laughter any longer. He was in tears, he was so tickled. Putting his hands under Sydney's behind, he lifted her straight up, pleased when her legs came around his waist.

“The door’s open, you demented man. Why are you laughing so hard? It wasn’t funny. She’s a she-devil,” she said as he tumbled her on the bed.

He got up and closed the door, locking it, then came back to Sydney. She had risen onto her elbows, staring at him with a disgruntled scowl. Still chuckling, he reached out and undid her pants.

Serious alarm filled her eyes. “You can’t be... Sawyer! What are you doing?”

“Having a snack,” he said as he peeled her pants and underwear down her legs. “Or maybe seeking some solace.” He handed her a pillow. “Better bite down on this. You know how noisy you get.”

“I’m so going to kill you later,” she told him on a sigh as he kissed the place where her leg met her torso. “Much, much later, though.”

He was going to have a word with Christie when he saw her again, tell her plainly to leave Sydney alone forever. But right now he was going to enjoy the woman he loved just because he could. Life was too short to waste worrying about anything else at the moment.

CHAPTER FIFTY-SIX

"I CAN'T BELIEVE YOU DID THAT," Sydney told him as they came downstairs sometime later. Her cheeks were still pink. He'd not been satisfied until she'd begged him for mercy, and even then, he'd taken his sweet time with his own orgasm.

When his brother Matt winked at them as he passed them on the stairs, she groaned, her cheeks flaming. "I told you everyone would know what we were doing."

Sawyer stopped her with a hand, concern on his face. "Does it bother you? That we were intimate here? I never would have done that if I'd known it bothered you."

"It doesn't, not really. I don't regret doing it," she told him in a low voice, moving closer as guests came in the front door. "It's just been a while since I was in a relationship and it's a little awkward, having people know. But I'm not sorry we did that. Please don't take my reaction to mean that I am."

He touched her cheek. "You're sure? Because I don't want you to ever feel like you can't say no to me, Sydney. Ever. Even after we're married."

She cupped her hands around his palm, leaning into his touch. "I like the way that sounds, 'after we're married,' I mean. And I do know I can say no. Do you really think I'd have a problem turning you down if I wasn't interested or up to the challenge? If I say yes, it's because I want to."

"Well, I am legendary. Women do follow me from other states," he said with a grin, wincing when she pinched him. "Your body might not let you say no."

She sighed with exasperation. "I love you."

"I love you. But we definitely are attracting attention now. Hi." He nodded at the three people standing at the foot of the stairs.

Sydney turned, a polite if embarrassed smile on her face. But when she saw who it was, she froze. "Adam? Helen, Ray? What are you doing here?"

Adam was staring up at her with, of all things, something akin to jealousy in his eyes while his parents were looking pleased if a bit apprehensive.

"Jordan was a client," Ray said as they came down the remaining steps. "What brings you here?"

Sydney accepted his and Helen's hugs. "He was Sawyer's dad. Sawyer, this is—"

"I know who it is." Before anyone could say or do anything, his fist flew out with a sharp jab, catching Adam under the jaw. He staggered back a few steps, then fell flat on his ass, looking up at Sawyer with stunned surprise as he touched his face.

Sydney's hands flew to her mouth and she stood there, wide-eyed, staring from Adam to Sawyer as Ray helped his son to his feet. He was shaking his head, but aside from a flare of anger in his eyes, he didn't say anything.

"What the hell? I don't even know you." Adam swayed on his feet but caught his balance. "What was that for?"

"Take your pick," Sawyer growled. "From what I understand, you have plenty sins to atone for."

Frank stepped in, hurrying to get between the men. "Nothing to see here, folks, sorry for the disturbance," he told the small crowd that had gathered in the foyer as he turned to Sawyer. "What the hell is wrong with you?" he hissed.

"It's been a long couple of weeks," Sawyer gritted. He still had yet to take his eyes off Adam. "Sorry."

Sydney was mortified. At the same time, she wanted to shove her finger in Adam's face and yell with triumph. Instead, she figured she might want to try to diffuse the tension.

"Adam's my ex-husband," she told Frank. "I'm sorry."

"We're going to find some ice," Ray said. "Come on, son. Let's get you out of here before any more of your chickens come home to roost." The slap he landed on Adam's shoulder wasn't quite gentle as he steered him toward the dining room.

Helen grimaced. "I supposed he had that coming, although I don't appreciate you punching my son. Are you the same Sawyer that Sydney's been working for in Hazard?"

"I am. She's spoken very highly of you and your husband. I am truly sorry for the embarrassment," he told her, inclining his head the direction the men had gone.

She shook her head. "You're awfully protective of Sydney to just be her boss. Not that she's not worth protecting."

"I'm not just her boss. We're engaged," he admitted.

Frank's eyebrows rose. "No kidding? Since when?"

"Three days ago. We didn't want to make an announcement given the circumstances," Sydney said, clasping Sawyer's hand.

He winced and sucked in a breath. "Ouch."

"Looks like you need some of that ice yourself, big brother," Frank said. "I'll get it and bring it to the patio. Helen, can I get you anything? Sydney?"

"The same, thanks," Sydney said after Helen asked for a sparkling water.

"So this is why you were so full of 'Sawyer this' and 'Sawyer that' when we'd talk," Helen said as they walked to the back of the house.

Sydney nodded. "It crept up on us, I guess you could say."

Helen's smile was a bit sad. "I'm glad. I've hated knowing you were alone. We only ever wanted the best for you, you know that, right?"

"I do."

Halfway down the house, Ray and Adam emerged from another door. Helen lifted a hand toward them. "I'd better go to them. I'd say it's been nice to meet you, but... I am sorry about your father," she told Sawyer.

"Thank you."

Sydney was relieved when Ray steered Adam in the other direction, and she did the same to Sawyer. "You silly man. What were you thinking?"

He leaned up against the concrete balustrade and shrugged, a broody scowl on his face as he looked after the Tates. "That I should have hit him harder?"

"Sawyer... what am I going to do with you?" she asked as Frank came out, bowl of ice and glasses of water in hand. He had a towel draped over his arm.

"Here. So why'd you hit him?" he asked as he set everything down on a nearby table. He spread the towel out and dumped some of the ice in it, deftly folding it into a bundle that he placed on Sawyer's hand.

"Because he hurt her." Sawyer sighed. "I didn't even think about where I was. I'm sorry, Frank."

"And here I thought the only ex's we'd have to worry about today would be Christie." He snorted, clearly amused. "You're lucky you just addled him. Congratulations, by the way, on the engagement."

Sydney eased the ice off Sawyer's knuckles to see how his hand looked. "Thank you. This looks like it's just bruised and scraped. I don't think you hit him hard enough to break it, thank God."

"I just gave him a little love tap," Sawyer said as Nan and his mother came out of the house. "Oh, boy."

Frank pulled Sydney aside while they lectured him. "I'm glad you two found each other."

She smiled. "Yeah? So am I. Even if he is an ornery bird sometimes. I'm sorry for the drama."

He waved it aside. "He's just like Dad. Consider that a warning—you'll have your hands full the next forty years or so."

"If I'm lucky," she said softly. "But so will he."

Frank grinned. "I kind of got that impression. I hate to see you two go back to Kentucky. I'd like to get to know you better, and I know I speak for the rest of the family when I say that."

She crossed her arms loosely over her chest. "It isn't that far of a drive. Sawyer said that you all as a family didn't get along that well. But that's not what I've seen here."

His brother shoved his hands in his pants pockets and shrugged. "It's better now than it was. There was a lot of tension between Dad and Sawyer. Dad carried a lot of guilt over the way Sawyer was raised, and that colored their relationship. He couldn't let go of it, even though I think Sawyer forgave him for any transgressions years ago."

That was so damned sad, Sydney thought. "Hopefully now things will have a chance to fully heal."

"I hope so. Well, I'd better see to the guests."

After he'd excused himself, she made her way back to Sawyer.

Elise was shaking her head. "Stubborn mule. Sydney, good luck with him, sweetheart. You'll need it." She kissed Sydney's cheek and went back inside.

Nan chuckled even as Sawyer gave an exasperated sigh. "He almost got himself grounded," she explained. "I'd like to have seen the altercation. Was it exciting?"

"No, it was scary. You could have hurt him, and then where would we be?" Sydney scolded even as she put her arms around Sawyer. "All those babies we're going to adopt would be left without a daddy."

He hugged her close. "I know. I wasn't thinking. I'm sorry."

"I know you are. And I'll love you forever for doing that for me." She tipped her face up for a quick kiss. "Among other things."

He brushed his cheek across her temple. "Imp."

"Don't you forget it."

CHAPTER FIFTY-SEVEN

ONCE THEY GOT BACK TO Kentucky, life slowly returned to normal. Since they'd been out of town for so long, Sarah decided to once again push the birthday party back, this time for two weeks. At Sunday dinner the week they returned, Owen good-naturedly joked that by the time the kids got to eat their cake it would be older than dirt, but Sarah had simply laughed at him, refusing to be swayed.

Knowing everyone in her family would be there, Sydney decided to seize the opportunity.

"What would you think about getting married at the farm when we have the party?" she asked Sawyer that night. They were curled up in his bed, holding each other as they wound down from the day. "I don't particularly want a big wedding unless you do. Danny could perform it, and we could sneak your family in."

"You mean not even tell them we're having a wedding until we show up and get hitched?" he asked. He raised up on an elbow. "Seriously?"

She nodded. "Unless you want the big shindig, yes. I don't particularly want to wait the months it's going to take to plan a big to-do, though."

He traced her hairline. "Sooner definitely works better for me. The faster I can make you swear to obey me, the happier I'll be."

Sydney reached down and grabbed him, making him grimace even as he chuckled. "You really think that's going to do one bit of good?" she whispered.

"No, ma'am. And I hope it doesn't. I wouldn't change anything about you, you know that, right? I love you."

She let her touch turn to a caress as they kissed. "I love you, too. So what do you say? Secret wedding?"

"Your grandparents will have to be in on it," he warned.

"I figured as much. As long as the groom's happy about it, we'll work everything else out."

"The groom is thrilled. Whatever steps we need to take to make you my wife, that's what we'll do."

Two weeks minus one day later, Sydney was sitting on the floor at the farmhouse putting the finishing touches on a glass-jar votive.

Noah, who'd been strong-armed into helping, was scowling. "Why do women feel like they have to have these frilly things at a wedding, anyhow?" he asked as he tied a bow onto a jar.

Sarah, who was tying said frilly bows and handing them to him, laughed. "Oh, Noah. You are such a man. This wedding is almost as simple as the one your grandfather and I had. I can hardly wait to see everyone's faces tomorrow when they show up and find out what's going on."

"You're telling me," Nan said from beside her. "I'm so excited to meet everyone."

"Speaking of everyone, Grandpa and Sawyer should be getting here any minute with Sawyer's brothers and Elise. Are you sure it's not too much trouble to put everyone up here, Grandma?" Sydney asked.

Sarah looked at her from over the top of her reading glasses. "We are not having this discussion again, young lady."

"Yeah, young lady," Noah drawled. "When are you going to have some great-grandbabies? I appreciate you taking the heat off me, by the way."

Instead of the joke making her laugh as he'd clearly expected it to, Sydney fell silent. She picked at the burlap ribbon around the jar in her lap.

"Syd? Did I say something wrong?" he asked.

She shook her head, swallowing against tears. "No. It's just... I'm late."

Sarah and Nan's indrawn breaths told her they understood, but Noah just blinked at her. "Late for what?"

Sydney cringed. "Really? You don't get that? Oh, geez, Noah, don't make me explain."

When he saw her acute embarrassment, realization set in. "You mean for your—ah, hell. I did not need to know that." He scrambled to his feet. "I'm getting some air."

Once the screen door had shut behind him, Sarah spoke. "Does Sawyer know? And just how late are we talking about?"

"Almost a month. I've not been able to tell him. I don't know what it means." She looked at Nan, who was frowning. "I don't know if Sawyer's mentioned anything to you about our family, about our... abilities."

"Not really, no. Sydney, you know he can't have children."

Sydney wet her lips. "I do know that. But that might not be true exactly. You see, this will probably sound like science fiction, but every now and then I have this ability to feel people's health. And once in a very rare while, I think I can heal them."

There was silence in the living room as Nan looked from her to Sarah, who nodded.

Nan's eyebrows shot up. "And Sawyer knows about this?"

"He does."

Nan gave a little shake of her head. "Can everyone in your family do that?"

"No. Mine isn't the only ability, but the rest aren't my secrets. I can't tell you. I hope you understand that."

"I do." She scooted to the edge of the couch, reaching

a hand out to tip Sydney's chin up. "Have you taken a test yet?"

"I'm afraid to. I've had one in my bag for a couple of weeks now, since right after we got back from Pittsburgh."

"Then don't you think it's time you did?"

"What if it's negative?" she whispered.

"What if it isn't?" Sarah countered.

"Maybe we're not ready to be parents. The adoption route takes time. If I'm…" She couldn't even bring herself to say pregnant. "That might be too soon for Sawyer."

Sarah rolled her eyes. "You aren't serious. Sydney Marie, go pee on the damned stick. Don't make me call your mother."

Nan snickered. "Does that work?" she asked Sarah.

"Apparently it does," Sydney said as she got to her feet. She closed her eyes, sending a fast prayer out to the universe. "If it's negative, you might have to explain it to Sawyer. I don't know if I can or not."

It took her ten minutes to get the courage up to take the test. There was no way it would be positive. None. She felt like she was cutting her heart out as she capped the end of the stick and laid it on the counter like the instructions directed. Unable to stand the pain, she fled the bathroom, only stopping to grab her shoes.

"I can't wait to find out, can't do this. It hurts too much," she told her grandmother before heading to the barn.

She hadn't been consciously trying to heal Sawyer when they were together. She knew first and foremost that it probably wouldn't do a damned bit of good. And secondly, he didn't deserve a wife who was constantly trying to change him. She knew that she had to accept his sterility as a done deal if she wanted to give their marriage a healthy start.

As to why she was so late, she figured it was probably a combination of stress and becoming sexually active again for the first time in years. There simply wasn't any way she was pregnant. No matter how much she wished she was.

CHAPTER FIFTY-EIGHT

INSIDE THE FARMHOUSE, SARAH AND Nan exchanged a look.

"Negative test or scared?" Nan asked.

"I don't know. Let's go see."

They'd just reached the bathroom when the sound of car doors closing echoed through the house, and Sawyer came in the front door, smiling.

"Where's Sydney?"

"Um, she went for a walk," Sarah told him. "To the barn, she said."

Sawyer, smart man, immediately picked up on her concern. "Sarah?"

In response, she went in the bathroom and picked up the test. "Well."

Sawyer and Nan peaked in, and she turned, handing the stick to him without a word.

He looked at it with a blank scowl. "What's this?"

"That's a pregnancy test," Sarah answered.

"I know *that*," he said, staring at it. "Whose is it?"

"Well, it sure isn't mine or Sarah's," Nan piped up. "What's it say?"

Sawyer raised his head. "The barn, you said?"

"Yes."

He turned and left without a word.

"Are you going to tell me or am I going to die of curiosity?" Nan asked Sarah.

She told her the results. "Though I'm not sure if that's good or bad. Let's go meet everyone, get them settled." And pray, she thought, even though she didn't say that out loud.

CHAPTER FIFTY-NINE

SAWYER'S HEART WAS NEARLY BEATING him to death by the time he reached the barn. He hesitated outside the doors, looking down at the test. In the twilight, he couldn't make out the results, but it had been seared onto his brain the moment he saw it in the house. Begging the universe he managed to find the right words, he opened the door and eased inside. The fairy lights they'd strung up for the wedding were on, giving the area a soft illumination.

Sydney was pacing at the far end of the wide aisle where they'd set the altar up for tomorrow. When she saw him, she closed her eyes, and he heard her sniff wetly.

"Why didn't you tell me you thought you were pregnant?" he asked quietly as he approached her.

"Because I didn't want to hurt you when the test was negative. I'm just late, that's all. I can't be pregnant. I know that."

He slid the test in the pocket of his jeans and walked up to her, wrapping his arms around her from the back. "How late?"

"Since Pittsburgh. Before, really. It's just stress. That's happened to me a couple of times. I shouldn't have said anything. I'm sorry."

He snuggled his face into the curve of her neck, exposed by the scoop neck of the shirt she wore. "I love you."

A tear splashed his arm as she nodded. "I love you, too. Can we just forget about this, please? Is everyone here?"

"Yeah. But it might be kind of hard to forget." He pulled the test out and brought it around to her waist in front. "Didn't you look at it?"

"What good is it going to do me to look at it?" she whispered. "Are you mad because I didn't tell you?"

"No, sweetheart. I understand why you didn't. But I really think you should look at this test."

Something in his voice must have gotten through to her because Sydney went very still. "Sawyer?"

"It's not negative."

When her knees went out from under her, he caught her easily and lowered her to the makeshift wood floor they'd put down earlier that day. Sitting behind her, he held her up.

"What?" she gasped.

He raised the test so she could see it. Very clearly, it was positive.

"We're pregnant," he whispered, kissing her temple. "Sydney, we're pregnant."

She burst into tears. "We can't be. How?" She took off her glasses and wiped her eyes, then reached up for the test, her hands shaking so badly he had to steady them as she looked at the tiny display screen. "How?"

"I don't know. That magic Campbell touch, maybe. And honestly, I don't care. As long as you're healthy and the baby's healthy, I can't ask for anything more."

Sydney turned and wrapped her arms around him, burying her face in his neck. "What about you? Oh, Sawyer. It has to be a mistake. What if it's some kind of weird fluke, and something's wrong? We need to get you checked out."

He'd explained to her that there was an increased risk of testicular cancer with his type of sterility, a conversation he now wished he'd skipped. "I never told you that in order to worry you. I told you because I wanted you to know what you were getting into. And maybe I'm wrong, but I don't think a positive pregnancy test can result from anything other than the presence of a baby."

She shook her head frantically, cupping his cheeks. "No. No, I read about a guy who took a test as a joke and it turned positive. He had cancer. You have to get checked out. We'll call first thing Monday. Promise me."

Sawyer kissed her. "Sydney, I'll pee on a damned stick as many times as you want me to. But think about it. *You* taking the test has nothing to do with me, other than the fact that I'm the one who got you pregnant. You *are* pregnant. This is real. We're having a baby."

The confused hope on her face as she stared up at him nearly undid him. "You think so?"

He laughed, wrapping his arms around her and rocking her back and forth. "Yeah, I think so."

"That might explain why your coffee's been making me sick lately," she said. He could tell she still wasn't convinced though. She looked up at him with a horrified gasp. "Oh, God. Sawyer, your family's here. How in the world are we going to explain this? They all know you can't... but you apparently can... unless they think I... Oh, God."

"We'll figure it out." He kissed her right between her eyebrows, then on each cheek in turn, and finally on the lips. "How far along are you, do you think? If you were already late in Pittsburgh, that'd make the conception date when?"

She flushed. "It'd have to be that first night, in the shower. That's the only time we were intimate without a condom before the trip. That and the second night we had Daniel." She looked down. "I guess *that* night would make more sense if you go from the assumption that my deep-seated fear and longing triggers the healing."

They'd made love quietly, desperately, that night, their lovemaking an intimate tempest that was what cued Sawyer in to how he really felt.

"That's the night I realized I loved you," he said softly.

"Watching you come apart in my arms, it was different than anything we'd shared before. I was wishing with everything in me that I could get you pregnant."

She leaned against him, holding tight. "So maybe it was the magic of *us* that did it, huh?"

"Maybe so." He sighed. "Like I said, it doesn't really matter to me how it happened. I just thank God that it has."

"I won't believe it until I see a doctor. And I won't relax until you do, too."

"Then we'll both try to get in on Monday. I love you, Sydney."

She kissed the underside of his chin. "I never thought I'd be happy like this. Even if there isn't a baby, I want you to know that. To know that I mean that. You're enough for me. Anything and anyone else is just a bonus."

"I do believe that. I hope you believe I feel the same way."

She nodded. "I do."

EPILOGUE

IN THE END, THEY DECIDED not to tell anyone else about the pregnancy test. Swearing Noah, Sarah, and Nan to secrecy, they went on with the wedding as planned. As simple as it was, the sheer joy of it so far surpassed her first wedding that Sydney had to keep pinching herself to make sure she wasn't dreaming.

"This is what we've always wanted for you," Emma told her when they had a moment alone after the ceremony. She touched Sydney's cheek, tears in her eyes. "My baby girl. You just shine with happiness. I couldn't ask for anything more for you. He adores you, you know."

"I do know, Mom. I adore him back."

"Your father's taking all the credit for this, by the way," Emma said as they looked out over the meadow. The festivities had moved from the barn to the picnic shelter, which was festooned with ribbons and sheer fabric. "I can't believe you all pulled this off without a word to anyone."

"You have no idea how many times I wanted to run over and see you and Zanny, tell you what we were planning," Sydney admitted. "But I wanted to surprise you more. And maybe I wanted to keep it to myself as long as I could. Kind of like a present."

"It's a good present. A very good present."

"There's another gift," Sydney said, pointing to Eli and

Noah, who were talking to each other with ease. “Are they really going to live together?”

“That’s the plan. I think it’ll be good for them. They can come at each other as equals now. Eli’s always been intimidated by Noah’s abilities, never saw them as a liability before. And Noah’s always been a bit jealous of Eli’s normalcy. Well, the playing field is level now. I’d like to see them regain the closeness they had when they were little.”

“Time will tell, I guess.” Sydney looked down at the gold band she wore on her left hand. “I never could have dreamed this.”

“I still feel that way about your father from time to time,” Emma admitted softly. “There’s nothing like it, kiddo, being loved by a good man, building a family with him.”

Instinctively, Sydney laid a hand on her belly. She didn’t even think about what she’d done until she noticed Emma’s astonished stare.

“Sydney?”

“I don’t know for sure. Please don’t say anything. I took the test yesterday.”

“Does Sawyer know?”

She nodded. “He’s convinced I am. I’m scared to death I’m not. We didn’t want to say anything until we know for sure. We’ll be going to the doctor as soon as we can get in.”

Emma bit her lip. “Forgive me for asking this, but is he sure it’s his? I mean, *I* know it’s his. *You* know it’s his. But...”

Sydney smiled. “He knows.” She looked out over the crowd and caught Sawyer’s eye. He was standing next to her father, Cade, and Grant, who’d driven up for the wedding, laughing at something Archer had said. The laughter faded into a twinkling smile as he started toward her.

“Good. Can I tell your father, or do you want me to wait?”

“Wait, please? It’ll only be a day or two.”

“A day or two what?” Sawyer said as he came up. He kissed her soundly, softly.

"Before we know. I kind of gave the game away."

"She touched her belly," Emma said. "I won't say anything, even though the suspense is going to drive me mad. Let me know as soon as you get the word?"

"We will," Sawyer assured her, "but it's just a formality. Now, if you'll excuse us for a few minutes, I'm going to sneak my wife behind the barn."

Emma rolled her eyes at them even as she laughed. "Good luck with that in this family."

The sounds of the gathering faded as they walked through the barn to the back side. Once they were through the doors, Sawyer slid them closed and held out his hands.

"Dance with me?"

Sydney tilted her head to the side, taking his hands. "Aren't we supposed to share our first dance in front of everyone? Not that I'm complaining."

He whirled her around, catching her in his arms. "I believe that's the tradition, yes. Shall we stop?"

"No." She slid her arms up around his neck, letting her breasts rest against him. "Kiss me?"

"Gladly."

By the time he pulled back, Sydney was ready to melt. "You do that very, very well," she whispered against his lips.

"I could say the same thing to you. And if your family and mine weren't on the other side of this barn..."

She pressed her fingers to his mouth. "Don't even go there. Tonight's going to have to be soon enough."

"I've never felt like this before about anyone," he told her, caressing her cheek. "I want you to know that. And it isn't just the lovemaking. You give me a piece of my soul back. I'd be utterly lost without you."

"I feel the same way about you. Every bit of pain I've had to go through to get here was worth it," she whispered. "To get to you."

Sawyer rested his forehead against hers. "Amen to that. I love you, wife."

"I love you, husband," she told him softly. "Words I never thought I'd hear or say. Precious words."

"Very much so."

She goosed him. "And to think, you didn't want to hire me."

Sawyer laughed and twirled her around and around. "I'm going to owe your father for that for the rest of my life. And that's a debt I'm all too happy to pay."

Looking up at the man she felt like she'd been in love with half her life, Sydney couldn't agree more. She had everything she'd ever wanted within arms reach. "I'm living my happily ever after," she mused. "And it's better than I could have imagined."

"Now we just have to help Rachel and Noah and Eli find theirs," he murmured as he kissed her again. "It's only fair that we meddle in their lives they way they did ours, don't you think?"

Sydney grinned. "Oh, absolutely. And I think I have a good idea where to start."

ALSO BY T. L. HADDIX

The Firefly Hollow Series:

Firefly Hollow
Butterfly Lane
Dragonfly Creek
Cattail Ridge
Cricket Cove
Stormking Road
Fern Valley
Snapdragon Way
Stardust Valley
Kathy

The Shadows Collection:

Secrets in the Shadows
Under the Moon's Shadow
Shadows from the Grave
Hidden in the Shadows
In the Heart's Shadow
Deception in the Shadows
Seduction in the Shadows
Domestic Disturbance (A Leroy/Shadows flash fiction)

Writing as Mallory Love:

Capturing Colleen
Seducing Samantha

You can connect with T.L. on Facebook and her website:

www.tlhaddix.com
www.facebook.com/tlhaddix